Creed

ISBN: 0-6158-0387-3
ISBN-13: 9780615803876

Creed

Kristen Ashley

Discover other titles by Kristen Ashley:

www.kristenashley.net

Warning

This book is an ADULT EROTIC romance featuring a (kind of) anti-hero *and* anti-heroine. This novel contains explicit erotic scenes that include elements of control and bondage as well as anal sex. The heroine, especially, in this novel lives life by her own rules with no apologies. In an effort not to spoil it for you, I will not explain further about the heroine but she is most definitely not your (or my, in my other books) "normal" heroine. Please read the Author's Note. There are also scenes of torture and rape in this novel so if you are squeamish about either or you do not enjoy the above sexual situations or characters, I would suggest that this novel is not for you.

Author's Note and Acknowledgements

Creed, as was the first novel in this series, **Knight**, is a departure from my usual novels. It is more erotic, exploring the building of trust and connection between two people in love.

This series was meant to explore anti-heroes, or men who are not your traditional hero. In other words, they do bad things, break the law and live by their own code which is not the normally acceptable code by which most of society lives.

When they came to me, the characters in this book threw me for a loop. Instead of an anti-hero, I got an interrupted hero and an anti-heroine. My Creed may skirt the law but Sylvie breaks it and makes no apologies for it.

Therefore, Sylvie is not soft, sweet, giggly or flirty. She is also not sassy. Sylvie is badass, kickass and makes no excuses. Life has led her to develop a hard shell with sharp edges in order to keep distant and protect herself from life's hurts but when she lets someone through… watch out. It's a love like no other.

I adore her.

I adore her so much, no kidding, I wanted to switch gears while writing this and call this book **Sylvie.** Alas, Creed came through just as strong and the beauty of his connection with and adoration of Sylvie wouldn't allow me to make that change.

That said, this is your warning that my Sylvie is not your usual romance novel heroine. She's one of the boys. She is, in a sense, like the female version of all my alphas from my novels all the way down to the language she uses.

I hope you give her a chance, and if you do, I hope she'll have you eating out of her hand.

Last but oh so not least, I want to thank my posse who again had my back in a lot of ways near and dear to my heart while I wrote this novel.

Kristen Ashley

You know who you are and you know all you've done.
To the moon and back, girlies.
For my readers, here you go...
Creed and his Sylvie.

Chapter 1
Black Expedition

I drove fast because she sounded tweaked.

Tweaked in her business was not good.

Tweaked in my business was not good either.

It was worse. She wasn't calling Knight. This meant bad things because it meant bad things were happening. Not bad. *Bad.*

If Knight knew something bad was going down he'd lose his mind, which meant someone might lose the use of an appendage. She knew, if I hit the scene, I'd have a mind to carpet stains.

Shit.

I screeched to a halt on the road outside her house in my blue 1968 Corvette Stingray then reversed, parallel parking expertly between two cars. In a second, I was out, hand to the gun under my leather jacket shoved in the holster attached to my belt at the small of my back. I shoved my keys in my pocket and approached the front door of her tiny house, my eyes peeled and scanning.

No noises, no sound.

It was late, after three in the morning. Her neighborhood was quiet. It was a nice neighborhood. Not flashy, not family. Just a neighborhood, if a bit rundown.

I hadn't run Serena's check. Another of Knight's team did it. I didn't know much about her, though I'd taken her to a few of her early appointments and stuck around until they were over. This was a service Knight provided to his new girls. Strike that; it was a service Knight insisted his girls have.

I pulled up what I knew about her and remembered she was an art student, earning cash to go to some fancy school in France. Parents gone, a car crash. If she wanted it, she had to do it on her own.

Fucking whacked, that shit. Sure, you couldn't pull together money to buy a plane ticket, pay tuition and living expenses in a different country by waiting tables unless you had a decade to do it.

But shit.

Each girl had their own story. Most of them were way worse than Serena's.

Which meant Serena might not be all there upstairs.

Please God, I thought, *do not let this bitch be seeing clients at her house.*

I checked in the window first, seeing light coming around the blinds, but they were closed. I couldn't get a lock on what was happening inside.

I moved to the door, stood to its side, reached out a hand and knocked hard twice.

"Serena!" I called. "It's Sylvie."

I heard the locks open immediately.

Shit, she was waiting at the door.

It was thrown open and I saw her.

Fuck.

I heard the blood roaring in my ears and didn't move except to speak.

"You need a doctor?" I asked.

She shook her head.

Then she whispered, "Sylvie—"

I cut her off, "You report this to Knight?"

"I... he'll..." she shook her head again, "no."

"You call someone other than me to help you out? Get you cleaned up?" I pressed on.

She nodded. "Cher. She's on her way. She'll be here soon."

Good. Cher. That bitch was smart, had her shit tight. She'd see to Serena.

I nodded back then, "Who was he?"

"He was... he was new."

I nodded again then, "Tell me you didn't see him here."

She shook her head. "Never."

At least there was that.

"He do more than what I can see?" I asked.

She closed her eyes. I held my breath. She opened her eyes.

"No," she whispered.

I studied her, not getting it.

She'd been worked over, eye swelling, lip fat and busted open but only a small tear. It didn't look like she needed stitches. It looked like it hurt like hell, but it wasn't that bad. Unacceptable, but not that bad.

Why didn't she call Knight? For this, Knight would make a statement then cut the asshole off. He wouldn't lose his mind.

She had to be lying.

"Serena, you gotta talk to me," I pushed. "Why'd you call me direct? Why haven't you reported this to Knight?"

"The girls say he gets angry," she replied.

"He does, and babe, he should. Your face is messed up. He does not offer protection so his girls can get messed up. He does not like that shit one bit. A statement needs to be made."

"He's scary when he's angry," she whispered.

That was the God's honest truth.

"Uh... just sayin', Serena, some asshole worked you over. He's a new client. You wanna tell me why you're protecting him from Knight?"

"I don't want Knight to get in trouble."

God. Serena was relatively new. This had never happened to her.

Right.

"That is not yours to worry about," I educated her.

"But—"

I leaned into the door and dropped my voice. "Serena, babe, it's not yours to worry about. It's what he does. It's who he is. That's why you're with him. If someone works you over, you report it to Knight. Immediately."

She held my eyes for a beat then nodded.

I went on, "Now, you meet this guy at his place, a hotel, what?"

"Hotel," she answered.

I nodded. "Where, when, how long you been home?"

She gave me the details.

I nodded again. "I'm paying him a visit, Serena, and I'm reporting this to Knight."

She bit her fat lip on the side where it wasn't as fat, then she stopped doing that and nodded back.

"How long before Cher gets here?" I asked.

"She said ten minutes and that was about ten minutes ago."

I gave her another nod.

"Ice," I whispered, dipping my head toward her face. "Take some painkillers. Lie down."

She nodded again then whispered back, "Thanks, Sylvie."

Kristen Ashley

I caught her eyes and locked my gaze with hers. "Anytime. Know it, babe."

She nodded yet again.

"Lock doors," I ordered. "I'll check in tomorrow."

"Okay, Sylvie."

"Ice," I repeated.

"Okay."

I looked meaningfully at the door. She closed it and I didn't move until I heard it lock.

Then I moved quickly to the car, but I didn't jog. I didn't run. I kept it controlled.

When I got in my car, I called Rhash, Knight's right hand man.

"Yo," he answered.

"Yo right back at 'cha," I replied. "Got good news and bad news. Which do you want first?"

"Good," Rhash replied, a tremor of humor in his voice.

"Right. I'm in an ass-kicking mood and I'm already in my car so there are no delays in going out to kick ass."

"Fuck," Rhash muttered, humor gone. He knew what this meant. "What's the bad news?"

"Serena got worked over and she called me."

"*Fuck*," Rhash clipped.

"Yeah," I agreed.

"How bad? She need Baldy? What?" he asked.

"She says not bad. Just beat up. Cher is coming to look after her. I need an address on her client tonight."

I waited for him to find it. He gave it to me and I programmed it into my GPS, then he asked, "There a reason she didn't call me or Knight?"

"Worried you'd lose your minds, get in trouble."

"Stupid," he muttered, sounding more than a little annoyed. "What's she think we get that ten percent for?"

This was a good question, and one I didn't have an answer to. In my experience, ladies of the evening didn't protect their protectors. If they were lucky, it was the other way around. They usually avoided them, if they could, or sought them out for not so good reasons, such as getting their fix.

Knight's girls weren't like that. I knew why. Hell, I definitely knew why.

It still was stupid.

"Got an ass to kick, Rhash," I reminded him.

"Need back up?" he asked.

"Feeling like kicking ass?"

"How bad was she?"

"Fat lip. Swollen eye," I told him.

"Then… fuck yeah."

I grinned.

That was why Knight inspired loyalty in his girls. Because he employed people like Rhashan and me who gave a shit.

"I'm starting at the hotel," I shared. "Meet me there."

"It'll take me about ten, fifteen. Wait for me. I don't want to miss anything."

I grinned again. Rhashan and all the guys thought it was hilarious to watch me work. This was because I was five foot two and cheated the gods by drinking a lot and eating whatever I wanted and still, I was thin. I had tits and nicely rounded ass. Neither in overabundance so, no doubt about it, I was slender. I wasn't girlie, but I wore my honey blonde hair long and wild and I also had a not-to-be-messed-with, once a week schedule of getting a manicure and pedicure.

Still, I could take down a man over a foot taller than me, with over a hundred pounds on me, and have him whining like a baby.

The guys thought this was hysterical, watching a man go down at the hands of a petite woman wearing nail polish. Sometimes, when I'd get the call-out, two or three of them would show just to watch.

I never disappointed.

"See you there," I said to Rhash.

"Yeah, later," he replied.

I flipped my phone shut, started up my girl. She purred for me while I waited the thirty seconds before I saw Cher pull up and park. I gave her a chin lift through the windshield and waited while she walked to Serena's house. After that, I waited until the door closed behind Cher.

Then my girl and I took off.

I had my back to the wall at the side of the door when I heard the elevator beep. I turned my head and watched Rhash walk out.

Rhashan was a huge, midnight skinned black man. Handsome. Fuck, they made few of them as good as Rhashan from head to toe. Smooth with a kick, like a good bourbon. You sucked it back then sucked in a breath to ease the warmth on its way down.

He'd recently married a woman I liked unreservedly, which was rare. It was known he liked to dominate, which was why I didn't dip my toe in midnight before he made the ultimate hook up with his new wife, Vivica.

No one controlled me. Not anymore.

That didn't mean I didn't enjoy the view immensely as he walked his muscled bulk my way.

When he got close, I lifted up a keycard between two fingers.

"Boss owes me a hundred, fifty," I noted.

Rhash's full lips quirked. "You get a receipt?"

I shot him a grin and jerked up my chin.

His eyes went to the door. "He in there?"

"According to my boy downstairs, who's one hundred and fifty dollars richer for handing me a keycard, he's not checked out," I told him.

He looked me up and down before he remarked, "This hotel, I don't get away without shelling out at least two fifty."

"You don't have tits." I pointed out the obvious and his lips again quirked.

Then his face got serious. "You lead?"

"Uh… am I Sylvia Bissenette?" I asked.

"Last time I checked," he answered.

That got him another grin.

He positioned and so did I, both of us unholstering our guns.

I slid in the keycard, got the green light, slid it out. I carefully turned the handle and cautiously moved into the dark room with Rhash at my back.

Within a minute, we'd ascertained the space was clear.

Rhash turned on a light and we both scanned the wrecked room with our eyes.

When I was done with my scan, my gaze went to Rhash and I noted his strong, square jaw was hard.

"She put up a fight," I remarked.

His eyes cut to me.

I was a loose part of the Knight Sebring team, not an official member. I was freelance. I had other jobs. But I was always on-call for Knight.

Being freelance didn't mean much to Knight's boys. For them, I took assignments, I took call, I was a member of the team. This meant we knew where each other lived. We drank together. We watched the Broncos together, usually at a bar. I was invited to Rhash's wedding. If I needed help on another one of my jobs, all I had to do was make a call and they had my back.

The fact that, outside work, our time spent together usually included alcohol meant we'd all shared.

So I knew Rhashan Banks had grown up rough. His Mom had him when she was sixteen. He had two sisters and a brother by the time his Mom was twenty-one. Each Banks kid had a different father and none of the dads stuck around.

Rhash was in a gang by twelve. His best friend got whacked during a turf war and died in his arms when Rhash was fifteen. Still, it took three more years and getting his girl pregnant before Rhash started to pull his shit together. She put the baby up for adoption, wanting nothing to do with it or a daddy who was destined for dead or incarcerated. She dumped his ass, had the baby, got rid of the baby then promptly went back on her grand schemes and got involved with another gang member, this one about seven huge steps down from Rhash. Her new guy didn't mind sharing. In fact, he passed her around to all his buds.

To deal with a life that turned total shit, she eventually got hooked on meth. Now she worked Colfax and her life expectancy wasn't very high, considering her pimp was an asshole, her strip was dangerous and her mind was always on her next fix.

Rhash fought his way out of that shit, eventually found Knight and lived every day knowing the kid he created with his girl was somewhere better. Knowing it and hating it because that better did not include his real mom or his real dad.

Somehow, all this shit got twisted in his head. The gang mentality wasn't gone. His loyalty was ingrained and extreme. It was just that now it was to Knight, Knight's team and Knight's mission.

Therefore, when he took in the evidence that one of Knight's girls fought back before getting a busted lip and a swollen eye, it pissed him off.

Rhashan Banks pissed-off was a little scary, and I say that even though not much scared me.

When he made no reply and I was done with his dark eyes burning holes into mine, I asked, "You got any cash on you?"

"Your tits wear off?" he asked back, and I fought back another grin.

"They're b-cups, Rhash. They look good but they only go so far covered up," I replied.

He twisted his torso and the light went out.

Then I heard him say, "Let's move."

We turned from the night clerk, who was two hundred dollars richer, and told us what we already knew from the empty, wrecked hotel room.

Serena's client had paid in cash. The credit card he put on file for incidentals cleared at the time of check in which was eight o'clock. When the clerk ran it again, it had been reported stolen. Plus he had checked in under a different name and address than he'd given us.

The false name and paying in cash was not surprising. Clients did their best not to leave trails.

The address and stolen credit card, not good.

This meant he felt safe to leave the room in that state, knowing they couldn't find him to charge him.

Knight had a stable of fifty-seven girls and shit happened. It was rare because Knight also had a reputation. Nevertheless, it happened sometimes. But no girl took a client without him being checked out. This was part of the work I did for Knight. He didn't dig deep, but he did dig. He never sent a girl out if the client was shady, had a record, cash flow problems or anything of concern turned up. We ran credit history, work history, financials, criminal records and we checked homes and places of work, all on the down low so as not to scare away clients.

In other words, this *particular* kind of shit did not happen.

Ever.

"His house," Rhash growled. "Meet you there. I'll text you details."

"Right," I muttered, walking beside him to the door. My head was tilted back, eyes up and aimed at his profile. I was assessing the level of his anger. I sensed it was not only increasing, but expanding to take in the guy who took his fist to Serena and whoever did the legwork on the client.

We were pushing out of the doors when I felt it.

Eyes on me.

I twisted my neck and shoved the door open with my gaze trained over my shoulder. I swept the reception area with not mild attention.

It was early morning; no one was there, that I could see, but the clerk.

Fuck.

I turned my attention to where I was going, heading for my girl in the lot.

This had been happening lately, too much. I long since learned how to sense it and read it. I might not be girlie, but I'd have to be blind not to see that I wasn't hard on the eyes. This meant I got a lot of looks.

This wasn't that, some guy who liked what he saw and wanted in there.

This was a different kind of watching.

It had been going on now for about a month, but every time I felt it, when I scanned or circled back to take a better look, I could find nothing.

I didn't like it, but there was nothing I could do if I couldn't discover the source.

Now I had a job to do and I didn't have the time to swing back into reception on the guise of asking the clerk more questions to see if someone was checking me out.

So I followed behind Rhash in his car with my eyes peeled, looking for a tail.

And finding nothing.

I stood in the empty living room trying to hold my shit.

"Who did the check?" I asked, my voice low with anger.

"Live," Rhash grunted, and I flipped open my phone, using my thumb on the keypad to scroll down my phonebook to Lively.

I heard Rhash hitting buttons on his own phone, I knew connecting with Knight.

We'd hit the client's house and found a for sale sign in the front yard. When we'd gone in, there was nothing there. Not a stick of furniture. Totally cleared out.

This gave me a bad feeling. This was not your random asshole that got off on paying for sex and roughing up women.

Stolen credit cards. False addresses.

This was bad.

Kristen Ashley

The phone rang four times in my ear before I connected.

"Pip, what the fuck? It's after four in the morning," Live muttered sleepily in my ear, using the shortened version of the nickname that the boys gave me. Pipsqueak.

The guys jacked around all the time. We were always fucking with each other, playing jokes, giving each other shit. It was just the way. Pipsqueak and Pip were not the nicknames for badass bitches like me who could kick ass, but what did I care? It was ironic and it sure as fuck could be worse. I knew this because one of Knight's men was nicknamed Tiny. This wasn't ironic and it didn't refer to his stature. He hated it but he put up with it, because if he didn't it would mean he not only had a small dick but also no balls, which would have been worse.

And anyway, he had a secret that I knew because one of his women shared. This was, his dick might be small but that didn't mean he didn't know what to do with his tongue and fingers. The way it was described, he made up for it in a big way.

I didn't delay in sharing what the fuck to Live.

"Serena was worked over tonight. Client paid for the hotel in cash, gave a fake name and a stolen credit card. Right now I'm standing in his living room with Rhash and it's empty. By empty I mean there's no furniture and there's a for sale sign in the yard."

"Fuck," he whispered.

"Baby, it's late. What the hell?" I heard in the background and knew this was Live's woman, Amy. She sounded sleepy and snippy. I'd never heard her sounding sleepy. I frequently heard her sounding snippy.

Incidentally, she was *not* one of the guys' women that I liked unreservedly, or at all. She was a ball buster. I didn't like women like her who happily accepted the dresses, shoes, jewelry and free cover to get into Knight's club, Slade, from her man. Amy didn't have any problems bitching about everything under the sun, including the fact Live had to work for the money it took to buy her dresses, shoes and jewelry.

"Yeah, fuck," I agreed, ignoring Amy, which was my usual tactic for dealing with her. "You do the full check?" I asked.

"Fuck yeah, I did. 'Course I did," Live told me, insulted. "There was furniture there when I checked him out, all through the house. There sure as fuck wasn't a for sale sign in the yard."

10

"Baby, what... the... *hell?*" Amy snapped, sounding less sleepy but definitely more snippy.

"Give me a minute, darlin'," Live replied to Amy. Then to me, "How bad's Serena?"

"Fat lip, swollen eye. Could be worse, but that isn't the point," I answered.

"Yeah," he agreed.

I heard Rhash's phone snap closed so my eyes went to him through the dark.

"Knight says meeting. Now. Slade. Get his ass in there, Sylvie," he rumbled, then didn't wait for me to respond. He stalked to the door.

I went back to the phone. "You hear that?"

"On my way," Live muttered.

"What?" I heard Amy ask, her voice going shrill. "Now?"

"Later," I said into the phone, then snapped it shut quickly in a successful effort to avoid hearing Live get his balls busted. I hoped she excelled at giving head or tasted like pure honey to be worth that shit.

I followed Rhash out the backdoor. We'd picked the lock and I made certain it was secure again before I moved around the house. As I approached my car, I watched Rhash give me a finger flick through the window as he drove away in his black Nissan Z.

I hit the sidewalk and was moving around the hood of my Corvette when I noted the big Ford Expedition motoring down the street the opposite direction from Rhash. My eyes locked on it, taking in the Arizona plates then moving up to the cab.

At the front of the hood of my Corvette, I stopped dead and my chest depressed like a boulder had landed on it.

The Expedition drove past, the driver not even glancing my way and my head turned, following it.

No fucking way.

No fucking way.

I'd seen him, this was true. I'd seen him dozens of times in the last sixteen years. Or, I had convinced myself I had.

But I hadn't.

He was gone.

There was no way after sixteen years he'd make his way from Kentucky to a street in Denver at after four o'clock in the morning at the same time I was on that street.

No way.

There was a time when I wanted it. I saw him everywhere, that was how much I wanted it. I wanted to see him again so he could take me away like he promised. Time passed and my life, that had been swirling, flushed down the toilet, and I wanted to see him again so I could scream in his face, kick him, beat him, share exactly what his betrayal meant to my heart and my life. How, when he left, a shit life that was only ever good when I was breathing his air turned even *more* shit.

That time was not now. I was over it. I'd gotten out, moved on. I lived my own life how I wanted to live it, not how someone forced me to live it. It wasn't easy. It was fucking hard. It nearly ended me.

But I did it and I was here. I liked my life.

And I didn't look back.

Not ever.

Not fucking ever.

So that wasn't him. It couldn't be him. It was my mind playing tricks on me.

Not the first time, and the way he fucked me over, I knew it wouldn't be the last.

I'd learned to live with it.

I came unstuck and rounded my girl. I got in, started her up and headed to Slade.

❧

I screeched to a halt in my driveway and threw open the door. I angled out, slammed the door and ran across my yard to my neighbor's.

Shit, I was five minutes late. And five minutes for Charlene was five minutes too many.

I knocked loud twice on her front door then turned the knob and walked in.

"I'm here! I'm here!" I shouted over what sounded like pandemonium. "I had work. Sorry I'm late."

He came around and slammed into my legs.

"Sylvie! Sylvie! Sylvie!" Adam cried. "Toads are slimy!"

Then he pounded a fist hard into my thigh and raced away.

I followed him, walking from the entry into the living room, rounding through the dining room before I hit the kitchen, which was bedlam.

Charlene was in a robe looking harassed. Adam was bumping repeatedly into the side of the counter. Theo was in his high chair, slamming his fists into the tray. Leslie was sitting in her booster seat, slamming her feet into the chair.

I went to Adam and gently led him away from the cabinets to the kitchen table, my eyes on Charlene.

"Sorry, I should have called," I said quietly. "Something went down. I got here as soon as I could. You go shower. I've got this."

Her eyes were brimming with tears, none of which had flowed over yet. That would happen in the shower. She'd go to work with puffy, red eyes again and hope they didn't notice she was strung out emotionally and physically.

"Thanks, Sylvie," she whispered before she took off and thus began the morning ritual.

"Cocoa Puffs!" Leslie shouted, still banging her feet into the chair.

"Right, Cocoa Puffs," I agreed. "And you'll get them if you stop making so much noise. Adam, up," I ordered, guiding him carefully into his chair. Then I got down to business.

I'd lived next to Charlene since I bought my house four years ago. Six weeks ago, her husband Dan took off on her. They went to bed and when she woke up he was gone, and so were most of his clothes, the flat screen TV they'd just bought, the string of pearls he'd given her two anniversaries before and, upon inspection, half their checking and savings accounts.

He hadn't cleaned her out. He'd left everything else.

He'd also left her with Adam, who was six and had Down syndrome, Leslie, who was three and Theo who was one and a half. He also left her a mortgage, daycare and special schools bills she couldn't afford on her salary. She had a job as a bank teller and family that all lived in New Mexico.

She was fucked financially, heartbroken and barely holding it together.

She said, over wine that faded into tequila and tears, that she had no idea Dan was over it. Money wasn't great. They were always struggling, but they had a good family and lots of love.

It was my opinion that many women lived in denial and Charlene was one of them. Her husband's eyes followed my ass enough that she couldn't miss it. She just chose to ignore it. Dan would often stare off into space as if he was imagining himself somewhere else, not there. And for the last year, the rare times I was home to notice it, he got home from work later and later.

She was pretty clueless, and her being surprised by Dan's defection was proof of this fact. But she was a fun drunk, loved her kids and her husband and she always took care of my cat when I went to Vegas or hit a beach. She made me a huge tin of Christmas cookies and brought it over with eggnog every year for Christmas. She also made me a massive birthday cake and brought it over with a premium bottle of bourbon or tequila.

Further, she was open and friendly. She told me she only ever wanted the simple life. A husband, a home, kids. She knew Adam was Down's before he was born and she didn't care. Didn't give it a second thought. Before Dan left, she was happy as a clam. Adam's special needs didn't seem to touch their lives. He was high functioning, but he still needed more care and attention. She never complained.

"Pure joy," she told me on a smile. "Wake up to it, go to bed with it and it comes from Adam. How lucky can I get?"

She meant that shit. That was Charlene.

And that was probably why, last year, on the fifteenth anniversary of it happening, when she brought over birthday cake and bourbon, I got sauced with her and laid it out.

All of it.

Everything about me.

Then I let it out, bawling like an idiot for the first time in years, clutching onto her like I could fuse onto her healthy, happy family cheerfulness.

I could count my friends on two hands.

But I could count those I was tight with on two fingers.

Knight and Charlene.

The only two people who knew everything about me.

So when Dan took off on Charlene, I stepped in. Every morning I came over, and while Charlene got ready for work, I got the kids breakfast, got them dressed and helped Charlene get them in the car so she could get them to their different schools and daycare. If I was around in the evenings, I lent a hand then hung to give her some company. I'd also corralled Rhash's woman Vivica and

Knight's woman Anya into helping her out a couple of times, looking after the kids so I could take Charlene out to get her hammered and forget her husband was a dickhead and that life could be fun.

Dan had not contacted her, not once in six weeks. My guess, he was wind. She'd never hear from him again. I'd offered to track his ass down so, at the very least, she could divorce him and hang a massive child support payment around his rat bastard neck, but she refused.

She was certain he'd see the error of his ways and come back, tail between his legs.

I was certain he was banging as much tail as he could find in an effort to turn his thoughts from the fact he was a total fucking douchebag, and he'd never come home to a lifetime of shit he was not man enough to deal with. Not to mention guilt over the fact that he'd given up and fucked over a decent, kind, good woman who loved him. Charlene wouldn't serve up that guilt. But he'd feel it. And he'd do all in his power to avoid it.

Thus I'd already done a few searches and made a few calls. If he turned up, I'd be all over his ass whether Charlene said yes or not.

She showered and got ready for work. I fed the kids, cleaned them up and got them dressed. This was not an easy task, but I was not a mom who needed to be at work on time at the same time worrying about how I was going to pay bills, so I had nothing on my mind but them and making it fun, which I did.

When Charlene was ready, we corralled them and got them out to her sedan.

"Work?" she asked me why I was late as she was strapping Theo in his car seat.

"Yeah," I answered, strapping Adam into his.

Her eyes found mine over the roof of the car and I saw her brows go up. "Bad?"

"Not good," I told her.

She pressed her lips together. She knew my history, she knew my work. She didn't agree with it, but she was a good friend. She kept her mouth shut. Or, at least, she didn't lecture me too often. Just enough for me to get her and for her not to be *that* annoying.

I leaned in and blew a raspberry on Adam's neck.

He giggled and shoved at me, shouting, "Sylvie! Toads are slimy! Raspberries too!"

I grinned at him and looked into the backseat to check that Leslie was secure. Then I tossed a smile at Adam who smiled back so huge I was sure I could see all his teeth.

Yeah. Pure joy. The world would be a poorer place without Adam in it.

Or, at least, mine would.

I leaned in, touched my forehead to his, pulled back and slammed the door.

I rounded the hood of her car on my way home when Charlene said what she always said.

"Thanks, honey."

My eyes caught hers as I passed her.

"You, me, them, until the me in that equation isn't needed anymore. Know it."

I watched her pull in a breath to control the tears.

I rolled my eyes and muttered, "Such a girl," and kept walking.

"You are too, you know!" she shouted at my back as I sauntered across her yard toward my house.

I lifted a hand and flicked out two fingers.

"And by the way, you keep walking through my yard, you're gonna wear my grass down to dirt!" she kept shouting.

"Such a girl!" I shouted back, not bothering to turn. "Bitch, bitch, bitch."

"Whatever," she yelled, and I grinned.

I hit my front door, pulled out my keys and watched as they drove away, both Leslie and Adam waving at me through their windows.

I waved back and let myself in, so focused on Charlene and her kids, so exhausted from zero sleep, mind so consumed by what Knight shared in the meeting that I missed something I normally would never miss.

The black Expedition parked right across the street from my house.

I locked the door behind me and walked directly to my bedroom. When I hit the door, Gun, who was curled in a ball pressed at the bottom edge of my pillow, looked up at me.

I was wrong earlier. I could count those I was tight with on three fingers.

Knight, Charlene and my cat, Gunsmoke.

She was white with a round head, kind of flat-ish ears and her fur was unbelievably thick. She looked like a big fat cat, but she wasn't. She just had a shit ton of short, thick fur. It also had a shimmer of gray at the very ends with vague gray rings on her tail. She was talkative. She was loving. She was superior. And she liked me and only me.

Not true. She adored Adam.

But she couldn't bear Leslie, and especially Theo. She might let them in when they weren't so loud and manically active. Now it was just me and Adam, who was also full of exuberance and energy, but not around Gun. He was quiet and gentle with Gun and she showed her appreciation.

She watched me walk in, sit my ass on the side of the bed and pull off my boots and socks. She then scooted away when I got up, turned toward the bed, fell forward and did a face plant in it.

And as I closed my eyes, sleep claiming me, I felt her curl up in the dent of my waist.

I knew she was probably hungry. It was time for breakfast.

But she was my Gun. She knew me. She had my back.

She'd wait.

Chapter 2

The Cutest Boy in Town

A cold, dark night in the hills of Kentucky, twenty-eight years earlier, Sylvie is six...

I heard them yelling.

"*Fuck you!*"

"*You wish, dirtbag! Fuck you! You piece of shit!*"

"*Don't call me a piece of shit!*"

"*Don't tell me what I can say!*"

"*You eat my food, live in my house, suck my dick for diamonds, I'll do whatever the fuck I want!*"

"*I hope you have a good memory, asshole, because the last blowjob you got was the last you'll get from me! I. Am. GONE!*"

Then I heard it, the thump, and I jumped.

I knew what that meant.

I knew what it meant.

I knew. I knew. I knew.

She'd have bruises tomorrow and walk funny.

I didn't like it when she had bruises and walked funny.

"Come on, Bootsie, come on," I whispered, and my doggie, a sweet, white, West Highland Terrier, cocked her head as I waved to her on my way to the door. She didn't want to come. She always tried to keep me in the room. She didn't like the yelling either, I knew it. She was a dog; she couldn't tell me, but I still knew it. She also knew what would happen if we got caught. She was there, and Daddy had even kicked her once when they found us.

But I couldn't stay. I couldn't listen anymore. We'd only been caught a few times, but we'd gone walking loads. I didn't like getting caught, but I heard the words in my head over and over again. I never forgot them. I didn't need any more of the words.

"*NO!*" I heard her screech.

"*Last blowjob I'll get?*" Daddy roared back. "*We'll see about that, bitch!*"

No more words.

We had *to go.*

"Come on," I kept whispering and slid out the door, careful. I had to be careful. They couldn't catch me.

That would be bad.

Bootsie followed.

I did what I always did, being careful. Before I put on my jeans, boots and coat, I took off Bootsie's collar. You could hear it jingling.

They couldn't hear it jingling.

I closed my door and we crept through my Daddy's big house; quiet, so quiet. I'd learned not to make a noise, where to put my feet so they'd always hit carpet even in the dark.

We got to the backdoor and slid out, me and Bootsie.

Quickly, as quick as we could, we crossed the backyard. I could see the stables off to the side, Daddy's horses shut tight against the cold. The pool was covered for the winter. Snow on the ground. I always worried Bootsie would fall in the pool under that cover and not be able to get out.

I hated winter.

I didn't like summers much, either.

Quiet, slow, I opened the back gate because it could creak if you didn't do it careful-like. And I was always careful.

I'd learned.

I closed the gate behind us so they wouldn't see it open. They might notice. They had before.

Or Daddy had.

That had been a bad night.

So I closed the gate. Always.

Bootsie and I moved through the snow and the trees. We did it fast. It felt good out there. The cold on my face, in my mouth, up my nose. I didn't know why. It didn't feel good normally, just nights like tonight.

I liked the quiet after all that noise, too. I special-liked it after I'd hear the thump.

And I liked the cold up my nose.

Breathing it in.

And in.

And in.

Bootsie and I kept going through the woods and I wondered what would happen if we didn't stop. Daddy hunted but he never took me. He said girls weren't put on this earth to hunt. He said pretty little girls were put on this earth to do other things, like be pretty.

Daddy said I was very pretty, but that wasn't something you *did*. That was just something you *were*.

So I didn't hunt with Daddy, or fish with him, or do any of the things he did with his buddies that sounded like all sorts of fun. I went to ballet classes, which I hated. The teacher was mean and had a stick she'd bang against the wood floors, and I didn't like the sound and I had to wear stupid outfits.

Daddy didn't listen when I said I'd rather go fishing.

Going fishing, he told me, wasn't for pretty little girls, either.

But I liked the lake. I liked water. I liked boats.

I liked all that a whole lot better than ballet.

Daddy didn't care.

Maybe Bootsie and I could walk to the lake. Maybe we could even walk to the ocean. I'd been to the ocean once, and I liked it. The sounds were good, the waves hitting the shore. I liked the sand under my feet; hard, tingly but still soft and fluffy. The sun felt better at the beach, but that was because there was a breeze. It was hot and cool. I liked having both. Not hot and still. I didn't like that.

Bootsie and me could walk to the beach. We could walk all the way to the ocean. Just go on and on and on. Maybe we'd find someone nice who'd give us food. If it took a long time, we'd find berries. I found wild strawberries all the time when summer was new. Sometimes I could even find raspberries when it was old. We'd find nice people and berries and walk to the beach. Just keep going until all we could see was water forever and ever.

Bootsie would like the beach.

Then again, Bootsie liked anywhere just as long as it had me.

This was what I was thinking when my feet went out from under me. I heard and was terrified by the cry I let out and the sounds of Bootsie barking as I went down. I tried to stop, threw my arms out, but I just rolled, my body banging against stuff, my coat catching on things, the sting of the snow hitting the skin of my face as I just kept going.

I landed, and it hurt because I landed against a tree.

"Ouch," I whispered, hearing Bootsie's barking come toward me.

21

Kristen Ashley

We were far away. We'd never walked this far. I'd never noticed that ridge.

We'd walked too far.

Still, I worried Daddy would hear my cry and Bootsie's barking.

The tumble made my body feel funny. Tight but tingly. Still, I turned my head to see Bootsie jumping through the snow down the slope I'd fallen over, yapping the whole way.

She needed to be quiet.

Before I could say anything to her, tell her to be quiet, I felt something under my arms then I wasn't lying in the snow anymore.

I was up on my feet and being turned.

This scared me so much I didn't move, didn't speak. Just looked at the heavy plaid shirt in front of me, knowing Daddy would find me. Knowing whoever caught me would call him. Knowing, when they did, Daddy would be *mad*.

"Quiet, dog." I heard a firm, low, boy's voice say, and my head tipped back.

Then I didn't move or speak for another reason.

This was because, right in front of me, his hands still on my sides, was Tucker Creed.

Tucker Creed.

The cutest boy in town.

Chapter 3
Pretty Cat

Present day...

I opened my eyes and felt it.

Shit.

Fuck.

Shit.

Someone was in the room with me and that someone was not Gun.

I rolled quickly over the bed, angling my hips so I didn't roll right over Gun as my hand went to the weapon still holstered on my belt at the small of my back.

I fell over the side of the bed, getting my feet under me and coming up in a crouch immediately, hands up, arms resting on the bed, gun pointed across the room.

I saw him and froze solid.

No fucking way.

No fucking way.

Jesus, I was dreaming.

Fuck, I had to be dreaming.

His eyes on me, he was unarmed. His back to the wall, one knee bent, the sole of his boot also to the wall. Arms crossed on his chest, he held my gaze steady, direct, intense and whispered, "Sylvie."

At the sound of my name coming from his lips, raw washed through me, a feeling I last felt drunk on my couch in Charlene's arms on my birthday last year.

A feeling I'd felt time and again before I learned how not to feel it anymore.

A feeling that threatened to shred me now.

A feeling that, with lots of practice, I buried.

"Tucker Creed?" I asked.

His arms came uncrossed only so he could lift his hands in the air, which I was guessing was his confirmation that he was, indeed, Tucker Creed. My first love, my protector, my savior.

My betrayer.

He crossed his arms again and requested, "You wanna stop aiming your weapon at me?"

Actually, no. I didn't. I wanted to keep aiming my gun at him, and I might also want to pull the trigger.

I was not wrong last night. That was him in the Expedition.

And I knew it was him watching me at the hotel. It was also his eyes I felt for the last month.

I knew it.

I fucking knew it.

And I didn't get it.

Even though I preferred to aim my gun at him, I still stood. As I did I reached behind me to re-holster my gun, at the same time keeping my eyes on him and asking, "What the fuck?"

He looked to the bed then back to me before he shared, "Pretty cat."

I looked to the bed to see Gun sitting on her ass, tail sweeping the covers, curious eyes on Tucker Creed. It was the first time since I got her that I lamented my choice of cat over Rottweiler.

I looked back to Creed, and when I did it hit me that this fucking *asshole* had accepted all I had to give him, everything that was me. He took it then took off and left me to the wolves, and pretty much the first thing he said to me was I had a pretty cat.

"Are you shitting me?" I asked.

His face changed and his mouth moved.

"We gotta talk."

We had to talk?

Sixteen years, out-of-the-blue he's in my bedroom and he tells me I have a pretty cat and we had to talk.

Oh yeah, he was totally fucking shitting me.

I studied him.

The last time I saw him he was twenty-three. Now, he was thirty-nine. One look and I saw either life had not been kind or it had been full of adventure of the dangerous variety.

He'd always been tall, even as a little kid. Back in the day, when he was mine, or I thought he was mine, I'd loved that. He grew to be six foot one. He towered over me. He had broad shoulders, a wide chest, narrow hips, thick thighs. I loved that too. The power of his body. Growing up with him, watching him hone it and learn how to use it.

He'd had a rough life, like I did, since he was born. So rough, we used to discuss in a way that was a joke—but also wasn't, but it *was* a release—which one of us had it rougher. We never came to a conclusion. He'd learned to take care of himself. I'd got him early so I learned he'd take care of me. Being big, learning fast, he was good at both, taking care of himself and me.

Or, I thought that, too.

In the end, I'd been wrong.

Now, he was still tall, but he was broader, wider. He'd bulked out, and not a little bit. He wasn't a behemoth, but one look at him, simply his size would make some men ill-at-ease and most would leave a wide berth.

But there was more.

His skin was tanned, leathery. Creases fanned from the sides of his eyes, worn there not through smiling. There were more at the sides of his mouth, along his forehead.

He had a scar that scored through his upper lip, mid right side. He had another one that slashed over his cheekbone, up his temple and disappeared into his hair, but you could see it didn't end there. This was because his brown hair was white in a thin stripe along the side of his head leading from the scar at his temple and stopping where his skull curved to the back. It wasn't gray with age. In fact, he had no gray in his hair even at his age. Someone had got him good with a knife. They meant harm and got interrupted in their endeavor of attempting to kill him.

No, life had not been kind to Tucker Creed.

I didn't know what to think of this. The only thought that came to mind was *good*.

He had on a plaid shirt in light blues, grays and greens mixed with white over a white t-shirt, faded jeans and light brown boots that had an almost yellowish tinge to the suede. His clothes were clean; they hung on him well, but they were not new or fashionable. He bought them for the purposes of covering his body, comfort and nothing else.

His hair was a mess and I felt a sting looking at it because it always was a mess, even back in the day. He rarely got it cut. It hung well past his collar and was always flopping in his eyes. That was no different now, except it wasn't flopping in his eyes. Though I knew, if he bent his neck forward even a fraction of an inch, it would.

Although he wore the years that passed from top to toe, his eyes had not changed. Sky blue, bright, the color so stark in his tan, rugged face that it seemed to glimmer.

Eyes I saw in my dreams, even now, if I admitted it to myself.

Eyes I saw in my head on the rare occasion I let my mind wander and it went there, to the glory days tarnished with betrayal.

Eyes that I remembered trusting as he looked down at me and moved inside me. The first man I took, and when I did I was sure he'd be the last.

He was not.

Not by a long shot.

"Were they going for the eye?" I asked, dipping my head toward his, my eyes on the scar on his cheekbone, and I noted his entire body gave a weird jolt.

Then he answered, "Brain, but their path was through the eye."

My gaze moved from his scar to his eyes. "You jerked."

"I like my brain as it is."

"Good call," I noted.

He began to push from the wall. "Sylvie—"

Oh no. I didn't know why he was here. What I did know was that we were not going to do this.

The time to do this was sixteen years ago.

The time we would never fucking do this was now.

I began to move around the bed. "Got a cat to feed, a shower to take and shit to do. What I don't got is time to talk."

Especially not with you, I finished, but only in my head.

"Sebring's meeting is at two and before that, we gotta talk."

Fuck.

Fuck!

I stopped dead and looked at him. "What?"

I asked the question even though I knew the answer.

Last night, Knight had told Rhash and me he'd heard rumblings of trouble. A takeover.

The work I did for Knight was rarely trouble. It was legwork, checks on clients and girls. Providing security, presence, escorting girls to and from appointments. Sometimes stuff went down in his club and he needed a team to take care of. Shit happened and did, if someone was stupid enough to try it or thought they could pay or bully the girls into keeping their mouths shut after they'd misused them. But usually work for Knight was a mundane payday.

The meeting that included the boys had mostly been Knight wanting to know how the shit with Serena got so fucked. Live had reported he'd done the routine and didn't cut corners. Knight had interrogated the rest of the team about all new clients and their background checks.

After that, he'd dismissed everyone but Rhash and me and shared that he had a gut feeling Serena was the beginning. He'd had someone come to him on the hush-hush saying they were hearing something was brewing. An old nemesis was back in town. Knight had fucked him over years ago and he was setting up to fuck back. Knight's brother was also back in town, and although he seemed to be toeing the family line, they'd had issues. Nick, Knight's brother, used to work for Knight. He knew the operation and Knight wouldn't put it past him to sell information.

Knight was also concerned about a mole.

That meant, he'd told us, he'd brought in outside talent. Someone objective. Someone not on the team.

Someone Knight wanted me to partner with to investigate Knight's operation and assess the danger, inside and out, and neutralize it if we found something while Rhash kept an eye on business.

The outside talent Knight brought in was Tucker Creed.

"Talked with Sebring after your meeting earlier," he stated, confirming what I knew. "He told me he told you. After that, I shared with him we had history and I was gonna have a word with you 'cause if we're gonna work together, we need to talk about that history."

I stared at him, my brain moving fast.

I did what I did for Knight Sebring because I knew how it felt, to spread your legs for someone because you were forced to take him for whatever reason forcing you to do it. I had no Knight Sebring to protect me from his bullshit, his demands, his temper. I had no Rhash or Live or Tiny to swoop in and teach him a lesson on one of the numerous occasions he did something I did not like.

There was no denying Knight and his boys operated outside the bounds of law.

In my mind, there was also no denying what they did was providing a needed service.

Until I learned the hard way how to protect myself, I would have done anything for the kind of protection they provided the girls.

Now I provided that protection. I got paid for it. I broke the law to do it. I conspired to break the law, making it safe for them to do it. And I did not give one fuck.

This meant, if there was some asshole out there that wanted to take over Knight's operation, I had to do what I had to do to stop it.

Even take a partner.

I was down with that.

Until now.

"We're not working together," I told him, moving out of the room and feeling him following me.

"He considered assigning this to you but you're tight with his team, might not be able to be objective. But more, Sebring doesn't want you out there on your own," Creed said to my back.

"He's protective. He'll get over it," I said to the bathroom as I walked into it.

I went right to my toothbrush.

Creed stopped in the doorway and leaned a shoulder against the jamb.

"Sebring strikes me as a man who likes things to go the way he wants 'em to go," Creed noted, and he was not wrong.

"I'll have a chat with him," I muttered to the basin as I grabbed my toothbrush and turned on the faucet.

His voice changed. It was deep. There was roughness to it with an edge of smooth, and that was also a change. It had been deep and smooth back in the day. Now that hint of rough said he smoked. It said he drank. It said he lived as jagged as his voice.

But when it came at me just then, there was a vein of soft that brought back the raw.

"Sylvie, we need to—"

I turned my head to him, toothpaste in hand and cut him off to declare, "I don't do partners."

"You did," he returned immediately, his eyes watching me closely. "But he died."

That sent raw through me again for two reasons.

One, because he was right. My partner died and he did it leaving a wife, a kid and one on the way. Stupid fuck enlisted. Enlisted when we were at fucking *war*. "Gonna do my bit," he said. Fucking fucker got out of the Marines, set up a life where there was a possibility, not a probability, that people would shoot at him. And then he went *back* to the probability, re-enlisting, and got himself shot dead.

The other reason was because I knew Creed had checked me out, and I didn't like that. I didn't like him knowing anything about me. I figured Knight hired him, he was good at what he did.

So he knew.

Everything.

I turned back to the mirror and loaded up my toothbrush. "Yeah, I did. He died. Learned that lesson. Now I don't do partners."

"This shit is what Knight thinks it is, the ride's gonna be bumpy. You need someone at your back," he replied.

Maybe, but it sure as hell would not be him.

Before shoving the toothbrush in my mouth, my eyes went to the mirror and I returned, "Need it, I got Knight or Rhash," then I started brushing.

Creed appeared in the mirror behind me and my eyes went up to his in the mirror.

"He might have a mole. As far as his team's concerned, it's business as usual for both of them," he told me something Knight explained last night. "Banks nor Sebring are available to you."

I shrugged.

"Sylvie, I've already been workin' this job a month. I know that team better than you do."

That pissed me off enough to pull the brush out, spit out foam then catch his eyes in the mirror again. "No fucking way. You may think you do and they may have secrets they haven't shared, but no amount of digging you could do in a month tells you more than what I know working side by side with those guys for years. You've lived the life, Creed. It's written all over you. You know that. You had something on one of them, Knight would already have that intel. So you don't have shit." After delivering that, I shoved the brush back in and kept at my teeth.

"You're right," he confirmed. "That doesn't mean there isn't something to get."

29

I shrugged again.

"You know what hangs in the balance," he stated, and I held his eyes.

I knew, but he told me anyway.

"Scenario one, Knight keeps business open and another girl gets it worse than Serena last night. He keeps it open, that shit escalates and girls get hurt. Scenario two, he shuts it down. Okay for him, but if he can't neutralize the threat in a timely manner, that means first, he's gotta let boys go. He doesn't need a team that big when there's no girls to look after. Second, the girls are fucked. They got no jobs, they got no money, then they look for alternate ways to get paid without a man or a five foot two powerhouse at their back. You know Sebring. He won't put them in danger. He'll shut down. That club turns over a mint. He'll survive. Those girls won't."

I stopped brushing. I spit, rinsed and looked back to his eyes in the mirror as I shoved my brush in the holder. "So I'll find the mole, if there is one, and I'll track down the trouble and put it out of commission. You've been looking into me, Creed. You know what I'm capable of. This assignment is not outside my skill level."

"Two working together is safer and shuts this shit down faster than one," he shot back.

Unfortunately, this was true.

"Then I know a couple guys who I can work with," I returned. "They're local. They can hit the ground running. I'll talk with Knight about them."

"Again, I've had the job a month. I don't have to hit the ground running, Sylvie. Right now, it's you who's catching up."

Fuck.

Fuck!

Exactly how was this happening?

Exactly how in *the fuck* was I standing in my bathroom, brushing my teeth, Tucker Fucking *Creed* at my back after I hadn't seen him for sixteen *fucking* years, talking to me about partnering on a job with him and not groveling or writhing in pain after I kicked his ass?

I knew how.

Because that was then, but that was over. And this was now.

This was now.

That was over.

"Fine," I agreed and watched a weird flare in his eyes, but I ignored that. I turned to face him and kept talking. "Got shit to do. We'll meet with Knight. After, you'll catch me up."

"No, now we gotta get shit outta the way, so as we work, it doesn't get *in* the way."

"No shit to get out of the way," I replied and moved out from in front of him and deeper into the bathroom.

This got me another eye flare, which wasn't weird. It was annoyed.

"Sylvie—"

I shook my head. "I don't just work for Knight, you know. I got things I gotta get done. It's late. I don't have a lot of time. You wanna help out, you can feed Gun on your way out."

"I ride along on your shit, we talk before the meeting, which means after we can get down to it."

This was, for anyone other than Tucker Creed, an excellent suggestion.

Since it was Tucker Creed, I shook my head. "Not gonna happen. I work alone." He opened his mouth to speak so I finished quickly, "Except for this gig for Knight, I work alone."

He didn't move.

I did, to put my hands to the hem of my shirt, and I did this as I asked, "You not moving, does that mean you aren't gonna help out and feed my cat?"

"I know," he whispered, and for the first time in a long time I had to hold back a flinch.

But I managed it and kept the mask in place.

"No shit?" I asked.

"We need to talk, Sylvie." He leaned forward an inch. "He told me—"

Oh no.

Fuck no.

I whipped my shirt off and tossed it aside. Creed stopped speaking abruptly and his eyes dropped to my torso as my hands moved to my belt.

"Learn this about me, partner, and I suggest you do it now," I told him. "I do not go back. Eyes ahead. Feet moving forward. I don't ever fucking go back. I don't talk about it. I don't think about it." I undid the button on my jeans and pulled the zip down. "You were in my life a long time ago. I've lived two full lifetimes since then, each entirely different. I like the one I'm in now. I'm not going back to the ones before. I didn't like them as much."

His eyes shot back to mine and his lips whispered, "Sylvie—"

It was my turn to lean in an inch. "Deal breaker. You're all fired up to discuss that shit, this is done. I'll tell Knight to find you another partner. He'll understand. We're tight. He'll give me that and not one thing will change between us. You keep your mouth shut about that shit, eyes forward, feet moving ahead, mind on the job, we'll be fine."

His gaze moved over my face and it took its time.

Then he said quietly, "You're serious."

"Serious as shit," I replied immediately then pulled down my jeans.

I stepped out of them and straightened, hands to my panties.

"You gonna hang while I shower?" I asked on a tilt of my head.

His eyes were locked to mine. "I'm ride-along with you," he declared.

"Man, I work alone."

"Not anymore."

I took my fingers out of the waistband of my panties and planted my hands on my hips. "Deal is Knight's job and only Knight's job."

"Deal is, we're partners. We learn to work together so we don't get dead workin' together. That means we take every opportunity to work together. Sebring's footin' the bill and you got yourself extra hands, eyes and brains on your other jobs that have shit to do with him. Honest to God, you gonna turn your back on that?"

"Yes," I returned instantly.

"Then that tells me that hard shell with sharp edges you grew isn't about life but about protecting yourself," he shot back. "Which means you won't let me in because of the shit we share. That means it's between us. And that means, we need to take each other's back, with that shit between us, we're fucked. And that... *partner,* means, if that shit's between us, you aren't lookin' forward. That's bullshit. You got your eyes trained way the fuck back."

Fucking fuck, fuck, *fuck.*

I held his gaze.

Then I told him, "Full can. Wet food. Cat bowls in the cupboard by the stove. She likes a clean one every day. And, by the way, I get out of the shower, before we hit the road, toast would be good. Don't skimp on the butter and ignore the grape jelly. The kids eat that. I like orange marmalade and don't skimp on that either."

His head jerked to the side. "The kids?"

"Don't fuck with me, partner, you know exactly who I'm talking about."

"Adam, Leslie and Theo. Neighbor's kids," he stated immediately. "Then there's Josh and Dora, your dead partner's kids."

Oh yeah. He'd looked into me, but he was still fishing.

I didn't know what to make of that so I didn't make anything of it.

"You get more visitors than the Pope," he remarked.

Yeah, he'd looked into me.

My eyes went down to see Gun slink into the room, rubbing her fluffy side against Creed's jeans-covered ankle.

Damn cat. Figured. She only liked me and Adam, and now, apparently, Creed. She didn't give the side-rub to anyone she didn't like.

Shit.

I got rid of this asshole, me and my cat were having a chat.

I looked back up at Creed.

"Cat's hungry," I reminded him, then I put my hands in my panties and yanked them down.

By the time I straightened, Creed was gone and I just caught Gun's hind end rounding the door.

I didn't bother closing the bathroom door to take my shower. He'd seen it before. It'd been years, but he'd seen it. So had a number of other men.

Anyway, if he had a mind to my privacy, he'd keep well away, and I needed that right about then.

Before I stepped in, I shouted, "Don't forget the coffee! Strong!"

"Strong!" Tucker *Fucking* Creed shouted back.

Tucker Fucking Creed making coffee in my kitchen.

Jesus.

I got in the shower and kept it buried where it should be. No tequila. No bourbon. Nothing would work it out.

The job would get done then we would be done.

Then he would be gone and I would move on.

Again.

We stood in my front yard, me in a tight, ribbed, grass green tank, low rider jeans, wide brown belt, gun at the back and brown cowboy boots with a piece of toast in one hand, a travel mug of coffee in the other, Creed carrying another one of my mugs.

My mug in Creed's long-fingered, veined hand with the stark, pale nicks of scars around his knuckles. Strong hands. Capable hands. Experienced hands.

Christ.

"Uh… no," I told him. "I drive. You ride."

"No offense, Sylvie, but you drive like a lunatic and the interior of your car was made for people like you; small who like to make a lot of noise. I'm not folding into that death trap. I drive. You ride."

I stared at him. "That is not gonna happen."

"Yeah, it is."

"No, it isn't."

"Not me that's got shit to do," he reminded me.

Fuck!

"Seein' as you're part Grandpa, I'll check my foot," I allowed.

"And you'll stop at stop signs."

I shrugged. "Sure."

"That would be, come to a complete halt."

Fuck!

"God granted me peripheral vision, Creed. I can see someone coming. I'll slow and roll through like normal. You'll be fine."

"Jesus, Sylvie, the slow and roll doesn't work. A stop sign is put up for a reason."

I cocked my head to the side and narrowed my eyes. "When did you get a stick planted up your ass?"

He cocked his head to the side and regarded me closely. "We talkin' about our pasts now?"

Fuck, fuck, fuck!

"Okay, I'll stop at stop signs," I gave in.

"And you won't turn on red if there's a sign that says you can't turn on red," he kept pushing.

He *so totally* followed me.

Often.

Shit.

My stare turned to a glare. I bit off a huge chunk of buttery, marmalade coated toast and said sharply through it, "Fine."

"Speed limit, as in, you'll go the."

I chewed, swallowed and asked through slitted eyes, "Jesus, *are* you a Grandpa?"

"Daughter's twelve, son's ten, so no, not yet, thank fuck."

I didn't even blink. It cost me, but I didn't even blink.

Fuck, he had kids.

Fuck, that killed.

"Ten miles over," I offered.

"Five miles," he countered.

"Seven."

He grinned and I didn't blink again, but that killed too. With me, he used to grin a lot, smile a lot, laugh a lot. Even so, each one was precious. He'd been beautiful. All of those transformed his features so he was magnificent.

Age and scars hadn't changed that. Not even a little bit. He still had great, even, strong white teeth. Fantastic lips. Strong, expressive features.

Magnificent.

"Deal," he grunted and moved to my girl.

I moved to her too, and juggled my breakfast (even though it was past noon) in order to get in. With the coffee between my thighs and the toast between my teeth, I started her up and pulled out maybe a *hair* faster than was needed.

That said, that was how I usually pulled out.

"Jesus," Creed muttered.

I bit back a smile and changed gears. I shot forward on a screech of tires then took a bite out of my toast and drove one handed.

"Right, catch me up," I ordered.

"You first," he replied.

I glanced to the side.

Shit, Tucker Creed was sitting beside me in my car.

Shit!

I buried that and asked, "Me first, what?"

"You first. I'm ride-along, maybe it would be good to know what I'm ridin' into."

"Hit The Retreat. Check in at the office. If there's time, check in on Serena. After that, Knight," I told him.

35

Kristen Ashley

"You still on The Retreat job?" he asked, exposing just how much he'd looked into me, which meant just how often he'd followed me.

I'd never tagged a tail.

Damn.

"Man, I'm *always* on The Retreat job," I informed him. "Every third asshole who cheats on his wife takes his bitch to The Retreat. My ass is in the parking lot there so often, management suggested they paint my name in a parking spot so it'll be reserved."

"Not good for business, a PI's name in a parking spot," Creed muttered.

"That's why I declined. That's me, looking out for the local adult resort."

I heard his chuckle, and it was different than I remembered too. Not just deep and smooth. The rough was in it. It made it sexier. A lot fucking sexier.

Shit.

"You ever been there?" he asked.

"Where?" I asked back.

"The Retreat," he answered.

"Partner, were you talking in your sleep thirty seconds ago?"

"I meant as a client, not an investigator."

Oh yeah, I had. Rubber mattresses. Fake silk sheets. Velvet comforters. Mirrors on the ceiling. Hot tubs in every room. "Environment chambers" where you could fuck in a gentle rain, breeze or both. Swings. Love machines. Steam rooms. Twelve channels of porn. Rooms available at matinee rates.

I'd *so totally* been there.

"So we *are* talking about our pasts?" I asked and he was silent. "Advice," I went on. "You feel like an adventure, call the top in the environment chamber. Seems like it'd be awesome, but that water hitting your face all the time is distracting."

That got more silence, which worked for me because it meant he shut up.

It stopped working for me when it went on a long time. He had a month of a possible hostile takeover of Knight's business to catch me up on and he couldn't do it in sign language when my eyes were on the road. This was because I couldn't see his hands and I didn't know sign language.

I glanced his way again, mouth open to say something, then I glanced straight ahead and shut my mouth.

I did this because his stubbled jaw was tight and his head was turned slightly to look out the side window.

36

Unhappy thoughts. Unhappy thoughts I did not give one shit about.

"Rule," I said quietly into the car. "You don't wanna know, don't ask."

"Deal," he muttered immediately, and that killed, too.

I knew why. For some reason, it fucked him up that I'd had experience of The Retreat. Why this would be, I did not know. *He* disappeared on *me,* and he'd done it nearly sixteen freaking years ago. He couldn't think I'd been holding out, pining for him all that time. He'd looked into me, he knew I didn't. At first, I didn't have a choice. Then I did, and I sure as fuck took advantage of it.

I wasn't going to think about that, either.

"You wanna fill me in on what you've learned for the last month?" I asked as I kept moving us toward The Retreat.

"Yeah," Creed answered. "You know Drake Nair?"

"Yup," I replied.

"You know who he is to Knight?"

"Been in Denver awhile, Creed, and almost all that time, I've known Knight."

"So you know Knight stole his stable *and* his club right out from under him."

"Yup," I repeated.

"And you know he's back in town."

"Didn't until last night, but yeah, Knight filled Rhash and me in. Rhash already knew. He flew under my radar. Nair's half asshole, half moron and since most people can't think very well with their ass, even though they try, he's not much of a threat, so can't say I pay a lot of attention to him."

"Asshole with money gets other people to think for him," Creed replied as I took a turn onto Colfax.

"This is true," I muttered before switching gears and shoving the last bite of toast in my mouth.

"Been watchin', Nick hasn't got near him. Nick doesn't keep good company, though. He's not doin' blow all the time now, but he doesn't have great friends. Been too busy, and without a partner, only had so much time, couldn't make a connection. That doesn't mean the connection between Nick and Nair isn't there."

"Right," I said through a full mouth, then finished chewing and swallowing before I asked, "Now tell me what else has kept you busy."

"Makin' sure you and Rhashan Banks are clean."

Kristen Ashley

My head whipped to the side and I stared two full seconds before I looked back at the road, feeling like I'd been punched in the gut.

I thought he'd looked into me because that was what I'd do. I had a prospective partner pinned to me, I'd know him inside and out before I got anywhere near the job.

I didn't think for one second Knight set him on me.

Or Rhash.

"Knight set you on Rhash and me?"

"Knight said it was a waste of time. *I* investigated you and Rhashan. Shit like this, no stone unturned. He's blinded by history and loyalty. He hired me because I'm not."

"Well, just to confirm," my voice was barbed, "neither of us would fuck Knight. Ever."

"Any way that could be?" he asked, and I glanced at him again before looking at the road.

"Don't wanna know, partner, don't ask," I said quietly, and felt his eyes on me.

"This shit, I *need* to know. He's deep with his woman. You two got history I haven't learned, affects everything, including us working together. You two hook up?"

"No," I replied.

"Ever?" he asked.

"No," I repeated.

"Wanted it?" he pushed. "Either one of you."

"Yeah, absolutely. We discussed it, found we weren't compatible, but that was years ago. One night we both had too much to drink. The other part of that incompatibility is that you fuck up what we got with sex, it'll never be the same, and what we got is worth *never* fucking up. You with me?"

"Yeah," he muttered.

"Then I'll make sure you're totally with me. I'm tight with Anya too. We're solid. She has no reason to know Knight and I even discussed that shit, even one night when we were getting hammered and letting it all hang out. She doesn't need that thought in her head. He's not deep with her, Creed. She's his life. Their daughter is his life. His family is the most precious thing to him; a man who's got everything so he's also got a lot to choose from, and his two girls

38

are his choice. Do not fuck that and do not put me in the position where I'm even a *little* responsible for fucking that."

"She the jealous type?" he asked.

"Don't know and seriously do not want to find out. There's even the barest possibility of losing that, Knight will lose me. I got two people who mean something to me, Creed, and he's one of them. You take half of my world away from me... for sixteen years, you were a memory for me and that's what I'll make you for your kids, too. Except you'll never stroll back into their bedrooms while they're sleeping. You still with me?"

He was silent a beat before, "Two people in your life who mean something to you?"

"Yeah."

"That's it?"

"Yeah."

"Banks?"

"He's not the other one. We're tight but not that tight." He was silent again and this lasted more than a beat so I prompted, "Did you get me?"

"I got you, Sylvie," he answered quietly.

I flipped the left turn signal on and slowed, stopped, waiting for my opening and pulled into the parking lot of The Retreat. I found my spot and reversed expertly in it. I switched off the ignition then I reached behind Creed's seat to grab my camera. I rested it on my thigh and grabbed my coffee. I threw back a slug, returned it then yanked out my cell, found the number and hit go.

It rang twice in my ear before I heard, "You're killin' me."

I grinned into the phone as I stared at the building. "C'mon, buddy, what would you do without my incentives?"

"They find out I'm giving you info, they'll find other places for their rendezvous."

"There are no other places in Denver who rent for an afternoon and have rubber mattresses, Clyde," I reminded him then continued. "Looking for a guy, five ten, salt and pepper, glasses, paunch, suit, drives a Chevy mini-van."

"No mini-van," Clyde stated.

"He been in before?"

"Fuck," Clyde muttered.

He had.

"Wednesday's his day, yeah?" I asked.

"Fuck," Clyde muttered.

"Crisp bill, Clyde."

"They usually get here around one."

I looked at my watch. Five minutes.

"Right," I said into the phone. "I'll be in the office with your money after they check in and get to their room."

"Fuck. You're killin' me." Clyde was still muttering.

"They ever quit coming?" I asked.

He didn't answer my question because they didn't. They always kept coming in more ways than one.

Instead, he said, "See you in ten minutes."

I grinned again and flipped my phone shut.

"Clyde the day clerk?" Creed asked as I shoved my phone back in my back pocket, grabbed my coffee and the camera. I took a sip of it as I switched the camera on.

"Yup," I answered as I shoved the coffee back between my thighs then I looked to him. "So, the last month, Drake Nair on radar but nothing, Nick Sebring on radar but nothing and you ascertained that Rhash and I would never fuck Knight. You get anything else?"

"Lively did the full check on your girl's client last night," he replied. "I followed him through it even though he didn't know it. When you hit that house last night, I was as surprised to see the for sale sign in the yard as you were."

This was good to know.

"So Live isn't falling down on the job," I surmised.

"That's still up for debate. I just know none of the team has deposited any-thing unusual in their accounts. They've also not purchased anything unusual, high ticket items or even medium range toys. Half-assed tails, they aren't off the beaten path or normal routines. Phone records show nothin' either. So if there's a mole, he's playin' it smart and that means we dig deep."

"There's no mole," I told him firmly.

"We still gotta look, Sylvie," he returned, his eyes holding mine.

"Yeah, and that sucks for me because these are my boys. If they ever find out I did this shit, I'm a rat. They'll get over it, the loyalty they have to Knight, but it'll take a while and I may never have their trust like I've got it now."

"But you'll do that for Knight."

I nodded. "I'll do it for Knight."

He kept his eyes locked with mine as he said softly, "And the girls."

I nodded again and didn't speak softly when I agreed, "And the girls."

He didn't look away and he didn't speak for long moments. I knew what he was thinking as he looked at me.

He knew why I'd risk a rap sheet for those girls.

Then he spoke.

"New deal."

I rolled my eyes and when I stopped rolling them, I stated, "Jesus, partner, I can't keep up."

He didn't reply to my comment.

Instead, he said, "I work the team. You work Nick and Nair."

I didn't suck in breath, but I held it because that was cool. Way cool.

Creed kept talking. "We stay tight. Meet often, talk often, debrief, and you need me, I'm there. I need you, you come when I call. But I look into the boys. That way you're not a rat. If they find out you worked this, they'll find out you didn't work them. Even if I turn up nothin', I'll undoubtedly turn up somethin'. Everyone has secrets. I uncover them and they don't pertain to this investigation, you're none the wiser. They haven't shared with you, when this is over, they'll know you *don't* know. They can trust you got nothin' on them. They can trust you didn't turn traitor. Keeps you solid with the team."

Yeah, that was cool, and that was huge because it stated firmly *he* was cool. He got it. He got the team. He got the importance of the team. And he got me.

"Deal," I whispered.

His eyes moved over my face then over my shoulder and he muttered, "Mini-van."

I looked over my shoulder and watched the mini-van drive into the lot and past my car. It parked two spots down. My target got out the driver's side door as a Nissan sedan drove in and passed my 'Vette to park just beyond the mini-van. My target waited for his piece, and thinking quickly, I moved my travel mug to the floor.

When they began walking toward reception they'd have to walk in front of my car.

This meant they might see us and wonder why we were sitting in the car and not going at it on a rubber mattress covered in fake silk sheets, all this accessible only feet away.

Therefore, my hand shot out tagging Creed around the neck. I angled across the emergency brake, pulling him sharply to me and crushed my mouth to his.

One second elapsed before two strong arms curled around me, tightened and hauled me across the brake. He twisted me so my back was to his hard thighs and Creed hunched over me, his mouth pressing hard against mine. One of my arms angled across his back, the fingers of my other hand drove into his hair and curled, fisting the thick softness in my hand.

Ten more seconds elapsed, and my heart was thundering in my chest so hard I could feel it in my throat when his head came up.

I forced myself to recover quickly and quip, "Way to sell it, partner."

He grinned down at me. My heart squeezed at seeing it so damned close and he replied on a murmur, "Gonna do it, go big."

"We share that motto," I informed him.

"Good to know," he returned.

"I gotta position. Got photos to take," I reminded him, seeing as he wasn't letting me go.

"New plan. You go in and pay off Clyde. I'll take the camera, get in the room and get your client enough evidence to nail his balls to the wall. When I'm done, I'll meet you at reception."

"I'm all for nailing a lying, cheating asshole's balls to the wall, but usually shots of them entering the room work."

"Shots of him entering something else would work better."

I couldn't argue with that.

But I could argue something else. "Man, you're a mountain. No way you're gonna get in one of those rooms and not be seen."

"Trust me."

It was the wrong thing to say. Absolutely, one hundred percent. He knew it and I knew it. We both knew the other knew it because both our bodies tensed so tight, I could feel with the slightest movement my tendons would snap, and I sensed the same with him.

Still, I buried it. We had to work together. We had to partner up. Which meant I had to trust him.

This sucked, but it was my experience that a lot of shit in life sucked. This was just the most recent.

So I forced myself to relax and said, "Right. Meet you in reception."

He lifted up, taking me with him and twisting me in my seat. I retrieved the camera that fell to the floor at my feet, as well as my travel mug. I handed him the camera and avoided his eyes, trying not to look like I was avoiding his eyes.

He angled out his side.

I angled out mine.

He moved right.

I moved left toward reception.

Clyde rolled his eyes when I entered.

"Please, a hundred dollars for a two minute phone call?" I asked as I walked toward the reception desk. "I am not a pain in your ass."

"No, you're killin' me," he returned.

"No, I'm sending your kids to college," I retorted, pulling out my money clip and handing him the bill.

He snatched it out of my hand and it disappeared in a blink.

Bullshit moaning weasel.

My eyes went to the TV sitting angled toward him at the end of the reception desk. I leaned into my forearms on the desk and checked it out.

"Classic porn," I muttered. "Odd choice."

"Seen all the others, like, a gazillion times," Clyde muttered back, and I grinned.

I had no doubt.

"We havin' a party?" Clyde asked, because I usually paid him off then took off, and I looked from the porn to him.

He was balding and not liking it, thus growing a line of hair way too long in order to do the comb-over, a tactic that men should abandon. I didn't know when they'd get that bald was beautiful. All you had to do was have the balls to carry it off.

Clyde clearly didn't have those kinds of balls. Then again, he was slender, narrow-shouldered, had an unfortunately shaped nose with a hook at the end *and* a bump on the ridge, and squirrelly eyes. Thus, just physically, there were a myriad of reasons he lacked confidence. Not physically; he was a whiner, not a good trait in anyone, man or woman.

It was my experience anyone could work anything. A man or woman could be what convention said was ugly or overweight, and if they held their shoulders straight, looked you in the eye and had a ready, genuine smile, that

43

shit melted away. The light shone from within, and if you had the balls to shine it, all anyone would see was beauty.

Alas, people did not get this, and Clyde was one of those people.

"Waiting for my partner," I answered and his brows shot up.

"You got a partner?" he asked.

"Yup," I replied.

"Since when?"

"Since a couple of hours ago."

"I give it a week," he muttered, his eyes sliding back to the TV.

I hoped it would last a day. I worried it would last a month.

I moved to a chair and sat my ass in it. I lifted my boots up to rest crossed at the ankles on the coffee table scattered with Retreat brochures and settled in. I killed time by calling Serena to make sure she was okay (she was, kind of). Calling Knight and leaving a message that I'd connected with Creed and we were on the job. And last, calling Live to check in to make certain he wasn't beating himself up too much. The last call lasted a while because he was beating himself up too much, and it took some time and an arsenal of my teasing to get him to feel better.

I'd barely flipped the phone shut on Live when I heard a tap on the window and I looked there to see Creed outside, crooking a finger at me.

"The summons," I said to Clyde. "Gotta go."

"Don't come back now, ya hear?" Clyde returned, and it was my turn to roll my eyes since he was full of it. Sure, if his bosses found out he was doing what he was doing, he was shit out of luck *and* a job. He was also a survivor so his bosses would never learn, and he averaged a hundred extra dollars a week for doing nothing so he'd keep doing it. Unfortunately, he'd also keep bitching about it.

I didn't bother with a wave or retort as I walked out and stopped on the sidewalk next to Creed.

"Well?" I asked.

His answer was to turn the camera's back to me with an image on it.

I leaned in and checked it out.

"Whoa, soccer dad likes pony play," I murmured. "Ride 'em cowboy." I heard Creed's chuckle and looked up at him. "How'd you get in?" I asked.

"They had other things on their mind and the TV blaring loud. Got in through the bathroom window," he answered and I felt my eyes get big.

"Shit, man, those are high *and* tight."

"Upper body strength and determination go a long way," he replied.

He was not wrong about that and visibly had the former while the latter was demonstrated on the camera.

"Right on," I stated, lifting up my hand in an invitation for a high five.

He stared at my hand and didn't move.

"Seriously?" I asked. "You gonna leave me hanging?"

His sky blue eyes came to mine, and again I held my breath as his hand moved. He gave me a high five, but when his big hand clapped against mine, it stayed there. His fingers shoved through, linking with mine, bringing our hands down. Then he shifted them so we were palm to palm, fingers curled around the sides. This he took straight into another shift where we had our fingers curled together from tips to knuckles in our palms. He then used my hand to pump our arms twice, so hard I was forced to take a step into him.

Then he let me go.

I forced air in my lungs.

Then I joked, "I'm learning good things about you, partner. Jive handshake master. I like it."

He shook his head grinning and tossing the camera in the air. My hands shot out to catch it so it wouldn't fall, and seeing as I was engaged in this endeavor, he had the chance to start sauntering toward my girl.

I took a moment to watch, mostly because his shirt hung really good from his shoulders. It was untucked so it mostly covered his ass, but his movement hinted at a fine one. And I was coming to the conclusion I seriously liked his boots.

Once I processed this information, I followed him.

I stood at the big one-way window in Knight's office that faced down to Knight's now empty nightclub and watched Creed stroll across the vast space toward the front door.

The meeting was done. Rhash met Creed. Creed gave his brief. We discussed our plans and now Rhash was gone, Creed was off to work the boys, and I was going to spend the rest of the afternoon finding and surveilling Nick Sebring.

I felt Knight get close but I didn't take my eyes from the window as I watched Creed walk out the front door.

"It's him," Knight murmured.

"It's him," I confirmed.

"Fuck, babe, you never shared his name. I had no fuckin' clue. I did, that contract would not have been signed."

I looked up at him. He was scary handsome in all the ways those two words could communicate. That was, he was incredibly good-looking; tall, dark-haired, striking blue eyes that were a deeper and more vivid blue than Creed's, but they were no less effective. His features were not beautiful, they were aggressively masculine. He was also scary because he just *was* aggressively masculine in a way that no woman or man could mistake. Just like with Creed, with one look at Knight, you knew you did not play with him, you did not mess with him. If you couldn't deal with all that was him, you avoided him.

It was hot. Luckily, since we'd made our decision that drunken night years ago and he was in way deep with his woman, he was like a brother to me, so his hot didn't affect me, our relationship or the job I did for him, other than the inescapable fact I couldn't mistake it.

"It's cool," I assured him. "We're cool. We'll get this done. No worries."

His eyes moved over my face as his lips muttered, "Why don't I believe that?"

"Knight, you know me. I'm about the job. No joke, we'll get this done."

Finally, his gaze locked with mine. "I want this job done, you know that. What I don't want, in gettin' that, is you shredded in the process."

Seriously, I loved Knight Sebring.

"I'm good," I said softly.

Knight studied me again before nodding and saying, "Word is he's the best."

I found this interesting.

"We got the best in Denver, so I'm surprised you didn't go to Nightingale Investigations," I remarked.

"Who do you think told me they heard that shit on the street?" Knight asked, and I felt my brows go up.

"Lee Nightingale?" I asked back.

"Yeah, but he's covered in work. He recommended Hawk Delgado, but I had a sit down with him. Delgado isn't about finesse like Nightingale can be so we decided it wouldn't work. It was Delgado who recommended Creed."

Liam "Lee" Nightingale of Nightingale Investigations was a badass private investigator-slash-bounty hunter-slash-anything goes man with a team of badasses to back him up. He'd contracted with me and I'd worked jobs with them when he needed a woman. I liked him, respected him and his team. They took pretty much any job that came along as long as the client could pay the hefty invoice, which meant the lawfulness of their activities was a bit vague. That said, they had close ties with law enforcement so it was a helluva lot less vague than Knight's.

Cabe "Hawk" Delgado, on the other hand, was a badass commando with a team of badasses to back him up. His jobs were usually more covert, intense and often out of town. I'd done one job with him and his team in town and that shit was extreme. It was kickass fun but it was extreme. Since most of his work was out of town, I didn't have a lock on the looseness of his morals.

In movie terms, Lee Nightingale was James Bond, except more kickass and super cool. He didn't bother messing with gadgets when he could just shoot someone. He was also a Broncos fan, and I had a feeling, when he had the time, James Bond watched rugby.

Hawk Delgado was John Rambo without exceptions, notwithstanding the headband.

What I knew about both of them was regardless of what they thought about his business, they were smart enough not to make an enemy of Knight Sebring, and he returned the favor. There was mutual respect, but no discussion about Knight's operations. I never asked how they felt, but then again, even if I did, they'd never tell.

My brows stayed up. "Hawk Delgado knows Creed?"

Knight nodded.

"You know their connection?" I asked.

"Worked jobs together."

"Those would be?" I pushed.

"They would be for you to ask Creed, Sylvie," he stated. "You got it in you to put that shit behind you, you gotta get to know your partner. I'll tell you this: it's fucked how shit works, but he's you, except male and maybe a little scarier. The shingle says PI. The word says his resume has a lot of blank spots and his

Kristen Ashley

skill set is varied. He doesn't take the job if he doesn't believe in the mission and like or respect who he's workin' for." Knight grinned. "But he charges a fuckuva lot more than you do."

My eyes went back to the window to take in the empty club and I muttered, "He's got kids to support."

Knight was silent.

I let this stretch, then threw him a grin and started toward the door, saying, "Got shit to do."

I had my hand on the handle when Knight called my name and I turned back.

"You need to bail, do it," he stated. "You're still mine, I'm still yours. Nothin', woman, not this shit, not you needin' to protect yourself from history in your face, not anything comes between you and me."

That meant the world, but he knew it so I didn't have to say it.

I jerked up my chin, but assured him again, "I'm looking forward. It's cool, Knight, trust me."

"You may be lookin' forward, babe, but that direction right now means most of what you see is history. You can't deal, you can't. Understood and it's all good."

Seriously, I fucking loved this guy.

Still, I griped, "Jeez, man, it was sixteen years ago. I'm totally over it."

"Anya left me or I lost her, I'd never get over it so don't bullshit me," he shot back. "There's only one, we both know it, and Tucker Creed was your one. So you aren't over it. That doesn't mean you can't cope. But you *won't* cope if you deny that somewhere inside you can't."

It kinda sucked he was hot, rich, cool *and* smart.

"Heartfelt, badass lecture over?" I asked, and his lips twitched.

"Yeah."

"Terrific. Got shit to do," I muttered and threw open the door.

"Sylvie," he called and I whirled on a snapped, "*What?*"

"Bottom of my soul," he whispered across the room, eyes locked to mine.

I sucked in breath through my nose before I whispered back, "Bottom of mine."

Then, before he could *really* get to me, I took off.

Chapter 4
Orange Sherbet Push-Ups

A cold, dark night in the hills of Kentucky, twenty-eight years earlier, Sylvie is six, Creed is eleven...

I stared up in Tucker Creed's pretty blue eyes that I could see were a pretty blue even in the dark.

Everyone in town knew Tucker Creed, his Momma and his dead Daddy. I'd even heard about them, all of them.

When his Daddy died, my Daddy told me the whole town went to his funeral. This was because he was a hero. He had the medals to prove it and *everything.*

My Daddy didn't talk about Tucker's Momma straight to me, but I heard him talking about her.

What I heard was him saying, "Winona Creed is a slut, a total fucking whore. If Brand Creed was alive today, he'd beat her bloody and the bitch would deserve it."

I wasn't certain sure what "slut" and "whore" meant, but obviously they weren't good. And I wasn't certain sure Brand Creed, Tucker's Daddy, would beat his wife bloody. That didn't seem like what a hero would do at all.

Looking up in eleven year old Tucker Creed's eyes in his cute boy's face, I could believe his Daddy was a hero. He was so tall. So handsome. His eyes so pretty. He looked like a hero, too. Now I knew what all the older girls at church were talking about all the times, and there were lots, when they talked about him. He was everything they said.

And more.

"I cannot believe you are SUCH a DICK!"

I heard the words and my body jerked hard, my eyes flying to the side.

Oh no, the words.

The words were here, too.

Suddenly, I felt hands over my ears. My eyes flew back and when they did, all I could see was Tucker Creed.

"Fuck you, you fuckin' cunt! Fuck YOU!"

That was a man. A man and a woman saying the words, and gosh, I didn't know one of them, but it sounded a lot worse than Daddy and my stepmom's.

My eyes slid to the side and I saw them outside the little, rickety house with its gutters falling down. The outside light was on. I could see the paint on the sides of the house and around the windows nicked and chipped. The screen hadn't been switched out of the side door since summer, which was crazy, and the screen had come loose on one end, hanging down. I could see the house was a whole lot smaller than Daddy's and mine. Then again, everyone in town, even me, knew the Creeds didn't have a lot of money, and my Daddy and Granddaddy and all the ones before made certain that everyone knew we did.

I could also see a man and a woman outside in the snow. She was barefoot. He had his jacket on. She was pushing him. He shoved back and she fell on her bottom in the snow.

I gasped.

I just heard the words.

I never saw. Never, never, *ever*.

Tucker Creed jerked me around so his back was to the house and I couldn't see anymore. Then he started walking, fast, making me walk backwards, his hands still covering my ears.

Silently, Bootsie followed us.

He came out like I did. He came out to get away from the words. He came out so he wouldn't *see*.

"You don't like the words," I whispered, and watched his head move funny, hard, fast, like a twitch.

"The words?"

"Mean words," I told him as he kept pushing us back.

"*Fuck you, motherfucker!*" the woman shouted. "*You leave, don't come back!*"

"*I time it right, you got a bottle of Jack in you, you'll lie back and spread so fast, my head will spin, then you'll spin that tired, used cunt of yours ON my fuckin' head!*" the man shouted back.

Tucker kept pushing me into the woods, his hands over my ears, clenching kind of tight but not hurting, his body blocking the view.

Then his mouth came to my ear.

"I don't like the words."

He didn't like the words. Like me.

"I don't either," I whispered in his ear.

"*Time it for TWO bottles, asshole. That's what it'll take for you to get me to spread!*" she screamed.

Tucker kept pushing us back, asking, "You got the words?"

I nodded, his hands moving with my head. "Daddy and his new wife."

Tucker kept pushing us then he said, "We're in the sun."

I blinked.

"What?" I asked.

"We're in the sun. On the pier. By the lake."

"*Get off me, bitch!*" the man shouted. I closed my eyes tight, but my hands came up, lifting high. I put them over his ears.

"We're in the sun," I agreed, seeing it, feeling it.

We were on the pier on the lake in the sun.

Tucker kept pushing me backwards. "We'll do cannonballs off the pier. My splashes'll be bigger than yours."

I kept my eyes shut, kept moving back with him, feeling Bootsie against my leg following us. I was also feeling the sun, the warmth, seeing the lake in my head, Tucker in swim trunks doing a cannonball off the pier.

"No way, my cannonballs are *the best*," I told him.

"Not as good as mine," he said.

"Better," I replied. I kept talking in his ear as he kept moving us back. "I'll bring a picnic. In a big basket. We'll swim and we won't wait thirty minutes after we eat."

"We won't wait."

"We'll jump in right after we eat. Bologna sandwiches. With cheese. And Ruffles, they have ridges. The cheesy kind. We'll drink as much Coke as we want. Cans and cans of it. And we'll eat frozen Snickers bars," I said.

"Frozen Snickers bars. Sounds good."

"Takes forever to eat them. It's great."

"Bologna sandwiches and frozen Snickers bars," he agreed.

"Cannonballs and sun and water," I said. "And nothing else."

"Nothing else," he agreed again.

"No one else," I told him.

"Just us," he said.

"Just us." I nodded, moving his hands with my head. "And Bootsie, my doggie."

"And your dog."

Kristen Ashley

We were moving up the incline I fell down, and it made me think things I didn't like.

I started to shiver.

"I been gone a long time, Tucker," I whispered. "Daddy might find out I'm gone. He doesn't like it when I take my walks."

"Then let's get you home, Sylvie."

He knew my name. I didn't know how. I didn't care. I just liked how it sounded when he said it.

We'd made it almost to the top when he let my ears go but took my hand, turned me and kept us walking. I heard him give a low, quiet whistle and Bootsie trotted with us.

"It happen a lot?" he asked in a soft voice.

"Unh-hunh," I answered and felt his hand squeeze mine.

"Your Momma... does it—?" I stopped talking when his hand squeezed mine again and he answered, "Yeah. Lots."

I didn't like that. I didn't like the words for me. I didn't like them for him, either.

I squeezed his hand back.

He kept walking me toward my house.

"You know where I live?" I asked.

"Everyone knows all about the Bissenettes," he answered in a way that was kind of funny. A kind of funny that didn't feel good.

I didn't say anything.

We kept walking, Bootsie at my side, and we did this a long time.

Then Tucker asked, "You go out when it happens?"

"Unh-hunh," I repeated.

"He ever catch you?"

"Yeah," I whispered, and the word was shaky, but his hand gave mine another squeeze so I knew he knew why my voice was shaky. That squeeze made me feel better.

I saw the fence that surrounded our backyard in front of me and Tucker was leading me to the gate.

He didn't say anything more until we got there. I thought he'd stop and I'd just go in, but he stopped and didn't let me go. He tugged my hand in a gentle way, like when I tugged at Bootsie when I wanted to pet her and she wasn't close enough to me.

52

I liked it.

I looked up as he turned into me.

"Next time you gotta get away, Sylvie, you come to me."

My breathing felt funny.

"What?" I whispered.

"It gets bad, you gotta get away, you come to me. I'll take care of you."

I stared at him.

"What?" I whispered again.

"We'll talk about the lake and cannonballs and how I'm gonna buy you orange sherbet push-ups from Merlin's store when summer comes."

Oh wow.

I *loved* orange sherbet push-ups. They were *the best.*

I had this feeling, deep, deep in my belly, that Tucker buying them for me would make them better.

"I'll freeze Snickers bars for you," I promised.

"Sounds good. I like Doritos. Cool Ranch."

"Okay. Ruffles for me. Doritos for you," I planned.

"Yeah," he agreed.

"Yeah." I nodded.

I stared up at him and felt my nose sting even as I heard my voice come out in a super, super quiet whisper.

"You'll take care of me?"

"My Dad said you always got something if you're not alone. We were alone. Now, we're not alone."

That thing deep in my belly felt funny, but it also felt nice.

"I don't like being alone," I whispered.

"You're not anymore."

That felt nice too. Nicer than my birthdays. Nicer even than Christmas!

I nodded.

His hand gave mine a squeeze. "Go in. Be careful."

I nodded again.

"Happens again, Sylvie, my room is on the right side, first window at the back. Just knock on the window. I'll hear you."

I nodded again.

"Don't let them see you," he whispered.

And I nodded again.

His hand gave mine a squeeze before he let me go.

He opened the door of the gate and he did it super slow, being careful, and I was thankful.

I started through, Bootsie at my side, and looked back at him.

I smiled.

He smiled back.

Wow.

It was the most beautiful thing I ever saw.

Then I slipped through the door. Tucker closed it slow and careful behind me and I did what I would do normally, but also what Tucker told me.

I got in and to my bed and didn't let them see me.

Chapter 5
Winner Takes All

Present day...

I opened my front door and smelled garlic.

Fuck.

Seriously?

I turned and tossed my keys on the table beside the front door. I pulled my gun and holster out of my belt at the back, set it on the table and moved to the left into my living room.

A huge, tan leather duffel was sitting, gapping open on my couch.

Fuck.

Fuck!

Seriously?

My eyes moved around the room and I saw the ashtrays had been cleaned, the beer bottles and dirty dishes cleared away and even the throws on the couches folded. My eyes moved up and I noted the wonky, hot pink, star-shaped fairy lights I had wrapped around my mantelpiece in disarray had been straightened and artfully draped.

They looked awesome.

Shit.

I stalked the other way, through my dining room, which still had the mess of magazines, newspapers and mail that had accumulated for the last month (maybe two) on the top of my dining room table. I stalked through the room even though, over the opened bar that delineated it from the kitchen, I saw Creed at my stove, his back to me.

"Uh, partner, I'm thinking I missed a memo," I stated.

He twisted at the waist to look at me.

"You feed your cat once a day?" he asked, and I stopped opposite the bar and planted my hands on my hips.

"Yeah," I answered.

"She says two," Creed informed me.

Shit. He spoke cat. This was not good. Gun knew *all* my secrets.

"Don't let her bullshit you," I ordered. "Though, if she's been good, when I get home she gets five cat treats."

"What constitutes bein' good?"

"She's breathing."

He threw back his head and burst out laughing, the heady gorgeous sound of it filling the space, bouncing off the walls, slamming into me so hard, it made my legs get weak.

Therefore, I stalked to the fridge to get a beer.

"You like ziti?" Creed asked as I yanked open the fridge door.

"Yeah, I like ziti," I answered. I closed the door coming out with a beer in my hand and went on. "What I don't like is your bag on my couch. What's the deal?"

He continued to stir sauce as his eyes came to me. "The deal is, we got a job to do and to do it we gotta get close with zero time to find that. So we gotta find the time to find that."

"How 'bout I eat your ziti and we put together a puzzle and find it before you leave and find a hotel room?"

"Too late," he replied. "Went over to meet Charlene and the kids. I told them I'm here, gonna be here awhile, I know about her situation and I'm on call if she needs anything. She seemed excited, and not just 'cause she needs the help. Apparently, she's worried about your way of life and thinks you're gonna die lonely. Also, her bathroom faucet is dripping. Something's rattling in her car. And that motherfucker who left her didn't switch the storm windows out to screens before he hauled ass. It's hot and she can't afford to run the air conditioning. So tomorrow, I'm gonna be busy."

I stood completely still, staring at him and waiting while I made the superhuman effort to keep my head from exploding.

This took a while, and Creed kept stirring the sauce even though his eyes didn't leave me.

Once I ascertained my head wasn't going to explode, or more aptly, I wasn't going to attack and indulge in an attempt to break his neck, I whispered, "That was not cool."

"I work and I don't fuck around when I do. There is no cool and uncool in a job. You do what you gotta do," he returned.

"You didn't have to do that," I shot back, but did it still whispering.

"I disagree," he replied.

"Explain, *exactly,* how that was okay."

"This was Arizona, you'd be deep in my life. You know the shit I care about, the people that mean something to me. You'd do what you can to make certain I didn't get taken away from any of it. That's how it's okay. You had a partner, his wife and kids are still a part of your life. You get me," he told me.

"I have your back. You have my word on that so you don't need that shit."

"Now I have your back for more than the fact I don't wanna see anything happen to you, but it's deeper. Way fuckin' deeper, and you know exactly how. They'd suffer and they'd suffer huge if you weren't there in the morning. So, shit goes down, no matter what it is, I'll bust my ass to make sure you're there in the morning."

Fuck.

Fuck!

He made sense. It was Asshole Invasive Sense (yes, meriting capital letters), but it was still sense.

Jesus.

I put the bottle cap edge to the counter, slammed the butt of my palm on it and the cap went flying. I ignored it and threw back a hefty pull.

When I dropped my hand, I knew he knew he'd won because he asked, "Anything on Nick?"

I gave in by answering, "Nothing, except I'm shocked to find Nick Sebring is boring." I rounded the bar, putting needed space between Creed and me. "His brother could be sitting and writing a letter and he'd be fascinating to watch. Nick. No. He's got a desk job. Works it, went home, made dinner, put on the game. That's it."

"So I take it tomorrow you're switchin' to Nair," he surmised.

"Fuck yeah," I confirmed, my eyes to a pile of folders on the edge of the counter that I not only didn't put there, I had no idea what they were.

He saw what I was looking at and I knew this when he invited, "That's everything I got on Nick, Nair and this investigation. Take it, read it. I'll cook. When I'm done, I'll bring you your food, we'll eat and while we do, I'll answer any questions you have."

I looked up at him and said quietly, "You're not staying here."

"I'm not leaving," he said quietly back.

We locked eyes.

I tried again. "There's no reason for you to stay here."

"Way you tell it," he fired back instantly, "no reason for me to go either."

Fuck.

Fuck!

I had to get back on my game. He was screwing me at every turn.

I broke eye contact, sucked back more beer, grabbed the folders and stalked through the kitchen to the back.

My house was shit. The bathroom suite was pink, put in during what I was guessing was the '50's, and the tub and basin had rust stains. The carpet was shag. There was wood paneling from the '70's in every room and my kitchen appliances were all avocado.

I didn't care. I made decent money, but in my job early retirement was necessary. You couldn't carry on doing what I did for eternity. You had a brain in your head, you quit doing it before the age of fifty hit your life's horizon. So I lived small, but still content, and socked back everything I could. The house was sturdy. It had personality that was mostly my mess, my cat and me. I spent very little time there and thus it worked.

It was the back room that sold me on the place.

It wasn't a walled in patio. It also wasn't *not* one. It had big windows so it seemed outside even though it was inside. Narrow, it had concrete floors I'd strewn with thick, bright, braided rugs. There was an old, slouchy, comfortable-as-all-fuck couch that had tons of big, slouchy pillows on it. Two wicker chairs angled across from it, more slouchy pillows on those. A big upright chest at the wall to the side of the door from the kitchen that had everything you needed in it; corkscrew, bottle opener, lighters, cigs, extra ashtrays, condoms. The shelves covered with green, trailing, brightly potted plants that even I couldn't manage to kill, and I forgot to water them frequently.

I loved it back there. If I was home, I was back there. I even had two space heaters back there so when it was winter I could still be there.

So I went back there, grabbed a pack of smoky treats, a lighter, ashtray and camped out on the couch with my beer and the folders.

What seemed minutes later, but I knew by how much I'd read wasn't, Creed came out with a plate of food that smelled divine in one hand and another cold one in the other.

"You shouldn't smoke," he muttered, handing me the plate and setting my beer on the table in front of me.

"You shouldn't either," I threw out my guess and his eyes caught mine.

"That's why I know you shouldn't do it," he replied, confirming my guess and moving back into the house.

I looked at the ziti. It was baked. There was tons of cheese, some of it baked brown. It reeked of garlic and I knew at a glance it would be delicious.

I set the plate aside and put the file that was open on my lap on the low, rectangular table in front of me. I grabbed the plate again, nabbed the fork stuck in the food, sat back and commenced eating. Upon my first bite it was confirmed. It was delicious.

Creed joined me, sitting in the wicker chair furthest from the door, putting his booted feet up to the edge of the table and his eyes to me.

He shoved a big fork full of ziti in his mouth and asked through it, "Questions?"

I didn't have any. He was thorough. He didn't miss a trick. This was added proof he was skilled, talented and experienced.

"You did a shit ton of work and got a month of nothing," I told him something he already knew.

"This is why I know the ride's gonna get bumpy," he replied then shoved more ziti in his mouth.

I shoved more in mine, chewed and swallowed.

"So, no questions about the file, let's get this closeness crap outta the way," I suggested and he grinned while still chewing.

Then he invited, "Shoot."

"Arizona?" I asked.

"Phoenix," he answered.

I shoved more ziti in my mouth, buying time to find it so I could ask it.

Then I found it and asked it, "Married?"

"Divorced. Six years."

Six years, divorced. His oldest child was twelve. I wondered how long he was married before the divorce. In other words, his first child was born four years after he left me so I wondered how long it took him to replace me.

I didn't ask this. It was clear we had to talk about our pasts, get to know each other. There was no avoiding it. But there were places we weren't going to go.

I nodded then continued, "You work out of state often?"

"If the job feels good and the pay is right, yeah."

"How long you been in state?"

Kristen Ashley

His eyes held mine even as he shoved more ziti in his mouth, chewed and swallowed.

He was preparing me.

He didn't have to. I was already braced.

Then he gave it to me. "Left Kentucky, went to Michigan. Moved from Michigan to South Carolina. Met Chelle there. Her parents moved to Arizona, she got pregnant. Wanted to be close, we moved there."

"Chelle?"

"Ex."

"Right," I muttered. I leaned forward, grabbed my beer, sat back and took a swig before I looked back at him. "See your kids often?"

"Often as I can."

"Close?"

His eyes grew sharper on my face before he answered, but when he answered, with the words he said, this warning would be lost on me.

"Yeah, with both. Kara's gettin' to a stage, doesn't get along with her Mom so I try to be around, and if I can't, I'm a phone call away. Something she takes advantage of so it's good for me since I connect with her often, though it sucks why she feels the need to do it. Brand's all me, top to toe to heart to mind, all my boy."

His casual, yet careful, words pierced through me like spears and I froze in an effort to contain the pain.

Then the pain engulfed me and I couldn't contain it anymore.

As it swallowed me into its dark, fiery pit, I tossed my plate of ziti on the table. It went skidding across the files and flew over the other side. I drew my other arm back and brought it forward in a sidearm slice, releasing my beer so it sailed past him and shattered against the low wall under the windows at his back, foaming beer spraying in wide spatter all around.

His feet came off the table and I knew by his eyes, he knew.

He knew.

He didn't forget.

That motherfucker *knew*.

"Sylvie, let me——" he started.

"You named her kids my names," I whispered, my breaths coming heavy.

"Sylvie——"

Shit, fuck, *shit*.

60

I couldn't take it.

We'd talked about it. We'd talked. Frequently. Talked. Dreamed. Planned. *Frequently.*

I told him, we had a girl, she'd be named Kara. We had a boy, we'd name him after his Dad.

Those were my names.

My fucking names!

"*You named her kids my names!*" I screamed then attacked.

Launching myself over the table, I hit him in the chest. His chair slammed back, taking us and his plate with it, ziti smushed between us, but I did not give one... single... solitary... *fuck.*

He named another woman's children *my names!*

That fucking motherfucker!

I shot up to straddling him, my knees in the back of the chair, my arm coming back in preparation to land a blow. He shot up with me, arms coming around me, effectively taking away my target. He pulled me to him, rolled the both of us free of the chair then kicked it and I heard it slide and crash against something that stopped it.

I'd learned early and quick that my size was a major detriment to pretty much anything, especially if it was physical. I was in shape, no doubt about it, but I was small, thin and a woman. So I had to aim true, be willing not to fight fair and be smart, fast, ballsy and sly.

I was so pissed, I lost sight of all that and Creed immediately gained the advantage. If I didn't pull my shit together, his weight, height and power would have me defenseless in seconds.

But there was no way *in fuck* he was winning this.

No way.

No fucking *way.*

Therefore, I lifted my head and sank my teeth in his neck so hard, I tasted blood.

"*Fuck!*" he ground out. He reared back and I went with him, using his momentum to take him to his back. I shot up, straddling him again and didn't delay in pulling back an arm and landing a fisted blow to his cheekbone.

He grunted and his head shot to the side.

I didn't get a second one in. He got his hand around my wrist and rolled me to my back, him on top of me.

Kristen Ashley

I got my boot planted in the floor and rolled him so I was on top. I grabbed both sides of his head and lifted it in preparation for a head butt when he came totally up, knifing at the waist. I automatically held on, my hands fisting in his hair.

"Calm the fuck down and let me explain," he growled.

"Fuck you!" I shouted. I let go with one hand and brought it low, shoved it up the back of his shirt and scored my nails through his flesh.

"Jesus," he hissed. He shifted to his knees and immediately fell forward so my back slammed into the edge of the coffee table before it went skidding. Then my back hit floor and Creed's body pinned me.

Not good. I had his weight on me and his hips between my legs so I couldn't get a knee to his crotch. He reached back and pulled my arm from around him, his other hand going to my other wrist and yanking my hand out of his hair. He pulled them around and between us, locking them there.

We grappled, pushed, pulled, shoved, both of us growling, grunting and hissing, me rocking my hips and planting my feet, arching my back, nearly rolling him but not succeeding.

Fuck, he was going to win.

Fuck, I had to fight dirty.

I lifted my head. He reared back to avoid my teeth, but couldn't get back fast enough. I got my mouth on him and didn't use my teeth. I used my tongue.

The element of surprise worked.

He stilled instantly.

It was a tactical error.

Not on his part, on mine.

He smelled good. He tasted good and fuck me, he *felt* good.

The pain of his further betrayal, one even more unforgivable than the last, still consumed me and it had to go. It had to go and I knew only two ways to stop it. Two ways I'd blindly turned to over the years. Two ways that didn't work for long but they worked for a while.

Without thinking, to dull the pain, I needed one of those ways.

So I went for it and licked up his neck to below his ear and God, *God,* the scent of him, the feel of him on my tongue, the taste of him…

God.

Suddenly and instantly, something altogether different consumed me.

62

I bucked my hips, put my weight into my foot on the floor and rolled him so I was on top. I went right in, my teeth to the collar of his tee, my fingers curling into it. I used both until I got the tear then my mouth went away and I ripped it all the way down.

His hands curled in at my waist. "Sylvie—" he murmured but I bent. My mouth to the sleek, muscled skin of his chest, I liked the feel of him against my lips so much my tongue snaked out.

Oh yeah. So good. Fucking beautiful.

I took more. Across his collarbone, down, to his nipple I sucked deep and his hands slid from my waist to become arms wrapped tight around me.

"Baby—" he whispered and I jerked up, slammed my mouth down on his and darted my tongue between his lips.

He took it and let me take, hard, deep, fuck, *fuck,* he tasted of beer and ziti and Creed. I remembered that taste, could swear it tipped my tongue countless times for going on two decades. I missed it and I loved it.

Loved it.

The kiss went wild. His hands went into my hair, holding my mouth to his then he took his turn to take from mine.

I gave him a taste then shafted up. His hands fell away from my hair. My hands went to my tank and ripped it off.

He had one second to take in my torso before I bent back to him and it was done. Even if I had the strength to fight it, I wouldn't have tried.

We tore at each other's clothes, shoes, tossing them aside. Rolling, hands everywhere, mouths, tongues. I couldn't see. I couldn't think. I could only taste and feel.

I eventually got between his legs and didn't hesitate, didn't play, didn't fuck around. I sucked his hard, thick, long cock deep, the head hit the back of my throat and my lips hit hair.

"*Jesus,*" he groaned then angled up. I lost purchase only suddenly to be flying through the air, twisted, brought down on his body facing his crotch, rolled and yeah, oh fucking *yeah,* he was over me. His mouth was between my legs, his knees at either side of my head, he was voracious, rabid, eating fierce, his tongue thrusting deep, his mouth sucking my clit hard.

God, so good, so goddamned good, nothing better. No. Not nothing. *No one.* No one fucking better.

Kristen Ashley

I lifted my hands to his ass, pulling myself up and taking his cock in my mouth. He didn't make me work. His hips moved under my hands and he fucked my face as he ate me and his mouth worked me harder. He went down to his forearms beside my hips, shoved his hands under my ass and pulled up so he could devour me. My knees cocked, thighs spread wide. I opened them wider and took his cock as he took my pussy until it built so huge I couldn't take it anymore. I released his cock, dropped to my back on a low whimpered moan and I lost his mouth.

I rolled to him instantly, hands on him, vaguely watching him reach for his jeans, yank out his wallet.

"Creed," I whispered, and even I heard the depths of my need.

His big hand fanned against the side of my face, gliding back into my hair as he looked down at me, his face hot, hard and fucking beautiful.

"Two seconds, baby," he whispered back. His hand went away, the condom came out and I spread my legs in preparation.

He positioned on his knees between my legs, I watched him roll on the condom then I knifed up, curving my arms around him and he didn't delay. His torso pressed into mine, I fell back, bringing him with me and he slid inside.

My neck arched and my knees lifted, my thighs pressing deep into his hips as I moaned, "Fuck yes."

He moved. I rounded him with my limbs, righted my neck, lifted my head and ran my tongue soothingly along the angry bite where I'd marked his neck.

I shifted my lips and in his ear whispered, "Harder."

"Soft, slow," he whispered in mine.

"Fast, hard."

"Soft and slow, baby."

I squeezed with three limbs as I squeezed him inside and dug my nails in his back, running them up.

"*Fuck*," he groaned and went faster and harder.

"Yes," I breathed, and he went even faster and harder.

"You like the taste of you?" he asked, his breath coming fast.

"Is it on you?"

"Yeah."

"Then yeah."

"*Fuck*," he groaned again. He lifted his head, I turned mine and he took my mouth.

64

I took his.

I tasted me on him and I whimpered into his mouth.

He fucked me harder and faster.

I pulled a leg from around him, shoved my foot into the floor and rolled him to his back. Then I rode him, even harder and faster, concentrating on giving it to him, to me, so he took over taking my mouth.

His lips broke from mine. His big hand at the back of my head, he shoved my face in his neck and growled, "Harder, baby."

I went harder.

Faster.

He kept growling. "Fuck, need more. I gotta fuck you."

"I fuck you," I panted, my breaths hitching, my blood singing.

It was building. Again.

Yes, it was building *huge*.

"Gotta fuck you," Creed ground out. Then he flipped me to my back and took over, hips grinding, and that felt so fucking good, so deep, so rough. It was so goddamned beautiful my mouth opened slowly, my head gliding back, exposing my throat and his lips and tongue took it.

His hands went to my hips, yanking me up to take him deeper.

"Yes," I whispered.

His hands slid up the sides of my thighs to my knees and up, swinging my calves in. I dug my heels in and held on tight as his hands moved to my arms, lifting them up over my head. He circled my wrists, pressed them into the rug and I froze, my head righting, my eyes locked to his face.

My voice was ragged, and not with sex, when I demanded, "Don't hold me down."

His head was tipped down, his eyes to our bodies, but at the sound of my voice, my tone, they shot to my face and his hips stilled on an inward thrust.

"Creed, don't hold me down!" I snapped, and he let my wrists go as a flash shot through his eyes.

He moved one hand to the side my face, his eyes also moving over it, and his voice was ragged too. Not with sex, not with what had been in mine, but the emotion ran just as deep when he whispered, "Jesus, baby."

"Fuck me, Creed," I demanded, and his gaze came to mine.

"Let's slow it down," he said gently.

"Fuck me," I repeated.

Kristen Ashley

"Sylvie, baby—"

I lifted my head and took his lower lip between my teeth giving it a nip. I released it, and face close, eyes all we could see, I bit out, "Creed. *Fuck me.*"

We held each other's eyes.

Then he moved, gathering me in his arms. He got to his knees then to his feet. His cock still deep inside me, he took two long strides. Then I was back to the couch and he was fucking me.

He went for my mouth but I turned my head and shoved my face in his neck, holding on with my arms and legs, tight. Tipping my hips to meet his thrusts, I erased everything from my brain but what was going on between my legs. I searched for it, reached for it and found it, my head rearing back into the cushions as I cried out my release. The pleasure, as it always did, driving away the pain.

Only bigger. Better.

Much bigger.

Way better.

I kept tight hold of him, burying my face back in his neck and keeping it there until Creed found his.

I gave him time, counting the seconds, waiting until his breath started to even then I ordered, "Get off me." His head came up and I felt his eyes, but I kept mine to his throat and repeated, "Get off me."

"I think what just happened proves we need to talk, Sylvie," he said softly. At his words, I heaved and twisted. He slid out and I took him to his side, back to the back of the couch.

I reared away, but not so far that I couldn't plant my hand in his chest and shove hard.

He got up on a forearm. His other hand circled my wrist tight and held mine to his chest as his eyes kept mine captive.

"You're a total asshole," I hissed.

He didn't reply, not for long seconds. Then he said quietly, "I had you, but in the end, you checked out. I was just a cock."

"They're all just cocks," I retorted.

He shook his head and his fingers tightened around my wrist as he leaned into me. "I had you."

"No one has me."

"I had you."

66

I leaned into him and snapped, "No one *ever* has me." I ignored the flash in his eyes and I ignored how easy it was to read, how hard it was to see that in his eyes. I ignored all of it and yanked at my hand.

He didn't release me.

"Let me go," I demanded harshly.

He let me go.

I jumped off the couch and moved to my clothes. I pulled on the tank and my jeans and left my panties, bra, socks and boots where they lay.

By the time I turned back, he had his jeans up and half buttoned.

I looked from his crotch to his eyes.

"Guest bedroom is a pit, but you dig deep enough, you'll find a bed. You look hard enough, you'll find sheets for the bed. I'm going out. Sweet dreams."

I moved toward the door, trying to decide if it was a bourbon or tequila night.

"I couldn't have you, I'd have that."

His words made me stop dead but I didn't turn. I didn't move.

Years passed.

Then he spoke again, quieter.

"I never thought I'd see you again. I couldn't have you, I'd have that part of you. That part of us. Kids named what we agreed, so every time I said the names of the kids I loved, I'd remember you and I'd have that part of you with me."

Jesus.

He could not be serious.

Jesus.

Someone kill me.

I turned then and looked him straight in the eye.

"You are so full of shit."

"I am?"

"Yeah," I clipped.

"You believe that, I'll give you her number. You call Chelle. Ask why she divorced me."

I hitched a hip just as I put a hand to it and asked flippantly, "That'll be interesting, Creed. What'll she tell me?"

"That she filed for the same reason you lost your mind tonight. She filed when she found out why I insisted on naming our kids. She filed because of why

Kristen Ashley

I named our kids those names. And she filed because she was done bein' married to man who was in love with a fuckin' ghost."

It took effort, but I just managed to ignore his verbal blows pummeling the breath clean out of me.

"So you're an equal opportunity asshole, doing that to her at the same time you did it to me," I noted.

"Yep," he agreed. "Still don't give a fuck, which is why it's good she's shot of me. Decent woman. Never should have done it to her. I got them, I got her part of them, and I got you in them. The way I saw it, I had a lifetime of livin' without what I most wanted, made certain I got all I wanted outta that. I like it like that, and I'd do it again."

Seriously, this dickhead could not be believed.

"You *are* an asshole," I bit off.

"Didn't deny it. Live with it every day. You don't have to repeat it."

"How'd she find out?"

"I told her. On your birthday seven years ago. The one day she never got. The one day every year I'd get shitfaced hammered out of my mind, all alone, just me. Difference that year was she didn't let me be. She pushed it. So she got it. *All* of it. Best thing that ever happened to her. Finally meant she could be free of the asshole that's me."

"Lucky her. Now she probably celebrates my birthday."

"No," he shook his head. "For me it was you. For her it was me."

Fuck. Fuck. *Fuck!*

I ignored that and stated, "I wasn't a ghost, Creed." I motioned to myself with my free hand. "As you can see, I'm alive and well."

"You were a ghost to me."

"Your choice."

"No it wasn't," he returned immediately. "Dig deep and you know it."

I felt my eyes narrow. I leaned in and hissed, "I don't know shit."

"Know this," he growled and turned his back to me. It was a move so surprising, I didn't have a chance not only to retreat, but even to brace.

At what I saw, I couldn't control it. I sucked in a sharp, audible breath.

I'd drawn blood on his back as well as his neck, and you could see other scratch marks.

None of them marred the tattoo that spanned the entirety of his skin.

A pier.

A lake.

A horizon.

The sun shining.

And along the pier a name spelled out in flowers up the indent of his lower spine.

"Sylvie".

He turned to face me again, but my eyes stayed at the wall of his chest, the vision of his back burned in my brain.

"I been back not even a whole fuckin' day, Sylvie," he went on, and my eyes cut to his face. "And we're fuckin' on the floor of your back room amidst a pile of fuckin' ziti."

"You fucking motherfucker," I whispered.

He ignored me and asked, "You get yet that we need to talk?"

I shook my head and ignored the pit in my stomach.

"We're not gonna talk."

He tore a hand through his hair and bit out, "Fuck, Sylvie."

"We are *not* gonna talk," I repeated with added emphasis.

His hand swept out in an arc indicating the couch and the floor. "So, that's not gonna happen again?"

"You're really fucking good at giving head so, no. I won't say that. I'll take seconds. Even thirds."

His brows shot up and his escalating anger slithered through the room. "You gotta be shittin' me."

"I'm not." I tilted my head. "Unless it wasn't good for you. If it wasn't then I'll take my attention elsewhere."

His anger gathered, grew, built, filled the room.

We held each other's eyes in silence.

Creed broke it by asking something that wasn't his to have.

"Why don't you like to be held down?"

It wasn't his to have, but still, in a way, he deserved it so I gave it to him.

"He held me down. He also tied me down. I didn't like it."

His hard jaw got harder and a muscle ticked there.

Then he whispered, "You didn't like it."

"I didn't like anything he did to me."

His entire face got hard, and the muscle moved to leap in his cheek.

Then he remarked, "So now they're all just cocks."

I jerked up my chin. "Yup."

"And you want me to be one of them."

"Uh… Creed, hello?" I swung out an arm to indicate the room. "You already are."

He shook his head. "No getting in there?"

I shook mine too. "Nope. Not you. Not anyone. But especially not you."

"You won't dig deep," he said quietly.

"I know what's buried there, so no. No fucking way. I leave that be."

We both went quiet again.

He broke it again.

"It was good for me."

I nodded. "Glad I'm not losing my touch."

His eyes went cold, but his lips said, "I'll take seconds and thirds and whatever you're willin' to give me."

"That was hot, baby, so it's good to know this partnership has all sorts of advantages," I replied.

He crossed his arms on his chest, but didn't for a millisecond release my eyes as he whispered, "Baby, just you wait and see."

"Oo, exciting," I whispered back sarcastically.

"You bet your ass," he returned.

"Are we done?" I asked, then carried on. "See, something else to learn about me. When I'm done, I'm usually done, and either he goes or I do. Since we're both staying I'm still ready to go. So are you through with me?"

"Not even close."

"Good news," I retorted. "But just to be clear, I'm up for seconds. You seem pissed. Angry sex works for me, but I'm guessing you're beyond that. So, what I'm asking is, for now, you through with me?"

"Yeah," he jerked up his chin. "For now."

"Best get supplied, baby," I warned. "That was just a teaser. I get in the mood, I can go all night. The emergency condom in your wallet isn't gonna cut it."

"Drugstore just got scratched on our itinerary for tomorrow. First stop."

"Works for me."

"Right. You done bein' a bullshit badass?" he asked.

I shrugged. "Sure."

"Good. But don't lose the bullshit smartass. She makes me hard."

"I'll keep her at the ready."

"You know the beauty of this?" he asked cuttingly.

"No, handsome, tell me," I invited mockingly sweet.

"This was exactly how your father and stepmother talked when they weren't fighting. Remember? You told me all about it."

His aim was true.

Right through the heart.

"I see," I whispered. "We're not fighting fair."

"Nope," he confirmed, and made his point by lifting a hand and touching the tips of his fingers to my mark on his neck. He dropped his hand and went on, "All's fair. No rules. No holds barred. Winner takes all."

My shoulders straightened. I wrapped my arms around my belly and I kept my eyes locked to his when I said softly, "Six years, Creed. Six years, every day, every minute, every second, I lost whole pieces of me. After I got loose, I made certain I don't ever lose. Not fucking *ever*. You just entered a game you cannot win."

"You got loose, you get any of that back?" he asked.

"Not that first fuckin' piece."

"So you're tellin' me my Sylvie is gone."

His Sylvie.

Motherfucking *asshole*.

"Long gone," I verified.

"Right," he muttered like he didn't believe me.

"Right," I repeated firmly.

"So who was that who smiled big at that Down's kid this morning like he started her day, and touched her forehead to his making him look like she started his?"

No way I was going to let him get to me.

"That was Adam's Sylvie."

"You ran across the yard like you'd just received a bomb threat, baby, not like you were five minutes late to help your girl. You don't miss a day even if you have to haul your ass over there hungover. You dropped a job when Josh got sick and your dead partner's wife had to work so you could look after him. She doesn't know it, but it's you that puts red and white roses with a blue ribbon on his grave every fuckin' Sunday. And you took me on just so you could take Knight's back. That wasn't Adam's Sylvie. It's not Charlene's Sylvie. It's not

71

even Knight's Sylvie. It's just plain Sylvie. The one I knew. She's not gone. She's standing right in front of me."

"You hold onto that, Creed, you're gonna get fucked."

"Jesus, I hope so."

I clamped my mouth shut.

Then I unclamped it to declare, "I feel the need to get drunk. We'll pick this up tomorrow."

"You need a ride home from the bar, you just call me," he invited.

"Handsome, you'll never hear from me. To get down to your name in my phone, I've got two whole letters."

It was his turn to clamp his mouth shut.

I took that as my cue to go.

So I did.

I stopped in order to glare at Gun, who was curled up in the seat of a dining room chair fast asleep. My glare was for her being in the mood to nap and thus deserting me in my hour of need. However, since she was snoozing, she missed my glare. Still, it made me feel better.

I also stopped to yank on another pair of socks and boots and grab my keys.

But me, my jeans, tank, boots and socks, commando and braless, walked right out the door, and like we had many, *many* times before, we took on the night.

Chapter 6
The Best Birthday Ever

A sunny summer by a lake in Kentucky, twenty-seven years earlier. Creed is twelve, Sylvie is seven. It's her birthday...

I peddled my bike quick over the trail in the trees to get to the lake.

I didn't want to miss him.

We didn't get to do this a lot. It was hard to get away from Daddy, but when he was at work, my stepmom was usually drinking that clear stuff straight from the bottle, so it wasn't hard to get away from her. I just had to be careful and Tuck told me we couldn't be greedy. Greedy was stupid. The more chances we took, the more chances we took on getting caught.

So we only did it special.

Like today.

My birthday.

This didn't count the nights. Tuck said I could come anytime at night, I just had to be careful.

So I did.

Whenever the words came, me and Bootsie would sneak out of the house and go to Tuck's. I'd knock on the window, and always, my knuckles would barely hit the glass before it flew up. Sometimes he'd stick his head out and tell me he'd meet me in the woods. If his Mom was gone, he'd stick the whole top of his body out the window, grab me under my arms and pull me in. Then he'd go back out, hanging almost all the way out, so every time he did it I was scared he'd fall, but he never did. And he did this so he could grab Bootsie and bring her in with us.

In the woods or in his bedroom we'd talk, and even though he was a whole lot older than me, we always had tons of stuff to talk about. What we liked to eat. TV programs we liked to watch. Movies we'd seen. Folks in town. He'd talk about his Dad. I'd talk about my Mom and my visits with her when she'd come get me and take me to Lexington for her weekends with me.

If we spent time in the woods or in his bedroom, no matter what, he'd walk me home to the back gate of the fence around my backyard.

The lake came into view and I saw him, his tanned bare back to me, sitting on the end of the pier. And just like always, seeing him made my belly feel funny. The kind of funny it felt right before you got on a ride at the carnival or amusement park. That kind of funny.

I stopped my bike by his. I jumped off, grabbed the stuff in my basket and laid my bike on its side in the grass.

Then I raced down the path to the pier, jumped up on it and raced down the wood planks.

Tuck turned and watched me, his lips curled up.

I stopped at the end and my, "Hi!" sounded breathy.

"Hi," Tuck replied.

I shoved the frozen Snickers bars at him. "Brought 'em!" I cried and then flipped off my shoes and sat down beside him at the end of the pier.

His legs were dangling down. So long, his feet were covered in water up past his ankles. My legs were so short I had to point my toes for the water to skim the tips.

He took a Snickers bar and started to rip it open.

I ripped open mine and bit hard into the frozen caramel and nougat.

"I couldn't make a picnic. She was in the kitchen," I told him through Snickers bar.

"That's okay, Sylvie," he told me through a mouth full of his.

"But she's, you know…" I didn't tell him what he knew and kept talking. "So she's out of it. We can swim and do it for a long time. Daddy's away on business and she'll probably be sleeping when I get home so we can spend all day here if we want."

"Your Dad's gone on your birthday?"

The way he said that made me turn my head and look up at him.

"Yeah."

He stared at me then looked back at the water. He lifted his Snickers bar to his mouth and bit off a huge chunk.

I felt bad since he didn't have a Dad, and I knew, with the way he talked about him, that what he would want most in the whole world was his Dad being there for his birthday. I didn't really care if Daddy was at mine. In fact, he always made me wear dresses that were too fancy on my birthday, so it felt mean, but I was kinda glad he wasn't.

We sat together and sifted our feet through the water, staring at it and chewing on our Snickers bars. And we did this until Tuck finished his. He shoved the wrapper in his cutoff jeans shorts pocket. Then he dug in his other one and I watched him come out with a little, white cardboard box.

He handed it to me.

"Happy birthday, Sylvie."

I stared down at the box then I looked up at him. "Wow."

He grinned at me.

I liked presents, and I liked it more that he gave me one, but that grin would have been enough for me.

"We don't have wrapping paper and I used all my allowance on that so I couldn't buy any," he told me.

"That's okay!" I chirped. I threw off the top of the box and looked down at the gold necklace with the tiny twinkling green jewel hanging off the chain, this attached to a little sheet of plastic.

"They said that's a peridot. Your birthstone," Tuck's voice came at me.

I tipped my head back to look at him. "I like it. Green's my favorite color."

He grinned at me again.

"I'm gonna wear it always, Tuck," I whispered. I was about to pull it out so I could put it on, but his face went funny and he shook his head.

"It's cheap, Sylvie," he said quiet. "The girl I bought it from said you can't get it wet. It'll make your skin turn green."

"I don't care," I told him.

"Your Dad will," he told me.

He would.

Darn.

I looked back down at the necklace and said soft, "I'll wear it all the other times when I'm not in the water."

"Okay," he replied.

I looked up at him and smiled.

Then I jumped up to my feet and ran back to my bike. I put the necklace in the basket with my Snickers wrapper because Tuck said his Dad said that littering was bad and you should never do it. So we never did.

I ran back down the pier pulling off my t-shirt and stopping to tug off my shorts. I had my bathing suit underneath.

"*Cannonball!*" I yelled and dashed down the rest of the pier. I jumped straight off the end as high in the air as I could get. I curled my arms around my tucked legs and hit the warm water.

I barely surfaced before I heard and saw Tuck hit the water beside me.

I smiled.

He surfaced, took one stroke and made it to me, then he ducked me.

I came up laughing.

We did cannonballs and dives and had ducking contests and floated and had swimming contests that Tuck let me win because it was my birthday, and we did it for hours.

When I got home, my stepmom was asleep so I didn't get caught being gone and spending the day with Tuck at the lake.

It was the best birthday ever.

Ever.

Chapter 7
I'm What You Need

Present day...

My eyes opened and I stared at the alarm clock amongst the junk on my nightstand.

Fuck.

Last night I picked bourbon. I should have picked tequila.

I pulled myself out of bed, then I lugged myself down the hall to the bathroom. I used the facilities and washed my face, brushed my teeth, downed numerous gulps of water cupped in my hand and was walking out when I heard the front door open and close.

Right. Well then. There it was.

God did not answer my prayers and make yesterday a bad dream like that whole season of *Dallas* where Bobby was dead and then, *poof*, the next season he's in the shower.

It would appear that yesterday, Tucker Creed actually did come back into my life, I agreed to partner up with him then ended the evening eating his food and fucking him.

Shit.

Great.

I wandered into the living room, through the entry and rounded the wall into the dining room.

There I saw a bakery box on the counter and a hot guy behind it. A hot guy with a small raised bruise on his cheekbone, an angry bite mark on his neck, a white, paper coffee cup in one hand, and, to my expert donut discerning eye, a Boston cream in the other.

His assessing eyes came to me. "Mornin'."

"Guh," I mumbled and ignored his quick grin by looking down at my cat, who had her face in her food bowl.

I stopped and stared. Hard.

Gun felt it and looked up at me.

Kristen Ashley

"Meow," she defended herself, and she had a right. She was a cat. Food was food, whoever gave it to you.

Still, I returned, "Traitor."

I heard a chuckle. My eyes cut to Creed then down to the big box, and I continued wandering his way, asking, "Did you buy donuts for the whole block in an effort to get your partner close in order to have dozens more reasons to keep me not dead?"

"No, I bought enough donuts to make Charlene and her kids happy for a morning."

Shit, they were going to love that. These days, donuts did it for them. Then again, they were the kind of family. Simple pleasures always did. Save Dan, the Douchebag, of course.

I stopped opposite the counter and looked back up at him. "Have I told you you're an asshole today?"

"You just got up, so no."

"You're an asshole."

He grinned again.

I threw open the baker's box and plucked out a glazed. I usually went for the fancy, complicated donuts. It was feeling like a glazed day.

I bit into it and looked back at Creed, saying through sugar and fried dough, "Coffee?"

He scooted a white paper cup across the counter toward me.

I picked it up, sipped and closed my eyes.

Ah, *good.*

"What was that about me bein' an asshole?" Creed asked.

I opened my eyes, but only to narrow them on him.

He burst out laughing and I glared at him while he did. But I multitasked, glaring while taking another bite of donut and sucking back another sip of coffee.

He stopped laughing and trained his eyes on me. "Have a good night?"

"No. I lost two hundred dollars playing pool."

"Meet your match?"

"No. I suck at pool. Fuck drunk texting. Drunk pool betting is where your shit will get burned."

That got me a full blown smile before he asked, "Where's your 'Vette?"

"A parking lot outside The X, hopefully resting easy under the benevolent eye of the Kickass Car God."

"I'm sure she'll be fine," he reassured me.

I took another huge bite of donut, chewed twice and said through partially chewed dough, "I hope so." More chewing then, "She isn't, I'll curl up in the closet and I swear, I won't come out for a week." More chewing, I swallowed, then, "And, just saying, I'll take my gun with me, and if you open the door for any purpose other than to toss in food and beer, I'll shoot you."

Through another grin, he muttered, "I'll take that under advisement."

"Don't think I'm joking."

He kept grinning.

Then his grin faded before he asked, "How'd you get home?"

"Don't know. Ride for a blowjob. I think he was blond though."

His anger instantly started slithering through the room.

"Don't play with me," he whispered. "You think my ass didn't wait for yours to get home?" he asked, and before I could answer, he went on. "She was a redhead, way too much makeup, and you both giggled your way all the way up to the door. Though she was giggling like a lunatic, she walked straight back to her car so she wasn't loaded, like you."

"She wasn't a she, she was a he."

"She had way more tits and ass than you."

"Foam rubber, Creed. The X is a gay bar. She's a drag queen. Her name is Uqueesha."

The Creed anger snake retreated and his brows shot up.

"That bitch was a dude?"

I nodded. "That bitch was a dude."

"Fuck, didn't call that," he muttered.

"Maybe Grandpa needs his eyes checked," I muttered back, and those eyes that I insinuated needed checked narrowed on me.

I took another bite of donut and grinned big through dough.

He took a bite of his and chased it with coffee.

Then before I could stop it, right after I swallowed, I asked, "You waited for me to get home?"

He said nothing, just looked at me.

Suddenly, standing at the bar to my kitchen, it felt weirdly like the sun was shining warm down on me.

Creed twisted his neck and looked at the microwave before his eyes came back to me and he said quietly, "Got ten minutes to go time for next door, baby."

Those rays of invisible sun heated my skin, taking the warm straight through me.

I shoved the last bite of donut in my mouth and put my coffee down on the counter. I rounded it chewing, then swallowing, as I headed straight to him. He turned to me, his chin dipped, his eyes never leaving me, even when my hands went to his neck, one sliding up and back. I went up on my toes, pressed deep and pulled him down to me.

I kissed him hard, my tongue sliding in his mouth and glazed mixed with Boston cream.

It was divine.

I pushed him back, back, kissing him, holding on, and he slammed into the side counter.

His arms closed around me, pulling me up off my toes, off my fucking feet. He pivoted, crossing the kitchen until my back slammed against the refrigerator.

I used his shoulders as leverage, clutching hard, pulling up, my hand in his hair holding his head to me as the kiss went wild and deep. I lifted my legs and wrapped them around his hips, using my back to push away from the fridge. I leaned in hard and he moved back until he crashed into the counter facing the dining room.

I tore my mouth from his, lifting my head to find both my arms wrapped around his. My breath was coming fast and shallow, my chest heaving with the effort, just like Creed.

Hair had fallen over his forehead and was mixing with the brow and lashes of one of his bright, blue eyes. It was strangely cute on a man who was not even a modicum of cute but hard, rugged and all male.

It was also hot.

And it was all kinds of sexy.

Shit.

"I gotta get dressed and get over to Charlene's," I whispered, not moving an inch, not letting go.

"I'm coming with," he whispered back.

"Suit yourself."

"That's what'll suit me."

was out of the bathroom, so they went down there to look at the faucet. Charlene got done getting ready and found me.

This brought us to now.

"Can I help you fix it?" Adam cried loudly and excitedly, jumping up and down twice.

"Need a part, pal," Creed's deep, smooth voice with the rough edge sounded down the hall. "But I'll get it, come back tonight, and you can help me then."

Great.

"I can help!" Adam shouted, jumped again, and Creed's smile got bigger, brighter, sexier, and, fuck me, sweeter.

I pulled away from the door and turned to Charlene who was examining me.

"You give him that bite mark?" she asked quietly.

"Um… yes," I answered.

"The bruise on his cheekbone?" she went on.

"Things got outta hand," I whispered.

"How out of hand?" she whispered back.

"He pissed me off. I attacked him. Got a bite and punch in. He defended himself. Things got heated in a different way. He gave me an orgasm after introducing me to bewilderingly good head and rough, hard sex, during which he carried me partway across a room still inside me, and shortly after, I returned the favor. With the orgasm, I mean. I didn't carry him across a room."

Her eyes went huge and she muttered, "Holy crap."

I would use different words, but I still agreed with an, "Unh-hunh."

Her face changed, her eyes going warm and worried, before she said quietly, "I know it's him, Sylvie."

Unlike Knight, I'd told Charlene his name.

She kept talking. "Knew it was him yesterday when he came over and introduced himself. I played it cool, though I have no clue how since I was," she leaned in and hissed, "*freaking out*. Are you okay?"

I nodded and moved further into the kitchen, murmuring, "I'm cool."

"Sylvie—"

I turned to her. "He has to matter for it to matter, and babe, he quit mattering a long time ago."

This was the conclusion I'd come to the night before. I was off my game because I was letting him get to me, like he meant something when he didn't. Not anymore.

So I had to let that go, and when I did that I would get a partner who knew what he was doing. I would work with him to make Knight's troubles go away. In the meantime, I could jump a hot guy whenever I felt like it.

This was not a bad deal.

The rest was done and had been a long time.

I just had to get over the shock of it, and I'd done that over bourbon and pool with a bunch of gay guys and drag queens, which was the best way to go about that. Or one of them.

"Sylvie, when you told me—" Charlene started.

I stepped close to her. "When I told you, it was my birthday. That was our day. That was *the* day. And I was drunk. Being over it doesn't mean being *over it*. Shit like that," I shrugged, "you never get over. But you can deal. I'm gonna deal. He lives in Arizona, has kids and a life down there, and he's a fucking great lay. You know me. I don't get involved but I do have fun. So I won't get involved, but I will have fun."

"The guys you pick up, honey, they aren't Tucker Creed."

I shrugged again. "They aren't anyone. Neither is he. A memory come back to life, who'll eventually become another memory. Might as well make it a good one this time."

She bit her lip, looking doubtful before she let it go to whisper, "Be careful."

I grinned. "Careful's my middle name."

She rolled her eyes at my blatant lie then shook her head, and doing so caught sight of the microwave.

"Crap!" she snapped. "Right!" she called loudly to the house at large. "Car! School! We gotta go!"

She moved into the dining room where Theo was chewing on something, diapered ass to the floor. I moved there, straight to Leslie, who was sitting on a booster seat at the dining room table, coloring. Creed and Adam appeared in the kitchen as we were heading out.

We got the kids in the car and I was still being a goof with Leslie when I heard Creed ask Charlene, "Sylvie got a set of keys to your house?"

I gave Leslie one last smile and touched her nose with my finger before pulling out of her car door as Charlene answered, "Yeah."

"I'll change the windows out today. Tonight, I'll deal with the faucet and look at your car," he told her. "Good for you?"

"Definitely, Tucker, thank you," she replied, and her gratitude was genuine. Dan was gone, but even when he was around Dan was a lazy-ass motherfucker. Creed, for Charlene, was a godsend.

I slammed the car door, moved to Adam's window and pressed my hand to it before I bent and pressed my mouth to it and blew my lips wide, making him and Leslie giggle.

After doing this, I moved around the hood of her car to the other side where Creed was standing as Charlene went on. "And thanks for the donuts."

I watched Creed jerk up his chin.

"Later, babe," I called as I walked by him.

"Later, honey," Charlene called back. I lifted a hand and kept going as I heard her say, "Bye, Tucker. Thanks again."

"No problem," he muttered, and I knew he was following me.

I stopped at my front door, Creed at my side, and I waved as they drove away.

Badasses, apparently, didn't wave, because Creed didn't. But when I turned to look up at him I saw that they watched cars drive away while smiling.

"Your agenda for the day?" I asked, and he looked down at me.

"First up, drugstore," his smooth, rough voice answered, giving me a quiver.

"Excellent," I muttered. "Next?"

"Got a lead yesterday. Following it. You?"

"A lead?" I prompted and he shook his head.

"Let me see if it pans out, Sylvie."

Oh shit. Oh no. Oh *shit*.

That could mean bad things if he had a lead on one of the guys.

I buried that and nodded. "Okay, me. Nair."

"He doesn't get out of bed before noon," Creed shared.

"Right. Okay. Me, drive-by of Nair's to get the lay of the land. Then office. Then check in on Serena. Back to Nair."

"Check in with me, too," he ordered. I nodded and he went on, "The part of your business I help you do is not this, but heads up, saw your girl had job applications on her counter. Part-time. How the fuck she thinks she's gonna manage part-time on top of full-time and three kids, got no clue. What I do know is, you do all your own admin and you got the money not to have to. It also doesn't take full-time help. It's none of my business. Shit like this can go sour amongst friends. But you set her up, she can do it at home. Extra money for her, bullshit work you don't wanna do gone for you."

Fuck, that was genius, and it sucked because it was his idea and I wish I'd thought of it myself.

I jerked up my chin. "I'll talk to her."

"You're at the office, grab any files you got on the jobs I may need to get involved in with you. Bring 'em home. I'll look 'em over."

I nodded.

"Now you'll give me her key so I can see to her windows before I head out."

I jerked up my chin again, walked in and opened the drawer to the table by the side of it. I grabbed the keys and tossed them to him.

He caught them, then his other hand snaked out, nabbed me around the neck and yanked me to him. He bent low and his mouth crashed down on mine whereupon he laid a deep, wet, long one on me that ended with me arched into his body with my hands fisted in his hair.

He pulled his mouth from mine, looked directly in my eyes and muttered, "Later."

He let me go and took off.

I took in a deep breath.

Then I headed to the shower to get ready to start my day.

Gun was sitting on the top of my couch, tail sweeping the back.

"Meow," she said.

"Not you too," I replied.

"Meow," she repeated.

"Whatever," I muttered, not needing a lecture from my cat and pulling off my clothes as I moved. I was naked by the time I hit the bathroom, which meant no delay in the shower, so I turned on the water, waited for it to get warm and stepped right in.

It wasn't until I was in my uniform (tank, jeans, belt, cowboy boots, long hair drying wild, a swipe of mascara and line of eyeliner) and I was standing in my driveway staring at the lone Expedition when it hit me I didn't have a car.

So I turned on my boot and headed to Charlene's to ask Creed to take me to my car.

⚜

I was sitting in my 'Vette parked on the street, nursing a chocolate malt and staring at the house out my side window, when I sensed movement. My eyes went to my rearview mirror and I saw a huge, shiny, black Ford Expedition pull in behind me.

I rolled my eyes, grabbed my phone and flipped it open. I went to the top of my recent calls list and hit go before putting it to my ear.

"Sylvie," Creed answered after one ring.

"Partner, I checked in before I rolled out to get here. No reason to physically check up on me. Reminder, I've been doing this awhile."

His response was, "Come back and get in my truck."

"No. You got something to say you can't say over the phone, come and get in my car."

"Truck, Sylvie."

"'Vette, Creed."

Silence.

I dug in. Creed did too.

Patience was one of the many virtues I did not have.

"Fine," I bit out. "Truck."

I flipped the phone shut, threw open my door and me, my phone and my malt angled out. We jogged to his truck. I threw open the door and climbed in.

I turned to him to see him grinning a crowing-because-he-won-(again)-grin.

I checked the eye roll and asked, "I'm here. What?"

"You know a woman named Amy?"

I forgot to be in a snit at Creed and his superiority. I felt my eyes get round as my mouth breathed, "Fuck me."

His gaze moved over my face before it locked with mine and he muttered, "You know her."

"No shit?" I asked.

"Pillow talk, baby," he answered softly.

Blood roared in my ears as I sat back in the seat. I faced forward and sucked up malt so fast, I had to close my eyes against the ice cream headache. Then I pulled the straw from my mouth and clipped, "That stupid *bitch*."

"She's in with Nair," he told me, and I turned my head to look at him. "I'm here because I got her phone wired. She just called him and she's heading over."

"That stupid bitch," I repeated.

"Far as I could tell, Lively is a loyal soldier. But Nair was getting info from somewhere. It's her."

"Money?" I asked.

"Don't know. When I wasn't concentrating on you, Banks, Nick and Nair, I honed in on Lively. Had my eye on him, which means I've had occasion to have my eye on him when he's with her. The little I saw of Knight's men with their women, they don't chose nagging, greedy bitches. Gut told me he had a weak spot, seein' as he'd have that in his bed. I paid more attention, wasn't wrong. His weak spot is her and his inability to get shot of her even though she's a serious pain in his ass. Heard them have a fight in a restaurant a coupla nights ago. She doesn't like his hours. She likes that he's well paid but she's not real fond of him workin' for his money. Could be, she's gettin' money from Nair for info. Could be, she's workin' with him to close Sebring down so Lively will have more time to devote to her. Could be both."

"She's greedy, she's a bitch and she's a nag, Creed, but she's not stupid. Yeah, it's known she pitches a fit when Live has to work when she doesn't want him to, but she's not so dumb to think they'll live large if he doesn't have a fucking job. She's in it for the money."

He nodded. His eyes went over my shoulder and he jerked up his chin.

I turned my head to see a red Mazda roll into Drake Nair's driveway, a brunette I knew at the wheel.

Amy, the stupid bitch.

I heard the noises a camera made when pictures were being taken and looked back at Creed. He had an expensive digital to his eye. I turned back to Nair's house to see Amy get out of the Mazda and approach the front door. The camera noises kept going as she did and continued up until she disappeared inside. Then they stopped.

"You good to be my eyes while I get close?" he asked.

"Fuck yeah," I answered.

"Let's move," he muttered and threw open his door.

I stored my shit, threw open mine and jumped out.

"I approach from the north," he said to me as we crossed the street. "His study is that side. I'll start there and move on if he doesn't meet her there. Catch up."

"I'll go south, perimeter check, see if anyone's around. Been here about fifteen minutes before you and didn't see any activity. I'll meet you north."

"Right," he muttered and started jogging toward Nair's neighbor to the north's yard.

I did the same to the south. I did a wide sweep, jumped a fence, crossed Nair's backyard and rounded the side, seeing Creed crouched low under a window, but his head was at the edge, camera to his face.

I whistled low when I got close, his head turned to me then he shook it.

I crouched low beside him, my back to the house, eyes on a continual scan.

"In the study?" I asked.

"Yep," he answered.

"And you were shaking your head because?" I prompted.

I heard camera sounds and the hint of disgust in his voice. "You don't wanna know."

I always wanted to know.

I twisted, shot up and looked into the window.

He was right. I didn't want to know.

I twisted back, shot down and muttered, "Gross."

I just heard a hint of humor when he mumbled, "I told you you didn't wanna know."

"FYI, that put me off the blowjob I had planned for you tonight," I informed him, seeing as what I just saw was Amy on her knees going at Nair, who was not attractive (but he was hairy and he had skinny legs).

"Fuck, I hope he doesn't eat her," Creed murmured.

That got me a tingle. Yes, even after what I saw. Mostly because it said Creed didn't want to be put off *his* plans for tonight, and I liked his plans.

I scanned. Creed kept silent but his camera didn't.

After a while, he broke his silence with, "That'll mean dry cleaning."

"Creed!" I hissed. "Don't gross me out."

"Just sayin', there's times when a woman should learn to swallow."

I turned and punched him in the arm. He chuckled.

Kristen Ashley

Then he muttered, "Time for business. Thank fuck, he's not reciprocating the gesture."

"Our day just brightened."

"Comin' home with donuts for you and people you give a shit about, seein' you in those little shorts and tight cami, no matter that you were hungover, nothin' could darken my day. Not even that shit."

Sneak attack, and I held my breath until my chest burned.

Creed's camera sounded.

"Cash," he muttered. "Wads of it. More than a blowjob is worth."

"Even if that includes reimbursement for dry cleaning?"

I felt his eyes and looked up to see he'd lowered down from the window and was looking at me.

"Yeah, and then some. She's the leak."

I nodded. Poor Live. For whatever reason, he dug her. This would strike deep.

"Truck," Creed grunted. I jerked up my chin and we both moved.

I'd learned that if you were somewhere you weren't supposed to be, if you acted like you were supposed to be there, people assumed you were. So I always did that, and noted, as Creed and I walked to his truck, free and easy, he followed the same school of thought.

We both angled in and I turned immediately to him. "You calling this into Knight?"

"Yeah. You wanna stay on Nair or come with me while I have a chat with him?"

"Get more done, we separate."

He nodded. "Nick's still a wildcard."

"Yup," I agreed.

"But Nair's pullin' the strings."

"Yup," I agreed again.

"Your plan?"

"Stay on Nair."

"Right," he muttered. "I finish with Knight, I'm on Nick."

"After what I saw, I'm beginning to miss Nick. He's boring but he's not gross."

Creed grinned at me.

My eyes dropped to his mouth then my body angled across the cab. I grabbed him at both sides of his head, pulled him to me and kissed him hard, wet, hot and long.

I let him go, grabbed the shit I stowed and threw open the door, muttering, "Later."

"Later, baby," I heard him mutter back.

I sashayed to my car and I did it deliberately. I felt his eyes on me as I went, and they felt fucking great. I got in, settled in and he pulled out. My car was too low to see him as he drove by, which was a shame.

I sucked back mostly melted malt, which still tasted great, and turned my eyes to the house.

Ten minutes later, Amy left and drove away.

Half an hour after that, Nair got in his ridiculously yellow Lotus and drove away.

I followed.

⚭

Hours later, I sat on my barstool, sipping beer, watching Creed play pool and thinking.

I was thinking about what I saw earlier. Creed walking into Charlene's house with a bucket of chicken and a bag of fixin's, all of which made the kids and Charlene (who not only didn't have to cook, but also didn't have to pay for it) go wild.

I was thinking of taking turns with Charlene, hanging around the corner of the doorway in order to watch Creed, with not only Adam but also Leslie, in the bathroom.

I was thinking he had a lot of patience, a lot of good humor, and I hadn't heard Adam or Leslie laugh that much since their Dad left.

I was thinking of sitting on the couch in front of the window in Charlene's living room with Theo climbing over me, Charlene beside me, and watching Creed's ass as he bent over the opened hood of her car. And I did this while thinking how much cooler it was in her house now that the windows were open and the breeze could get through.

I was thinking I liked all I was thinking about.

Shit.

Kristen Ashley

I stopped thinking when I saw Creed put the end of his pool cue down, give his opponent a look and lift his hand, palm up.

The dude he'd been playing was pissed. He should be. He lost.

He said a few words to Creed that only a blind person would miss were angry, and Creed showed no reaction whatsoever.

Total badass.

Bills were passed over without a whole lot of sportsmanlike conduct.

Creed turned from the pool table without a backward glance. He walked down the steps and crossed the bar to me. He stopped in front of me and shoved the bills down my tank, straight into the cup of my bra.

I felt my clit swell along with my nipples.

He dipped his face close, his eyes never leaving me.

"Time to go home, baby."

Fuck yeah, it was.

I smiled.

⚜

I was on my knees at the side of the bed between Creed's spread thighs and I was working his beautiful cock.

Fucking hell, I liked his cock. Big, thick, long, hard and silky. Beautiful, every inch. All of them.

I pulled up, lips tight around the rim of the tip, and while rolling it with the tip of my tongue, I sucked deep and *hard.*

"Jesus," I heard him groan. Then, before I knew it, I had hands in my pits and I was flying through the air.

I landed on my front in the bed and I didn't have the chance to get used to my change in circumstances before my hips jerked violently. I heard the rip and my panties were gone.

I rolled and looked up at Creed, who was looming over me.

"I wasn't done," I informed him.

"You're done," he growled.

"I totally wasn't—"

I stopped talking because my head shot back, seeing as his fingers glided through the wet between my legs and he started finger fucking me.

"Fuck," I breathed.

92

He got closer. I felt his heat and hard body at my side and his fingers worked me faster, driving deeper.

I moved my hand between my legs to curl around his so I could feel.

I felt Creed's lips skim my chest before they disappeared, and then his mouth was at my ear.

"Tank off, baby," he whispered, his fingers not ceasing for a nanosecond in their delicious activity.

I yanked off my tank.

"Bra," he grunted.

I arched my back, twisted my arms behind me, released the clip and tore off my bra, tossing it aside.

The instant I was done, his mouth closed over a nipple.

My back left the bed. I ground my hips down on his hand and shoved my breast deeper into his mouth.

My free hand slid into his hair and I moaned, "Oh God, yes. My God, *yes.*"

I rode his hand, my hips bucking and jerking against his fingers.

His thumb tweaked my clit and I gasped loudly as sensations tore through me.

His mouth released my nipple.

My chin dipped down and my eyes locked on his.

"Don't stop," I begged.

He shoved his fingers up deep and tight. "Want my dick there," he growled.

Right.

I was good with that.

"Condom," I breathed.

He dipped his head and ran his tongue from the base of my throat down my chest, between my breasts, over my belly, and he didn't move his fingers until his tongue slid through my wet heat.

My neck and back arched and a long, silent moan escaped my throat.

He moved away. It took me a minute to recover as I heard sounds of foil ripping then my eyes opened when he stated low, "Call it."

I looked at him. "Call what?"

His hand shot out, hooking me at the back of the neck, pulling me up off the bed. His other arm curled around my back and he tucked me close against his body.

"Until I know what you can take, and what you can't, you call it."

Kristen Ashley

Warm rays of sun hit me.

"What?" I whispered.

"You want me to fuck you, you wanna ride me, you want it on your knees. Against the wall. On the floor. Bent over the back of your couch." He paused, his face got closer, his voice more impatient as he demanded, "Baby... *call it.*"

My invisible sun warmed me deep to my soul.

"On your back, Creed," I whispered.

He dropped us to our sides, rolled and lifted me even as I positioned my legs. I grabbed his cock and he lowered me down as I guided it inside.

Fuck yeah.

I started moving, my eyes on him, his pinned to me.

"Hands to the headboard," I demanded. I watched his eyes flash and I ground down and kept grinding.

He lifted his hands to the headboard and I watched his fingers curl around.

My eyes went back to his face and I saw his jaw was hard.

He didn't like that. That wasn't his gig.

But he did it.

For me.

Fucking hell.

The heat of the rays of my sun burned deep.

I bent to him and kept moving on his cock as I explored the skin of his neck, shoulders and collarbone with my mouth.

I ended at my scabbed-over mark on his neck and licked it.

His hips started bucking up to meet my downward glides.

"Yeah, baby," I whispered in his ear.

Suddenly, both our bodies jerked up the bed and my head flew up to see he'd pulled us both up. His arms were now cocked, the muscles flexed and straining in his biceps, the veins in his forearms had popped out.

I looked to his face as our hips met over and over, rough, hard, fast, deep, beautiful.

"You wanna touch me," I said softly.

"Want your tits in my hands, your tongue in my mouth."

"Take it," I breathed.

His hands immediately moved, but only one curved around my breast. The other one dove into my hair and crushed my mouth down on his. His
94

tongue spiked out and I took it. It curled around my tongue, then he sucked deep so my tongue was in his mouth and I gave it.

His thumb slid across my nipple hard and I took that, too, moaning down his throat, our hips moving faster. His finger met his thumb and rolled. The kiss, already wild, went out-of-control and I had to lift a hand and curl my fingers around my headboard. The power of his hips increased so much, if I didn't, he'd throw me off.

It was coming. Fuck, holy shit, it was coming.

I tore my mouth from his and my head flew back.

"Ride 'em, cowgirl," he murmured, and it was the first time *in my life* I came while smiling.

◦✷◦

My head dropped forward as it left me. My hands were curled around the top of my headboard and I still felt Creed's mouth between my legs. His head to the pillows, I was sitting on his face, his tongue lapping at me, sweet, gentle, even tender.

Fuck me.

I shifted my hips. He got the message. His fingers, already curved around my hips, pulled me down the length of his body and I collapsed on him.

"Right, you got a Costco around here?" he asked, and sated, relaxed, in a total happy zone, this question threw me.

So I muttered into his neck, "What?"

"You weren't fuckin' around. You *can* go all night. This means I need to find condoms in bulk."

My body started shaking on his with my laughter and I lifted my head to look down at him. "I'm not sure Costco sells condoms in bulk."

"Worth a fly-by to check and see," he muttered, and I kept laughing but collapsed back into him.

He waited until I quit laughing then his arms gave me a squeeze.

"You got the plan?"

I nodded. "Knight's business as usual. No one's the wiser we got the goods on Amy and Nair except Lively, who will pass along bogus intel. Set up. You need to work on Charlene's car after you pick up the part tomorrow morning.

I'm on Nick. Tomorrow afternoon, another search of his place. After that, we regroup."

"You got it."

"You tired Grandpa?"

He was silent.

Then, "Shit, seriously?"

I lifted my head and smiled down at him. "No. I'm wiped."

He pressed his head into the pillow and looked back at the headboard muttering, "Thank God."

"God's not in my headboard, Creed."

He looked back at me, grinning. "Disagree. Saw some heavenly action tonight."

He was not wrong.

I tipped my head to the side and dipped my voice low when I asked, "You wanna sleep in here tonight?"

His voice was dipped low and a flash went through his eyes. His arms tightened again when he replied, "Yeah."

"I don't cuddle," I told him.

His arms tightened again, but this seemed reflexive, before he muttered, "Right."

"He cuddled."

Another flash went through his eyes as his jaw hardened. Then he unclenched it to repeat a muttered, "Right."

"You can manage that, you're welcome here until you go back to the Grand Canyon State."

One of his hands slid up my back, over my shoulder and up my neck to curl around the side of my head before he whispered, "I'll take it, Sylvie."

It was my turn to mutter, "Right," and I did before I shifted off him.

I turned off my light.

Creed turned off his.

I pulled the sheet up to my waist and settled on my belly. My head turned away from him, knee crooked. I didn't know how he settled.

"I like morning sex," I warned into the dark.

"Fuck me," he muttered.

"That's what I'm saying."

I heard him chuckle.

Then my body tensed as I felt the tips of his fingers glide over my hip, my ass to my waist in a super soft touch before they moved away.

"'Night, partner," he murmured.

"'Night, Creed," I murmured back.

Five minutes later, Gun joined us, curling in the crook of my leg.

By the sounds he made, Creed fell asleep before me.

It took me a while.

Mostly because, over and over in my head, I heard his voice saying, *call it,* and saw in my mind's eye his hands curling around my headboard.

I adjusted minutely, reaching out to Gun and sifting my fingers through her thick, soft fur.

"Fuck," I whispered.

She started purring.

I fell asleep.

Creed

"Fuck," Creed heard her whisper.

He squeezed his eyes tight.

He heard her cat start purring.

He cuddled.

Creed opened his eyes.

It took some time, but the cat quit purring so he could hear Sylvie's breaths come deep.

He shifted out of bed and moved to her dresser. Carefully, he opened the drawer where he found it while he was doing his search a month before.

He dug back behind her tees and his fingers hit it.

He pulled it out, moved to the window and stood in it, letting the moonlight light the wooden box as he flipped it open.

His put his finger in, flicking through the chains there.

Eleven necklaces. Eleven peridot pendants.

He flipped the box shut and his eyes went to the bed.

Her cat's head was up and Creed knew she was looking at him.

Sylvie kept his necklaces. She cared.

She kept them.

Kristen Ashley

She cared.

He fucked her twice that night, made her come four times. She was there but she was not. He could be anybody.

But if she kept those fucking necklaces, somewhere in her, she cared.

He put the box back, grabbed his shit and left the room. He dumped it on the floor in her wreck of a guest bedroom, climbed into the double there and settled on his back.

He shoved one hand between his head and the pillow. He lifted the other one and traced the scar on his cheek then through his hair, his fingers pressing deep, feeling the ridge along the skin under his hair, over his skull until it stopped.

The memory played in his head like it did thousands of times before, his voice coming back, pained, weak.

Promise me.

The bastard promised.

He'd lied.

Creed rolled to his side.

He didn't cuddle Chelle. He gave her that until she fell asleep and then he set her away.

He'd fucked her over, huge. He'd tried, but a dead man felt nothing. Creed had nothing to give. He wanted to. She deserved it. But it just wasn't there.

He couldn't sleep next to Sylvie, his Sylvie, and not hold her.

So he didn't.

Chapter 8

I'm Creed

A cold, dark autumn night in Kentucky, twenty-six years earlier. Creed is thirteen, Sylvie is eight...

Bootsie yapped and I opened my eyes.

Darkness.

Silence.

Then I heard it, like a tap on the window.

Oh boy. This had never happened before.

I threw the covers back and jumped out of bed. I ran to the window, threw it up, stuck my head out in the cold and looked down.

Tucker was standing in our side yard.

Wow! This never happened before!

I waved then pointed to me and down. He nodded and started walking toward the backyard.

I pulled the window down and ran to my closet. It was cold and I went to Tuck's once without mittens and a hat and he got mad at me. So even though I had to be quiet, I pulled on socks, boots and my coat over my nightgown, then added my mittens and a hat.

I bent down to Bootsie. "This is different, Bootsie. You don't get to come this time." She whined a bit and I put my mittened finger to my lips and said, "Sh." I dropped my hand and continued, "I'll be back real soon, promise."

I gave her fur a ruffle and kissed the top of her head. Then super careful, but as quick as I could, I dashed down the hall, the stairs, through the house and outside.

Tuck was standing at the partially opened back gate.

I ran across the yard, and when I was close enough, he reached right down, grabbed my hand and pulled me through the gate. He closed it slowly behind us then he moved, real fast, dragging me with him through the woods.

It was then I knew this wasn't fun. This wasn't like meeting him at the lake. This wasn't like when I went to his house with the squirt guns, got him out of bed and we had a squirt gun fight at night, in the dark, in the woods.

This was something bad.

When we were well away from the house and no way Daddy could hear, I asked, "Tuck, what's the matter?"

He let me go, but he didn't stop walking. He walked to a tree, slammed his opened hand on it then slammed his shoulder into it and turned around. He then slammed his back against it and slid down to his behind, pulled his knees up and dropped his head.

Oh yes. This was something bad.

I rushed to him and got down on my knees beside him.

"Tuck, what happened?" I asked.

"Sheriff brought Mom home." He told his lap, stopped then kept going, "Again."

I got it then. His Mom got drunk all the time and she got pulled over for driving that way. Tuck told me they took her license away. Now she had to walk, take a bike or get a ride everywhere. It put her in a bad mood and she took this out on Tuck.

I got closer and put my hand on his knee. "Oh, Tuck, I'm sorry."

His head came up, turned and his eyes came to me. "She lost her job, Sylvie. Two days ago."

I didn't know a lot about these things, but I knew that wasn't good. They didn't have a lot already. I knew, Mrs. Creed without a job, now they'd have less.

"Tuck," I whispered.

He shook his head. "Not Tuck. *Creed*."

"What?"

"Sheriff's deputy had a partner. They got Mom in on the couch, but I heard 'em talkin' outside. Said they didn't get it. Said she was a mess. Said she *always* was a mess. Said, 'cept her bein' pretty, they didn't get why Dad liked her. Said she was trouble. Too much. Not worth it. Even too much for Brand Creed. Said she was good for nothin'. Said they hoped her boy, *me,* was more like Brand than her."

He stopped talking so I whispered, "Okay."

"Mom gave me the name Tucker," he told me. "Dad used to tease her. Said she was crazy, namin' me Tucker. 'Least I gave him Creed,' he'd say, laughin', grinnin' big at her, makin' her roll her eyes right before she'd giggle and give

100

him a hug. So that's who I am. I'm not what my Mom gave me. I'm what my Dad gave me. I'm Creed."

"Creed," I agreed.

He looked away and muttered, "Done bein' Tuck. Done bein' crazy, drunk Winona's boy. I'm Brand Creed's boy. I'm Creed."

"You're Creed," I told him.

He turned his face further away and I had a feeling he was trying not to cry, or not to let me see him cry, so I gave him that. Boys did that and I didn't know why, but I did know it was important.

I sat next to him, though. Got close, shoved my shoulder into him and started wiggling it so he had to put his arm around me. When he did, I pressed even closer. He got kinda stiff for a second then he relaxed and his arm curved tight around me so I rested my cheek against his shoulder.

But I didn't say anything. Sometimes, when I was trying not to cry and someone said something, it'd make me cry.

So I just pressed close.

We stayed this way a long time. It wasn't comfortable but it was warm and it still felt good.

Finally, he said something.

"You know, I lost him, too."

"I know Tu... I mean, Creed."

"She acts like she's the only one."

"I know."

"It's been years and I still find her drunk, smellin' bad and passed out on the stupid couch with a stupid bottle, booze drenched in the carpet, his picture in her hand."

I pressed closer.

"I lost him too," he whispered.

"I know, Creed."

He pulled in a loud breath.

Then he said quiet, "You gotta get home."

I didn't want to, but I agreed, "Yeah."

We got up and he took my hand as we walked back to the gate. He stopped me like he always did outside. Then his eyes dropped to my throat, his hand let mine go and he lifted it and twitched the pendant there.

He looked back at me and grinned. "You're always wearin' one 'a those."

I nodded.

"Even if they don't match your outfit," he kept talking.

I grinned back. I liked it that he noticed. It felt good.

"I like them," I said. "And they've never turned my skin green."

He shook his head, still grinning and told me, "You're a goof."

I shoved his shoulder and told him, "*You're* a goof."

He shoved me back and replied, "You're a *bigger* goof."

I smiled big and said, "Yeah."

"Go to bed, goof."

"Okay. You go home, goof."

He shook his head again then opened the gate for me.

I started to slide through but turned back and looked up at him.

"Creed is the best name *ever*," I whispered. "I always thought so. Always. I'm glad you're Creed, but you always have been, you know."

I heard him pull in another breath.

Then he whispered, "Go to bed, Sylvie."

I grinned up at him. "Okay, Creed."

I slipped through the gate, hearing it latch quietly behind me.

Then I stole through the yard, the house. I took off my warm clothes, changed my nightgown that had mud stains on the knees and seat, hid the dirty one under my mattress and I went to bed.

Chapter 9
You Can't Breathe without Me

<hr>

Present day, four days later...

My eyes opened and all I could see was Creed's tattooed back in front of me.

The last four days I woke up alone to Creed making breakfast in the kitchen. Clearly, he was an early riser. I was not but did it for Charlene, though I got up at the last possible second.

Last night, though, we went out. I got a shade past tipsy, and when we came home, I attacked. It had been energetic, or more energetic than usual. It had lasted a long time, or even longer than normal. And it only stopped when we both passed out, or when I did.

I must have done him in. Now, he was out.

Sleep slowly leaving me, recent memories moved through my head.

These were mostly about working and spending time with Creed. Learning he wasn't good at his job. He was *very* good. He was a good partner; communicative, amusing, alert, sharp. Working with him was a lot like working with Ron, my dead partner. I could trust him because he knew what he was doing. We worked shit through, planned our moves, broke stuff down, and when we did, he listened to me. I wasn't just another gun, someone he was putting up with or a liability. I was a colleague. He treated me with respect, wasn't overly protective and never acted like I was a girl.

A couple of nights ago he'd shared in my back room over beers, takeout cheeseburgers and onion rings, that he'd had more experience than me, falling into the work within months of moving to Michigan. I'd shared that I'd started my training with Ron when I met him at a gun shop and range when I was buying my first gun about a week after I moved to Denver. I also shared that Ron offered to teach me how to shoot, and shortly after that he took me on. We became partners and he'd taught me everything I knew.

I further learned about Creed that whatever happened sixteen years ago, he was a decent guy. Or good at playing one.

He went with me every day to Charlene's, even over the weekend, and there were no more donuts or Cocoa Puffs. Eggs and bacon that he made. Pancakes. Oatmeal. He was good with the kids, and especially Adam.

I knew this when, two days before, Adam had broken a figurine, kinda went weird about it, and before Charlene or I could wade in, Creed did, calming Adam and then going so far as cleaning up the figurine.

He also took them to lunch on Sunday, then to the park, while I went to Ron's grave, giving Charlene the house to herself to clean and then relax. It was a cool thing to do. They had to be a hand full, but they came back excited and intact and Charlene called me that night to say they all were dead to the world within seconds of their heads hitting the pillows.

With all this, and more, it was coming clear there was a lot to this new Tucker Creed.

He did dishes. Put his towel on the towel rail. Rinsed out beer bottles before he recycled them, and not only took out the trash but asked when trash day was and hauled the bins to the curb. He even went beyond the call of duty and, Saturday, took time out to mow mine and Charlene's lawns.

Truth be told, I was a little worried about this. Worried Charlene would get used to the extra help and then Creed would go to Arizona and there'd be no one to fix her car or mow her lawn.

If I admitted it to myself, which I didn't, I also worried about the fact that I really liked working with him. And more, I liked having him around. And, needless to say, I freaking hated mowing my lawn, so I liked not having to do that.

I missed Ron. I didn't mind working jobs alone, but there was no denying it was better to work them with someone else. It wasn't the additional brainpower and firepower. It was the company. Knowing you weren't in it alone even when you were separated. I missed that. I'd been alone a long time and the only times since Creed left I didn't feel alone had been when I was working with Ron or spending time with Knight or Charlene. It was cool to wake up knowing your day would include someone else in a way that was integral to life.

Creed read all my open case files. Sat down with me, made suggestions. We planned and we worked my shit together as well as Knight's. Work got done and it shifted easily from me on my own to us working together. Life fell naturally into an order that was solid, comfortable. It was good. Too good.

Last, it was also good getting it steady and abundantly, and it was better since that "it" was so fucking great.

I liked sex once it was about what I wanted, and not what someone was taking from me. I lost myself in it. I was able to move total concentration to the good shit my body was feeling, which meant I had no space to concentrate on the bad shit that was always at the edge of my mind.

It was better with Creed.

I couldn't get enough of him. He couldn't get enough of me. We jumped each other frequently. Sometimes to fuck, sometimes to grope, sometimes just to kiss... and hard. He didn't leave my presence, not even the room, without hooking me behind my neck, pulling my mouth to his and kissing me deep. I returned the favor. We'd done it on the couch in the back room (again), on the floor of the hall, in the shower and in my bed.

It was wild but not abandoned. This was because I sensed him letting me guide it. I didn't explore the boundaries of this power he was willing to give me by making him do something he didn't like, not again. He'd demonstrated he'd do that for me once. It touched me in a place I was denying, so I didn't push it because I was unwilling to go there again. That didn't mean I didn't feel him handing the reins over to me.

He took, absolutely. He flipped me when he wanted the top, he adjusted us when he was ready for a new position, he took my mouth when he wanted it. But there was always an underlying alertness, and if I gave the barest indication something wasn't working for me, he backed off and did something else.

It wasn't gentle. It wasn't making love. It was fucking.

But, because of what Creed gave me, it was more. It skimmed the edge of making love because fucking was fucking, but when you gave even a hint of more, which he did every time, it was something else.

And it was dangerous.

I knew it but I was powerless to stop it. This was not because it was Tucker Creed (or I was telling myself that). This was how I'd lived my life when I got free. I played with fire. I didn't mind getting burned. It was a reminder that I was alive and it was a way to bury shit that, if it surfaced, would destroy me.

So as the days passed, I was finding it harder to hold him distant. I was finding it harder to convince myself he didn't mean anything to me. I was finding it harder to deny that the new Tucker Creed wasn't getting to me.

Right then, that tattoo nearly all I could see, my sleepy brain filled with all I'd experienced with him recently and waking up for the first time in my life beside him, I lost hold on all that. I lost control of my ability to separate the Creed that used to be from the Creed that was sleeping beside me. I lost the stranglehold I had on me.

I had my head on the pillow but my body was close to his, my side brushing his, my eyes level to his shoulder. His head was turned away from me.

We were both on our stomachs, his leg crooked, my leg crooked with his, the inside of my thigh resting on top of the back of his other leg, which was straight. I had my arm curled around his back.

Yes, *me* cuddling *Creed* (kind of).

The sheets were over our legs, and when I lifted my head slightly and looked down, I saw they were mostly over Creed's ass. But I could see the top of it wasn't covered. None of mine was.

My eyes moved up, my arm shifting, and I caught the flowered "Sylvie" in the dent of his lower spine.

Seeing my name inked in that vulnerable dent in his spine, a vulnerability surrounded by the power of his defined muscles, the beauty of the image of our place, my body moved before I told it to do so. My mouth hit his back at the lake, then it glided down. His body twitched, shifted, and I put my hands to him, one between his shoulders, one at his ass and pressed down lightly.

"Sylvie." It came out as a sleepy growl and went straight between my legs.

My lips kept moving down his back, over his waist. Soaking in the tat, soaking in our place, soaking in us. Then my lips moved up the curve of his ass. Pushing the sheet down, I bared my teeth and nipped his flesh.

"*Fuck*," he whispered, his big, powerful body shifting again.

Against his skin, I murmured, "Stay still, baby."

"Fuck," he whispered again, and I shoved my hand between his legs, curled it up and found his cock.

It was hard.

Yes. I loved that. I wanted it. *Needed it.* Already.

My mouth drifted up and there I was.

Sylvie.

In flowers.

On our pier.

Slow, so fucking slow, taking my time, my hand wrapped tight around his hard cock, I traced my flowered letters with my tongue.

I got to the "i" and Creed was done.

He rolled, disengaging me. He knifed up and grabbed me, pulled me over him, his hand at his cock. He slammed me down, impaling me.

My head shot back.

Yes. Just what I needed.

Exactly what I needed.

His hands slid up my back, his fingers curling around my shoulders holding me down as his forearms pressed deep, holding me to him.

He felt good, hard, big, filling me.

I was gone. Seriously gone. Already close. I had to move.

I righted my head and looked at him. "Gotta move, Creed," I whispered.

"What'd he take from you?" he whispered back.

His tattoo in my head, our place still on my lips, my name in his skin on my tongue. All I was learning that was him filling my head. His cock inside me. I worked against those odds and tried to bury it.

I failed.

Still, I breathed, "Don't. Let me move."

"Tell me what he took from you. I'm giving it back."

Shit.

"Creed—"

His hips bucked up and my breath hitched.

God, that felt *great*.

"You wanna move, baby, tell me what he took from you."

"Don't wanna, *gotta,*" I whispered, pressing my breasts into his skin and dragging my nails lightly down his back; two things I knew, fucking Creed copiously the last few days, he liked. A lot.

It didn't work.

"He held you down, Sylvie. I'm gonna hold you down. I'm gonna show you it's good. You can trust it. You can enjoy it. I'm gonna give you that back."

"Please—"

"He tied you down. I'm gonna tie you to the bed, baby, and you're gonna love it."

Fuck.

I needed *to move* and his words, the heat behind them, the determination weren't helping matters.

"Baby—"

"When I'm done, you will fear nothing. Never again. I'm gonna give that back to you. Now, what else did he take from you?"

"Creed—"

His hips bucked up and it pulsed through me.

"What did he take from you?"

I shoved my face in his neck and ground my hips into his.

"Sylvie—"

"My ass."

His fingers at my shoulders dug in.

"He took your ass?" he growled.

"Yeah," I breathed. Then, on a plea, "I need to move."

"Didn't make it good for you?"

"That shit's not good, Creed."

"That shit's fuckin' awesome, Sylvie," he returned, his voice rumbling through me. "I get you ready, you'll come so hard with me up your ass, you'll think you're comin' out of your skin."

Serious to God. I didn't know how, that was *not* my gig, but the way Creed was talking about it, it was *not* helping.

"I need *to move,* baby."

"What else did he take?"

"Creed—"

His hips bucked up and I whimpered.

"What else did he take, Sylvie?"

"He hit me."

Creed's body stilled underneath me, and it did this so completely it felt like all the air in the room stilled with him.

"What?" he asked.

"He hit me."

"While he was fuckin' you?"

His anger wasn't slithering through the room and the room wasn't stilled anymore.

It was vibrating with fury. Every fucking centimeter.

I lifted my head, but before I could look at him and answer in the affirmative, I was on my back and Creed was pounding into me.

Finally!

I opened my mouth to speak but didn't say a word because his slammed down on mine.

He fucked me hard and kissed me harder. Then he fucked me harder and I kissed him deep. Then I lifted my knees high, wrapped my calves around him and groaned down his throat as all he gave me washed over me.

He didn't break the contact of our mouths even while I came, while he kept thrusting hard and deep or when his heavy grunts drove down my throat with his own release.

When he was done, coming down, he slammed up hard and planted himself so deep, I swear, it was like he wanted to fuse with me.

Then his mouth slid down my cheek to my ear and his voice was gruff with his orgasm and emotion when he whispered, "My tat means to you what it means to me." I closed my eyes tight, mentally kicking myself for giving that away, and moved my hands to his shoulders. But he pressed his entire body into me, negating my shove before it even began. "Kept you close every day, every night, right with me, and now you know it. You just don't know what to do with it."

Shit, how did I let this happen?

Shit. I just had to wake up to him and I was open, bare. Fuck!

"Get off me," I whispered.

He lifted his head and his face, harsh and intense, looked down at me. "And you won't know what to do with it until you talk to me."

"Sex, work, food, beer then you're back to Arizona, partner," I reminded him.

"I'd move here. I'd move to the goddamned, fucking *moon* to wake up to you in my bed."

Holy shit!

"Just came inside you, Sylvie, no condom. That was just you and me, nothing in between. *Nothing.* And you know exactly what I fuckin' mean," he remarked and I blinked.

Shit. How did *that* happen?

Shit!

He pulled out, rolled off and I closed my legs. I turned to the side, curled my knees up and tried to sort out the ten thousand thoughts crashing in my head. The priority of which was Creed's badass sperm, likely Olympic-class swimming with pinpoint accuracy, inside me, and whether I was up-to-date on my birth control pills.

Fuck!

Letting my mind wander to heretofore unknown unsafe sex was a mistake. I was doing that and therefore not processing the fact that he was prowling to my mirror. I also didn't process the fact that he snatched a long scarf I had dangling on it and was prowling back, twisting it and doing something with it in his hands.

But I processed his knee hitting the bed and his hand capturing my arm.

I shot up and tried to pull away.

"What the fuck?" I clipped. He looped the scarf over my hand and it tightened at my wrist. Even as I pulled and struggled, before I knew it, he'd tied the other end to my headboard.

My eyes shot to him and rage shot through my system.

"You fucking *fucker!*" I screeched.

"Look at my hand, Sylvie," he ordered, calm as could be, the *fucking fucker!*

"Fuck you!" I yelled. My other hand went toward my wrist tied to the bed, but he batted it gently away. My eyes shot back to him. "Let me untie it!"

"Look at my goddamned hand, Sylvie," he bit out, calm a fleeting memory.

"Fuck you!"

He moved. My eyes moved to where he moved, and I saw his fingers tug at the end of the scarf. A slight yank and my wrist was instantly released.

I froze and stared.

Then I wasn't frozen anymore, but not because I moved. Because Creed's hand wrapped around the back of my neck, he pulled me to him and both his arms closed around me, plastering me to his body.

"*That's* how you do it," he growled in my face. "You do it so you get tweaked, you still got control and you can get yourself loose any fuckin' time you want. You do it and you have a safe word so it goes places you don't like, you say it and it… fuckin'… *stops.* The guy who did that shit to you, Sylvie, he was a goddamned animal, takin' from you what you didn't want to give. Not all men are. In fact, most men aren't. And I'm a man who's not."

"Let go of me," I snapped.

"I gave it time. Your mouth on my tat, I'm done with givin' it time. You're not gonna dig deep, I'm diggin' in there for you."

"That is not gonna happen."

"It is. You don't wanna talk. I will. He promised me, Sylvie."

My body went solid before I tried to jerk away, but his arms only tightened so tight I could barely breathe.

His face got close and his voice got low. "He promised me. I would never, *ever* fuckin' leave you to him unless he promised me."

I glared into his eyes.

"He lied," he whispered.

"We're done," I hissed. "You're out. We partner but you're gone. Outta my life. Outta my house. Outta my bed. Outta everything but the job."

"No fuckin' way, and you know what?"

"I don't care what," I clipped.

He ignored me. "The way I know it's no fuckin' way is because you won't be able to let me go. I can leave. I can be gone. You can try to make it just about the job but you won't be able to do it. I know that because you didn't kick my ass out, Sylvie. Not completely. You're keepin' it about the job and that shit is *not* about Knight. It's about finding a way to stay connected to me. You're foolin' yourself, baby, but you sure as hell aren't foolin' me. I been dead for sixteen fuckin' years, suckin' in air and not gettin' any oxygen until I sat down with Knight Sebring and he told me the names of his team. Then, finally, fuckin' *finally,* I was breathin' again. And you know, don't fuckin' bullshit me, *you know* you been dead until you woke up that morning, rolled off your bed and aimed your gun at me. Try to deny it, Sylvie, but your tongue traced your name on our pier on my skin because you needed that. You need me. You won't stay away and you won't let me go because, baby, you can't breathe without me."

Then he let me go. I fell to my hand in the bed and watched as he moved through the room, bending and tagging his shit before he walked right out.

I reached low and yanked the sheet up.

Shit. Fuck. *Shit!*

Okay, get my head together. Okay, see to Charlene and the kids. Get to Knight. Explain. Get to the airport. Get the fuck out of here.

My body jolted when Creed stormed back into the room wearing nothing but his jeans.

He stopped, planted his hands on his hips and demanded to know, "You know where he is?"

I stared at him, not keeping up, before I asked, "Who?"

"Dixon," he bit off.

My head jerked. "Who?"

He leaned forward, his face suffused with hard fury. "Jason *fucking* Dixon. The animal who did that to you."

Cold washed through me. Ice cold.

Oh no. I didn't like this.

I did *not* fucking like this.

And I didn't like it because I had no freaking clue what he was talking about, but he seemed to know.

Just whatever he knew was not right.

"What?" I whispered.

Creed ignored my question and asked his own. "He still in Kentucky? Or did you just get the fuck out and don't know?"

"Jason Dixon married Peggy Linklater six months after you took off. By the time I left, they had two kids and she was pregnant with the third."

It was the truth, but it was the wrong thing to say. I knew this because it seemed every muscle in his body stood out in deep relief, such was the effort he was making not to move.

I got up on my knees holding the sheet to me. "Creed—"

"He wanted you," he growled and that cold crept deep.

"I know," I whispered.

"Dixon had a thing for you," he told me.

"I know."

"We fought about him," he reminded me.

"I know," I repeated.

"You told me it was only me."

Oh God. Oh shit. What the fuck *was* this?

"It *was* only you."

"You bled for me."

Oh *God*. Oh *shit*. What the fuck *was* this?

"Creed—"

"Did he lie or was it you?"

I shook my head. "This is… we're not going over this. This shit is history."

"Can't fake blood," he told me. "You gave me your virginity."

"Yes," I snapped. "What is this shit? Of course I did. You know that. Jason Dixon? What the fuck are you talking about?"

He didn't answer. He asked, "Who did it to you?"

"You know. You told me you knew," I reminded him.

"He told me it was Dixon."

"It wasn't Jason Dixon."

"He told me it was Dixon," he repeated.

Jesus, God, *what was this?*

"It wasn't Jason Dixon."

"Then who was it?" he demanded.

"We're not doing this, Creed," I fired back.

He leaned forward and roared, *"Who did it to you, Sylvie?"*

"Richard Scott did it to me!"

He stared at me a beat, two, three, then he turned and I watched in fascination as the muscles worked in his back while he threw a powerhouse punch to the wall, his fist going clean through the paneling, the drywall, everything.

He pulled it out and twisted back to me as I deep breathed.

"Do *not* make me waste my fuckin' time diggin' for it," he growled.

"It's mine, not yours. You were gone. You left me to that."

"I did fuckin' *not* and you know it. How in *the fuck* did you go from me to Richard fuckin' Scott? The only drug dealing pimp in the goddamned county."

"You know."

"I don't fuckin' know."

"Maybe not then, but you know now. I know you do. You looked into me."

"Sylvie, I didn't have time to dig that deep. I thought you hooked up with Dixon. I didn't fuckin' know about Scott, so," he leaned toward me again and thundered, *"tell me!"*

I shook my head. "Don't bullshit me. You know. You know what I do for Knight and why. It's about the girls."

"Yeah, Sylvie, I know that because *you're you* and watchin' you for a month I know, as much as you shovel the bullshit, that hasn't changed. You got a heart of gold. You always had a heart of gold. Somethin' matters to you, you'll do anything. Only difference now is you do it with a gun clipped to your belt. Now, *tell me how you got hooked up with fuckin' Scott!"* he shouted the last.

"Daddy owed him money, Creed," I hissed. "That's how."

A muscle in his cheek jerked then he asked, "He pimp you?"

I shook my head. "He liked me all to himself."

"How'd you get away?"

"I stuck him with a knife. *His* knife, incidentally. Luckily, they declared it self-defense because, before I did, he beat the fucking shit out of me. I survived, Creed. Richard didn't."

His chest heaved with his breathing. Mine did too. I felt it moving under my hand clutching the sheet to me.

"You're talkin', Sylvie, you ready to listen to me?" he asked tightly.

"No," I answered firmly. "No. You wanna talk, *you* listen, but I'm not gonna fucking listen, Creed. He *sold* me. Daddy *sold* me. You left me to that shit and I don't give one fuck why you did it. You did it. I was a captive for six fucking years. I had a car. A home. But no freedom. He bought my clothes, made me wear them. I had no choice. He told me what I could eat. He fucked me. He held me down. He tied me down. He took my ass. He slapped me while he pounded inside me, all of it dry because he did nothing for me and that... shit... *stings*. And he beat me. Repeatedly. To get away, I had to kill him before he killed me. I can still feel his blood warm on my hands. God, so much blood. I had no idea a body had that much blood. It was all over the bed. All over him. All over *me*. He *owned* me until I took his life to get mine back. That's why no one else gets me. I killed a man to get me back and I'm keeping me."

"It was Scott," he whispered.

"Yeah, it was Scott," I confirmed.

"No, Sylvie," he shook his head, then lifted his hand and pointed to the scar on his face before he scored his finger through his hair along the streak of white. "It was Scott's men, not your father's, who did this to me and drove me away from you. Your Dad just was in on it."

Oh my *fucking* God.

What was he talking about?

"You're ready," he went on, "you'll get the story. Warning, it lasted a fuckuva lot less time but it was no less ugly."

After he delivered that, he turned on his bare foot and prowled out.

I sat in my bed and shivered.

That was, I sat in bed and shivered until I heard the front door slam.

Then me and my sheet went to the kitchen and we got the bourbon. Then me and my sheet went to the back room and we got my cigs.

Then me and my sheet went back to bed.

"Sylvie."

"Fuggov," I slurred.

"Sylvie, babe, look at me."

"Fug... *ov!*" I shouted, lurching toward the voice then collapsing in bed.

"He do this to you?" I heard growled as I blinked.

"Who?"

"Creed."

"Scott."

"What?"

"Richard Scott didid to me. Daddeh didid to me. Creed jus' lef' me."

"Fuck," I heard whispered, then I felt my hair pulled gently away from my face and lips at my ear. "I knew this would shred you."

"Go 'way, Knide," I mumbled into my pillow.

Knight didn't go away. "Five days, you're shredded."

"Ah'll be okay," I muttered. "Ah always am."

"You haven't been okay for sixteen years."

Fuck, *that* was the truth.

"Ah havin been okay for *forever.*"

I blinked and my hazy vision vanished.

This was because I passed out.

I put the cigarette to my lips, took a deep drag and blew out the smoke, my eyes trained out the window of my back room to the dark night.

I knew someone was there well before I heard Anya call from the door to the kitchen, "Sylvie?"

"Here," I muttered.

Quiet.

Then, softly, "Knight sent me to check on you. He gave me the key."

Kristen Ashley

"That's cool."

"You okay?"

No, I fucking was not.

"Yup."

She walked through the dark and I watched her shadow move and fold into the other chair across from me.

"How's Kat?" I asked about their daughter.

"She's good. Knight's folks are here from Hawaii. They're babysitting so I could have a rare night at Slade."

"Have fun?" I asked.

"Yeah. Good night. Great night, actually."

"Good," I muttered.

She was silent.

Then she asked, "You still drinking?"

"I think drunk off my fucking ass, passed out by noon, missing helping out Charlene for the first time since Dan the Douchebag took off on her and seriously hanging by three is enough. I'm laying off the sauce."

At least for the night.

"Charlene got worried. Came over. You were passed out. She had to get back to work so it was her that called Knight," Anya told me.

I nodded to the window and took another drag from my cigarette, blowing the smoke out the screen.

"Sylvie, please talk to me," she whispered.

I could trust her, and it was time. I did it more because I could trust her and less because it was time. All I knew was, I had to unload this shit on somebody, she was available, and lucky me, I could trust her.

Therefore, I asked, "Knight tell you about me?"

"Will you be angry at Knight if I say yes?"

"No."

"Then yes."

I nodded, took another drag then reached to my side and crushed out the cigarette. "So he told you about Creed."

"I'll admit, I got the recent update." Then quieter, "He was worried about you, Sylvie, and apparently, there was a reason for him to worry."

116

"There's about one thing Knight Sebring could do that would piss me off and that's fucking you over, so don't worry about me being mad at him because you two talk. I'm not. That's cool."

She was silent.

I was, too.

I spent my silence fighting the urge to grab another cigarette. I was not a heavy smoker unless I was drinking. Casual. I should quit. But she wasn't one. She'd even made Knight quit. So it was uncool for me to smoke around her, even in my own house. She walked in on me having one, that was one thing. Another to chain smoke when she was four feet away.

When she remained silent, I took my mind off my need for another smoke and stopped being that way.

"He wants to talk. Tell me why he left me all those years ago," I shared.

"Okay," she whispered.

"Doesn't turn back the years," I told her.

"You're right."

"Doesn't erase what happened to me," I carried on.

"You're right about that, too."

I pulled in breath through my nose and stared at my dark yard.

Gun came into the room, and I knew that because she jumped up on my chair. Then she shoved her way into the space between my thighs and my torso, which was snug since I had my body twisted sideways in the chair and my feet in the seat. Still, when she wanted something, she was determined and she got it. So she got it, curled up and started purring.

I started stroking.

Then I started talking again.

"He has a scar on his cheekbone, a streak of white through his hair where the knife went through. He said they were going for his brain through his eye and he moved. He also said when he got it, it had something to do with him leaving me."

"Why don't you find out?" she asked cautiously.

"They could have tortured me back then and I'd never leave him. Obviously, they did something like that and he left me."

"You're guessing. My advice, honey, you shouldn't guess. You should *know*."

"Doesn't turn back the years," I muttered.

"You're right, it doesn't."

"Doesn't erase what happened to me."

"You're right, Sylvie," she whispered.

I fell silent.

Then I again broke the silence.

"He named his kids with another woman the names we chose for ours." I heard her sharply indrawn breath. "Yeah," I agreed. "That's about what I thought before I attacked him and tried to beat the shit out of him. That didn't work."

"Why would he do that?" she asked. "Did he explain?"

"Yup," I answered. "Said it was because he thought he'd never see me again. Said it was because he wanted to call the kids he loved the names we chose so he could remember me every time he did it. Fucking whacked *and* mean. His wife found out, divorced his ass, and seriously, I do not blame her."

She fell silent for long moments before she broke it.

"That's the most beautiful thing I've ever heard."

My head turned to stare at her shadow.

"What?" I breathed.

I watched her shadow lean toward me.

"Okay, maybe you won't like me after I tell you this, but if something happened to Knight and he was taken from me, I love our daughter enough to go on with life even though, in all honesty, huge important parts of mine would be over. Going on with life maybe would include having someone else in it, but I know this: there is no one for me but Knight. I'd be honest, and if the guy didn't get it, he'd have to move on, but that's the way it would be. I'd do everything in my power in some way to keep Knight alive, not only for Kat but for me. I'd need it so I'd do it. This would mean there probably wouldn't be anyone else for me. But what happened to you happened a long time ago, Sylvie. You were young, he was young. He was just trying to keep living at the same time keep you alive and with him in some way and, well, that's beautiful. You're right. It's also whacked and mean. But anything can be a lot of things, and it might be whacked and mean, but it's beautiful, too."

I looked back to the night.

"This doesn't matter," I said softly. "I can know what happened for him to leave me. Hell, maybe I could even understand. But it wouldn't matter. I am who I am now. No going back."

"There's never any going back. But you're not talking about that. You're talking about not moving forward."

I shook my head.

"You are, Sylvie," Anya stated firmly. "You're digging in and staying there. This isn't about history. This is about what could be."

"Even if he could explain shit, it'll always be between us."

"Only if you let it be."

I laughed without humor.

"You're scared," she whispered, and I turned my head back to her shadow.

"Fuck yeah," I whispered back.

"He left and your life unraveled."

"Yup."

"You can't do that again."

"Nope."

She sat back and again fell silent.

I looked back to the night.

We remained quiet a long time.

I broke it this time.

"I'm being a bad hostess. You want a drink?"

She stood. "Some other time, honey. I should get home to my family."

Her family.

She was a lucky bitch. Fortunately, she knew it.

"You mind if I don't see you out?" I asked.

There was a smile in her voice when she replied, "Not at all."

"Thanks for stopping by, Anya. Tell Knight I'm cool. All systems go tomorrow."

"I'll tell him."

I watched her walk to the darkened kitchen doorway as I stroked Gun.

Her shadow didn't disappear through it. It stopped and I knew she was turning back to me.

"One last thing, Sylvie. When I leave, I want you to think about your life right now. I know you like it. I know you've got people close to you. I know you have fun. But I want you to think of your happiest memory, the happiest in your whole life. Then I want you to compare it to the life you live now without Tucker Creed. My guess, your happiest memory includes him. My guess, even with that shit between you, you give it a shot, you'll go from the life you live

119

now, that you like, to something else. Something bigger, richer, better, *happier.* And you know it. You're just scared to lose it because you lost it once. Then, after all that, think about what your life would be if he was *never* in it. You'd never met. He'd never touched it. Then, honey, ask yourself how you would feel if you didn't have those moments. Last, I hope you'll come to the realization that, this time around, you're making the deliberate choice not to take a chance in order to have that beauty."

I stared at the shadowed door long after her silhouette left it, but I didn't see dark shadows. I saw sunny days, the lake, the pier, blankets over grass, young bodies rolling on them, tangled, twin beds in dark rooms that barely fit two bodies, whispered conversations, holding close.

My hands curled around Gun as my legs uncurled from the chair. I set my feet on the floor as I cuddled her close and walked through my dark house to my bedroom. I didn't bother with a light. I just dropped Gun gently on my bed and dug through my clothes on the floor until I found my jeans from last night.

I dug my phone out of the back pocket.

I flipped it open and the light from the screen made me wince.

I went to my phonebook, scrolled down and hit go.

I put it to my ear as my eyes went to the clock on my nightstand.

It was one seventeen in the morning.

The phone rang once.

"Sylvie," Creed greeted, sounding alert but growly.

"I'm ready," I whispered.

Silence.

Then, "I'll be there in ten."

Disconnect.

I flipped my phone shut.

Fuck.

Chapter 10
My Sylvie

***

A warm, late summer day in Kentucky, twenty-two years earlier. Creed is seventeen, Sylvie is eleven, one day away from being twelve...

I got off my bike, leaned it against the wall. I walked down the side of the building, pulled open the door, walked into the frozen milk stand and saw him right away.

Creed with his girlfriend, Natalie.

My stomach started hurting.

I began to turn around real quick but he was laughing. His head moved and he caught sight of me.

"Hey, Sylvie."

I gave a stupid wave then turned around and walked out the door.

But I ran to my bike.

I pulled it from the wall and started to get on when I heard, "Hey! Yo! Wait!"

I looked up and saw Creed's long legs were bringing him to me.

He was *so* beautiful.

As he got closer, my head went back, back, until he stopped in front of me.

"You not gettin' any ice cream?" he asked.

I shook my head. "No. I forgot. I gotta get home. The stepmonster is taking me shopping for my birthday."

This wasn't totally a lie. She was supposed to. She just hadn't got out of bed yet.

"Right," he muttered then grinned. "We on for the lake tomorrow?"

No way. He'd probably want to bring Natalie.

I shook my head. "Sorry, I should have... I forgot to tell you. I'm going over to my friend's house tomorrow. All day slumber party."

His head jerked to the side and his voice was quiet when he reminded me, "We always meet at the lake for your birthday, Sylvie."

"I'll meet you the day after, but I can't stay long."

"Come in the mornin', before you go to your friend's, just real quick," he urged.

"I… I can't. I'm going over there early."

"Then I'll meet you earlier."

"I—"

"Creed! You gonna buy me a cone or what?"

He twisted around to look behind him and I leaned to the side to look around him. I saw Natalie outside the door, one hand holding it open, one hand on her hitched hip. Her long, tanned legs on show in her short-shorts. Her big boobs making the material of her tight t-shirt stretch.

"In a second," Creed called back.

I was so intent on my study of the beautiful, tall, brunette Natalie and wishing I had brown hair and long legs and big boobs that I didn't notice him turn back to me.

"Hey," he said softly, and my eyes shot to him.

Then I quickly dropped my head and moved closer to my bike, mumbling, "Gotta go."

"Hey," he said it softly again, and slowly, my eyes lifted to him. When my eyes met his beautiful blue ones, he whispered, "You'll always be my girl."

He was just being nice.

I'd stopped being his girl a couple years ago. He had other ones now. Lots of them. Natalie was just the newest one.

I bit my lip and looked away, trying real hard not to cry.

"Hey," he whispered and I didn't want to, I could see the wet swimming in my eyes, but I pulled in a breath and looked back at him to find him closer and leaning down toward me. "You'll always be my Sylvie. Yeah?"

I sucked in a breath and nodded.

"Come to the lake. I'll meet you early," he ordered.

I nodded again.

He grinned, lifted a hand and touched the green stone hanging at my neck.

"Gotta give my Sylvie her necklace."

"Okay, Creed," I whispered.

He pulled only an inch away, but stopped and whispered, "It's always you and me."

I nodded again and felt my lips quivering.

He kept whispering, "Always me and my Sylvie, yeah?"

"Yeah," I whispered back.

He lifted a hand and tucked my hair behind my ear. "Careful ridin' home."

"'Kay, Creed."

"See you tomorrow."

"'Kay."

"Later."

"Bye."

I got on my bike.

He strode back to the frozen milk stand.

I cried all the way home.

Chapter 11
We Win

Present day. . .

"Sylvie?"

I stood completely still, the roaring in my ears deafening, my eyes opened but blinded, every nerve in my body vibrating like I was receiving way too many volts, but my lips moved.

"Stop talking."

"Baby." I felt two big hands settle gently on either side of my head.

"They didn't do that to you," I whispered.

"Sylvie—"

"Take it back."

"Ba—"

My hands shot straight down in fists. My head jerked back so far pain pulled at my neck and the words carved jagged through my throat as I shrieked, *"They did not do that to you!"*

His arms folded around my head as he yanked me to his body.

"We're done for tonight," he muttered into the top of my hair.

Oh God.

That wasn't it.

Oh God.

There was more.

My legs gave out under me but Creed caught me, lifting me up in his arms. I shoved my face in his neck as we moved through my house. Then we were in bed, Creed gathering me close, tucking me tight, curling over me so he was mostly on me. He was the only thing there was, the only thing I could see, the only thing I could feel.

"They didn't do that to you," I whispered into his throat, but it was a ragged plea.

"Quiet, Sylvie."

My body bucked violently as the sob tore through me.

Creed's hold tightened.

My fingers fisted in his shirt.

"They didn't do that to you. They didn't do that to you. They didn't do that to you. They didn't do that to you. They didn't do that to you. They didn't do that to you."

"Sh, baby."

I shushed.

He held me.

My tears quieted.

He still held me.

"Creed?" I called.

"Sleep, baby."

"Do you believe in God?"

"Sleep."

"Do you believe in God?"

"I don't know."

I sucked in a broken breath.

Then I whispered, "Right now, I don't either."

My eyes opened and I stared at the alarm clock.

Then I threw the covers back from the bed. I jumped up, rushed out of my room, down the hall and through the living room. I smelled bacon cooking, so instead of going right out the door, I ran into the dining room and stopped dead halfway in.

Creed was at my stove. He felt my presence and turned.

"Charlene," I whispered.

"I went over. It's all good. She's cool. Helped with the kids."

I stared at him and started trembling, head to toe shakes.

He didn't miss it.

"Come here, Sylvie."

"I need time..."

His head jerked then his eyes locked on me.

Cautiously, he replied, "Honest to Christ, give you anything. Anything, baby. But lost enough time. Can't give you that. Space, maybe. Time. No."

I shook my head. "No, I mean... I need time before you tell me the rest."

He closed his eyes. He did this slowly.

Then he opened them and whispered, "That, I can give."

I took off running, right at him, direct. I hit kitchen tile, turned and launched myself through the air.

Creed caught me.

My legs wrapped around his hips and my mouth hit his hard.

He dropped to a knee then he dropped me to my back.

We fucked on the kitchen floor.

And burned the bacon.

My fingertips moved over the scar, my lips chasing them all the way across his cheekbone, his temple and through his hair.

His hands at my ass tightened, his fingers digging deep.

I dropped my lips to his ear.

"He's dead."

"You said."

"No. I mean Daddy."

His fingers dug in deeper. "Too bad."

"Yeah."

"He buried in Kentucky?" he asked.

"Yup," I answered.

"Soon's we see to Knight's shit, road trip. We're fucking on his grave."

My head shot up and I looked down at him.

He grinned up at me.

My invisible sun's rays warmed me straight to my soul.

Only sun ever that lay on his back in a bed.

God, *God,* I missed my sun.

"He deserves it, baby, and I'm adventurous, but graveyard sex..." I paused. "I don't think I have it in me."

"Then we're fucking on that fuckin' golf course he loved so goddamned much."

"*That* I can do."

Creed gave me a smile.

"He told me his favorite hole was sixteen," I shared. "He said it was tough but beautiful."

"Right, on the green of sixteen, I'll drill *my* favorite hole."

He said this while smiling.

I burst out laughing.

I wandered into the back room with two fresh, cold ones. I got close to Creed sitting in one of the chairs, facing dusk. He ignored the beer I offered and hooked me around the waist, gave a rough yank and I landed in his lap. He curled his arm around me and lifted his long legs to rest his bare heels against the windowsill.

Only then did he take his beer.

He sucked some back. I sucked some back and my eyes moved over the detritus of the Chinese delivery we'd consumed that was spread across the low table. We ordered everything that struck our fancy, which meant we could have fed twelve.

Leftovers for days.

Right on.

I'd called Knight early, filled him in and told him we needed another day. He was down with that.

I knew he would be.

So all day it was Creed and me. His body. My body. Fucking. Drinking. Eating. Some talking. More fucking.

I had never had a boyfriend other than Tucker Creed. We'd made love once and he was taken away from me. So I didn't know make up sex could be so fucking great.

Especially when you had sixteen years to make up for.

"I want you to meet my kids."

My head jerked so I could look at him, even as my entire body tensed.

"What?" I whispered.

His eyes locked on mine. "I want you to meet my kids," he repeated.

"What, like, *now?*"

He grinned. "No Sylvie, they're an eighteen hour drive away so not now. Not tomorrow. After this job. After we're cool. I'll bring 'em up."

Oh shit.

"Creed—"

His arm gave me a squeeze.

"Sit on that. Don't react. Just sit on it. Think about it. There's time."

"Okay."

He held my gaze and didn't let go of the subject.

"Not sure where you are, but I'll state clear where I am. I gave you up once. It killed me. It was figuratively, but it still killed me. I'm not doin' that shit again. I'm further than you on this. In a way, I've been with you for over a month. You haven't even had a week. So you sit on knowin' in your future you'll meet and get to know my kids. But, just sayin', in your future, you'll meet and get to know my kids."

"Well, you're just sayin' that, I'll just say that sixteen years have passed so we should discuss that after, as you put it, we're cool."

"We're cool," he stated firmly. "We'll just be... cooler."

I grinned at him and muttered, "Right."

He grinned and muttered back, "Right."

I took a draw off my beer.

Creed wasn't done laying down the law.

"They took you from me, they took shit from you. They're dead. Now I'm givin' your shit back."

My eyes went back to him and I asked, "What?"

"Yesterday, what I said?" he stated this as a question, but stopped way before I knew what the fuck he was on about.

"Uh... babe, yesterday you said a lot."

"In bed," he added detail just not enough.

"You said a lot there, too."

"Sylvie, think back. What'd I say I was going to give you back?"

Oh that.

Shit.

"Creed—"

"Safe word's Geronimo. Remember that. Then we play."

How was he turning me on again? We'd been through at least six condoms, and that was just him. He didn't have the capacity to orgasm as much as I did, unlucky for him. I'd had twice that.

"Creed—"

His hand dropped so he could put his beer on the floor then it drove into the side of my hair, curled around the back and pulled my face close to his.

"You like sex, a lot. Far's I can see the only hang-ups you got, that animal gave you. You find, as we play, you got more, that's cool. Those're yours. I'll have a mind to that, but you do not fear what he taught you to fear. You and me work so you live easy. We work that shit out, we take it slow. I mean all of it. You find you can't work past it, that's okay with me, but we try. We try to get rid of that, of him. So it's just you and me, and when we fuck, the two of us are the only ones there and it's all sweet and easy."

"I'm thinking," I said gently, "this is just as much about you as it is about me."

"Fuck yeah," he agreed. "Straight up, I like adventure. I like control. I like ass play. We try it, you don't like it, we'll find what we like, but not him taking it from us. You with me?"

I was. Kind of.

Before I could tell him that, he went on, "Chelle didn't like any of that shit. She couldn't relax."

Oh no. We were hitting a danger zone.

"Uh… we're doing good here, Creed," I started. "I think we should maybe put the brakes on and coast the rest of the night on that goodness before we share deeper."

He lifted his chin but said softly, "My point, baby, is she couldn't relax, and that was on me. That was on me because you were in the room. She didn't get it fully until I gave it to her fully, but she's not a dumb woman. She understood. And she was fuckin' a man who had another woman's name inked in his skin. She didn't miss that, and not only because it's hard to miss. I don't want him in the room with you and me. Now, do you understand me?"

"Yeah," I whispered.

"Good," he whispered back.

I sucked back more beer. He grabbed his from the floor and did the same.

I trained my eyes to the dusk.

Then I asked it, "Just, you know, for the future, do you get along with her?"

"She puts up with me for the kids," he replied instantly. "Other than that, she avoids me. She's got another man's ring on her finger now. After they got married, she came over to my place, drunk off her ass, and gave it to me. Now

I'm the one in the room. He knows it, her man. Loves her, puts up with that shit. Sucks. She's a good woman. Probably not her intention, but she paid me back all the same. I live with that, what I did to her, to him, to them. Guilt lies heavy. I dicked her around, she lives with the pain of that every day. I live with the guilt of it every day."

I looked at him. "Can we work that out for you?"

Creed looked at me. "No. That's my penance and I deserve it."

"Life happens, Creed, and shit happens with it. We all can't live buried under the shit."

His brows shot up. "Seriously?"

"Well... yeah."

He grinned. "Baby, just days ago you were determined to live under your pile of shit. Are you free of it that easy?"

"We're not talking about me."

"We weren't. We are now."

I narrowed my eyes at him. "Stop being smart and logical. It's annoying."

He threw his head back and burst out laughing.

I turned away and sucked back beer.

"Sylvie," he called when he finished laughing.

"What?" I answered the window.

"Look at me."

I looked at him.

His eyes moved over my face then his hand came up to rest against the side of my head and his thumb moved over my face as he watched it. His hand slid down my neck, my chest to press flat where my heart was beating.

"Some people get to live life. Some people survive it. We're survivors. We can carve out our pieces of happy, and, I swear to God, baby, right now, you got my vow, for you and for me, the rest of our lives, I'll bust my ass to carve our piece of happy. But we're foolin' ourselves if we think we can set aside the shit that happened to us, the shit done to us, the shit we've done, and move on. It'll be with us forever. We just gotta learn to live with it. We bury it, deny it or pretend it isn't there, we're fucked. It'll surface and tear us to shreds. We acknowledge it and keep on keepin' the fuck on, we'll be good."

"You hurt a good woman," I noted cautiously.

"Not then, but now I'm glad it happened and it's done. Because if I was still tied to her when I got up here and found you, I'd get untied. Doesn't say much about me, but I've come to terms with the asshole I am. What it does say is what you mean to me. So it's good it happened and it's over. I'll hang onto that as I carry that weight."

That was as beautiful as it was horrible.

Life.

Or life as Creed and I knew it to be.

My eyes went to his throat and I whispered, "I killed a man."

"You saved a life."

My eyes went back to his. "What?"

"In my business, I've killed two. Both of them, I remember. Both of them stick with me. It is not for me to judge if they deserved to live or die, but in the situations we were in, it was them or me. I saved me. You saved you. I did not deliberately hurt Chelle, but I did it all the same. That'll stick with me. You killing that animal, that'll stick with you. You may not be grateful that it's with you, but I am because it means, right now, you're with me."

I stared into his eyes and said quietly, "He deserved it."

"Your call. You lived his shit. Way you tell it, I absolutely fuckin' agree."

I bent my neck and rested my forehead against his jaw.

Creed's arm tightened around me.

My eyes to his throat, I asked, "So, what are your plans for our piece of happy?"

"One day at a time. That day starts with me wakin' up beside you in bed. That's my piece of happy. I'll find yours and make sure you get your piece."

What he said worked for me.

I pulled in a breath.

Creed lifted his bottle to his lips and sucked down beer.

Then I gave him everything.

"I'm terrified out of my mind."

"Sucks, baby," he whispered. "But I get that and I'll help you work through it. For me, we had this one day and that was it, if I walked out your front door tomorrow and got shot dead, I'd die happy. And I'd die happy because, even for a day, I had you back with me. Seems I lived a dozen fuckin' lifetimes knowin' that would never be. Havin' it means everything to me. So I'm not scared. Two things in my whole life I wanted. My Dad back and you. Now, you're tucked close to me, so that works for me."

My sun's rays warmed me straight through.

I shifted my head to press my face in his neck.

Creed held on tighter.

He was chained to the floor, lying in the corner, the dried blood on his face, matting his hair.

Daddy was standing in the room with him and a bottle of water was on the floor between them, just out of his reach.

His lips were dry, crusted, chapped, split.

Daddy moved, toeing the water an inch closer, still out of reach.

"Give her up," Daddy demanded.

He lifted his head. His sky blue eyes vague with hunger, thirst and pain, he still directed them at Daddy.

The word was weak and it cracked in the middle.

But he said it.

"Never."

Daddy kicked the bottle of water and it flew across the room, liquid splashing everywhere, but none of it where it needed to be.

My body jerked then shot up to sitting in the bed. My knees came up, my hands went back into the mattress and I fell heavily into them.

"Sylvie?"

Creed's arm was heavy along my waist. The last thing I remembered before the dream was us whispering in bed, me tucked close, mostly under Creed, like he held me the night before when I was sobbing.

Clearly, we fell asleep cuddled close.

I felt the bed shift with him coming up on his forearm.

"Sylvie," his voice was firmer.

I didn't reply.

The dream still had a hold on me.

I threw back the covers and knifed out of bed. My movements frantic, I dashed to the dresser, yanked out panties and tugged them on awkwardly. I left that drawer open even as I opened another one and tagged a babydoll tee.

133

I pulled it over my head as I raced out of the room, down the hall through the living room, the entry and the dining room to the kitchen sink.

I snatched a glass from the cupboard and turned on the water. I filled it, put it to my lips and sucked it back. Water dribbled down the sides of my mouth, down my neck, wetting my tee.

When it was empty, I filled it again and repeat.

As I was drinking, I felt a warm body press against my back, hands on the edge of the sink in front of me. That body arched and I felt a face buried in my neck.

I emptied the glass, filled it again and repeat.

Creed didn't move.

I emptied the glass and dropped it into the sink with a crash.

"They could have killed you," I whispered.

"They didn't," he murmured against my neck.

"They could have killed you," I repeated.

One hand left the edge of the sink and snaked across my belly, but his face didn't leave my neck. "Baby, *they didn't.*"

"I read somewhere that it takes only three days to die of dehydration."

Creed didn't respond.

I told him something he knew better than me.

"They had you a month."

His lips went to my ear. "They're dead, Sylvie. We're here. We're together. We're breathin' and they are fuckin' *dead.*" I listened to him pull in a breath before he finished, "We win."

We win.

I dropped my head.

Creed's other hand left the edge of the sink and wrapped around my chest.

He held me that way a long time. Then he moved from me but took my hand, guided me gently from the sink and out of the kitchen, through the dining room into the living room where he took me to the couch. Positioning me with his hand in mine, he let me go, but put both his hands to my shoulders and pressed lightly.

I sat on the couch.

He leaned into me and framed my face with both hands. So close, his shadowed, scarred-for-me beauty was all I could see.

"Wait here. I'll be back," he whispered.

I nodded, moving his hands with my head.

His hands tipped my head forward. He kissed the hair at the top then he let me go. I watched his shadowed form leave the room.

He came back in less than a minute and I noted vaguely he was wearing jeans. He also was carrying a bag.

He came to the couch, upended it and a bunch of small, mismatched jewelry boxes fell out on the couch beside me.

"Knight gave me your name, I wasted no time findin' you. Saw you, then I flew home and got these," he murmured.

He tossed the bag to my coffee table and pawed through the boxes in the dark. He found the one he wanted, flipped it open, and with a tug, yanked out a necklace.

I stopped breathing.

The gold glinted in the moonlight. I saw the gemstone pendant hanging. I couldn't see the color in the shadows but I knew.

I knew.

He held it toward me.

"That was the one I didn't get to give to you by the lake on your eighteenth birthday."

I started shivering. My hand lifting up like it had a mind of its own, Creed draped the necklace over it, gem to my palm, before he went back to pawing through the boxes.

He found one, opened it, yanked out another necklace.

"This one I bought for your next birthday," he muttered and draped it, gem to my palm, over my still raised hand.

The tears hit my eyes.

Creed went back to pawing, found a box and tugged out another necklace.

"This one was when you turned twenty," he whispered.

Wet slid down my cheeks.

Back to the boxes again, again, until the necklaces draped over my hand numbered fifteen.

When he was done, his hand curled around mine, palm to palm, his fingers curved around the chains, and he leaned deep, his lips at my ear.

"You were gone, but I had more than the tat, Sylvie. I didn't get it then but I get it now. They never fuckin' took you away from me."

My breath hitched and my voice trembled as I told him, "I have the others."

"I know."

"They took you away from me."

His hand squeezed mine, the pendants and chains digging into my skin.

"I'm back, baby."

At his words and all they meant to me, nearly sixteen years of wanting just that, despairing I'd never have it, I lurched out of the couch, my free arm hooking around his neck. I barely got it positioned before I fell right back, pulling him down on me and into the couch.

Boxes went flying. His fingers scraped through the chains, gathering them. He lifted up and tossed them across our bodies toward the coffee table and he came back to me.

His mouth coming down, mine going up, we collided, lips opening, tongues out tangling. We kissed as his fingers curled into my panties at the sides. He tugged them down then tore his mouth from mine and moved away, yanking them off. His hands came to my hips, jerking them sideways. He got on his knees on the floor and pressed open my legs. His hands shoved under, fingers digging in my ass, he pulled me up as he went down and his mouth was on me.

My neck arched an my fingers slid into his hair. I pushed down as he pulled up and feasted on me.

Breathing hard, it came fast. It was going to consume me so I lifted my head and urgently whispered, "*Creed.*"

His head came up and he muttered, "Two seconds, Sylvie, condoms in the other room."

I pulled myself up, my hands reaching for his fly. "Fuck it."

"Sylvie."

My head dipped back as I undid buttons and my eyes found his. "I need you, baby."

He shoved my hands aside and took over for me. I tugged his jeans down over his hips even as he got up and put a knee into the couch. I spread my legs, he fell forward on his forearms beside me and thrust deep.

My mouth opened on a silent moan and I shoved it in his neck, my tongue coming out, tasting him there. I circled him and held tight with everything I had available to me.

"Baby, mouth."

That was Creed. I dropped my head back. Creed's mouth came to mine and he drove deep with his cock *and* his tongue.

My arms moved from around him, found his, trailed down and pulled hard so his weight hit me.

His head came up.

I laced my fingers in his and pulled both our arms over my head, twisting our hands so mine were to the cushions.

He ground deep with his cock and growled, "Fuck, baby."

"Take me."

"*Fuck. Baby.*"

It was guttural.

It was beautiful.

Creed pressed my hands into the cushions. His forearms pressed, too, beside mine. He took his weight off me, angling his body up, his hips still driving deep. I watched his shadowed head drop and he looked down the length of our bodies in order to watch as he fucked me.

My legs left him. I brought my knees high and his pounding went *deep*.

My moan sounded more like a cry and his eyes shot to my face.

"I love you, Sylvie," he grunted, driving hard, fast.

"Baby," I gasped. It was coming over me.

He dropped down, holding me still pinned to the couch, his lips sliding along my cheek to my ear.

"Born to love you, Sylvie."

I rocked my hips back to meet each thrust and panted, my fingers squeezing his holding mine down to the cushions.

"Born to love you, baby," he repeated. "Die lovin' you, my Sylvie."

My neck arched, my pussy clenched, my clit spasmed. My thighs pressed tight to his sides, his mouth went to my throat and I cried out his name as I came with Tucker Creed still drilling deep inside me.

Oh yeah.

Fuck yeah.

He was right.

We win.

Chapter 12
Wishing Away the Years

A late, cool, autumn night in Kentucky, eighteen years earlier. Creed is twenty-one, Sylvie is sixteen...

The house was silent as I walked through it in the dark. Daddy was away on business. The stepmonster was visiting her sister in Atlanta.

I was coming home from a date.

I opened the door to my bedroom and the minute I did, the light came on.

I let out a little scream, and when my eyes adjusted, I stared.

Creed was lounging on my bed, back to the headboard, long legs straight, booted feet crossed at the ankles.

"Missed your curfew," he said low and I blinked.

This had never happened before. As in ever. Not for ten whole years.

Still, it was Creed, and always with Creed and me, anything went, and as always I was happy to see him.

"Hey," I greeted, walking in and closing the door behind me, grinning at him. "What're you doing here?"

"Missed your curfew, Sylvie, by two fuckin' hours."

I stopped and stared at him. "What?"

"It's past midnight."

I tilted my head to the side. "So?"

He didn't answer my question, he asked one instead, "You out with Dixon?"

"Yeah. Why?"

"He's an asshole."

I shook my head. "No he's not, Creed. That's mean." I studied him, not liking the look on his face or the feel he was giving the room so I asked, "What is this? Why are you here and being weird?"

He lifted his feet, twisted his lower body and came off my bed, standing tall, and even though I wasn't close, I still had to tilt my head back to look at him.

"You're not that girl," he announced.

I put my hands on my hips. "What girl?"

"The *easy* girl."

My chest squeezed.

"*What?*" I breathed.

"Dixon is a dick," he stated.

"Stop saying stuff like that!" I snapped.

He took two steps to me and then rocked to a halt. "He's too old for you."

"He's eighteen."

"Too old," he decreed.

"This is crazy!" I hissed. "What's your problem?"

"That guy, Sylvie," he shook his head, "not a good guy. Only man richer in the county than his Daddy is *your* Daddy. He says everywhere he won't have to work a day in his life and still be rich. And you know what? He's right. And you know what else? Makes him an asshole dick that he's down with that."

I moved away from him, tossed my purse on a chair in the corner and whirled back to him. "I'm not marrying him, Creed, we've only had one date."

"Don't let there be another one."

I planted my hands on my hips again and shot back, "Not for you to say."

"Every girl he dates is easy, hopin' for access to the pool and the horse stables and the rides in his sports car. You already got that shit, Sylvie, you don't need him to give it to you."

"I'm not dating him because he's rich, Creed. I'm dating him because he's *cute.*"

"And you datin' him says somethin' about you, not him, and it's not good. So stop doin' it."

I threw out a hand asking, "You know what?" Then I didn't wait for him to answer and went on, "*You're* being a dick. This is none of your business!"

"You're my business, Sylvie."

"No, I'm not. Or at least this part of me isn't," I retorted and he leaned into me, his handsome face twisting in a strange way.

"Yeah, you are. All of you. You're *my* Sylvie."

I sucked in a breath and held it even as I felt every inch of my skin tingle.

He leaned back, scowling at me then he looked away.

Tearing a hand through his hair, he muttered, "Jacked. Even sick. Totally fuckin' illegal."

"What?" I whispered, and his eyes cut back to me.

140

"Do not go on another date with Jason Dixon."

"Why?" I asked.

"Because it means something to me."

I pulled in another breath and looked away.

"Sylvie," he called and I looked back. "Promise me."

I clenched my teeth. Then I nodded.

"Is that a promise?" he pushed.

"Yeah," I bit out.

He stared at me and I stared back.

We did this a long time.

He broke the silence.

"Dad would be pissed."

"About what?" I asked.

His striking blue eyes moved the length of me and my skin started tingling again.

Then they locked on mine.

"He'd be pissed at me... wishing away the years."

With that he left, slamming the door behind him.

I stared at the door and realized I was breathing heavily.

Then I closed my eyes tight, wondering what on earth all that was about.

I opened them and forced myself to get ready for bed.

But I did not sleep.

Chapter 13
Issues with My Man Being a Badass

Present day...

I walked into the bedroom and saw Creed in my bed, up on a forearm looking both pissed and sleepy.

Oh, and hot.

"Where the fuck you been?" he growled, and I stopped dead. When I didn't answer, just kept staring at him, he went on, "Baby, get this: woke up without you for sixteen years. Got you back for good yesterday. Don't wanna do that shit again. You get up, you wake me. Even if it's just to kiss me and tell me you're leavin' our bed. You with me?"

I kept staring at him.

"Sylvie," he continued growling. "Are you with me?"

I took off running, and close to the bed, took a flying leap, arms wide and landed flat on top of him.

He grunted and so did I. His hands had curled around my waist while I was on the downward plunge and his fingers dug in as I lifted my head to look down at him.

"Morning!" I chirped, and he started grinning but stopped when his eyes dropped to my throat.

I felt his entire body go stone-still.

"Fuck," he whispered.

"Love them," I told him.

His eyes came back to mine and they were agonized.

"Fuck," he repeated in a whisper.

I ignored the agony and dipped my face close.

"Every one of them," I whispered back.

"You wearin' them all?"

"All twenty-six. Even the ones you got me when I was a little girl. They're tight but I'm wearing them."

His hand went from my waist, pressing in, trailing up my body, then I felt his fingers weave through the tangle of chains.

I'd gotten up *way* early because they were calling me. So I left Creed in bed, went to my dresser, got the old, then went out to the living room to collect and inspect the new.

And every last one of them I put on.

"Dreamed of this," he murmured, his eyes glued to the chains. I dropped my head to rest my forehead on his. "Dreamed of seein' you again, my green at your neck."

"Guess today that makes me the woman who can make dreams come true," I remarked, trying to keep it light, and his eyes came to mine, so close, so blue. Gorgeous.

"Yeah," he said softly, and I watched a light ignite in his eyes. "Though, never dreamed of you wearin' all of them at once."

I pulled my head away and tucked my chin in my throat in the wasted effort of trying to see them, doing this muttering, "I don't know." I looked back at him and smiled. "I think they look *awesome*."

He smiled back and my smile got bigger, but his faded as he lifted both hands to either side of my head and held them there, his eyes moving over my face, his hands holding me steady.

"You love me?" he asked quietly.

I dipped my face close and answered quietly, "On a cold night, a long time ago, you put your hands almost exactly where they are right now, and I might have been six years old, but I fell hard. So, yeah. For over twenty-seven years, every day, every minute, every second, I've loved you, Tucker Creed."

His hands left my head and my back hit the bed because Creed flipped me there before he kissed me, hard, deep, long. A kiss filled with twenty-seven years of love and beauty.

It was the best kiss *of my life*.

"I'm seeing I'm gonna have issues with my man being a badass," I stated, standing in my front yard in my jeans, tee, boots and belt. With my coat of mascara, eyeliner, gun in its holster on my belt, travel mug in hand, I narrowed my gaze at Creed.

"Just get in the truck, Sylvie."

"'Vette, Creed."

"I drive."

"No, I drive," I shot back.

"*I* drive," he reiterated.

"Why, because you're a man?" I asked.

"No, because I lied yesterday. I'm not all right with bein' dead and havin' you back for one day. After this morning, I want another day, at least, and as I've already said, you're a lunatic behind the wheel. We're ending this day eating steak I'm grillin' and drinkin' beer then fucking. We're not ending it in a fiery ball of flame."

"I've never had an accident in my life," I informed him.

"And today, you won't have one either, even though you'll court it."

"I'm not that bad of a driver."

"Baby, *you are.*"

"Am not!" I snapped.

Creed looked to the heavens.

"We have a meeting with Knight in twenty minutes, Creed," I reminded him, and his eyes came back to me.

Then he crossed his arms on his chest.

I crossed mine on my chest and we went into stare down.

I may have mentioned patience wasn't one of my virtues. Actually, I didn't have many virtues, but patience definitely wasn't one of them.

So it was me who gave in.

But I did it grumping, "Oh, all right," and stomping to his truck.

I avoided looking at his face as we both angled in. I was in a good mood. I had my eighteenth birthday peridot at my neck (tough choice, but I decided on chronological) and the man I loved since I was six at my side so I didn't want my mood broken.

Creed pulled out of my driveway like a Grandpa.

I didn't inform him of this.

Instead, I shared, "Just so you know, I speak English. You don't have to macho-speak with shit like 'you with me' after you macho-speak with a bunch of bossing me around. I get you. I'm with you. Or if I'm not, I'll tell you."

145

"Noted," he muttered, but sounded like he was smiling.

I made the diplomatic decision not to look.

Then it hit me.

"You're not gonna stop talking like that are you?" I asked.

"Nope," he answered.

I sucked back coffee.

Then I turned on the radio.

"Switch it to news, baby," he ordered.

I absolutely did *not* switch it to news. I switched it to country with excellent timing. Kellie Pickler was just beginning to sing, "Tough".

"Sylvie, news," Creed in a way repeated.

"News is depressing. Kickass country bitches are awesome."

"Sylvie—"

I started singing. *Loud.*

Silence from the driver's seat.

Then a burst of laugher.

So that was when I kept singing, but did it smiling.

"You, a word. The rest of you, downstairs."

This was Knight, and on the first "you" he pointed a finger at Creed. We had just made it to his office at Slade. Rhash and Live were already there. Everyone but me looked at Creed. I glared at Knight.

I knew what this was about. Knight loved me. He hadn't told me but he'd shown me. He thought Creed "shredded" me. He was instigating a badass throw down that, I suspected, would include threats and intimidation as to what he'd do if Creed hurt me again, which had zero chance of working on Creed. Mostly because I knew in my soul Creed wouldn't hurt me. Partly because Creed was as badass as Knight, just a little more rough around the edges, and threats and intimidation didn't work on badasses. Still, Knight was going to say his piece.

I loved that. I loved him. I loved that about him.

But it was totally unnecessary and it could cut into our happy vibe, and I didn't want that to happen for me or Creed.

Knight's eyes sliced to me. "I'm having a word with Creed now, Sylvie."

"And I'm feeling a girlie tantrum coming on, Knight," I shot back.

He scowled at me.

I glared back.

Then he stated the God's honest truth.

"You know you don't have the patience to win this."

I rolled my eyes.

Then I decided to make a point. I walked right up to Creed, grabbed his head, pulled it down to me and laid a long, wet one on him.

We broke the kiss with Creed smiling so huge he looked in danger of laughing.

I tossed Knight an unhappy look, ignored Rhash and Live staring at me with huge eyes and sashayed to the door.

I was standing outside the door at the bottom of the stairs that led up to Knight's office when Rhash and Live lumbered down behind me.

"What the fuck was *that?*" Rhash asked upon arrival. He was clearly both curious and also wondering why I was making out with the hired investigator seeing as that was a *wee bit* unprofessional.

Quickly, succinctly, honestly and somewhat brutally, I laid it out.

All of it.

When I shut up, they were both staring at me.

"Holy fuck," Rhash whispered.

"They starved him, beat him, chained him and sliced him?" Live asked quietly. "For *a month?*"

"Yup," I answered. "But they're dead. We're not. I've got twenty-six peridot necklaces and had a morning that included," I lifted up my fingers with the count, "*three* orgasms. And this was *before* we went over to help out Charlene. So we win."

"Shit yeah, you do. Three?" Live was clearly impressed.

I grinned at him.

Rhash's voice rumbled to me and the tone made my eyes cut quickly to him.

"He promised him you'd be safe, he'd see to it you had a good life then he sold you into hell?"

One look at him and I could see Rhash was in the mood to be super scary.

"Rhash—"

I didn't say more because his hand shot out and tagged me at the back of my head. I did a face plant in his wide chest and his other arm closed tight around me.

All the air squeezed itself out of my lungs, and not because he was holding me too tight. Without a choice, though I wouldn't have taken another one, my arms stole around his bulk.

"Glad you won, Sylvie," he whispered into the top of my hair. I took in a deep breath, realizing that in the last two days the people I was tight with, that meant the world, had doubled to welcome back Creed and include Rhashan Banks.

"Thanks, babe," I whispered back.

He let me go and his eyes went right to Live. "You tell anyone I hugged Pip, I'll break your neck."

Live grinned at him and held up his hands. "Lips sealed."

I decided sharing time was over. At least for me.

That was why I asked Live, "You doin' okay?"

Something flashed across his face. He looked away, down to the floor then back at me. "No. Don't like breathin' that bitch's air. Don't like her touchin' me. Knight's keepin' me busy and away from her so I don't gotta spend a lot of time with her, but when I do, gotta keep up appearances. I'll be happy when this shit is done and I can get shot of her ass."

I got that, big time, so I nodded.

Rhash's phone beeped. He pulled it out, looked at it and then he shoved it back in his pants.

"Knight's done with Creed," he announced.

We all moved to and through the door and up the stairs, but it was probably only me who was hoping we didn't open the door to a bloodbath.

We didn't.

Creed had his back to the wall, arms crossed on his chest, feet crossed at the ankles looking like he was waiting patiently for his woman to get done in a shop so he could take her ass to a bar and get a beer.

Knight was leaning against his conference table with much the same look about him. My eyes did a scan of Creed first, then Knight, and they seemed hunky dory. In good spirits even, like they'd just got done talking about the Rockies chance at a pennant this year. This ticked me off so I stopped and crossed my arms on my own chest.

My eyes narrowed on Knight. "I know I have a vagina, but that doesn't negate the fact that I have a brain and a spine, so I can make my own decisions about my life and deal with the consequences. I'm also not real big on dudes talking about my shit behind my back."

He held my gaze steadily and replied, "Babe, cool it. You got a man who cares about you, namely me, this shit is gonna happen. Deal with it, because it's not *not* gonna happen because you throw a shit fit about it with a gun on your belt."

I opened my mouth to speak, but Creed cut in so I looked to him.

"Baby, it's cool. I'm not gonna be pissed after what you been through that for the last ten years you had a man who gives a shit about you at your back, and he doesn't delay in layin' it out that just because you got your man back he's still gonna have your back. He's cool. I'm cool. Now you need to be cool. You get me?"

At the, "You get me?" I rolled my eyes. At the same time, my phone rang.

I pulled it out, ignoring Creed's amused grin, and looked at the display. I felt my brows draw together as I flipped it open and put it to my ear.

"Hey, babe," I greeted.

"Sylvie."

At the sound of her voice, my back went straight and my eyes sliced to Creed. "Talk to me."

"I hurt."

Fuck. Fuck. *Fuck!*

I lifted a hand, my gaze going to Knight. I snapped, but he was already straightened away from the table and staring at me, alert. "Serena, where are you?"

"He just left. At the hotel. I hurt, Sylvie."

I heard the pain and tears in her voice.

Knight was already taking long strides to his desk and computer.

"You need Baldy?" I asked into the phone, looking down to my boots.

"Baldy?"

"Dr. Baldwin, Serena. You need him?"

"Yes."

Shit. Fuck. *Shit!*

I looked at Knight, nodded, and turned on my boot toward the door. "What hotel, babe? Room number. I'm on my way. So is Baldy."

She gave me the hotel name and room number as I jogged down the steps, hearing boots behind me.

"Hang tight, Serena. We'll be there, ten minutes," I told her as I ran across the nightclub, still hearing boots behind me.

"I don't think I can get up to answer the door." Her voice was weak.

Shit!

"Don't worry," I assured her. "We'll get it. Be there in ten."

"Okay, Sylvie," she whispered.

"Soon, baby," I whispered back.

We were out the door, running down the sidewalk to Creed's truck parked on the street. He beeped the locks, ran around the hood and we both angled in even as I flipped my phone closed and open again. I called Knight as I gave Creed the hotel name and preliminary directions. Creed pulled away from the curb *not* like a Grandpa, and I put the phone to my ear as I yanked the seatbelt around me.

Knight answered with, "Already called Baldy. He's on the way."

"You know where she is?" I asked.

"New rules. Girls report where they're goin', phone when they get there, phone when they leave, phone when the door to their house is locked behind them."

"Right. She's in room number six twelve," I told him.

"I'll text that to Baldy," he replied.

"Her client pay for an all-nighter?" I asked as Creed took a turn on red he wasn't supposed to, and it felt like the truck was going to go up on two wheels so we both leaned into it.

"Yeah," he answered. "Gotta go. Report back."

He disconnected and I flipped the phone shut.

Creed drove and I gave more directions.

Then he murmured, "Cab's full of your fury, baby, check it."

"Right," I muttered and sucked in breath.

Creed drove.

He pulled up and screeched to a halt in front of the hotel. The valet made the approach but I was out of the truck, running into the hotel and didn't look back.

Luckily, reception was clear except the clerk.

"Hi," I said when I arrived at the desk. "I have a friend in room six twelve who's diabetic and she forgot her insulin. She's in bad shape and I need to get up there and give it to her. She says she can't make it to the door. Can you give me a keycard to six twelve?"

He shook his head. "Sorry, against hotel policy. Not unless your name is registered to the room. Really sorry."

Fuck! I didn't bring my money roll with me.

I flipped open my phone but kept my eyes on him. "Can she call down, tell you it's okay?"

"Uh... I'm not sure—" he started.

Then his eyes flew down to the desk, so mine did too, and I saw a familiar, big, strong, veined, scarred hand sliding a fan of three one hundred dollar bills across the desk.

"Keycard. Room six twelve," Creed rumbled. My head tipped back and I looked at his hard profile as he finished, "And advice, don't say no to me."

Okay, maybe I wasn't going to have issues with my man being a badass. Especially when he was also my partner on a job and could get shit done by being scary.

The guy took Creed in for approximately a nanosecond then jumped to the stash of keycards, did whatever he had to do with the machine and handed it to Creed.

I turned and dashed through the lobby. Ignoring the elevators, I scanned for the sign, found it, darted that way and hit the stairs. My legs were short, but I still took them two at a time, hearing Creed hurtling up behind me. I hit the door to the sixth floor, winded, heart pumping and shoved through. I didn't slow down as I ran down the hall, scanning the signage to find the way to six twelve.

I stopped at one side of the door, Creed right behind me. He stopped at the other side.

"Gun," he grunted. I nodded, yanked mine out. He had his in his hand. He shoved in the keycard but his eyes cut to me. "You lead, Sylvie, but careful. This shit's a set up, you got no vest and today's not my day to lose you."

I nodded.

He pushed down the door handle and shoved in.

I moved into the room, gun down but at the ready, staying close to the inside wall, eyes peeled, slow, scanning. I turned my head left and peered around the door to the bathroom. It was clear so I kept moving in, feeling Creed just feet behind me. I hit the room proper, saw her, saw she was alone, saw the state she was in, stopped and lifted a hand back to Creed. I turned my head and shook it once.

He jerked up his chin, holstered his weapon and settled back.

I holstered my weapon and bustled in.

"Sylvie," she whispered through cut, swollen, bleeding lips as she looked up at me through slitted, nearly swollen shut eyes.

"Here, babe," I whispered, moving quickly, gently, efficiently, pulling the bloody sheet around her naked body. "Baldy's on his way. Knight knows what's happening. I'm here with my partner. His name is Creed. He's a good guy. In a second he's gonna come in. Let's get you decent."

A whimpering sob slid past her lips as I tucked the sheet around her bruised, bloodied, abused, violated body.

When I was done, I asked, "You okay for Creed to join us?"

"Yeah," she whispered.

I felt him move in and looked up at him as I sat on the bed and pulled her hair away from her face. "Ice, wet washcloth," I said softly. Creed's heated, infuriated eyes moved from Serena in the bed to me. He jerked up his chin, turned and disappeared.

I bent over Serena. "We're here. We'll take care of you, babe. We're here."

Another whimpering sob.

I heard a low whistle. My head came up and Creed tossed a wet cloth to me. I nabbed it and he disappeared again.

I folded it, pressed it light against her eyes and got another whimpering sob.

"We're here, baby," I whispered, stroking her hair.

"There's nowhere I don't hurt," she whispered back, and rage tore through me as blood rushed in my ears. It took effort, but I fought it back.

"We're here," I whispered. "You're not alone, Serena. We're here, baby."

After a short while the door opened. I looked to the opening of the hall and Creed filled it, ice bucket in his hands. He stopped close to me, handed me the bucket but held my eyes.

"Check it," he mouthed.

I nodded.

Then I checked it.

I bent back to Serena.

I paced the hall outside Serena's room, but while I moved my eyes were locked on Creed, who was on the phone with Knight. Baldy, or Dr. Baldwin—a good doctor, a good man, but one who accepted cash and kept his mouth shut—was in with Serena, as was a nurse he'd called in to assist him.

I'd heard Creed's side of the conversation and got from it there were two other girls who had since called in, both newish, both with all-nighter clients, both messed way the fuck up.

Pre-emptive strike. We fucked up.

"Right. Sylvie and I will take the girls," Creed said into the phone, eyes to me.

Oh no.

Fuck no.

That meant Creed and I were on check and security detail and would miss the action.

Again, fuck no.

I stomped to him, reached high, snagged the phone out of his hand and put it to my ear.

"Do not fucking bench me," I snapped into the phone.

"Sylvie—" Knight started.

"Offensive, Knight, and you fucking know it. Finesse is done. These assholes pay. Find Live. Find out where the fuck Amy is and I'm all over that fucking bitch until she talks to me."

"Babe, you know I trust you, but this kind of shit, you got a hot head. Give the girls your touch, keep them safe and—"

"Bullshit. I got more control than you *and* Rhash put together when shit like this goes down."

"I know you, remember?" he asked softly. "I can hear it in your voice. Your control has snapped, Sylvie. Rein it in and look after the girls."

"She told me there was nowhere that didn't hurt," I hissed, and Knight was silent. "Don't bench me," I repeated.

Knight took a beat then, "Don't make me regret this."

I lifted my head and jerked my chin up at Creed. He turned to Serena's door, used the keycard and went through, probably to brief Baldy we were leaving.

"You won't regret it," I promised Knight. "Get me the details on Amy. Two minutes, Creed and I are on the road."

I disconnected and Creed came out.

His eyes caught mine.

"Let's move," he grunted.

We moved.

I stood in the stall in the bathroom, peering out a small opening of the door.

Amy was having a martini lunch with her girls who also lived off a man's back. We clocked her. Creed told me he'd get her to the bathroom and my objective was to clear it so we could do our business there.

Luckily, no one came in while I waited, so when she did, red wine stains down her dress, a pissed-off look on her face, I had her.

Seriously, Creed was genius. I didn't know he managed it; probably bribed a waiter, but not only would red wine down your dress send you straight to the bathroom, it'd also leave a nasty stain. Amy deserved more than red wine stains on her dress, but that was where I came in.

"I cannot believe this *shit*," she hissed at the mirror, flipping her arms down, eyes to the stain reflected in the mirror.

I walked out of the stall and she turned to me then blinked.

"Wow, Sylvie. Hey," she greeted.

I glanced through her, walked to the door, rapped on it once and Creed slid in, closed the door and leaned against it.

"What the fuck?" Amy asked and I turned back to her. Her eyes went from Creed to me. "What's going—?"

I moved, and in a flash, I had her against the wall, my hand to her throat, my body pressed into hers. Her face had paled and her eyes were wide.

"The blowjob you gave Drake Nair pay for that dress or did you get it off Live's back?" I asked and her eyes got wider. "Oh yeah, bitch, we know. Mark this, Amy, you fucked up, not getting your name on the lease. Live, right now, is packing your shit up. You got the choice. You talk, I let you go and you go home and you'll find your shit in boxes. Or you don't talk, I let you go and you find your shit all over the goddamned grass."

"I…" Her eyes shifted side to side as her hand lifted to try and pull down on mine, but I just pushed her deeper into the wall with my hand and body. Her gaze came back to mine. "I don't know what you're talking about."

"I'll refresh your memory, but I'll do it by posting pictures of you on your knees, his dick in your mouth, side by side with pictures of you taking a roll of bills to every social network I can find and I'll tag you in it. By the time they take it down, it'll have gone viral. There will be sites it hits that *won't* take it down, and thousands of people will see you sucking cock for money. You'll walk down the street and never know when someone will recognize you. That's not enough, copies get couriered to your folks. Wonder what Daddy will think of seeing his girl getting her face fucked for cash."

Her eyes suddenly went hard and she bit out, "Fuck you, Sylvie."

"Wrong answer," I whispered. I let her go but grabbed her wrist, flipped her around and shoved her face first into the wall, yanking her arm up. She cried out, I got close and snarled in her ear, "Talk."

"I'll scream."

"Do it," I invited. "See that big guy against the door?"

She didn't answer.

I didn't wait and went on, "Well, that's my man and no one out there saw him or me. You scream, we vanish. You report this to the cops, we both got alibis. But you, *you* live with Knight Sebring's wrath breathing down your neck, and everywhere you go, every minute of the day, you fear the day he unleashes that wrath. If you can live down the blowjob pictures, you still got Knight to deal with. You talk right now, you're homeless and without a man to lead around by his dick. You don't, you bought yourself a life full of fear."

She didn't say anything.

I yanked up on her arm hard.

She whimpered.

"Don't test me. I might be small, but I'm strong and I'm pissed. I'll snap it," I whispered in her ear.

"He… he, I don't know much about it," she whispered back, straining against my hold, lifting up to her toes in her high-heeled shoes to alleviate the pain.

"Share what you know," I invited.

"Let go," she demanded.

"Not until you share."

"Not until you let go."

I yanked up again and she cried out.

"I got all day. You got a martini to get back to," I told her.

"I... *fuck*," she snapped. "He wants Knight's girls. Thinks, if they don't think they're safe, they'll defect. If it's bad enough and they just quit, he's fine. Just as long as he shuts down Knight and his girls."

"You know Nick?" I asked.

"Who?" she asked back.

"He work with a man named Nick?"

"No. I don't know. I never heard that name."

"Those clients last night, Amy, they weren't new," I told her.

"He's been planning this a long time," she told me.

"Are there more men in the system we gotta worry about?" I asked.

"I... don't know."

"How many men are there, Amy?" I pushed.

"I don't know," she repeated.

"Three men worked girls over last night. Are there more?"

"I don't know!"

I yanked up her arm and shoved her so deep into the wall, her face smushed against it.

"Now is the time to share," I advised softly. "I find out you withheld anything, Amy, this will not make me happy, and I'm a girl. Girls know girls. I'll know *exactly* what'll cut deep and I'll do that to you. You get me?"

"I don't know!" she snapped. "I just told him what Live told me about the new girls. He wanted to target the new girls. The other ones, the ones that have been around awhile, they were in the business, defected to Knight for protection and know the score. They wouldn't blink. The new ones would freak. He knew that. So I gave him their information."

Stupid, useless *bitch*.

"Do you know what else he's got planned?" I pushed.

"No!"

"You sure about that?" I prompted.

"I just told him about the new girls. That's it!"

I whipped her around again, grabbed both wrists and cocked her arms, shoving them into her chest and her back into the wall so hard her skull cracked against it. She blinked and winced in pain, but I got in her face.

"He beat her bloody, split open and swollen. He raped her between her legs and up her ass. He did the deed, but *you* did that to her, too. He's a man and men can be animals. You're a woman and we gotta look out for each other. What could bring you to do that to a sister?"

Her head tipped slightly to the side and her face got snide. "Can you rape a girl like that?"

Blood roared in my ears and it took everything I had not to spit in her face.

"You sucked cock for money," I reminded her. She flinched and I leaned in. "And you spread for Live for the same reasons. He might not have handed over cash direct after the act, but those girls got one on you, bitch, in a way that makes them so many steps up from you it isn't even funny. They're honest about being whores. You're just kidding yourself that you aren't one."

I shoved her against the wall and stepped away.

Her hands went to her wrists and rubbed.

"I don't see you again," I whispered. "You see me, you disappear. Do you understand?"

"Fuck you," she whispered back.

"Blowjob pictures, Amy."

She scrunched her face up and glared at me.

I continued, "I do not see you. I do not hear about you. Live doesn't. No one does. You have ceased to exist on the club scene in Denver. Yeah?"

"Yeah," she snapped.

I was done so I turned away from her to see Creed watching me blank-faced, arms crossed on his chest. He moved away from the door and opened it for me. I walked right through and we moved down the hall, through the restaurant, out and to his truck.

I called into Knight what I knew. He reported back they'd picked up Nair. I told him we'd be there in thirty.

I disconnected, filled in Creed, and suddenly he pulled into a parking lot. He drove to a section far away from the store without any cars around, stopped the truck and switched off the ignition.

I turned to him. "What——?"

Kristen Ashley

He'd already unbuckled his belt. He hit the release on mine, and before I knew what he was doing, he'd shoved his muscled bulk between the seats, reached through and yanked me between. He had me on my back across the seats, his mouth on mine and his hand went down the front of my pants, scraping past belt and straight into panties.

I gasped against his tongue and when his finger slid hard across my clit, I moaned.

He broke the kiss and his lips didn't leave mine as he muttered, "That was fuckin' *hot.*"

Maybe, but this was way hotter.

"Glad you approve," I breathed.

"Give me room to move, baby," he ordered, and my hands went directly to my jeans. I loosened the belt, unbuttoned the button and slid the zipper down.

Then my head shot back when Creed got room to move.

His mouth worked my throat, his hand worked my pussy, and my hands clutched his shirt. He didn't mess around and I came for him within minutes. As I came down, his mouth was still working my neck as his fingers slid, gentle and tender, through the wet between my legs.

His lips glided up to my ear as his fingers kept toying between my legs and he whispered, "You, sittin' on the end of the pier. Your sixteenth birthday. You got the same thing every year for ten years, but you acted every time like I didn't hand you some shit necklace, but the moon. I looked at you and it hit me it was you. It hit me that it could be no one else but you. You were born to be mine. I was born to be yours. And it hit me that it sucked huge I had to wait at least two years to make my move to claim you."

I closed my eyes, turned my head and pressed my face into his neck.

"Watchin' you work back there," Creed went on, "I get you. Huge parts of that Sylvie are gone. I loved them, but they're gone. But, baby, know this, the new parts of Sylvie that took her place are fuckin' *amazing.*" My heart squeezed and Creed lifted his head to grin down at me. "Seriously. I had to fight against gettin' hard, watchin' you work that bitch."

"I didn't even give her my good stuff," I informed him through my own grin, and his fingers slid around and in, driving deep.

My lips parted and Creed's dropped to brush them as he spoke.

"Then, baby, partnering with you is gonna be all kinds of good."

I lifted my head half an inch and kissed him.

He kissed me back.

We broke the kiss. His fingers slid out as he dropped his head to kiss my throat. He moved to shove himself through the two front seats as I righted my jeans and then I shoved myself through.

I was belting my seatbelt when Creed put the truck in gear and rolled.

I looked to the side, saw he had the tip of his middle and index fingers in his mouth and he was licking them clean.

My clit spasmed.

Oh yeah.

This partnering business was gonna be all kinds of good.

I held onto the headboard even though I really had no choice.

With two scarves tied to my wrists, their ends clutched between my palms and the headboard (in other words, within easy reach if I needed to release them), I couldn't move my hands.

I was on my knees in the pillows, ass tipped back, Creed behind me. His arms around me, both hands at my breasts, rolling and tugging my nipples as he powered deep.

My head flew back as the headboard rocked with his drives and my body's jerks.

This shit was *great*.

"You okay?" Creed grunted in my ear.

"Yeah," I breathed. "Harder."

He drilled up harder.

Oh yeah.

Yeah.

"Give me more, Sylvie," he growled, and I arched my back and tipped up my ass. "Yeah, baby," he approved and slammed in harder.

"Creed!" I gasped, so close, oh so fucking close.

He pulled out to the tip and stopped.

No!

I pressed back but he moved with me, withholding.

"Need you, baby, I'm close," I whispered.

He withheld. I only had the tip and his mouth came back to my ear.

"Keep your back arched, ass high, yeah, Sylvie?"

"Creed," I begged.

"Let me give you somethin' good," he urged, his voice rough, the smooth totally gone.

I swallowed then nodded.

I lost the tip and I bit my lip not to whimper.

His fingers swept my hair over one shoulder then, starting at the base of my scalp, one trailed down my neck, between my shoulders, slow, so fucking slow.

"Arch, tip that ass," he murmured, and I arched deeper for him, lifting my ass further. "Beautiful," he muttered, his finger going down my spine, down, between the cheeks of my ass, down through my wet. He tweaked my clit and my entire body jolted, the headboard banging.

Oh God. He was right. This was good. This was *hot*.

"You should see you," he whispered, and I felt both his hands at my hips. They went up my sides, light, over my ribs, light, and then they moved in to cup my breasts. "Give me those, Sylvie."

I pressed into his hands. His thumbs moved to rub over my nipples hard. My body jerked again and my heavy breaths grew heavier. Creed rewarded me, his thumbs circling my nipples, pressing deep, making me moan.

"Fuck, so fuckin' beautiful," he murmured, his hands moving to my back, pressing in more now, pushing me further down.

They moved over and curled around my ass, the thumbs sliding in, gliding along the sides of the cleft, one honed in and circled the sensitive skin and, fuck me, fuck me, I was so far gone, I wanted it so much I strained into it.

"Gonna take that," he muttered.

Oh yeah.

He pressed in tighter. "When you're ready, baby, gonna fuck that and play with you while I do. Rock your world."

"Do it now," I breathed.

His thumb moved away and I couldn't control the whimper before I felt his lips move over the ass cheek of my right side then up to the small of my back.

"Oh no," he whispered against my skin. "Got you tied and arched for me. Little at a time."

"I'm ready," I panted, and felt his lips move against the small of my back like he was smiling.

"Pleased, Sylvie, but when I fuck that, you're gonna be a whole lot more than ready."

Holy shit.

Something to look forward to.

My legs quivered.

His mouth disappeared and not a second later, his cock drove inside again. I came instantly and I came *hard*. Never better. Never bigger. Never.

Fabulous.

I took him through mine, I took him through his, and I stayed tied, on my knees, arched with ass tipped back as he pulled out but moved a hand between my legs and toyed with me gently until he was finished with me. Then he positioned under me and I thought he was going to take me with his mouth, but his long arms reached up, gently pulled the ties out from under my palms and he released me. With hands to my hips, he slid me down his body. When I was close, one of his hands slid into my hair to pull my face down to his and kiss me.

When he was done, he shoved my face in the side of his neck.

"You good?" he asked quietly.

"Yeah."

"How good?"

"Really fucking good."

His arms wrapped tight around me and he gave me a squeeze.

I pressed closer and brushed my lips against his skin before I whispered there, "Thank you."

"Baby, you don't have to thank me for makin' you come." His voice had a smile in it. "My pleasure, and I mean that in every way that can mean."

I lifted up and looked down at him.

I was not smiling, and his faded when he caught sight of my face.

"No," I said softly. "Thank you for making me feel safe, *then* giving that to me. Never, Creed, not once since him, did I give over total control to a man. You're the only one. I didn't think I could like it. You made me like it. No, fucking *love* it and want more. So," I dropped my face closer, "*thank you*."

I watched a wealth of emotions flash through his eyes before his hand pulled me down and he took my mouth again, rolling me, covering me with his body, kissing me long, wet, hard and deep.

Kristen Ashley

When he broke the kiss, his lips trailed over my cheek to my ear and his voice was hoarse when he promised, "You're always safe with me."

I held him tight. "I know."

"I'll erase him."

"You already are."

"Make your body sing."

"You already do."

"I love you, Sylvie."

"I love you back, Creed."

His head moved. I felt the edge of his teeth run light along my jaw then his lips came back to mine and he locked our eyes.

"Gonna claim back every inch of you," he vowed.

"You already have."

"No, I haven't. But I'm gonna."

I smiled against his lips. "Looking forward to that, baby."

He smiled back. "I got that. Nearly begged me to fuck your ass."

I shrugged under him. "You made it hot."

"Oh, it's hot," he promised.

I squirmed under him. He smiled against my mouth again. Then he touched his lips to mine and lifted his head an inch.

"Need provisions," he said quietly. "For you to like it, need you slick."

He was killing me.

"Sex shop, first stop tomorrow," I declared, and he threw back his head and burst out laughing.

I stilled and stared as his laughter shook my body and filled the room with its beauty.

When he sobered, he grinned down at me. Then his grin faded and his hand came up to curl around the side of my head.

"What?" he whispered.

"I missed you," I whispered back.

I watched him close his eyes slowly then his face disappeared in my neck.

We lay that way awhile before he rolled us to our sides but kept our bodies close.

When we settled, quietly he told me, "You got shit to think about."

"Like what?" I asked.

"Future shit."

Oh fuck.

"Creed—"

"Just fucked you again without a condom, baby."

Oh fuck!

"You got pills in your bathroom. You take 'em?" he asked.

"Um... sometimes," I answered, and he grinned. "Usually, I'm steady with that and condoms, always. You've put me off my game," I told him, and his grin got bigger. "We're on day two, Creed," I reminded him gently. "This is good. I like it. I missed you. I love you. I'm happy as all hell to have you back. But we gotta be better with that shit."

"Take your pills," he ordered. "Give me the heads up when you're back on track. I like to feel just you."

I nodded. I liked that too.

He kept talking. "Future shit you gotta think about is just that. I'll lay it out. I want a life with you. A home with you. Kids with you. All we should have had but did not get. Yet. I want you to get to know my kids and build a relationship with them. And, bonus I didn't expect, I enjoy workin' with you. You're good at what you do. You got energy. You believe in the job. You let that emotion make you better at it rather than clouding it, and I dig that. I got a business in Phoenix. You got one here. We gotta pick where we're gonna be. No pressure, but I don't wanna be far away from my kids or put them through the hassle of flyin' every other weekend to come and see me. But that doesn't mean we can't get creative and work something out. That's enough for now, but that's where I am, what you need to think about. No decisions today, tomorrow, next week. We'll talk when you're ready, but that's where I am."

"Okay," I replied.

"Okay," he whispered.

I decided it was time to switch subjects. "What's your take on today?"

He rolled to his back, but pulled my torso up on his as he did. He looked to the ceiling. I looked at his face.

"I get the play, but I still think you all jumped the gun." His eyes came to me. "Sebring does the job fueled by emotion. I don't know where it comes from, but he's got a fire in his belly. He was playin' it smart with finesse, diggin' deep, lookin' to make sure he got all the players. Beatin' the shit outta Nair until he gave all the names of the clients he planted to work over the girls and promised to get the fuck outta Denver might not solve the problem if Nick or some other fuckwad is in on this with him."

I nodded. "Takes care of the immediate problem, though," I noted.

"Maybe, maybe not." His eyes grew sharp on me, and when he went on, my body braced. "Torture doesn't work. Incentives do. Anyone will say anything to stop the pain. We have no idea if he gave us all the names of all the clients he planted. He swears he's workin' alone. We can't trust that either. The only thing we know since we've been watchin' him is that he hasn't directly approached the girls, but Knight's no further than he was before."

"Torture didn't make you say what they wanted you to say to stop the pain," I said quietly.

"Exactly. Torture does not work if you're usin' it on a true believer. Until they offered incentives, they got nothing," he replied, not quietly.

I pulled in a breath and moved us out of this. I couldn't deal with this. Not now.

"We've found nothing to even hint that Nair had a partner."

"That's the only thing I feel good about. My gut throughout this entire job said the man worked alone. He got info and he bought talent to do their thing with the girls, but this is not a man who inspires loyalty. Knight's business is fucked. He shouldn't be doin' it, but before I took this job, I looked into him and got nothing back but respect. Even know some cops on the DPD who had good words to say, no fuckin' joke. So, regardless that he does it, I couldn't sniff out one single enemy, outside Nair."

"Knight shouldn't be doing it?" I asked, and my tone made him focus more intently on me.

"I get you," he said gently. "And I'll say, straight up, in my job with the clients I take, I cross a lotta lines, so I am far from squeaky clean. But there is no denying what Knight Sebring does outside that club is not okay."

"I disagree," I retorted, and his arm around my back gave me a squeeze.

"I know you do, Sylvie. I know why you do. But now you know that I disagree with you."

"Do we have a problem with this?" I asked, and he shook his head against the pillows.

"Nope. Your life, your job, your choices. I fit into that life. I don't bend it to my will. Same goes for you with me. We got issues along the way, we discuss

164

and maybe agree to disagree. But if I accept you have reasons for making the decisions you make and vice versa, we'll be cool."

That was the right answer so I nodded and my body relaxed.

His arm gave me another squeeze.

"Do you know why Knight does it?" he asked.

"No. He hasn't shared and I don't care. He does it. He doesn't fuck around. He's committed and, honestly, Creed, this shit rarely happens. So he's good at what he does, whether you agree with it or not."

"Right," he muttered, and I braced again when his eyes went back to intent. "That visit to Serena, baby, before we came home, she wants out. The girls want out, you should help them and so should Knight."

"We do," I told him and continued, "And I will. So will Knight. He'll pay to make her physically healthy again. The girls will work with her to help her get over what happened or learn to live with it, then he'll work to pave her way in another life. She'll be okay."

His eyes got more intent and his arm tightened so I kept braced when he carried on.

"Just throwin' this out there, but the new ones come in, you should counsel them to different ways of goin' about life."

"I thought you accepted I had reasons for making the decisions I make?" I asked.

"I do. I also told you, we had issues along the way, we discuss them. And a woman finds herself in the position to approach Knight in order to have protection so she can sell her body, Sylvie, he or you should do what you can to show her another way before you take her on. It's the right thing to do."

"Okay, I get you," I told him. "And, you may not know this, but he does that already. I cannot say that he expends a lot of effort, and there is no doubt he could make more of one, but he doesn't just set them up. Sometimes they feel there are no other ways."

He shook his head and his arm came up, fingers sifting in my hair so he could pull my head closer to his.

"I had all access, Sylvie, demand that shit when I take a client, and Serena was hookin' to pay for art school. Can you tell me there's no other way?"

"She's twenty-five, Creed. She can also make life choices."

"You didn't answer my question."

Fuck.

"Okay," I gave in. "That was whacked."

"Yeah," he agreed.

"All the girls don't have reasons like that, Creed."

"Maybe not, but sometimes shit in life can make you blind to choices you don't know that you have. You and Sebring really wanna look after those girls, you help them open their eyes before they sell their bodies. Talk to him about making more of an effort."

"You know, you annoy me when you make sense," I shared, and his face lost its intensity when he grinned.

"Not much I can do about that, baby." His fingers twisted gently in my hair. "You gonna talk to him?"

"Yeah," I muttered.

"Be convincing," he ordered.

I rolled my eyes.

He kept being bossy.

"Now kiss me."

"No."

His brows went up. "No?"

"I'm not in the mood to kiss."

"What are you in the mood for?"

"I'm in the mood to suck you off."

His face got lazy and I got even more in the mood to suck him off.

"Want my mouth in your cunt while you do that," he growled.

"This would not be a hardship," I muttered.

"Top or bottom?" he asked.

"Top," I answered.

His hand slid down my back and lightly smacked my ass. "Bathroom. Want you clean when I eat you. Then come back, climb on and give me that pussy."

It was then I suspected my face got lazy.

I dropped my head and kissed his throat. Down, I kissed his chest.

Then I dashed to the bathroom and cleaned up. I dashed back, climbed on, gave him my pussy and took his cock.

Again, it was *fabulous*.

Chapter 14
Finally

A warm summer day in Kentucky, seventeen years earlier. Creed is twenty-two, Sylvie is seventeen ...

I was pacing the pier, my tanned, bare feet pounding against the wooden planks. I was dashing my fingers across my wet cheeks when I felt him and I whirled.

He was jogging through the grass wearing his usual old faded Levi's and a tee. I could see his beat-up pickup through the trees parked up on the lane.

I took off running down the pier, through the grass, and I didn't stop even as I felt his blue eyes move over me, his face harsh with worry. His arms started to swing wide and he stopped jogging just in time to brace when I hit him going full-tilt.

Those arms closed tight around me.

"Sylvie, baby, what the fuck?" he muttered in the top of my hair.

"Kah... Kah... Kah... *Creed*," I blubbered, pressing deep into him, my arms also wrapped around him tight.

When I didn't go on, he demanded, "Talk to me. I got your message. Got here as soon as I could. What happened?"

"Bah... Bah... *Bootsie*," I wailed, and my body shook with my sobs.

"Oh fuck," he murmured.

"She dah... dah... *died!*" I bawled.

His arms got tighter and I felt his lips pressed into the top of my hair as he whispered, "Oh baby."

I cried in his arms, mine holding as tight as his held me, my body shaking uncontrollably, and I did this for a while.

Then I arched back, looked in the direction of his face and cried, "She's the only one in that house I like! Now she's gone and I'm *all alone!*" after which I collapsed against him and started bawling again.

He bent and picked me up. I circled his neck with my arms, shoved my face in his neck and kept right on crying. We both went down and he settled me in his lap, his back against a tree. He stroked mine as I pressed close and kept sobbing. I did this for a while and Creed let me, stroking my back, sometimes my hair, sometimes shifting my hair away from my face, but not saying a word and holding me close the whole time.

My tears subsided to sniffles and whimpers but I didn't raise my head when I said, "I loved her."

"I know you did, Sylvie," he whispered. "She was a great dog."

"I have a whole year before I'm out of that house and I have to spend it all alone."

"Hey," he called gently, and I sucked in a trembling breath.

Then I asked, "What?"

"Look at me."

I straightened a bit in his lap and tilted my head back.

His hands came to either side of my face, fingers moving, shifting damp tendrils of hair away, wiping away wet, his eyes watching them move before he framed my face and looked deep in my eyes.

"When has my Sylvie ever been alone?" he asked softly.

I closed my eyes and my head dropped forward, my forehead hitting his chin.

He kissed me there then his lips moved against my skin, "You always got me."

I nodded, my forehead moving against his chin. "Yeah," I whispered.

"Where is she?" he asked.

I sucked in a shaky breath and pulled back an inch, tipping my head to catch his eyes.

"I wrapped her in a blanket. She's at home."

"Your Dad and the stepmonster?"

"He's golfing then having dinner with his cronies. She's shopping then drinks with her girls. He said he'd call the vet, but they said they couldn't come until tomorrow."

He looked over my shoulder and muttered, "Priceless. Pure Bissenette. His daughter's dog dies and he's fuckin' golfing."

"Creed," I called, and he looked back at me.

"I'll take you home. Get her. Take you both to my place. You say good-bye and I'll take care of her."

I stared at him.

God! He was so *wonderful.* Everything. *Everything.* He was everything to me.

"Thank you, Creed," I whispered.

"Gotta take care of my girl's Bootsie," he whispered back.

I looked deep into his beautiful, *beautiful* blue eyes.

Then I whispered again, "Thank you," leaned forward and touched my mouth to his.

On the way back, his hand suddenly slid up into my hair, moving fast. His fingers curved in and my head stopped its retreat.

His gaze bored into mine. Something about it was hot. So hot, I felt it burning me.

Mine bored back.

I moved forward, and it was only a couple of inches, but Creed met me halfway.

Then his mouth was on mine, mine was on his. His opened, mine followed suit, and his tongue slid inside.

Oh my God.

Oh my God!

Creed was kissing me!

And he tasted as beautiful as he… just… *was.*

Suddenly I was on my back in the grass, Creed's torso pressing me there, his tongue demanding something I wasn't sure how to give. I'd necked with guys, but not like this. Not like Creed was kissing me, but I just let him take what he wanted. As far as I was concerned, he could have anything from me. His big hands moved fast and warm at my sides. Every inch of skin on my body started tingling and I pressed up automatically, seeking more. Of what I didn't know.

Just Creed.

I just wanted more of Creed.

He tore his mouth from mine abruptly on a harsh, clipped, *"Fuck,"* and my arms tightened quickly when it felt like he was going to pull away. His eyes locked on mine. "Let go, Sylvie."

"Don't," I breathed.

"Sylvie, let go."

"Don't. Don't. *Don't.*"

One of his hands cupped the side of my face. "Baby, you gotta let go. This is not right."

I lifted my head an inch from the turf and whispered fiercely, "This is the most right thing in the world."

My words were true. I knew it. *I knew it.*

"You're beautiful," he told me. "You're beautiful, Sylvie. The most beautiful thing I've ever seen, but you're too young, baby. This is not right. You gotta let go."

"I'm never letting go."

"You gotta *let go.*"

My arms tightened hard around his neck. "Creed, I'm *never* letting go."

I watched him close his eyes tight. His head dropped, mine went back to the grass and he rested his forehead against mine.

Then he bit out, "*Goddamn it,*" and jerked up, but not away from me. He pulled me up with him until he was sitting again, back against the tree, me in his lap and his arms, facing him.

His arms left me, his hands shoved my hair back away from my face and he held me there, one hand on each side.

"This was not supposed to happen now," he told me.

"It happened," I shot back.

"*Fuck,*" he hissed, banging his head back against the tree and looking skyward. "What the fuck do I do now?" he asked the branches of the tree.

I lifted a hand to his face and brushed away the thick hank of hair that fell over his eye, and his head righted so he could look at me.

Then he said the five most precious words I ever heard *in my whole life.*

"I wanna make you mine."

I closed my eyes as joy and relief swept through me.

Finally!

I opened them, looked at him and lifted my hand to touch the peridot resting at the base of my neck.

"Too late. I already am."

His arms closed around me, one hand coming up to the back of my head again and shoving my face in his neck.

"Shit," he muttered before he pulled me back and looked down at me. "You sure?"

I nodded. "Absolutely."

He closed his eyes tight and dropped his forehead to mine again. "God, Sylvie."

I slid my head down to the side and pressed my face in his neck, my arms stealing around him, holding him tight.

He bent his neck and put his lips to my ear. "I wanna see you."

Those were the four second most precious words I ever heard *in my whole life*.

"Okay," I whispered.

"Regularly."

"Okay," I agreed quickly.

"We gotta be careful."

"We always did, Creed. It'll be okay. We've had tons of practice."

His arms gave me a squeeze.

"No one can know," he told me quietly.

"I know."

"This is us. You and me. Special. We do this, we take it slow, we do it smart. We don't fuck it up."

I didn't get that entirely, but still, I nodded. "Okay."

He knew me and gently pulled me back so I'd look at him.

When I caught his eyes, he explained softly, "I guide this, Sylvie, you follow my lead. Nothing changes between us except everything. You gotta understand, in the eyes of the law, I'm too old for you. In the eyes of God, I'm too old for you. And, bottom line, I'm too old for you. We can be together and we can do things, but we're taking it slow until I'm not too old for you. Do you understand me?"

I bit my lip, feeling my face get pink, but I nodded. I understood. He wasn't going to do it with me.

Not yet.

Then I whispered, "Can we kiss again?"

He grinned. "Fuck yeah."

I grinned back. "Good, that was really nice."

He started chuckling then he pulled me close and held me there for a long time.

He broke the moment by saying, "When we go pick up Bootsie, leave your parents a note. Say you're at a movie. You won't be home 'til late. Then you can have dinner and hang at my place with me. We'll watch a movie."

My first date with Creed.

It sounded perfect.

Except, of course, the part about Bootsie.

"Okay," I whispered.

"Let me see your face, Sylvie."

I pulled it out of the side of his neck, tipped it back and looked at him.

His hand came up and curved around my jaw, tipping my head back further. His dipped down and he brushed his mouth against mine.

It seemed I'd been waiting for years to be just like this with Creed.

And having it…

It was *divine*.

He moved back half an inch and, eyes locked with mine, he whispered, "My Sylvie."

I smiled and felt warm through and through, and not just from the Kentucky sun beating into me.

His hand slid back into my hair and tipped my head forward. He kissed the top of my hair and murmured there, "Let's take care of Bootsie."

Then he kissed me, got to his feet, taking me with him in his arms. And when he was up, he put me on my feet.

Hand in hand, we walked to his truck.

Hand in hand, me and Creed, the way I knew down deep in my heart we were always meant to be.

Finally.

Chapter 15
Give Me That

Present day...

"She's with Dixon."

Creed lay there, his sky blue eyes just staring. Not at the bacon sandwich he could smell, which was set just out of reach, but at Daddy.

He didn't believe it. He'd lost track of time. He'd been there days, maybe weeks, but he didn't believe. His Sylvie wouldn't do that. Not in a few days. Not in a few weeks. Not ever.

"She's with Dixon," Daddy went on. "Right now. It didn't take her long with you being gone to realize she's better than you. She's a Bissenette. You may have your Daddy's blood, but you've got more of Winona in you. I know this. I know it because you'd set your sights on a teenage girl. Fuck with her head. Take her virginity. You're trash, Tucker Creed. You were trash before that whore shoved you out. You're trash now. Jason Dixon isn't trash. Jason will give her everything you can't, never could, never will. Jason will hand her the moon."

Creed said not a word. He just lay there, staring.

Daddy got impatient and bent deep, leaning close.

"Promise to let her go, leave, never return, let her have the life she should have, and we'll feed you, we'll unchain you, get you medical attention for that cut. I'll give you ten thousand dollars and you can set up somewhere else. Promise to let her go, leave and never come back, never enter her life again, never phone her, never see her, and this will be over."

Creed spoke then.

And he did it to say in a cracked, parched, weak voice, "Never."

I shot up to sitting in bed, the room dark, Creed's strong arm along my stomach, and I was breathing heavily.

The dream still had me.

I threw the covers aside and started to catapult myself from the bed but Creed's arm tightened. Instead of jumping one way, I found myself flying the other. I landed in the bed on my back then Creed's weight was on me.

"It was a dream, baby," he whispered through the dark. "Just a dream. It's over."

It wasn't a dream. It was real. He told me. He told me all about it. Even the new stuff.

Now I knew everything.

I thought I was ready.

I'd never be ready.

It hit me I was shaking, so I did the only thing I could to get rid of the shakes. I wrapped my arms around his solid, warm bulk, lifted my head and shoved it in his neck taking in his scent, letting everything that was him envelope me.

"These dreams are kicking my ass," I whispered back.

"Just hold on," he murmured.

I sucked in breath, tightened my arms and held on.

The shaking left me and I found my mouth saying, "I don't want you to go."

It was early morning Friday, three days after the shit went down with Drake Nair. Outside of the three girls who got targeted needing a lot of TLC, things seemed settled. Creed and I were working my jobs as well as keeping an eye on Knight's business, but it seemed Nair had worked alone. Creed didn't trust it, not yet. He wanted to do more digging and he wanted to be around in case something went down. So he spoke to Knight, Knight agreed and we were still nosing.

But the weekend was upon us and it was Creed's weekend with his kids. He was flying back to Phoenix. He got them Friday afternoon and took them back to Chelle Sunday evening.

We'd discussed this and decided that this visit Creed would tell them about me and he'd take some time to tell Chelle. He didn't want her blindsided by the information coming from one of the kids that a woman named Sylvie was in his life. I thought that was cool of him to do, but I didn't envy him that conversation.

He wanted me to come with him, but I talked him into going alone. His kids stayed with him and he was okay with me staying with all of them, telling me his kids were good kids. They'd adjust, they loved their Dad, sense his happiness and be cool with it.

He obviously knew his kids better than me, but I disagreed. I thought they should get a heads up and not be confronted with me on their turf until they had time to prepare. Creed didn't like it, but he agreed. I had a feeling he agreed more because he thought I needed time to prepare to meet his kids, not the other way around, but whatever. He'd agreed. So he was leaving that day and wouldn't be home until late Sunday.

Now that the hour was nearly on us for him to leave, I didn't like it.

Not at all.

I didn't want him away from me.

Shit.

"Sylvie—"

I interrupted him, "Forget I said that. I didn't say that."

His hands came up to frame my face before he whispered, "Come with me."

God, it would be so easy to say yes.

"I don't want your kids—" I started.

He cut me off. "They'll love you."

I nodded against the pillows and I gave his body a squeeze.

"Yeah, they will," I agreed. "I'm good with kids, but this is different. This is about our future, all of our futures, and it should be handled with care."

"Baby, you don't think I got my kids' best interests at heart?" he asked.

"I'm not saying that," I replied quickly. "I just think we should finesse this. Give them time. Take it slow."

"Right," he muttered. Then he rolled, taking me with him so I was on top. He reached out a long arm and I blinked when the lights came on. When my eyes adjusted, I saw his on me. "Hotel," he stated.

"What?" I asked.

"We fly there together. Get you a rental car, a hotel where you can hang but not sleep. I go get the kids and talk to Chelle. I spend time with them Friday, tell them about you. Friday night, late, when they're in bed, you come to me, sleep with me, leave before they get up. Saturday, we do somethin' together. Maybe a water park. Somethin' fun. Somethin' they'll like. Somethin' not on their home turf. You take off, come back when they're asleep, leave again before they get up and we fly back together."

Had I said before that Creed was genius?

Creed was genius.

"That would work," I told him quietly and watched him grin.

"Will you be able to keep yourself occupied?" he asked.

I grinned back. "Totally."

"Then it's decided," he muttered, his eyes on my mouth.

"It's decided," I agreed, getting the words out about two seconds before his mouth hit mine, and he kissed me, deep and sweet.

When he lifted his head, he was not grinning. His gaze was intent, and I'd since learned from seeing that look before to brace. So I did.

"Beauty," he whispered.

"What?" I asked.

"Beauty. It's pure beauty you don't wanna be away from me. I don't like that, baby. I love it."

My hand slid up his chest to his neck where my fingers curled around. Once they reached their destination, they moved and slid up further into his hair. Then they put pressure on to bring his mouth back to me so I could kiss him.

When my tongue slid in his mouth, I planted a foot in the bed and rolled him.

Then I kissed other parts of him.

Suffice it to say, it took us a while to get back to sleep.

When we did, we both slept easy.

"I'm walking up to your house now," I said into my phone, hitching up the strap of the bag on my shoulder, and got a, "Gotcha. I'll be at the door," back from Creed.

Just an FYI, Phoenix in July was hot. Not your normal brand of hot. Hotter than the hinges of hell kind of hot. I'd never been in hot that hot. I didn't even know hot that hot existed. It was eleven thirty at night and the heat had not left the day.

Not good.

After we flew in and rented the car, I followed Creed to a nice hotel close to his house. We checked in, got the lay of the land and he took off to meet

Chelle for lunch prior to picking up Kara and Brand. I got changed directly into my bikini and made an appointment for a mani/pedi and facial for later that afternoon at the hotel spa. Then I hit the pool because, everyone knew, if you went to a place with palm trees, even if only for the weekend, you came back with a tan, including kickass bitches like me.

This was a mistake.

Lying by the pool was not relaxing and enjoyable. It was like baking in an oven. Even the water of the pool wasn't cool, but beyond warm. Although it provided relief, it wasn't much and didn't last long.

Therefore, I gave up on the tan and went back to my room, showered, did my spa treatments and hung out watching movies and ordering room service until Creed called to say the kids were in bed.

On the plane, I'd decided on a plan for the weekend, a weekend I'd spend mostly away from Creed and also meeting his kids.

I didn't normally plan. I usually flew by the seat of my pants. My dead partner Ron told me this was one of my three great skills. I could think on the fly better than anyone he'd ever seen, including during his stint in the Marines. I could cast a mean lure. And last, I was better than Marion in that arctic bar in *Raiders of the Lost Ark* during a one-on-one drinking contest.

But this was too important not to have my shit together. So my plan was this: tan and relax on Friday, hopefully get through Saturday without making his kids hate me, and discover Phoenix on Sunday to see if I wanted to be the one to make the move for Creed and his kids.

My time by the pool was, unfortunately, not conducive to me wanting to make the move for Creed and his kids. My time walking up to his house, albeit this lasted probably ten seconds, didn't help either.

I lifted my flip-flop clad foot to take the step into the covered front entry of his adobe-style, terracotta tile-roofed house. The door opened, Creed stood in it and I felt much better.

"Hey," I greeted quietly, grinning up at him.

Creed didn't reply. He leaned deep and reached out with an arm. He hooked me around the waist, took me off my feet and suddenly I was in the cool house. The door shut behind me, my back arched over his arm, my front plastered to his and Creed's mouth was on mine.

Yeah, feeling much better.

He lifted his head and when he caught my eyes he muttered, "You don't have to be quiet for the kids. They both sleep like the dead, and even if they didn't, their rooms are at the back of the house. Tonight they were wired because of our plans tomorrow so it took them a while to go to sleep, but now that they're out, they're out."

I nodded, He released me with one arm to step to my side and pull me into his place.

At first sight, my breath caught.

Holy shit.

My house was a place to exist and crash.

Creed's house was... *not.*

I stared.

It seemed half show home and half just plain home if you were relatively loaded and gave one serious shit about where you lived.

Man, Creed really must charge a fuckuva lot more than me.

I was stunned. Not much surprised me, but this... this did. Hugely.

Creed told me he had his Expedition as well as a nondescript Ford sedan to do work in during jobs he needed to be invisible. He also told me he had a Harley, a speedboat he took to the lake with his kids and a three bedroom house on a hill.

Of all of this, I was excited about the speedboat and Harley. The speedboat said good times on the water that included such things as inner tubes, skis and Creed wearing nothing but swim trunks. Who wouldn't like all that? A Harley elevated anyone's badass status about seven thousand levels. Owning a Harley and looking and acting like Creed made him even more badass than Ron, and Ron was a fucking Marine.

Creed did *not* tell me his "three bedroom house on a hill" was a showplace.

My eyes scanned as Creed moved us through.

To the left through an archway was a study. Handsome furniture with a modern bent, the space clearly used but organized, even tidy.

Straight ahead was open space and lots of it. It also screamed, *"Make no mistake! You're in the Southwest!"*

A long, rustic, wooden, rectangular dining room table with eight chairs was just in from the front door, and beyond the recessed study was an open plan kitchen with modern cabinets, shiny granite countertops and top-of-the-line appliances. The kitchen/dining room and living area was delineated by a red felt pool table.

Yes, a pool table. That was how vast the space was.

Past that was the living area with a big, comfy-looking sectional, accompanied by a massive chair and ottoman and an enormous flat screen TV in an enormous wall unit. The floors were shining wood throughout, except the kitchen was tile.

There were stunning prints with a southwest feel on the walls, but none of them were stereotypical. They were unusual and exquisite. Art deco desert landscapes that Creed would tell me later were by Ed Mell. Whimsical portraits by L. Carter Holman. Colorful cacti in bloom by Diana Madaras.

The entirety of the space had a feel of rustic as well as modern, mixed with a heavy hand of southwest. It was decorated in brick red, terracotta and cream with hints of turquoise, purple, golden yellow and sun burnt orange.

It was amazing.

Beyond the living space was the showstopper. Floor to ceiling windows with a view to a lit pool that looked more like a rocky grotto, including a small waterfall. All of this was surrounded by a massive pool deck and handsome deck furniture. There were manicured, graveled-in areas around the pool deck filled with palm trees, fruit trees and weird but attractive cacti. Since Creed's house was on a hill, the pool's backdrop beyond an adobe wall was the lights of north Phoenix.

The house was amazing.

The back patio and view were *awesome*.

In truth, the whole thing was. Well-appointed, well-decorated with personality and thoughtfulness. Open, airy, clean and tidy, but with a comfortable feel.

Therefore, like I mentioned, I was stunned.

The Creed I knew lived in the broken down house that he shared with his mother. A house that, when he grew older, he was constantly working on to keep the roof from leaking, the plumbing working and the space livable until we could take off on my eighteenth birthday, finally to start our lives. The furniture was old, worn, and in some cases, hand-me-down. Creed's Dad had inherited the property from his Dad and had died before he'd been able to give his family better. Winona Creed was a mess who could barely take care of herself and didn't bother taking care of her son or home. This included the fact she didn't clean, as in ever.

These thoughts entering my head, harking back I remembered something I'd forgotten.

Creed did clean. He vacuumed, did the dishes and did the laundry. He hated that house, and not just because it was ramshackle, but because it didn't smell good, didn't look good, and it was a pain in the ass to clean not only his own mess but that of a drunk of a mother who didn't give a shit. Like me but for different reasons, he couldn't wait to get out.

Still, even remembering that, it must be said I didn't know what I expected of single Dad Creed, but this definitely wasn't it.

We were standing at the windows looking out at his view when Creed murmured, "Hot as an oven now, baby, but come September through to May, that right there is paradise."

I looked up at him to see his eyes trained to the view. He must have felt my gaze because he tipped his down to me.

"What's the stringy cactus?" I asked.

"Ocotillo. Orange flowers, twice a year. The desert in bloom, outside you and my kids, is the most beautiful thing I've ever seen. You're here in March, Sylvie, I'll take you out. So pretty, you'll forget to breathe."

I held his eyes and forgot to breathe right then.

He liked it here, a lot. He'd found a home. He'd settled.

I forced myself to nod and looked back at the view before I turned out of his arm, took in all that lay behind me before looking back up at him and remarking, "You live in a showplace, Creed."

"You grew up in a showplace," he, for some reason, reminded me. "You grew up with that, and your Dad proved your whole life he didn't give one shit about you, and in the end proved it beyond doubt, usin' you to cover his ass. But I grew up in a pit with a Ma who proved daily she didn't give a shit about anyone but herself. My kids don't have to live with that. I left Chelle in a five bedroom house in a neighborhood in the west valley and she's still there. Her man moved in with her. It isn't like this. More family, less show. But it's clean, new, nice, in a neighborhood filled with people who give a shit about their home, kids, friends and neighbors. What goes on behind closed doors could be somethin' else, but that's the feel of the place. What my kids have with their Mom and here, though, is good and safe, and it surrounds them with the knowledge that someone gives a shit."

I stared up at him and said not a word.

He leaned down to me. "Way I see it, you escaped your traps with the way you live in Denver. This," he motioned to our surroundings with an arm, "is me escapin' mine. Bonus, I give good to my kids."

Bonus, I give good to my kids.

God, my new badass Creed, who was a great Dad, who gave a shit and had a cool house and the ability to take out the trash without being asked, was *awesome.*

Therefore, I stated, "I love you, Tucker Creed," and got to watch as he grinned.

Then he hooked a hand behind my neck, pulled me in and up and brushed his mouth to mine before lifting his head an inch, giving my neck a squeeze and asking, "Got no paneling or shag carpet, and the kitchen is cleaned more than once every year, but you think you could be happy here?"

I ignored his teasing. My eyes slowly slid from side to side then back to his beautiful blue ones whereupon I answered on a shrug, "Don't know. I might be able to make do."

Creed burst out laughing, but drowned the noise two seconds later by taking my mouth and laughing down my throat.

Then he showed me more of his house by taking my hand and guiding me to the master suite.

Like the rest of the house, it was awesome, except more, because it was all Creed.

Not to mention, it had a huge bed.

I twisted my neck and whispered, "Harder, baby. Faster."

Creed had an arm wrapped around my chest at an angle so his hand was curved around my breast, thumb circling the tip. His other hand was between my legs, fingers toying with my clit. We were on our sides. His front was pressed against my back and his cock was sliding slow and gentle between my legs.

"Slow, Sylvie. Sweet," he murmured. He twisted his own neck, lifted his head and slid his tongue down my neck.

I shivered and tipped my ass further to get more of him.

"Like that," he growled against my skin.

I did too. Oh yeah, I did too. All of it. Even the growl. Maybe *especially* the growl.

I focused hazily on the view of his pool and backyard through the floor to ceiling windows that made up one wall of his bedroom, and I realized he was making love to me. Making love to me in his bed, his home, his city.

I loved it. I loved the feel of it. I loved that he was giving it to me and I loved why. He wanted me to want to join my life to his here, and he wanted it badly. So he was trying to convince me, and he was using a really good way to go about that.

So I was going to give it to him. All of it.

I took him, strained into his touch, arched into his strokes, gave him exactly what he wanted, taking everything he had to give in return.

He slid out, moved slightly away, rolled me to my back and then rolled over me. I spread my legs for him. He settled on me and glided right back in. My neck arched at the feel of having him back even though I only lost him for mere moments. I loved taking him inside, being connected, as close as we could get.

I felt his hands at my sides moving up and automatically lifted my arms. Creed liked to hold me down. He did it often. And I had to say, I liked it too. It wasn't the same as what I'd experienced before. He enjoyed lifting up, watching his cock take me, our bodies moving together, joining. He liked taking control and allowing me to do nothing but accept all he gave.

To be honest, I wished we could do it with mirrors so I could see what he could see. So I could watch the strong, vital, massive power of his body moving over and thrusting into my petite one.

It was already hot. Watching him hold me down while he fucked me, that would be *smoking*.

As expected, his cock moved inside me as his hands trailed up my sides, over my pits, over my arms. Then his fingers curled around my wrists and he lifted up to gaze down at our linked bodies.

God, I loved it when he watched.

I bent my knees, feet in the bed, tipping up my hips and he slid in deeper.

Yeah, I loved that, too.

His eyes came to my face as he transferred my wrists to one hand. Still holding me down, his other hand slid down my arm, over to my neck and down my chest, between my breasts to my belly.

Nice. So fucking nice.

My breath escalated.

"Love you, baby," I whispered.

I saw his eyes go soft and his strong and white teeth came out to bite his lower lip. I liked that look so much, I arched my back, pulled my knees back and pressed the insides of my thighs to his hips as he bent his head and took my mouth.

The second he did, he started powering in harder, deeper, faster.

Fantastic.

Beautiful.

Only Creed could give this to me.

Only Creed.

Creed stopped kissing me when our breathing grew heavy. We were panting, he was grunting and I was moaning. Our lips brushed, our breaths mingled, our hips collided and his lips slid down my cheek to my ear.

"I want you here. I want you in my home, my bed, my life," he murmured, the smooth out of his voice. It was low and so rough with sex and emotion, it was abrasive, scoring through me.

"Baby—"

"I want your clothes in my closet. I wanna hear your voice in my house when you're talkin' on the phone. I want you sittin' beside me when we're watchin' TV. I want shit you like in my fridge. I want your razors in my shower. I want my roof over your head. Your car in my garage. I want to give you what I should have been giving you for sixteen years. As good as you deserve. A show-place. A place where I can make you happy."

God. He was killing me.

"Creed, let me—"

He didn't let me finish. He pressed on, driving in, our bodies jolting with his thrusts, his voice harsh in my ear.

"Give me that, Sylvie. Give me that, and swear to God, I'll give you everything."

"I—"

His head came up, his cock drove deep and stayed planted and his eyes burned into mine.

"All I'll ask. All I'll ever ask. You give me that and you got a lifetime of nothin' but take."

"Give me my hands, baby," I whispered, and he released my wrists immediately. I moved them to frame his face, lifted up so I was close and kept whispering, "You can have that. You can have anything from me, but only if I get to give as good as I get."

He shook his head, moving my hands with it and grinding his cock into me. It felt so good my lips parted.

Creed spoke.

"All I want is you. You make my home yours, you'll never have to give."

"It doesn't work that way, Creed."

He pulled out, slammed in, and his face jerked down toward mine so fast, I pressed my head into the pillow in an automatic response. I held my breath at the expression in his eyes, even as I gasped it in deeper when his hand slid down my belly and his thumb pressed hard against my clit.

"I vowed to you I'd take care of you. I vowed it. I thought I was doin' that when I left you. I wasn't. I need this, Sylvie, and you gotta give it to me."

"It's not—"

He started moving again, powering fast and deep, his thumb circling my clit, and my neck arched on a deep moan.

His lips went to my throat and my fingers slid into his hair. "You gotta give this to me," he demanded, voice thick.

"Creed—"

He went faster, deeper, harder.

Oh God.

My fingers in his hair fisted.

"Baby—" I breathed. It was building and it was going to overwhelm me.

"Give that to me, Sylvie," he ordered.

"Okay, yes," I gasped. "You have me. You can have anything."

"Fuck yeah," he grunted. His thumb pressing harder, his hips driving faster, his mouth took mine. He shoved his free arm under me, wrapped it around my hips, slammed me down as he powered up and I moaned my orgasm down his throat.

Two minutes later, he groaned his down mine.

He took a few moments to recover then rolled us, still connected, so I was on top and he was on his back.

I lifted my head to look down at him before I informed him, "You know, the rulebook states anything agreed through sexual manipulation is thrown out after the act."

I saw the white flash of his smile before one of his arms snaked around my waist and got tight while his other hand slid into my hair and pulled my face closer to his, whereupon he informed me, "Yeah, if you're makin' love with a normal guy. If you're doin' it with a badass, it's a totally different rulebook."

I had to admit, this was true.

"I'm a badass, too," I reminded him.

"You are," he agreed readily. Something, by the way, I truly believed that he believed. Something, by the way, I totally loved about him. "So, in future, baby, you got that option open to you."

Good to know, as well as something to look forward to when it was my turn to coerce something out of him.

"Right, then," I tipped my head to the side, "maybe you'll explain exactly what I agreed to."

His arm around me got tighter. His fingers flexed against my scalp and the white of his smile faded from his face.

"You know, Sylvie," he whispered.

He was right. I knew. I knew, back in the day, he was acutely aware that I had an in-ground pool, a stable full of horses, a fancy car, a huge house, a house-keeper; all provided to me by my piece of shit Daddy, and if I hooked my star to his, at first, he couldn't give me any of that.

I didn't care. He was right earlier. That was a trap from which I would move, after he left, to a prison.

But Creed was a man, all man, even back then, and he didn't see it that way. Not then and obviously not now. He never wanted me to feel loss. He never wanted me to have any reason to regret choosing him, and no matter how much I talked, how hard I tried to convince him I didn't need any of that shit, he didn't believe it. I was young, and he was worried following my heart was blinding me to reasonable life considerations an older person would take into account.

He was wrong then.

He was wrong now.

"You know, I'm a different Sylvie," I stated quietly.

"I know, baby."

"I can take care of myself."

"I know that, too."

Okay, now I was confused.

"Then... what?"

"My house. My furniture. My housecleaner, pool guy, gardener. Your body in my bed," he replied.

I didn't get it.

"What?"

"I take care of you," he answered. "I provide for you."

Uh-oh.

My body stiffened over his.

"Creed—"

"You work. You earn. You enjoy yourself. You do what you like. You buy me shit if you want. But I provide, Sylvie."

"That's crazy," I told him.

"It's what you just agreed," he told me.

"Okay, but it's crazy."

"It isn't."

"It is," I shot back. "I'm not seventeen and depending on you, Creed."

"Right," his voice was low and leaning toward angry impatience, "I get you. I get we lost that time. I get you're not seventeen anymore and you can take care of yourself. And I get that maybe to you it's crazy, but what you need to get is it's what I fuckin' *need*."

He meant that. He *needed* it.

Oh God, they messed him up. They messed *us* up. They fucked everything up even beyond what we already knew.

My voice was softer and my body relaxed into his, my hand coming up to wrap around the side of his neck when I said, "That was a long time ago, babe. I've lived. I've changed. You have, too. We're doing this, going forward in life together. I get what you're saying, but we're both different and we're different in good ways. We should embrace that."

"You're giving up Charlene, the kids, your partner's family and Knight to be here with me. That's your part. I take care of the rest."

"Please don't do that."

I said it in a rush, my voice suddenly edged with an anguish I felt coming from deep in my gut, tearing through me, leaving tatters in its wake, and I felt Creed's big body still under mine.

I went on, "My Dad did that to you. My Dad took those years away from us. Yeah, it's gonna suck, giving up my life in Denver, but it's you. It's always been you. I'd walk the Sahara to get to you. I'm not lovestruck and acting stupid. I know it's gonna be hard giving up my life in Denver, but I don't have kids. I don't live in a house like this. I don't have roots. I have relationships, and if relationships are good, it doesn't matter where you are in the world, they always stay strong."

He didn't listen to the last part and this would be clear when he stated, "You carry no guilt for what those motherfuckers did to me."

"I know, kind of," I semi-agreed. "But do you see where I'm coming from?"

Creed rolled, disengaging us, so I was on my back and his body was pressed into my side and partially over me.

"No kind of," he growled. "That was all Bissenette, what he did to you and what he did to me. These nightmares you're havin', don't let them take hold. You bear no responsibility for what happened to me."

I felt my body begin to shake and my voice was fragile and so totally not me, it felt like it came from some other me when I reminded him, "You wanted to leave that night. I made you—"

His big hand covered my mouth and his head dipped so he was all I could see. "He and his assholes *tortured* me. He *sold* you, his fuckin' *daughter,* to pay off a goddamned debt for fuckin' *blow.* Even if you weren't his daughter, Sylvie, that… shit… is… *whacked.* Who does that?" he asked.

He didn't wait for an answer, even though he pulled his hand from my mouth and wrapped it around my jaw as he kept talking.

"No one but people who are serious as shit fucked in the head. You could have no fuckin' clue when you left me that night what would happen to us the next fuckin' day. Where we were, what we knew, you made the right decision, Sylvie. You were a good person, a good daughter, tryin' to do right, and you made the right decision. It was him, baby. All fuckin' him. Do not take that shit on. You do, it'll fuck with you forever."

I stared in his eyes, and I did this a long time. Long enough for the shakes to subside, and I took in a deep breath.

"Okay," I whispered.

His body relaxed at my side. "Okay."

"So," I started to recap, "I give you Phoenix and living in an oven for a few months out of the year. You give me a fab pad with a pool, but the rest, can we agree to wing it? See how it goes."

He waited a beat before he muttered, "I can live with that."

I grinned at him and muttered back, "Good."

I saw his return grin before he bent his neck and touched his mouth to mine.

He lifted his head and whispered, "Gotta get rid of this condom, baby. Be back."

I nodded against the pillows. He bent his neck again to touch his lips to my throat before he started to roll off the bed.

But he stopped and looked back at me.

"Just to say," he began, "this house and all it is, all that's in it, it's about me, it's about givin' good to my kids. Absolutely. But make no mistake, Sylvie, no way in the back of my head while I was buildin' all this, buildin' my life, I didn't think I wished I was giving it to you."

After he dropped that bomb, he finished rolling away from me.

I had no retort, mostly because I'd stopped breathing.

I took in a deep breath in order to jumpstart my oxygen intake and rolled three times to the other side of his massive bed. I swung my hips around, put my feet to the floor and got out, reaching down. I pulled on my panties and cami and wandered to the windows.

Seriously, his view was fucking *fantastic*.

I felt him enter the room, heard his bare feet padding on the floor, then I felt his arms wrap around me from behind.

I relaxed into him.

Then I asked what I'd wanted to ask since I got there.

"How'd it go with Chelle and the kids?"

His body grew tight for a second, as did his arms before he sighed and relaxed.

I did not take this as a good sign.

"Heads up: Kara is gonna like you, probably rabidly. She's determined to like you. She's thrilled past anything healthy I got a woman in my life."

This was surprising news so I turned in his arms while he was still talking, curled mine around him and looked up at him as his chin dipped so he could look at me.

"Mostly, this is to stick it to her mother. I do not get what's goin' down between those two, but I figure what she fakes for you in order to hurt her Mom will eventually become genuine and not a way to fuck with Chelle. It's just that, now, that's where she's at."

"Oh… kay," I agreed slowly, not getting this either. Then again, my step-monster mostly ignored me and I returned the favor. We existed in the same house. She gave an effort that was all show when she thought she'd get something from my father in return. Usually, even when I was really young, she went her way and I went mine.

My Mom called her a scheming, greedy gold digger, which was what she was, seeing as she was Daddy's secretary before he divorced my mother to make her his wife. And I liked my Mom as best I could, seeing as my Dad devoted his life to all things fucked up, including doing everything within his formidable power to make my mother's life miserable, and that included keeping me away from her. He did this until she gave up the fight and took off to California. Before that, no way I'd use the stepmonster to screw with precious time with my Mom. No way in hell.

But, whatever. Kara Creed was not me. I was just going to have to deal.

"Brand's Brand," he went on, taking me from my thoughts. "He likes everyone. His response to me tellin' them about you was, 'Awesome cool, Dad'."

Creed said the last with a smile and kept talking.

"He likes people. He's social. Talkative. Even when he was a baby, he met people's eyes and smiled at them. Just like my Dad. Dad could and did talk to anybody. He never went anywhere where he didn't have a friend, mostly because he made friends if there wasn't one there already. Brand's just like that."

That sounded better, so I gave him a smile and a squeeze.

His expression grew thoughtful, and his gaze drifted over my head as he murmured, "Chelle's happy for me."

I blinked up at him. "Say again?"

He looked down at me. "She didn't do cartwheels, but yeah, you heard me. She was happy."

"You're kidding," I whispered, not having a good feeling about this.

189

Kristen Ashley

"Baby, your name is inked on my back and she loves me no matter I dicked her over. You don't know her, we haven't gotten deep about her, but I told you she's a good woman. When I say that, I mean she's a really fuckin' good woman. Funny, loving, smart, sweet. In a fucked up drunken speech, I gave it all to her. She knows about the lake, the pier, the necklaces, the promises, all our history. You're inked on my skin. I named her kids your names. That shit, our shit, our history, our connection was and is extreme. She gets that better than anyone but you and me, and she loves me. She can't have me, but she can be happy that I have what I need."

Okay, he was a man so he didn't get this shit, but women *so* did not work that way.

Ever.

"Okay," I said, but even I could hear I was full of shit.

His arms gave me a squeeze and his face dropped closer to mine. "You'll meet her and you'll see. She is not like other women. She's just Chelle."

"Mm-hmm," I mumbled and still sounded unconvincing.

He studied me then his mouth curled before he muttered, "Nothin' to do but wait and let you experience it yourself."

Something *not* to look forward to. Chelle Whatever-her-name-was-now was *so* not happy Creed had found me.

Shit.

I decided not to make any noise at all since even my mumbles were lame.

Creed gave me a squeeze as he said quietly, "Kids sleep late, but told them we were going to Wet 'n' Wild tomorrow so they got wound up. That means tomorrow is a Disneyland day where they'll be up early, rarin' to go. We gotta hit the sack so we can get up earlier than them, get you back to the hotel then you can come back"

"Right," I whispered.

I started to move away, but his arms got tight again and stayed that way so I looked back up at him.

"This shit, hotel, us separated, you comin' in under the radar, out early; thanks for doin' that for my kids, baby," he said quietly, and I tipped my head, pressed deep and held on tight right back.

"Anything, Creed."

I meant it.

Creed knew it.

190

I knew this because his face changed. His head moved. His mouth took mine and he kissed me deep and sweet.

After he lifted his head he let me go, but took my hand and moved us to the bed where we both moved in then he tucked me close.

"Love you, Sylvie," he muttered into the top of my hair.

"Love you back, Creed," I muttered to the skin over his collarbone.

His arms gave me another squeeze, and luckily, shortly after, tucked close to Creed, I fell into a dreamless sleep.

Creed

Creed's eyes opened and he saw the dawning sun but felt Sylvie in his arms, in his bed, in his home.

He pulled in a deep breath, his chest expanding, pressing into his woman's soft skin, soft body and he let that cut through him, leaving beauty in its wake.

Taking long moments of quiet, alone in the weak light of dawn, holding his Sylvie, finally. His eyes moved to the alarm clock on his nightstand.

Then he shifted carefully, moving slightly away to stare down at her. Her thick, long hair a tangle on his pillow, her profile relaxed in sleep.

Creed watched her.

Since having her back, this was not the first time he'd done this. In fact, he did it every day.

Every single day.

Because lying beside a still asleep Sylvie, he had her back. His little, sweet, funny, loving Sylvie who had no idea how beautiful she was. His Sylvie who had hope and love written all over her face. There she was, asleep right beside him. Those sharp edges sheathed, she was all soft, all beauty, all the memory of his Sylvie.

She told him that the old Sylvie was gone. He didn't tell her she was wrong, and he'd never tell her. He had the new Sylvie, and in these moments before her eyes opened and the day started, he had the old one, too.

And down the hall, his kids slept in his house on a hill, far away from fucking Kentucky and the memories buried there.

Therefore, Creed had it all.

Everything.

He lifted a hand to cup her cheek then slid her hair away from her face. He watched her features shift, her eyes flutter. She moved to her back. He saw the green gemstone twinkle at her neck and he felt the beauty of that in his gut.

"Is it time to get up already?" she asked, her voice soft and husky with sleep.

Creed shifted his fingers through her hair, pulling it down her chest, then he curved his hand around her ribs under her breast as he nodded.

"Damn," she muttered, arching her back in a little stretch.

He glided his hand up between her breasts, up her chest to the chain at her neck where he stopped and twisted it around his forefinger.

"You did it again," he murmured and she blinked.

"Did what?" she asked.

"Wakin' up beside me, in my bed, in my house. You did it again." When her brows drew together he finished, "My Sylvie, the dreamweaver, makin' dreams come true."

Her face went soft. Hope and happiness flashed in her eyes, and there he had it again. In those moments he had her back. His Sylvie, both of them, right there in his bed.

Yes, he had it all.

Everything.

Or he would when he had her mouth.

So he went about taking it, dipping his head even as he tugged gently on the chain to pull her to him.

Sylvie lifted up and met him halfway and there it was.

Tucker Creed had everything.

Absolutely everything.

Fucking *finally*.

Sylvie

"Shit, I'm nervous," I whispered.

It was early. I was standing at the front door in Creed's arms and he'd just finished kissing me a kind of good-bye, the "kind of" part being that I was returning in less than two hours.

"Don't be," he whispered back.

"Kids like me," I kept whispering. "But what if they're, like, the only two kids I've ever met who think I'm a loser?"

Creed grinned and his arms gave me a squeeze. "They'll love you, Sylvie. Honest to God. Don't worry."

Being back in Creed's arms always felt good. It made me feel safe in a way I hadn't since I lost him.

It just wasn't working then.

"Creed—"

He suddenly let me go and his hands came up to cup either side of my head and his face, already close, came to a breath away.

"My kids are not dumb," he announced, and I stared into his eyes.

"I didn't say they were." You guessed it. I was *still* whispering.

"Baby, they've seen my tat."

I pulled in breath.

He kept talking.

"It was not lost on them I was fakin' it with their Mom, and not just because we got divorced. Kids sense that shit. Trust me. It was not lost on them that things didn't get a whole lot better for me when she and I were done, and it will not be lost on them that you got the name inked on my skin and I'm finally fuckin' happy. One day, when they're older, when they know you better, when they can deal with the part of the story we'll share with them, we'll share it with them. They'll get it and be happy for both of us. That's what love is, Sylvie. That's family. I didn't know it because I didn't grow up with it. You didn't either. But havin' my kids, I get it. The change might take some gettin' used to, and I'm not sayin' the road won't turn rocky along the way. I just know my kids love me and they'll see me happy, so they'll love you at the very least for makin' me happy."

Right, that made me feel better.

"Okay," I agreed softly.

Creed's eyes roamed my face then his hands slid down to either side of my neck before he said softly back, "Can't wait to give you that."

"Give me what?"

"A family."

My heart lurched and it didn't feel bad. Not even a little bit.

He kept speaking.

"Just you wait, baby. Didn't live free and easy. Didn't feel totally alive. Not without you. But I got my kids and I had somethin' to live for, work for, keep goin' for." His thumbs moved out and stroked my jaws before his voice went rough to say, "Now, I got it all."

Jeez, he was killing me.

"Shut up or you'll make me cry like a girl, and I never cry like a girl, except when I find out my Dad was more of an asshole than I already knew him to be and the man I loved since I was six was tortured at his hands. Furthermore, crying makes me cranky. I don't need to be made cranky three hours before meeting your kids. Get me?"

He grinned and muttered, "Got you."

"Good," I muttered back.

He leaned in, pulling my head down to kiss the hair at the top before he moved back.

"Go, baby."

"Right, Creed."

I got up on my toes to brush my mouth to his. He let me go. I let him go. He opened the door and I hitched the strap of my bag up on my shoulder before I headed out into the furnace.

God. It wasn't even eight and it already had to be a hundred degrees.

I looked back over my shoulder as I walked down his walk and the heat assaulted me.

Creed was watching me move and Creed was smiling.

Suddenly, I didn't feel the heat.

Instead, I lifted an arm to give him a finger flick before I jogged to the car, feeling my long hair swaying over the skin of my shoulders and back.

I got in my rental and drove away to take a shower and prepare to meet Creed's kids and get wet at a water park in extreme heat.

And as I drove away, Creed stood in his open door, letting out the air conditioning and he kept watching me.

All the while, still smiling.

Chapter 16
I Absolutely Do

A cool autumn day in Kentucky, seventeen years earlier. Creed is twenty-two, Sylvie is seventeen...

Creed tore his mouth from mine.

"Sylvie, baby," he murmured.

Losing his lips, I moved mine to his neck, and I didn't know why I did it, I just did, I touched the tip of my tongue to his skin.

Oh my.

He tasted *beautiful.*

"Sylvie!"

At his sharp, rough tone, I dropped my head back to the blanket Creed laid over the grass under the trees by the lake and looked up at his handsome face.

"What?" I whispered, and my whisper was breathy.

He stared down at me then I felt his hand cup the side of my face, the pad of his thumb swept my lips and he whispered back, "Give me a break, baby."

I took in a shuddering breath trying to get my heart to stop beating so hard.

I didn't want to give him a break. I wanted to keep kissing him. No, I wanted *him* to keep kissing *me.* I wanted him to kiss me forever.

Forever.

He was that good of a kisser, for one. For another, he was Creed, and he was finally all mine.

I had no idea my face made it clear I not only wanted his kisses, but I wanted more. I would find out, in a way, when his hand moved away, he dropped his head and shoved his face in my neck.

"Fuckin' hell, you're killin' me."

That didn't sound good.

"I... I..." I swallowed. "Am I doing something wrong?" I whispered.

His head shot up and his hand returned to cup my face as he shook his head. "No, beautiful. No, baby," he assured me gently. "Maybe we should just take a break from neckin' for a while."

This was not a suggestion I liked, but I finally got it.

I was making him hard.

Oh my God! I was making Tucker Creed hard!

Me!

Sylvie Bissenette!

Oh my God!

He liked kissing me, too. Not like I thought he liked it. Like... *really*. Maybe even as much as I liked kissing him.

Wow.

I liked that.

I tried not to grin, but it didn't work too well. I knew this when his eyes dropped to my mouth and they went funny in a way that made my belly feel funny and also made me bite my lip.

His gaze came back to mine and he muttered dryly, "I see my girl gets it."

"Um..." I muttered back, and he grinned.

"Yeah, she gets it," he kept muttering then his face got closer. "I dig that you like you can do that to me, but just so you know, it feels good, gettin' excited. But for a guy, it can go bad." He saw it coming, my question, so he lifted up his chin slightly before shaking his head. "Not gonna explain. Not now, baby. Later, maybe. Not now." He rolled to his back, pulling me with him so I was lying partly to his side, partly on him and he lifted a hand to pull my hair away from my face before suggesting, "Let's just talk for a while."

I preferred kissing, but I could do that too.

So I agreed, "Okay." Then I studied his face and fell into the Creed and me that was and would always be. "Is everything okay with your Mom?"

His hand left my hair. His torso lifted up and he got up on his elbows behind him even as I stayed close. Once in position, he rolled his head around on his neck like he was trying to stretch away tension there.

He did that a lot when I brought up his Mom.

She was living with him again. She'd moved out, moved in with a man, but they'd got in a fight and now she was back. This, unfortunately, happened a lot. She'd find the man who was the love of her life, date him for a few weeks, move out then move back in when it went sour. Sometimes her being away lasted a few days. Sometimes, if Creed was lucky, it lasted months.

This time, it had lasted months.

Now it was over.

Creed did not like his Mom coming home because he didn't like her much. He also didn't like it because that meant I couldn't come over at night, eat with him, watch TV, neck on his couch before he walked me through the woods to my car that I'd park on the old abandoned lane that went nowhere.

He further didn't like it because she hadn't changed. She drank too much, didn't mind making a mess, but did mind cleaning up after herself.

He also didn't like it because when she got back she could be nasty. She didn't get that there was only one Brand Creed. She didn't get, after years and years and years, that she needed to learn to live with his loss and move on. She just continued to feel the pain and take it out on everyone around her.

Last, she was in and out of work, currently out, and Creed worked at the local tire factory. He was union, he told me, so the pay wasn't bad (I didn't get this, totally, but I did believe him). But no one wanted to work hard, come home and watch their Momma drink their paycheck while she made a mess and gave him stick (I *did* get this, totally).

Creed told me his Dad actually didn't leave the house to his Mom when he died, and when Creed turned eighteen, he owned it. So he could tell her to leave, kick her out.

But Creed wasn't that way.

He was Brand Creed's son through and through. He didn't have it in him to be mean, not even to a Momma who never was any good to him or for him or, really, anybody.

"No, Sylvie, it's not okay," he answered.

I scrunched up my nose.

He grinned.

I stopped scrunching my nose and grinned back.

Then I pressed closer. "I wish I could do something," I said quietly, and I did. Really, really badly.

"You can't, baby," he said quietly back. "My lot in life."

"Not forever," I told him, and his eyes held mine before they drifted beyond me.

"Seems like it'll be."

197

"No way," I told him firmly, and his gaze came back so I went on. "When I turn eighteen, we're out of here. We're going to get in your truck and *go*. Drive until we hit a place we both like and then stop and build a life without your Mom. Without my Dad. We're going to buy a house and have babies and no one will know us. No one will know I'm Sylvia Bissenette, A Bissenette of *The* Bissenettes, and no one will know you have anything to do with Winona Creed. We'll just be Creed and Sylvie. Just you and just me."

Creed's head tipped to the side slightly and his eyes were soft, but lit with a bright light when he asked gently, "You want babies?"

"Two. A girl and a boy," I replied immediately.

"Got it planned," he muttered, his eyes still soft but bright, his lips curled up at the edges.

"Yep." I grinned.

"Names?"

"Kara, the girl. Brand, the boy."

His lip curl faded and the soft went out of his eyes, but the bright went brighter.

"Brand?" he whispered.

"For your Daddy," I whispered back.

He stared at me. That bright in his eyes shining through me, shining deep and feeling sweet, like it wasn't autumn and there wasn't a nip in the air but it was summer and the sun was shining, warming me through.

"Make it tough," he muttered.

"What?" I asked.

"You make it tough not to kiss you," he explained, and my belly curled.

I liked that, too.

I bit my lip.

Creed grinned at me and teased, "So, the hope is, you're namin' your boy Brand, you intend for me to be the Daddy."

That was such a stupid question, I released my lip, narrowed my eyes at him and slapped his arm.

He burst out laughing, lifted up off his elbows and his arms curled around me. He fell back twisting so he was now lying mostly on my side.

I liked lying on him.

I liked this a whole lot better.

Therefore, I lost my exasperation. I lifted a hand and slid the hair away that had fallen over his forehead. The minute I dropped my hand, the hair fell right back and I couldn't help but smile.

"You know what love is?"

Creed asked that and my eyes shot from the hair on his forehead to his eyes.

"I..." I swallowed again. Then, holding his eyes, I whispered, "Yes. I do. I know what love is, Creed."

I felt his big hand curl warm on the side of my face before I felt the pad of his thumb sweep across my lips again. He watched it move as he replied, "I do too, baby." His eyes came to mine. "I absolutely do."

I sighed.

Creed bent his head to touch his mouth to mine before, unfortunately, he pulled away.

But when he did, my heart leaped when he whispered, "Kara and Brand. I like that."

I felt my eyes get soft before I whispered back, "Good."

Chapter 17
It Always Would Be

Present day...

I was one of those people who, when I was wrong, I'd admit I was wrong.

Right then, floating on an inner tube on the lazy river at Wet 'n' Wild in Phoenix, Arizona after having a squirt gun fight with Creed, Brand and Kara, which was after we went down copious water slides (including one the kids called "the toilet bowl", which had this kickass swirly thing going on), which was after we had lunch, which was after we horsed around in the wave pool... I was *loving* Phoenix.

I was getting a tan.

I had my man back.

And he was right, he had great kids.

But, meeting Kara and Brand, the surprises kept coming.

First was the fact that I expected them to look exactly like Creed. In my mind, badass genes would beat out pretty much everything.

They didn't look exactly like Creed. Apparently, badass genes knew enough to bow to traits that would create a superior being.

In other words, his kids were gorgeous.

Kara had thick, gleaming, long, straight brunette hair and a twelve year old girl's slim, tall, almost boyish body. She had perfect, dark arched brows and the features of her face, which were still girlish but would clearly mature into great beauty, bore absolutely no resemblance to Creed's. They might be Chelle's, they might just be Kara's. From Brand's looks, I couldn't tell.

Brand also had thick dark hair, and although ten years old, he was tall and had his father's exact build. His features didn't resemble his father or his sister so they, too, were either from his mother or all Brand.

Luckily for them, both kids inherited Creed's unusual bright blue eyes, and with their dark hair and tanned skin (which said they weren't adverse to the heat like I was), their eyes were startlingly beautiful. Even more so than Creed's which, until I saw them, I would have said was impossible.

Another surprise was Creed's brand of parenting.

Neither of us grew up with good role models, and when Creed wanted to spring me on his children with very little warning, I thought he was the cool, laidback Dad. Maybe, I had to admit, *too* cool and laidback.

He was not.

I'd forgotten that Creed's Dad died when Creed was ten, so there was plenty of time for the first Brand Creed to make his mark on his son. Although I'd never met Creed's Dad, it was clear to see his father had done just that.

Creed wasn't exactly strict, but he definitely wasn't Weekend Daddy who spoiled his kids when he had them and let shit slide. I noted this when he didn't give in when Kara strode into the park and immediately wanted to go shopping in the gift shop. He also didn't give in when Brand wanted to order enough food at lunch to feed an Army. Creed wasn't a jerk about it. His refusals were quiet and gentle. They were also firm and his kids minded him immediately, clearly because they were the norm.

Further, they packed their own bags and carried them to the car, and they did this without Creed telling them to. They were polite, and when Kara forgot to say thank you to the waitress for bringing our drinks, Creed gave her a subdued but meaningful Dad Look, which prompted a quick remedy to her lapse in courtesy. And when a squabble seemed to be beginning to break out in the backseat on our way to the park, all he had to say was a quiet, low, "Stop... now," and the burgeoning squabble ended immediately. The mood in the backseat didn't turn jovial, but they stopped bickering.

Creed, whose language was as foul as mine, also didn't cuss around his kids. Also, although he held my hand on more than one occasion, obviously (and thankfully) his message was plain that public displays of affection were to be kept at an appropriate minimum.

I didn't expect Creed to be a bad Dad. He made it clear he loved his children and they were a huge, important part of his life, and any Dad who felt that way couldn't be all bad.

I also didn't expect him to be a *Dad,* showing love and care at the same time guiding with a firm hand.

I had to say, I liked it.

But truthfully, I thought Creed was thinking positively, even hopefully (but not rationally) about what he expected their reaction would be to me.

I was wrong about this, too.

From the instant I met him at Creed's house, Brand was exactly as Creed described him. Open and friendly but also talkative. *Very* talkative. The kid had a lot to say, but fortunately it was interesting, and a lot of the time damned funny.

Kara was the same, except from the very little I knew of her, not rabid about it. It seemed genuine, albeit watchful.

And it was clear they both adored their Dad, though this was not a surprise.

The only thing that made me pause was Kara's adoration of her father *was* what could be described as rabid. It shone from her eyes, was reflected in her features. She loved him and she clearly missed him being away, and not away as in a job in Denver, but away as in not seeing him every day. She was not a spoiled Daddy's Little Princess, but there was something there that was off, just not right, and part of that was that it seemed Creed didn't see it. Or perhaps he was acting normal in the hopes that would help her work through it.

Regardless, I couldn't ask about it, not with her around. And when Creed was around, Kara was. Whereas Brand was independent, did his own thing, quickly found other kids his age he could befriend and go off and do things with, Kara stuck to her Dad like glue.

Thus me being in the lazy river, giving Kara time with Creed without me being there.

I tipped my shade-covered eyes up to the sun and figured it was heading to late afternoon. I didn't know exactly, but I reckoned I'd been on the lazy river for a good long while. During lunch, Creed had pulled a fast one, suggesting he make his dandan noodles for the four of us for dinner when we got home. I was supposed to go to the hotel after the water park, but Creed made his "suggestion" in such a way I couldn't protest. It was sly at the same time it was sweet since he didn't want me to leave him and he wanted me to spend more time with his kids.

That said, I figured a day at Wet 'n' Wild with me around was enough for one weekend.

Creed obviously disagreed.

Clearly, Creed's dandan noodles were a treat and the kids would put up with anything, even their dad's "new" girlfriend eating noodles with them, seeing as they agreed enthusiastically. I didn't know what dandan noodles entailed, but I did know it entailed a trip to the grocery store. So I also figured my time was up in the lazy river and I should haul my ass out and find Creed and his kids.

As I floated around a bend, I'd discover I wouldn't have to find him since he was standing where you entered and exited the gently flowing water. His arms were crossed on his chest. His hair was wet but curling around his neck as it dried. And his blue boardshorts with white stitching and blue flip-flops were the only things hiding his beautiful, tall, broad-shouldered, sculpted, tanned, badass body.

Incidentally, they were doing a poor job of it since the waistband of the shorts fit snug and low along his flat, defined abs, and waist and his cut hipbones leading into the shorts would make pretty much anyone who had a vagina wonder what they led to. Luckily, it was only me and my vagina who would know the details.

Taking in all that was him, I felt shivers in four places that were so strong, they defied even the Phoenix heat.

His shaded eyes caught mine. His face behind his sunglasses was impassive and I watched as his hand came up, his finger pointing at me then it turned and he crooked it. Once.

More shivers and my nipples got hard.

I stared at him as I drifted toward him thinking two things.

First, no man since Richard Scott would ever get away with crooking his finger at me, and Richard only got away with it because he was a dick who beat me repeatedly. Since him, I'd break a crooked finger before I obeyed such a bossy, arrogant, wordless command.

Not Creed. Oh no. It made me near desperate to jump him.

The second thing was, top to toe, all of him, and the all there was of him, that every female from sixteen to sixty in the vicinity was staring at and wanted for their own, was all mine.

Not only that, it always was and always would be.

At that, I didn't feel a shiver. I felt a warmth that wasn't coming from the Phoenix sun, but my own personal one, directed straight at me from behind Creed's shades.

I was closing in, preparing to exit my inner tube, when Kara in her cute girl's bikini sidled up to her Dad's side. The warmth I felt increased when Creed's shades unlocked from mine, he looked down at his girl, his mouth curved into a gentle smile and his arm naturally slid around her shoulders.

Yeah, he was a good Dad. He loved his girl. He loved his kids.

I got out of the water. His shades came back to me and my lungs hollowed out when I saw the gentle grin still playing at his mouth. His rugged, scarred face was relaxed and contentment was stamped on his features.

He also loved me.

And he was happy.

Tucker Creed hadn't had a day like today, not ever, not in his life, not even way back when, when it was just him and me.

And this made him happy.

So dandan noodles it was, and I wasn't even going to give him any stick for pulling a fast one.

I moved to him and Kara, smiling back, trying to ignore the wet but still hot pool deck burning the bottoms of my feet, wondering where I left my flip-flops as I came to a halt in front of them.

His deep, smooth voice with its hint of rough came right at me.

"Time to go home."

Home.

I'd never had that. Not ever, not in my life, not even way back when, when it was just Creed and me.

My smile got bigger.

"And they were all, 'It's too hot,' and I was all, 'Wusses, it's *not* too hot. There's a breeze. This is a walk in the park to me. I could run in this heat. I could *sleep* in this heat.'"

Brand and I were sitting at Creed's island with Brand talking a mile a minute, while Kara and Creed were making what they told me was called a "pizzookie". The pizzookie, as described, was a phenomenon whose existence I was shocked I'd not only never heard of before, but also had never partaken of, copiously. Apparently, you took store bought cookie dough, sprayed a cake tin, scrunched a bunch of dough in the bottom, baked it until it was just cooked but mostly gooey, plopped a shitload of ice cream on top and ate it out of the pan. If you were feeling saucy, Kara further explained, you could do this with brownie dough.

See?

A phenomenon. Delicious *and* genius. If it was as good as it sounded, I could make and consume one every night.

I couldn't wait.

Dandan noodles were a hit. Eating them, I found that I'd had them before at restaurants, but I would never consider making them at home. Then again, Creed had always been good in the kitchen. He'd learned to cook out of necessity because his Mom didn't and he'd always had a knack for it.

I'd learned to cook at the crack of Richard's whip, and thus I avoided it. I could cook and do it well. I just hated doing it because time spent in the kitchen reminded me of Richard. And that was never good.

Grocery shopping with the Creeds before the noodles was a stitch. This was partly because Brand was riding a water park high and sweeping us along with his wave, being a total goof and cracking jokes that were so bad, they were hysterical.

But it was Creed who had us doubled over in an aisle when he inexplicably started roaring with laughter so uncontrolled he couldn't even speak. He just pointed at a display of DVDs in the center of the aisle that had a label that said "Family Friendly Movies", but were a variety of documentaries on natural disasters and serial killers. Obviously, we all saw the humor and joined in. It took us ten minutes to pull our shit together and move on, considering the fact both Brand and Kara kept making suggestions about family friendly movies that should be added, such as an in-depth perusal into the Third Reich (Kara's idea, and she even used the words "in-depth perusal") and the Spanish Inquisition (Brand's idea).

When we got back to the house, I found it was cool being in Creed's house with his kids. Even being there only weekends, they were comfortable and there was a kickass family vibe that not only was awesome to see Creed had, but was awesome to feel.

I wasn't a part of it. It was way too early. But both kids included me, and it felt more than a little nice.

Once we dumped our stuff, got in showers and changed, the division of labor fell naturally. Kara helped her Dad in the kitchen in a way so practiced I knew it was the norm while Brand entertained me.

We'd had the noodles and were onto dessert, and Brand was regaling me with stories of how his cousins (Chelle had a brother and a sister, both with kids), who came from Maine for vacation that summer, couldn't get on in the heat. Something Brand thought made them wusses, and something, as a native Phoenician, he was proud he could do, no sweat (literally).

"Son, they're not wusses," Creed broke in as Kara pulled the pizzookie out of the oven, and Creed tossed a hot pad across the kitchen to land on the island in front of Brand and me. "They're just not used to it," he finished.

"Yeah, but they complained about it, like... *a lot.* Like... *all the time.* That says *wuss,*" Brand disagreed.

"Can't argue with that," Creed muttered, and I silently concurred.

Kara put the pizzookie on the hot pad. Creed opened the freezer to get out the ice cream and I stared at the pizzookie, mentally making it my first priority to hit King Soopers and buy cookie dough and ice cream when I got home.

"Totally," Kara muttered after her father, now reaching for spoons. "It's too hot," she fake whined. "I feel the heat coming through my shoes." She looked at me as she handed me a spoon and went on, "We don't complain the ocean's too salty when we go visit them."

Brand snorted before he said, "The ocean's too salty. I am *so totally* using that when we go back to Maine."

"And the air's too heavy," Kara added.

"And the breeze is too breezy," Brand put in on a boy mini-giggle.

"How about the Creeds don't bellyache or even pretend to be wusses, but suck it up like true Creeds?" Creed suggested, turning away from the fridge.

Kara grinned at her brother, handed him a spoon, and all got quiet as Creed arrived with the ice cream. He opened it up, scooped it out and piled it on.

I watched him do this with avid fascination.

Holy shit.

Seriously.

I was full of noodles and I still was considering taking all three of them out so I could have that shit all to myself.

Five minutes later, I would lament I didn't make this move. This was because, with what was clearly abundant practice, the three Creeds fell on that pizzookie like chocolate chip cookie dough was being outlawed the next day. It was every man and his spoon for himself. With difficulty, spoons clinking against spoons, I got a load on mine and got it in my mouth, but before I got it back to the pan, swear to God, more than half the pizzookie was gone.

Apparently, Creed gently drilling manners into his children did not include allowing the guest to have a head start on the pizzookie, or even a clear go (or two).

As I was trying quickly to form a strategy to get my spoon in there, I heard Creed order with mouth full, "Don't be shy, baby."

I made the mistake of looking at him to see him grinning, mouth still full, then he swallowed and honed back in on the pan. By the time my eyes got back there, I estimated there were approximately five bites left.

"Can't be shy when pizzookie is on the line." Brand murmured his advice then shoved pizzookie in his mouth. Kara and Creed's spoons scooped out more and I went in, got a load and hoisted it to my mouth.

By the time I went back, mouth barely having taken its first chew, it was all gone.

I'd had two bites and the entire ten inch cake pan was full when we started.

I looked around the island at the chewing, grinning Creeds, the young male version having melted chocolate and cookie crumbs on his lips.

Okay, right.

I might only have had two bites, but next time, I'd do better. Definitely.

And I liked this pizzookie crazy family.

Seriously.

"What'd I say?"

This was Creed, on his back in his bed, me straddling him. His hands on my bare ass, his cock still inside me, and we'd just spent several minutes, hands groping, faces nuzzling, post-orgasm.

I stopped licking his neck and lifted my head to look down at him.

After pizzookie and some Diamondbacks baseball, I'd left under enthusiastic, heartwarmingly authentic, "See you later, Sylvies," from Kara and Brand. Then, three hours later, I came back to have sex and sleep with Creed.

Now he was asking me a question and I didn't know what he was talking about.

"What?" I asked.

His hands slid from my ass, up my back, out over my ribs then up, up, up to frame my face. "The kids. They like you."

"Not enough to give me a clear go at the pizzookie."

Creed grinned.

I kept talking but quieter.

"Kids tend to like thirty-four year old women who go all out in a squirt gun fight and don't mind looking stupid and accidentally running into the pelican that shoots water out of its mouth."

One of his hands moved down to curl around my neck. The other one slid into my hair at the side, through it and down the back where his arm ended curling around me as he replied, "Yeah, they do. Being a big goof goes down good with kids, but it was more than that, baby. They just like you."

I hoped his latter words were true, but I was stuck on his earlier words.

"I'm not a big goof. I'm a badass, even with a squirt gun. I totally kicked both their asses."

"Baby, you ran into that pelican and they nailed you," he reminded me.

"Sure, but I recovered and rallied *huge*."

His grin came back. "Yeah, and that's when *I* nailed you."

My eyes narrowed, "Creed, hot stuff, *you* didn't nail me until ten minutes ago."

His grin got bigger. "I nailed you then, too."

I disagreed. "It was totally a tie in the squirt gun fight."

He disagreed with me disagreeing. "I kicked your ass. You were drenched."

"You did not, the pelican kicked my ass," I shot back.

His body started shaking under mine as he asked, "Seriously? You're okay with the fake pelican squirting water out of its mouth kicking your ass and you're not okay with me doing it?"

Absolutely.

Seeing as this could go on all night, I decided to put a stop to it by announcing, "Paintball tiebreaker when we get back to Denver."

"Beautiful. I don't play at business unless I got swim trunks on and my kids with me."

The breath went out of me at his calling me "beautiful". Something he hadn't done in sixteen years. Something I loved back then. Something I missed. Something I loved having back so much, it hurt.

"Sylvie?" he called.

Kristen Ashley

I focused through the exquisite pain and saw the amusement had faded from his face and his eyes were intent on me.

I didn't share.

I just whispered, "Then, baby, you're missing out. Business is business and fun is fun, and paintball is a freaking *blast*."

He ignored me and asked, "Where were you?"

I knew what he was asking but I didn't answer. Instead, I told him, "I'm right here, with you."

"Five seconds ago, you were somewhere else."

"Creed—"

His hand at my neck slid back into my hair and his arm around me gave me a squeeze while he prompted gently, "Sylvie, asked you a question."

I pressed my lips together then slid my hands up his chest. One stopped at his neck, the other one I wrapped around his jaw and watched as my thumb traced the edge of his lower lip.

When my thumb was retracing its path, I looked into his eyes and whispered, "I missed you calling me 'beautiful'."

"I missed havin' you close so I could call you that," he whispered back.

I shifted off his cock but moved down his body so I could lay my cheek on his chest, and both his arms went around me.

"It'll never stop hitting us," I said softly.

"Don't 'spect so," Creed said softly back.

"Sometimes it doesn't feel like winning when that sucker punch comes and we're reminded of how much we lost," I told him, then felt, weirdly, his body shaking under mine like he was laughing.

I lifted up and looked down at him.

Yes, laughing.

"This is funny?" I asked quietly.

His hands came back to frame my face and he replied just as quietly through his waning laughter, "Baby, I hauled you into my house last night, kissed you at the door. I made love to you in my bed. I woke up to you. I spent the day with you and my kids. I watched you go down over the pizzookie. You barely got your spoon in there. And, ten minutes ago, I watched you ride my cock hard and make yourself come before you made me do the same. No way, after what they took from us, no way am I gonna let them make me feel that isn't anything but what it is. Us winning."

210

Shit, he was right.

He also wasn't done.

"Wish I was a better man," he said quietly. "Dad'd be pissed at me, he knew I was even thinkin' this, but, I get the chance, I'll spit on your father's grave, what he did to you, what he did to me. But, if I don't get that chance," his hands at my face pressed in and his voice dipped low, the smooth sliding clean out of it, his expression shifting to intense, "I'll take this. I'll take this every day, and every day I'll know in the end I beat that bastard. He might not have been alive to see it, but I beat his goddamned, motherfucking ass."

Seriously, he was hot when he was being all vengeful badass.

Thinking that, it hit me.

I loved the Creed that was, and he was still in there, with his kids, with me.

But without what happened to us, this Creed would never have been.

And I loved this Creed in a way that maybe time had dulled the feeling I had before, even though it didn't feel that way. Because I loved the man under me in a way that wasn't just meant to be. It wasn't a way we were born to be. It was in a way that *needed* to be.

With sudden clarity it hit me that I was always a bit of this Sylvie. I liked clothes and I gossiped with my girls and I put on makeup, even now. But I was not the daughter my father wanted, who adored ballet and wore ribbons in her hair and didn't beg him to let me go fishing with him every time he went out with his buddies.

So maybe the Sylvie-due-to-circumstances I became was the Sylvie I was supposed to be.

And Creed had always had badass in him. He was his father's son. We even talked about him joining the military when we got wherever we were going to go, settled in and he was okay with the possibility of leaving me to go on assignment.

So maybe due to circumstances, he became the Creed he was supposed to be.

And because the universe wasn't right without us together, we became that way then we came back together.

On this thought, I pressed closer and asked, "Do you think that shit had to happen so I could be who I am with who you came to be?"

Both his hands slid into my hair and fisted gently at the back of it, none of the intensity shifting out of his face when he replied, "Fuck… *no. My* Sylvie, who had my back and stood by my side as best she could from the age of six to the age of eighteen, did not deserve years of torture and living with the knowledge a man is dead at her hand, and I didn't deserve the shit dished out to me, either. What I think is, it's life. Life can be shit. We had our shit. We'll have more of it. Though, God willing, not that fuckin' bad, and we made our way back together because together is the way we're born to be. But," his hands in my hair pulled me closer and his voice dipped lower, "you wanna think it was supposed to happen that way. That makes you feel better. Think it. I just don't agree."

"The me that I am right now though, Creed, feels like the Sylvie I was meant to be," I pointed out.

"Yeah, you are," he agreed. "Comfortable in your skin. Good at what you do. You enjoy it. You like the way you live. I can see that. But you could have become this Sylvie without that shit buried in your soul," he replied and I tipped my head to the side.

"Would you be down with that?"

He lifted his head an inch from the pillow so our faces were mega close and he whispered, "Then and now, beautiful, I'll take you any way you come to me." His hands in my hair shook my head gently. "*Any* way. I love this Sylvie. I loved that Sylvie. I just love *you,* baby."

And I just loved him.

Any way he came to me.

To share this, I shoved my face in his neck.

Creed got the message and I knew this when his arms circled me and he gave me a mighty squeeze.

He allowed seconds to tick by before he murmured, "Gotta let you go, need to deal with this condom."

"Right," I murmured back and shifted off him.

He kissed my shoulder before he exited the bed. I had pulled on my panties and camisole by the time he got back.

Creed turned off the lone light we had on and pulled me into him, tucking me close, and I took us full circle.

"I'm glad your kids like me, Creed."

"What'd I say?" he asked in reply.

I pressed in closer, grinning at his shadowed skin.

Creed's arms around me tightened then loosened and I relaxed into him. Finally, I gave it to him.

"Just so you know, you haven't changed much, but I'd take you any way you came to me, too," I whispered. "I loved you then. I love you now. I just love you, Creed."

I heard him draw a breath as I felt his chest expand with it.

Then he released it and I felt his lips brush the top of my hair.

"Good to know," he muttered there.

I smiled at his shadowed skin again before I took a deep breath. And in my man's arms, after a day of fun and relaxation, a night of good food and then great fucking, I slipped straight into sleep.

Daddy showed him the picture. Me, wearing heels, a dress Creed had never seen, my hair done up in a way I never did it, looking older, like the days he'd spent there were years. I had Dixon's arm around my waist, my hand lay on his chest and my head was resting on his shoulder.

"I told you," Daddy whispered, his voice ugly in his glee. "Right from your arms to Jason's. Right to Jason."

Creed tried to focus through the hunger, the pain, the discomfort, the smell. He couldn't see my face. He could barely see my profile.

But he knew I'd never go to Dixon.

Never.

Daddy went on, "He'll make her happy. I promise you. I promise you, Tucker. He'll make her happy. I'll see to it. She'll be happy in a way you never could make her be."

Creed closed his eyes.

Daddy lost patience, his fingers shoving in Creed's hair, yanking his head back and the pain spiked along the slice in his scalp. *"Look at it!"*

He opened his eyes and there I was.

His Sylvie.

Even in another man's arms, he drank me in.

"That's where she's meant to be," Daddy told him.

Creed knew Daddy was wrong.

That wasn't where I was meant to be.

Because we were meant to be.

"He'll make her happy," Daddy continued. "I promise you that. You promise to vanish from her life, I promise, I *vow*, Sylvie will be happy."

Creed's eyes moved from the photo to Daddy and he whispered, his voice hoarse and weak, "He'll never make her happy."

Daddy yanked again on his hair, arching his neck back. More pain, this excruciating, tearing through his entire scalp, down his neck and spine.

But Creed didn't even groan.

All he said was, "Never."

I shot up to sitting, the dream still having a hold on me, but I didn't get the chance to dart out of bed and do anything crazy.

This was because Creed had me on my back with him on me, his hands moving soothingly over my skin and his lips whispering, "Just a dream. Just a dream, baby."

I wrapped my arms around him and held on tight through the shakes that trembled through me.

He rolled us to our sides and silently held me through the shakes, one hand drifting up and down my back, one hand sifting through my hair until the shakes left me.

Only then did he speak.

"This shit has got to stop."

I tipped my head back and whispered, "I'll get through it, Creed."

I saw his darkened chin dip down and he replied, "Yeah. You will. By talkin' to somebody. I don't care who it is as long as it's a professional."

I felt my body get tight. "I'm not gonna go see somebody."

"Yeah you are."

I pulled up so we were face to face. "I'll be fine," I told him. "I'll get through it."

He disagreed. "Not on your own, you won't."

"Creed, it's just bad dreams."

"Sylvie, you got the beginnings of PTSD."

It was then I felt my body go still.

Then I returned firmly, "I do not. It's not a big deal. It's just dreams."

"It's not just dreams, baby."

"It is. That shit didn't happen *to me*," I reminded him. "It happened *to you*."

"You're right. The shit you're dreamin' about, it happened to me. What that shit led to, what's buried and what's fuckin' with your head, even if it isn't comin' out, is what happened to you after that happened to me. You're dealin' with a new load of fucked up shit on top of the old load you haven't sorted through, and your head is focusing on what you *didn't* experience in order to avoid what you *did*."

Oh God, now he was making sense.

"That's whacked," I scoffed to cover the fact he was freaking me out, and Creed rolled into me and on me.

"It fuckin' isn't," he growled. "Trust me, that shit happened to me so I fuckin' know. Years after that, Sylvie, *years*, that shit did a number on me. You think I didn't have nightmares? You think I didn't wake up in a cold sweat time and time a-fuckin'-gain? You think, to this day, I don't always carry water with me in my fuckin' car? I hear the sound of chains, my gut gets tight. To. This. *Day*. You were sold to an animal, an owned human being forced to do what he wanted you to do in ways *no* woman should have to perform and ended up killin' him with a knife. You don't do that shit and move to Denver and everything is cool. You process it. If you're smart, you find the tools to deal with it because it's always fuckin' there. You just gotta learn to control it before it controls you."

I hated that he went through that, all of it, but also this new nuance he shared with me.

And I hated it when he made sense.

But I wasn't ready to give in. "I can't talk about this now. I need sleep then I need to get back to the hotel."

"Yeah, you need to do both of those things, but you can do them after you agree to see somebody."

"Creed—"

"Sylvie."

I fell silent.

He did, too.

We stared at each other in the dark.

God! I wished I was more patient.

"Fine," I snapped.

I felt his body relax, which sucked because I hadn't noticed how tense he was. His tenseness communicated eloquently that my dreams were bothering him, maybe even more than they bothered me, and that didn't suck. That sucked *huge*.

"Good," he muttered.

Whatever.

"Will you get off me so I can sleep?" I requested.

"Sure," he agreed, his voice lighter, the smooth back in it. He tipped his head and touched his mouth to mine before he moved off me.

I was tucked close before I made my effort to save face after giving in.

"You know, you're a pain in the ass."

"Yeah, I know," he informed me. "My kids tell me that shit all the time, though they use different words. And they say it when I make decisions based on the fact that I love them and I want them to live the best life they can, even if that row is hard to hoe. Don't give a shit when they gripe. Won't give a shit when you do either."

Again.

Whatever.

"You can stop talking now," I invited.

"Wasn't me who broke the silence by tellin' you that you're a pain in my ass."

I decided to take his anorexically-veiled meaning and try silence.

Creed wasn't done.

"Though, just sayin', you're also a pain in my ass."

"You're still talking," I pointed out.

He stopped talking, but his body started moving and I knew he was silently chuckling.

A-freaking-gain.

Whatever!

I was too annoyed to notice that even after the dream, Creed had led me so far from its residue, I fell right to sleep.

"Chelle picks them up at three. Come to the house at three thirty so we can head to the airport."

We were standing at Creed's front door and he was giving me directions I already had, something I was realizing I'd have to learn to live with because, apparently, badasses were bossy even when they didn't need to be.

And repetitive.

"Right," I muttered.

"You get lost, don't like Cave Creek, call me. You can hit Cooper'stown for lunch then head back out here."

Creed had given me some ideas of what to check out during my time alone in Phoenix and I'd picked two top contenders. One was Cave Creek, which was a town just out of the city, and with its desert location, history and copious bars and restaurants, it sounded like the place for me. The other choice was Alice Cooper's restaurant, Cooper'stown, which was downtown and sounded like it had great food with seriously cool swag.

"I won't get lost," I told him, but this was a lie. I probably would. I got lost all the time, even with sat-nav because I routinely made the decision to distrust sat-nav and went my own way and got lost, which was why I got sat-nav to begin with. It didn't make sense, but then again, a lot of things about me didn't make sense. I'd learned to roll with it.

Creed stared at me a beat then repeated, "Take the one-oh-one to Cave Creek Road, baby. It's not hard. If you make it hard and get lost, call me."

I stared at him but I did it with narrowed eyes and repeated, "I won't get lost."

"You will."

"It's easy to get there, Creed."

"You forget, I followed your ass, frequently, for a month. My count, while I was followin' you, you got lost five times. Take the one-oh-one to Cave Creek Road, you get lost, call me. You with me?"

Annoying!

"Just asking, we established your kids like me, will they stop liking me if I wake them up on a Sunday morning by kicking your ass in the dining room?"

He grinned. "No, probably not seeing as you got absolutely no prayer in hell at kickin' my ass and they'll find it amusing to watch you try."

I cocked my head to the side. "That a challenge?"

His grin got bigger. "Yep."

"I accept."

His grin changed and I felt the change spasm through me as he dipped his head close to mine and whispered, "I take you, I fuck your ass after I make it so you beg me to do it. You take me, you get to tie me to the bed and do whatever you want to me."

Holy shit!

I was *so totally* winning this. All that was Creed at my mercy?

Yeah. So. Totally. *Winning*. This.

"You're on," I whispered back.

"Don't tire yourself out, baby. We play out the challenge tonight."

Oh yeah.

I smiled slow. "I'll be ready."

His face dipped closer. "Yeah you will. After I pin you, I'll make sure of it, beautiful."

Another spasm shot through me before I asked, "You gonna make me have a spontaneous orgasm at the front door or are you gonna let me go get lost in Phoenix?"

The sexy swept clean free of his face. His hands came up to frame mine and his face stayed close when he answered quietly, "I'll never let you go, but I'll let you leave... for now."

Seriously, he had to quit saying shit like that. He was killing me.

"FYI, babe, I'm not a woman prone to liking fervent avowals of adoration," I told him in an effort to get him to stop making me feel squishy happy like a big girl.

His hands framing my face pulled me closer. "Bullshit, Sylvie. I say that shit, light hits your eyes. You love that shit, you feed off it and I'm gonna give it to you until you're addicted to it and can't live without it." His thumbs swept my cheekbones and his voice went velvet rough. "But don't worry. I swear, I won't make you have to."

He was wrong.

Not about my bullshit. He was totally right about that.

He was wrong about having to give it to me until I was addicted to it.

I already was.

"Let me go, hot stuff," I whispered, lifting my hands to curl my fingers around his wrists. "It's getting late."

Frustration flashed briefly in his eyes before he nodded and pulled me closer while lifting up his head so I felt his lips on my forehead. Then he tipped my head back and I felt his lips touch mine. Finally, he let me go and stepped away but grabbed my hand while his other opened the door, and he walked me out to his front step.

He squeezed my hand and I looked up at him.

"Later, Sylvie."

"Later, babe."

I got up on tiptoe. He bent for me and I touched my mouth to his.

When I pulled back, his eyes were looking deep into mine and I could see the light in them, happiness and hope in his rugged, scarred features, the feeling I felt in my soul reflected in his face, a look he just told me I gave back.

Yeah, I was addicted.

Totally.

And so was Creed.

Then again, that was always the way.

And, hope to God, it always would be.

Chapter 18
My Whole World

A cold winter evening in Kentucky, seventeen years earlier. Creed is twenty-two, Sylvie is seventeen...

Once I heard him get her down, I stole out of Creed's bedroom, down the hall and cautiously looked around the corner into the empty living room. I didn't enter it until I saw Creed walk in, and at the look on his face, I took a deep breath and moved into the room.

His angry eyes came to me.

I bit my lip, let it go and asked, "How is she?"

"Drunk and fuckin' passed out. The usual. How do you think she'd fuckin' be?"

I bit my lip again and took a deep breath before I moved to him.

Our evening had been interrupted by a call from the Sheriff telling Creed to come and get his Momma. She was smashed, as usual, making a ruckus, as usual, and before the Sheriff was forced to arrest her, Creed had to do something about it. So he hauled himself out to his truck and did something about it.

As usual.

This happened at least once a week.

Luckily, my father was working a lot, out of town on business. The step-monster mostly didn't know I existed and Winona usually started drinking early so I could be there often and stay late for Creed.

I was walking toward him when Creed, his eyes still angry, his tall body still tense, stated, "Saw Dixon."

I didn't know what this meant, I only knew the way he said it didn't mean good things, so I stopped.

"Jason?" I asked.

With his eyes on me like that I felt stupid, and also like I sounded stupid.

"Yeah, *Jason*," he spit out Jason's name. "Not old enough to drink there, but anywhere in the county they'll serve a Dixon just like they'd serve a Bissenette."

Oh boy.

Kristen Ashley

Not this again.

We were making plans. When I turned eighteen, we were going to leave. That day, my birthday. Gone.

But Creed had problems with what I would give up when we were gone. He was putting away money, saving it as best he could on his salary while having to take care of his Mom. Even so, he knew and I knew that what we would have when we started out wouldn't be what I had now.

I didn't care, not even a little bit. I just wanted a dog as soon as we could afford to have one. The rest, just having Creed, I knew I would have all I would need.

Creed didn't believe me. He was sure I'd miss my car, my pool, the horses, the allowance Daddy gave me. He kept telling me it wouldn't be months, it would be years before he could give anything like that to me. He promised... no, *vowed* I'd have it back one day, but it would take a while before he could give it to me.

He felt it would be a devastating loss for me. I knew he did because he talked about it all the time. He wanted to make sure I was sure. He wanted to make sure I wouldn't think, one day, I'd made a mistake.

But there was more.

Since his Dad died, he'd lived a long time being Winona's son. It was crazy, but he didn't think he was good enough for me, and me giving up all I had would make me realize it, too.

Nothing I said made him understand that was totally crazy. So I had decided just to show him. He'd get it eventually.

I hoped.

"Creed—"

Creed cut me off, "Doesn't know you're mine. No one knows you're mine. Was closin' in on hammered, braggin' about doin' you. Braggin' about a Dixon finally nailin' a Bissenette. Braggin' a lot and doin' it *loud*."

I felt my neck get tight and my shoulders straighten as I asked quietly, "Are you joking?"

"Do I look like I'm jokin'?"

No, he absolutely did not.

"Why would he do that?" I asked.

"Don't know. Maybe because he's a dick. Or maybe because he nailed you," Creed answered.

222

At that, my neck got so tight, I felt the muscles would snap at the same time I felt my stomach tie itself in a knot.

"Now, please, tell me you're joking," I whispered my plea.

He didn't answer my plea. He asked crudely, "He do you, Sylvie?"

I shook my head and was still whispering when I replied, "I'm going to pretend you didn't ask that."

"Don't, beautiful, not until you answer me."

I kept shaking my head, the hurt beginning to dig deep. "Don't call me that when you're angry."

"Don't avoid the question and fuckin' answer me," he retorted.

I stared at Creed and he stared right back.

When I felt the tears prick my eyes, I turned to go back to his room to get my coat and purse, and I did this muttering, "I'm leaving."

I didn't make it. In the hall, Creed caught my arm and pulled me around to face him.

"Why are you avoiding the question, Sylvie?" he asked low, his voice angry.

I tried to twist my arm away but his fingers tightened. So I stopped trying, leaned in and asked back, "Why are you asking the question, Creed?"

"You dated him," he reminded me.

"Yeah," I leaned in further, "*once.*"

"You sure it was only once?" he pressed.

I twisted and yanked my arm from his hold but stayed leaned into him. "Uh... *yeah,* Creed. It was only a year ago. I think I remember a year ago."

"He's into you, still. Everyone knows it, mostly because the dickhead won't shut up about it."

"Okay, but I'm not into him," I returned then threw my hands out to indicate the hall and us in it, making my point even as I said it out loud. "I'm into *you.*"

Creed ignored this and asked, "That night you came home late, that one date you said you had, was it then? Did he do you then?"

I shook my head again, my heart pumping, the tears still stinging my eyes, and it was taking everything to keep them from falling. "He didn't do me at all, and by the way, it doesn't feel really good that you keep asking when I already answered this question, Creed."

"Dixon gets what he wants."

Why were we still talking about this? Why didn't he believe me? He always believed me. I'd never lied to him and he knew it. Why this? Why now?

"Well, he didn't get me!" I snapped.

"How do I know that?" he pushed.

My heart started pumping even harder. I felt the wet hit my eyes, but now it was taking everything to stop from screaming.

Creed didn't notice, he kept going, "You told me that night you'd stop seein' him. How do I know you did? How do I know even if you did, you didn't give him somethin' that night that should be all for me?"

"Maybe because I'm Sylvia Bissenette and *not* Winona Creed?" I asked sarcastically.

It came right out of my mouth before I could stop it. I knew it was mean, a cheap shot and I was so angry, so hurt, I didn't care.

Except that night, my first and only date with Jason, when I came home to Creed in my bedroom, I'd never seen anything like this come from Creed. Even back then, he'd been nicer to me. Angry at me being late, frustrated that I was too young and he had to wait for me. I knew this now because he'd told me, but he wasn't mean.

I saw his head jerk slightly to the side at my nasty words, but I was done with this conversation, *so* done, and I was leaving.

Therefore, I whirled and dashed to his room, but by the time I grabbed my coat and purse, he was standing in the doorway.

I stomped right to within two feet of him and stopped.

"Out of my way, Creed," I demanded. "I'm going home."

"He suits you, not me."

I went still and stared at his face, feeling his quiet, strangely husky words burn all over my skin like acid.

Then I lifted a hand, planted it in his chest and shoved him before I got close, tipping my head way back and glaring up at him, hissing, "Tucker Creed, for a smart guy you are so... very... *stupid.*"

His hand came up, fingers curling around my wrist, holding it to his chest and he whispered back, "You know it. I know it. Everyone in the county knows it."

"I know no such thing," I bit out.

"Bissenettes and Dixons, you two get together, it'd be the wedding of the century."

Was he crazy?

I ripped my hand from his and stepped back. I twisted my torso and threw my coat and purse on his bed before twisting back and semi-shouting, "You've gone totally insane!"

"Winona Creed's son with anyone, *not* the wedding of fuckin' anything."

He had. He'd gone totally insane.

"You're crazy," I snapped.

"Am I wrong?" he asked.

I put my hands on my hips and returned sharply, "No, you aren't wrong. Absolutely not. If a Bissenette married a Dixon in this county, it would be the wedding of the century."

I watched his jaw get hard and it hurt to see pain slash through his features, but I kept talking.

"But it'll have to be some *other* Bissenette, Creed. *Not* me. *I* belong to you. You belong to me. If I married Jason, it might be the wedding of the century, but it would go against all that was *meant to be*. Even back then when I was dating him, I hoped, heck, I *prayed* no girl would catch your eye before I got old enough to make you see me, and how much I wanted you for *mine*. And the first time you kissed me I thought finally, *finally* everything was as it was meant to be." I threw up my hands. "The earth might stop rotating around the sun if I left you or you left me and I did something crazy and got together with Jason. So if I felt like that then, and, heads up, Creed, I felt like that a year ago and two years ago and ten years ago, why would I ever give something that important to a guy like Jason Dixon when, from the minute I understood it was mine to give, I knew it was you I wanted to have it?"

"It's mine to have?" he whispered.

Oh my God!

Why wasn't he listening to me?

I planted my hands on my hips again and felt my brows draw together. "Yes, it always was and always will be... until you take it, of course. Which, by the way, if it was up," I leaned in, "*to me*," I pointed behind me to the bed, "you could take it *right now*." I leaned back and threw my arms out to the sides. "But *nooooo*, you say we wait until it's legal. So that's on *you*," I pointed at him, "not *me*."

"Baby, don't tempt me like that." Creed was still whispering, his eyes intense, burning through me. It didn't feel like acid this time, but a *whole lot different*.

But I was sick of waiting. I was sick of necking and feeling his hands over my clothes and not *on me*. Feeling his heat and his hard muscle through his clothes and him not allowing me to dip in, get skin and not feeling *Creed*. Feeling all he made me feel; sitting at his kitchenette eating his spaghetti or on his couch watching TV and just doing that, knowing I had most of what I wanted, what I needed, what I'd longed for what seemed like all my life but wanting *everything*.

I was sick of it. Sick to death of waiting.

"Warning, Creed, from here until my eighteenth birthday there's going to be a lot of tempting," I shot back. His body moved like he was going to take a step toward me, but he halted, his big frame rocking, and I watched his hands ball into fists.

"It burns," he said low, and the way he did I held my breath. "Every time. Every time I walk you to your car and watch you drive away from me, it burns."

I let out my breath in a whoosh and whispered, "Creed."

"It burns, knowing you're goin' back to a Daddy who doesn't give a shit. Goin' back to your stepmom who's a worse drunk than the woman sleepin' across this house, she's just better at hiding it. Goin' back to listenin' to him take his hands to her, still, fuckin' *still*."

He leaned forward on the last word then sucked in breath before he leaned back and went on.

"It burns that you gotta listen to them talk the way they do, cuttin' each other to the quick, layin' into each other until they bleed, *daily*. It burns I can't protect you from that. I can't protect you when I see you in town in a dress he wants you to wear, a dress that's not *my* Sylvie. It burns so deep, the need to take you away, put you in my truck, deliver you from that shit and I can't. All I got... all I got, Sylvie, is livin' for the nights you'll come to me. The nights I can make sure you got a decent meal in your belly, because that bitch sure isn't gonna fuckin' feed you, and your Daddy doesn't care. The nights I can show you someone, one single person on this whole goddamned earth loves you, lives for you. Your Momma married that man, gave up on you, moved to California, and now you get a fifty dollar check every birthday and Christmas, and maybe a phone call, if you're lucky. You got no one, like me. That's the way it is, that's the way it's always been. So I live for the nights when I have you because I'm all you got, and baby, you're all I got, too. That's the way it is, that's the way it's always been and that's the way it always will be."

"You protect me," I told him softly.

"Not enough," he retorted harshly.

"Creed—"

"So, baby, don't," he talked over me. "Don't do anything to fuck this up. We got seven months. Seven months to wait it out then we'll be free. Free of your Daddy. Free of my Ma. Free of this hellhole. Free to just *be*."

"Okay," I whispered instantly.

We stood, me in Creed's room, Creed in the doorway, staring at each other.

"You protect me," I repeated, still whispering.

"Not enough," he repeated too, not whispering.

"If I didn't have you—"

"You got me," he clipped.

I took a step toward him, stopped and said, "I know. But if I didn't have you, I don't know where I'd be."

"Right back at 'cha, beautiful."

I licked my lips, then pressed them together before I unpressed them and said quietly, "You asked me not to date Jason again, I didn't. And he didn't get anything from me. I swear."

I watched Creed's chest expand with his breath, then he crossed his arms on it and nodded.

"Can we stop fighting now? I don't like it," I whispered.

I saw his face get soft before he ordered gently, "Come here, Sylvie."

I didn't hesitate. I went there. When I got close, Creed's arms uncrossed and I walked right into them. It was his turn not to hesitate, and they folded right around me.

Against the hair at the top of my head, he promised, "We get through this shit, we get away, I'll give you a beautiful life, baby. I promise. I fuckin' swear, a year, two, all this shit will be a memory, and you might not have everything you're used to, but what we do have will be beauty."

I nodded, my cheek sliding against his flannel shirt, my arms wrapping around him tight.

"I'll give you beauty, too," I promised back.

"You already do," he whispered, and my belly dipped.

227

"And I'll give you Kara and Brand," I went on.

"Lookin' forward to that, baby." He was still whispering. One of his arms left me and his hand came to my chin. He lifted my face up to look into his grinning one. "Look forward to makin' 'em just as much."

That made me feel tingly and I grinned back.

I felt my grin fade and I pressed close before I said softly, "I love you a whole lot, Tucker Creed."

His grin faded. His hand at my chin disappeared so both arms could wrap back around me and he gave me a squeeze before he replied, just as softly, "You're my world, Sylvie. Always have been. Always will be."

I pulled a breath in through my nose, gave him a smile that even I could feel was crooked and trembling. I closed my eyes tight and shoved my face into his chest.

Like always when I was there, his arms gave me yet another squeeze and he became what I was to him. Everything. My whole world.

As always.

As it always would be.

Chapter 19
Worth Every Fuckin' Minute

Present day...

I was showered and getting ready to check out of the hotel room, take off and discover what Phoenix had to offer, when a knock came at the hotel door.

I walked to the door, looked out the peephole and stared at the beauty pageant-beautiful, tall woman with dark arched brows and gleaming, straight brunette hair standing outside.

A woman who looked a lot like Kara Creed.

Shit.

Fuck.

Shit.

I sucked in breath and tamped down my irritation. I arranged my features and pulled open the door.

She looked right into my eyes with her unusual light brown ones. The rest of her would make a less badass woman quail. She was built, all hips and tits and a tiny waist. Fashionable clothes, the fit, style and colors suiting her. Perfect skin that didn't often get touched by the sun, or she wore SPF makeup.

She was everything that was not me.

She said not a word. I didn't either, but she knew I met her daughter and I'd be all kinds of stupid not to see the resemblance, so I decided not to play dumb.

We checked each other out for a while and finally, I spoke.

"Hey."

Lame, yes, but what else did you say?

"You're Sylvie," she replied.

"And you're Chelle," I returned.

She lifted up her chin, exposing a long, slim, elegant neck.

I tipped my head to the side. "How did you find me?"

She didn't hesitate to answer. "Only one nice hotel close to Tucker. He wouldn't put you in anything but the best he could find. The best of the best isn't close and he wouldn't have you anywhere that wasn't close." She shrugged. "So here I am."

She knew Creed. That wasn't a surprise. They'd been married. She also knew how he felt about me. That, also, wasn't a surprise. He'd told her.

But she called him Tucker.

Weird.

"And they gave you my room number?" I asked.

"For two hundred dollars," she answered.

Seemed she paid Creed loads of attention, and not just about me.

Time to move this on.

"Okay, Chelle, what can I do for you?" I asked.

"You can let me in," she replied.

I shook my head, but did it gently and dipped my voice low. "I don't think—"

She lifted up a slim, elegant hand, slim, elegant gold bangles clanking as she did so, and dipped her voice low, too. "I'm not here to be ugly, Sylvie. I promise. I just want to talk."

"About what?" I pressed.

"About things I'd rather not say in the hall."

Goddamn it!

If I didn't let her in, I'd seem bitchy. That said, I totally didn't want to let her in.

I had no choice, really, and that sucked.

I stepped back, opening the door as I did and moved aside.

She walked in and it looked like swanning, but I had the feeling that long-legged grace came naturally.

I closed the door, followed her, and when I arrived in the bedroom area, I saw she'd stopped and was examining my zipped up, beat-up, leather satchel.

I stopped well away and offered, "Do you want me to make some coffee? I've got one of those little pots and plenty of java."

She looked to me and shook her head. "I'm good."

I nodded and fell silent. She was here, I didn't invite her. It was up to her to lead.

She regarded me closely. "I'm not what you expected," she stated quietly.

"Nope," I agreed, giving her no more.

I actually didn't know what I expected. Creed was hot, successful and all man. He could get anyone, even someone as beautiful as Chelle. But she was way more polished and stylish than I would expect would turn the eye of a man like Creed.

She pulled in a delicate breath and asked, "He hasn't spoken of me?"

Shit. I didn't want to be doing this, but I really didn't want to get into this crap. So I had to put on the brakes before we even really started.

"Okay," I threw out a hand, "I don't want this to go bad. From what I know, you understand what's happening. Not a little bit of it, all of it. So I think you get I'm gonna be around as in around... *a lot.*"

She didn't flinch, but that didn't mean I didn't catch how much that cost her.

"So," I went on, "I wanna be careful here, I don't wanna create bad blood. You and Creed get on, so I'm gonna try not to fuck that up. So don't take offense when I say this, but giving you the honesty, I'm not gonna talk to you about what Creed and I talk about. I'll say this. I know a little bit about you. I know you both love your kids. I know you've made good ones. I know you got a new man. I know you know about me and I know the break with Creed wasn't good for you. Can we leave it at that?"

She didn't answer me.

Instead, she stated, "He wanted no memory of you."

I didn't get this so I asked, "What?"

She swept her hand up and down her front. "After you, he told me it took years, but when he couldn't bear it anymore, the nightmares, the anguish, the longing, in an attempt to bury it, he fucked everything that moved. After you, he told me, he did everything he could do to drown out the memory of you. After you, there were no blondes. After you, there were no women who were slim and little and looked like they needed protecting. After you, those women ceased to exist. He didn't even look at them. He wanted no memory of you."

Okay, I liked this and hated it, in equal measure.

"Do you know why that was?" I asked, and she nodded but I went on, "If you really do, Chelle, you know that was more than being about me."

"True. But we both know it was mostly about you."

Okay, she was probably right about that.

I pulled in breath, opened my mouth to speak, but she got there before me. And when she spoke, she was whispering.

"I have never..." she swallowed, "not in my life, not in all the time with him, except when the kids were born, I have never, *ever* seen him the way he was at lunch on Friday."

I shut my mouth.

She closed her eyes and I saw her draw in breath through her nose before she opened them again and continued whispering.

"Please, don't hurt him."

That was so unexpected I felt my body give a small jerk.

Then I started, "Chelle—"

She shook her head and raised her hand. "You're everything to him."

I shook my head too and returned, "I was. Now, I know he feels the way I feel about being back together, but he's got your kids and he adores them."

She nodded. "I know that. I know that, Sylvie, but we both know the love we have for a child is not the same as the love of a lifetime. I know he loves them. He'd do anything for them. That's not what we're talking about. That's a different kind of everything. And if he's told you even a little bit about me, you know I love him. I want the best for him. That will never change, he's with me or he's not. I know from what he told me, you're the best for him. You were with him since the beginning, you came into his life just a year after his Dad died. So that girl before, that girl that became the woman he loved was everything to him. But time has passed. Now, I need to know you're still the woman who will see to him, who will make him look like he looked at lunch, even though he tried to hide it so he wouldn't hurt me. Who made him look like I've only seen twice in my life, and that was when Kara and Brand were new to this world and placed in his arms. Who made him look happy."

Holy shit.

Creed was not wrong. She actually *was* happy he found me again.

"Okay, Chelle, gotta say you're kinda freakin' me out," I admitted.

Her body gave a start then her lips twitched. "There it is. He didn't tell you much about me."

I grinned. "He did. I just didn't believe him."

Her lips tipped up, but she didn't commit fully to the smile before they untipped and she said softly, "You can believe him."

I had to say, this was pretty cool. And since it was, since she put it out there, since she paid two hundred dollars to do it and since she did really care a lot about Creed, I gave it to her.

232

"He's my world. I've been lost for sixteen years without him. Lost, broken and lonely. Having him back makes me feel whole again. I'd die for him."

"I hope you don't have to, but... good," she replied.

I grinned at her. "I hope I don't have to either. That would suck."

She gave me a small grin back before she looked at my satchel then back at me. "Okay, well, I um... that's kind of all I wanted to say or, uh... to hear. I don't want to take up too much of your time so I'll just head out."

I nodded and stepped aside so she could pass. I followed her down the short hall and stopped away from the door where she stopped, hand on the handle, her head tipped down to look at it. She stood there a beat like that and didn't move so I was about to call her name before her head snapped up and, not taking her hand from the handle, she turned to me.

"He didn't tell you."

Oh crap. This wasn't good. Not only that she was clearly about to impart something on me that Creed had not gotten around to telling me, but the look on her face that said not good things.

"Chelle, I don't think—"

"It's very him not to tell you," she cut me off to say.

"If there's something you've figured out he hasn't told me, maybe we should let Creed tell me."

"He might not and you should know. I know you don't know already because you aren't angry. You aren't acting like a bitch."

Okay, seriously did not like this.

"Again, how about we let Creed tell me."

She ignored me. "He's a good man. He feels guilt he shouldn't feel. I did it to myself."

"Chelle—"

"I deliberately got pregnant with Kara in order to trap him into marrying me."

Holy shit!

I stared, mouth hanging open and everything.

Unfortunately, words kept coming through her lips.

"I knew he didn't love me. I always knew he didn't love me. But I loved him. Too much. I did that to him and he loves Kara, Brand, and when I got pregnant I knew something was wrong. He was battling with something in his past. He didn't tell me what it was, but I knew it was holding him back from living a full life. So I got pregnant, convinced him to try to get on with his life, and he settled for me. I knew it the whole time, Sylvie. He'd never gotten over you, though I didn't know the issue was you. And if I hadn't done that to him, he'd still be alone. He could have come to you free and clear. You could have your own kids you'd named those names. It could have—"

"Please stop," I interrupted her, and before she could begin again I kept going. "I gotta say, it isn't cool, doing that to a man, not deliberately. Shit happens, I get that, but deliberately?" I shook my head. "And babe, I can tell you get that he feels shit for breaking your heart, but there's no going back now. There's only forward, and this is between you and Creed. You need to sit down with him and talk. It isn't fair to any man to carry the load he's carrying from breaking it off with you when the whole time you knew it was a possibility."

She turned fully to me. "I've talked to him. He won't listen."

There it was. The reason she was telling me this.

She wanted me to intervene.

I had to put a stop to this and pronto.

"Right," I began, "this is new, for you, him, me and we gotta feel this out as we go along, but I can say at this juncture I'm uncomfortable with being a Creed-slash-Chelle go-between. If you're here to corral me into helping you two work out your issues, just saying, again giving you the honesty, I got enough to deal with right now with Creed back in my life, things at home, at the same time hoping your kids like me. I can't be that for you, and I'm not sure I ever want that role. If you want it, you gotta do it yourself. I'm not saying I don't want to be involved in things as they crop up down the road. I'm going to be a member of this family, and, babe, not to hurt you, but Creed and I'll be building our own. But I get there will always be a Creed and Chelle that raise two great kids. And although you got your man and Creed has me, you two have to keep your shit together so you can do your best job raising those two kids, and that doesn't involve me. It doesn't involve your man. It involves you and Creed. You with me?"

She studied me then replied quietly, "I'm with you, Sylvie."

I nodded then continued, "We got a job, you, me, Creed and your man, to be cool always for your kids. You probably know Creed had a revolving door of father figures and my stepmom was a loser. No kid deserves that, and I never wanna do that to a kid, especially not kids that are Creed's. So let's find ways to figure that out so they don't feel this, and just know they have a lot of love centered around two great parents who want the best for them."

I saw her eyes warm before she told me, "I think we can do that job."

"I know we can," I returned.

She held my gaze then nodded before saying, "I'm glad you feel that way, Sylvie, because that's the way I was hoping it would be. Every, uh... ex-wife who's a Mom always fears when her ex finds another woman and what that will bring. I'm pleased it brought you."

I grinned again and stated, "You trapped him or not, babe, he got you pregnant so he *did* choose you, so let's just say Tucker Creed has good taste."

She grinned back. "Yeah, let's say that." At my nod, she finished, "I should get going."

"Later, Chelle."

"'Bye, Sylvie."

She turned to go, but I stopped her by calling her name and she turned back. "Just out of curiosity, and if it's personal between you two, you don't have to tell me, but why do you call him Tucker?"

Her brows drew together and she said, "I was wondering why you called him Creed. Only people on the job call him Creed."

Strange.

I decided, since he hadn't shared, I wouldn't so I just said, "Throw back from the old days."

"Ah," she mumbled, but I got the sense she either didn't get it or didn't believe me, but she let it go with a, "Well, see you, Sylvie."

"Yeah. See you, Chelle."

She took off.

I waited for a bit before I left the room to check out. I wasn't going to tell Creed about Chelle's visit. Not yet. I didn't know what his response would be and I didn't want to piss him off or upset him when he had his kids. There would be plenty of time to tell him and not ruin the last hours he'd have with them for two weeks.

Instead, I shook it off and took on Phoenix.

Kristen Ashley

"She calls you Tucker."

Creed and I were back in Denver, at my place, in the back room. I'd just told Creed about Chelle's visit. I was sitting on the couch, Creed was standing at the window staring out, partaking of one of his rare cigarettes (he was trying to quit; he was also trying to talk me into doing the same) and blowing the smoke out the screen.

I waited until we were not on the go or in a public place to share about Chelle. Once I'd shared, he'd gone to his bag, grabbed his smokes, came back and lapsed into brooding silence, staring out the window.

I let him have some time and did this studying him.

It had been a long time since I'd seen this Creed.

Back in the day, we both knew our clandestine time together was precious so we made the most of it. It didn't happen often, but he had a lot on his mind back then: us taking off, what would become of his mother when we were gone, what would become of us. So he could go quiet, retreat into his head, think thoughts he didn't want to share. I knew this because I asked him to share and he didn't, no matter how I tried to break through. Eventually I learned that I didn't need to try. He would sort out what he needed to sort out and come back to me.

Watching him, it struck me that it might make me a freak, but I missed this, and I suspected he hadn't changed. He'd sort it out without me prying, let me in when it was his time and I just needed to roll with it. So I didn't change how I dealt with it and let him have his time.

Though, considering I wasn't a patient woman and sitting in a silent room stroking my cat and watching a man smoke and stare out the window, no matter how hot he was or how much I loved him, was kinda boring.

Therefore, I quit giving him time and mentioned his ex calling him Tucker.

He turned his head, his eyes coming to me. Then he turned his body, took two steps, bent low and stubbed his cigarette out in the ashtray on the coffee table.

When he straightened, eyes back to me, he answered, "No woman calls me Creed. Only men… and you."

"Okay," I replied, not getting it, but also thinking his somber mood meant he wasn't up to explaining it.

I was wrong because Creed kept talking.

236

"Tried to keep the name, found women calling me that reminded me that I'd never again hear you do it. It reminded me of that night in the woods when we were kids and I told you I was who I was going to be. It reminded me of how you were there for me. How you were always there for me and how I'd never have that again, either. So I went back to Tucker. Men call me Creed 'cause that's what men do."

I nodded then asked, "So Chelle doesn't know you're Creed?"

He shook his head. "No one in my life knows but you."

Okay, it was dawning on me I was seriously a freak because I liked that, a lot. I liked having that all to myself. There was a day when Creed was all mine. Now, with our histories changing, his body was all mine but his love was shared. I didn't mind that. Even back then, I knew when we started a family I'd have to share him. That didn't mean I didn't like us having a piece of our past that was unaltered. No one understood, it was all ours.

"That wasn't cool."

Creed's words seemed to come out of nowhere and made me focus on him again.

"What?"

"It wasn't Chelle. I'm surprised as fuck she pulled that shit on you, and it wasn't cool."

I shook my head but said, "I didn't like it at first either, babe, but it ended all right. She wasn't there to be a bitch. She was there to—"

Creed moved to the wicker chair, sat in it and lifted his long legs to put his boots on the table while interrupting, "I know why she was there, and why she was there wasn't cool." He flipped out a hand. "Don't know, haven't lived through this shit, never expected to have a woman in my life I gave a shit enough about to live through it, so I don't know how it should go. How I'd have liked it to go is me introducing you to her. Me having control of the situation. Me being at your back. Not you enduring a sneak attack which, luckily, because you are who you are and Chelle is who she is, didn't go south. One or the other of you was having a bad day, it could have."

"I can handle shit like that, baby," I said softly.

He shook his head but replied, "I get that. I get you can take care of yourself. What you need to get is that I'm me and you're you, and no matter you can handle yourself and a gun and you got a tough skin, that doesn't mean I'm down with you going it alone. Not with this. Not with anything. We always had each other. We lost that. We both feel that deep. Now we have that back and Chelle doesn't get to take that away from you. No one does."

Seriously, could this guy get any better?

I stared at him and he held my gaze steady as I did.

No, he couldn't get any better. Then again, he was always the best.

I decided to move us on and asked, "So what are you gonna do?"

"I'm gonna sleep on it, call her tomorrow and tell her how I feel about it," Creed answered. "Then I'm gonna tell her not to do it again. Then I'm gonna tell her I want the kids to get to know you better and us to have more time to get settled before she and I sit down and figure out what's next for our kids, and while we take that time, she needs to back off. And last, I'm gonna tell her she never approaches you unless you invite it or there's somethin' necessary goin' on with the kids and she has to do it."

"You don't have to go that far, Creed. I liked her," I told him. "She gave no indication we wouldn't get along. Honestly, it wasn't that big of a deal."

I watched as he took his boots off the coffee table, put them to the floor and leaned toward me, elbows to knees, his face turning from serious to "right now, pay some major fucking attention to me" serious.

"As I said," he started quietly, "I get you can take care of yourself. When I said that five seconds ago and explained, you didn't get me. So I'll make it clear this time. I get you can take care of yourself, Sylvie. What you need to come to terms with is, no matter how badass you are, I'm gonna take care of you, too. You can spout a bunch of bullshit about your experience, your skills, your fear- lessness but that will not mean shit to me. You're not only my woman, you're Sylvie. When I say I have your back, I don't mean it in the way you're used to with the guys you work with. I mean I have your back as your man. I look out for you in all ways I can do that, including emotionally. So, you liked Chelle. This is not a surprise. She's likeable. But I control that fuckin' situation so I can control any hurt or upset that might come to you, and I mean control it as in stop it. Now are you with me?"

I held his eyes and realized I had a choice. I could hold onto my badass and make an issue of this or I could let Creed do what Creed felt he needed to do.

I knew I could take care of myself and his protection was unnecessary. He just told me he knew it, but he needed to make his position clear anyway.

It meant more to him to take care of me as my man than it meant to me to retain my status of badass. I'd weathered a six year hurricane and didn't come out unscathed. Through that, Creed had not been there to take care of me. For him, that struck deep. Further, I was his Sylvie as I was now, and still the Sylvie I was to him way back then.

He needed this. I didn't need to make a point that might be valid, but considering his emotion, however valid, it was unnecessary.

Not to mention, it felt seriously fucking good to have that part of Creed back, too. The one who looked out for me, protected me. I'd proved I could carry the burden, but that didn't mean it didn't feel great to share the load *and* be back in the position to return the favor.

So I made my choice and answered, "I get you. I also love you, Creed."

His face relaxed before he replied, "Right back at 'cha, beautiful."

I closed my eyes, hearing those words, feeling them warm my skin, loving every syllable.

It was a mistake. I barely had them closed before Gun suddenly scattered. This was because I felt a shoulder in my belly and I was up in the air. I rallied quickly, but not quickly enough before I was falling backward toward the floor, Creed coming with me, and automatically my arms circled him. One of his hands cupped the back of my head before I hit floor then both of his hands went to my shoulders. As his body held the rest of mine down, his hands put on pressure, pinning my shoulders to the floor.

"Pinned," he whispered, and I felt my eyes narrow as his lips smiled. "I win."

"I wasn't ready," I pointed out the obvious.

"I told you we'd play out the challenge tonight. You had fair warning. But doesn't matter, you should always be ready."

He was not wrong and that sucked.

I scowled up into his face as his eyes roamed mine, then he rolled so I was on top.

He lifted a hand and pulled the hair away from one side of my face as he said, "You're not ready, baby, we'll do something else."

"Can I tie you to the bed and do whatever I want to you?" I tried.

He grinned and my nipples tingled but he answered, "No. You gotta win that."

Shit.

His other hand came up to pull back the hair on the other side of my face and he repeated, "If you're not ready, we won't do it."

I wasn't a squelcher, but I didn't know if that sucked or if I was in for the experience of a lifetime. What I did know was that I trusted Creed either to make it not only good but phenomenal, or to back off if it wasn't working.

To communicate all this, I stated, "I don't renege on a deal."

His head tilted slightly to the side and he asked softly, "You ready?"

"You gonna make me ready?" I asked back and got another grin, this one *way* different.

"Oh yeah."

That got another nipple tingle, but this one didn't stop at my nipples. It traveled south.

Therefore my, "Then... yeah. I'm ready," came out breathy.

His hands fisted in my hair, his face hardened with something that was seriously hot, and his lips ordered, "Then up. Get to the living room and get naked."

I was right.

Seriously hot.

"The living room?" I asked.

"Baby, what'd I say?" Creed asked in return.

I stared down at him, still feeling the tingle.

Then I did as Creed said.

∽✞∽

I was naked on my knees on the back of the couch. Creed was standing in front of me wearing nothing but jeans. I had my legs spread and Creed had his hand between them, toying with my clit. I had my hand flat against his hard crotch and I was rubbing. Through this, we were kissing hard, wet and hot as we had been for a good long time.

He was toying, taking his time. Giving me nothing; hints, whispered caresses, making me go for it and taking it away, which made me happy for the scraps he was giving me, at the same time desperate to have everything. He'd been doing this for a long time, too.

Needless to say, I was primed. I had his tongue in my mouth and his hand between my legs, but I wanted his fingers or other parts of his anatomy inside me, and I was at a point where I didn't care where he put them.

Before I could tear my mouth from his and inform him of this fact he tore his from mine, and suddenly I wasn't on my knees facing him. I was turned, my knees at the back edge of the couch, and I had Creed's hand between my shoulder blades, pushing down until I was face to the cushions, ass in the air. It was not a position I'd ever been in, but albeit somewhat acrobatic, it wasn't uncomfortable.

"Stay that way, baby. Do not move. I'll be back," his rough growl came at me and I did a full body shiver.

I didn't like bossy. I didn't like to be ordered around. I didn't like to be controlled.

That was to say, I didn't like it from anyone, not anyone, but Creed.

So this was *hot*. Phoenix hot. Remember for the rest of your life that time you did it in the living room hot.

I did as he said and felt Creed leave the room. Then I felt him come back and position behind me. A second later I heard a soft "funf" of something hitting the couch then his hands were on me, oiled, slippery, warm, *amazing*.

Oh yeah. I was right. This was *hot*.

His hands traveled the skin of my waist, up my back, down my sides then they disappeared. I heard a cap pop, another soft "funf, and his hands were back. Slicker, warmer, roaming everywhere, oiling my entire back, my sides, ribs, waist and around where he rubbed the oil into my breasts, thumbs circling my nipples making me squirm. Back to the bottle and more oil, over my hips, down the outsides of my thighs.

Those thighs started trembling.

Back to the bottle, another "funf", then more oil over the insides of my thighs and up over the cheeks of my ass.

"Spread wide, baby. Give me all you got," Creed murmured, his voice rough.

I slid my legs wide without hesitation.

I moaned into the cushions as his slick hand slid between the cleft of my ass, through my wet and over my pulsing clit. His finger rolled, gentle, soft, mind-boggling, and my hands slid out so my fingers could curl around the edge of the couch cushion to hold on.

"You can get a hand up here, Sylvie, I want your finger here. Soft, sweet, like this," he kept touching me, showing me what he wanted. "You make yourself come, baby, I won't be pleased."

This was another challenge that I was willing to accept, but wasn't so sure I could best it. Still, I was going to try. So I braced my torso on the couch and put my hand between my legs. Creed's fingers gave mine access but they didn't go away. Covering mine, he felt as I touched myself, and I knew he liked it when he growled and pressed his hard, jeans covered cock against my thigh.

"My Sylvie," he murmured, his other slippery hand roaming my slick skin, "so beautiful, so sweet, so fuckin' hot."

Shivers drifted up my spine. My hard, throbbing nipples brushed the upholstery of the couch making them throb harder and Creed's hand drifted back through the wet then away. He went back to the bottle and I felt the oil dripping directly onto my skin, sliding down my spine, between the cheeks of my ass, drenching me. I felt more shivers and it took everything not to press harder, deeper, roll my hips into my hand, strain them to him.

I was coated in oil, so were his hands as they moved over me, pressing in, circling, fingers curling so his knuckles could dig deep into my muscles, turning me on and relaxing me at the same time. A sexy massage. An erotic rubdown.

So when it happened, I was ready to take him as his slippery fingertip slid inside my ass.

My body tensed, except the muscles of my legs quivered. My ass reflexively tipped up, pushed out to get more and his finger slid in a little deeper.

Another moan into the couch.

Oh God, that was good.

Oh God, how was that good?

"You want more?" Creed's thick voice came at me.

"Yes," I breathed into the couch.

"Say please, Sylvie."

Oh God, that was even hotter.

I took too long, enjoying how hot it was, and I knew this because his finger slid out.

Crazy, insane but I wanted it back.

"Please," I gasped, tipping my ass up, an invitation.

His hand slid across my cheek, cupping it, the pads of his fingers digging in, and his voice was husky when he muttered, "Good, beautiful. Now take your hand away, hold onto the couch. I'm gonna work you, and when you want my cock, you ask for it and you do it nice. Yeah?"

As I said, I didn't mind this bossy Creed. No way. No fucking way.

"Yeah," I replied immediately.

"Stop touching yourself, Sylvie."

Okay, shit. I didn't want to do that, but I did it.

It was the right thing to do. I was rewarded immediately. When my hand slid away, his hand slid in and he finger fucked my pussy as I felt a finger slide slightly inside my ass.

"You want more, say please," Creed ordered, fucking me hard between my legs with his fingers.

"Please," I begged, moving my hips with his hand, and he gave me more.

God, shit, he was right. This was awesome. Amazing. Fantastic. So good, it felt like I was going to come out of my skin.

"More?" he asked.

Oh yeah. More. Definitely more.

"More," I gasped, holding onto the edge of the couch, the fabric torture against my hard nipples, my legs trembling so hard they were shivering.

"What do you say?" Creed prompted.

"Please," I whimpered, and he didn't delay, he gave me more.

He kept doing it without me asking and I was on the edge, so close, so fucking close, and he pulled out, then tweaked my clit. Then his fingers wrapped around the outsides of my thighs.

"You don't come like this, baby," he growled. "You come with me inside you."

"Take my ass," I replied instantly.

"Ask nice," he ordered just as quickly.

"Take my ass, Creed, please."

I felt his hands clench my flesh before he demanded, "Finger to your clit, baby. Make yourself come while I fuck your ass."

I nearly slid off the front of the couch as I hurried to do what I was told and my whole body was quaking, ready, fevered. I felt the sleek, oil-slickened head of his cock prod and push; slow, firm, back, then more. Gentle, careful until he pushed through with the tip then he slid slowly all the way in and he had me. Every bit of me. The one last part he didn't have yet was now Creed's.

"Fuck, you're beautiful everywhere," he groaned as he started fucking my ass. "Harder baby. Take yourself there."

I pressed harder, deeper. I rolled, bucked, reared into his smooth, deep strokes, his hands curled around my hips pulling me to him, pushing me away at the same time holding me steady on the couch.

It built, and God, it was too much. It was too huge. I couldn't take it. It was burning through me. It was going to consume me.

"Creed," I panted into the couch, panic rising as the pleasure swelled. Wild, uninhibited pleasure that felt like it was going to destroy me, and I lifted up onto a hand in the couch, arm straight.

"Work yourself, Sylvie," Creed grunted, going faster, getting impatient. One hand slid around my hip to cover mine between my legs, he pushed in, rolled then twitched our fingers as he kept at my ass and it overwhelmed me.

My head shot back, my muscles seized and my cry pierced the room as I experienced the most intense, overpowering, extraordinary orgasm I'd ever had in my life.

It kept hold of me as Creed kept fucking me. His fingers kept at my clit and one orgasm rolled into another. I was on my third when Creed's other arm sliced around the front of my hips, pulling me to him, burying himself inside me, and I heard his deep, rumbling groan.

I kept still, staring unseeing at the couch, feeling him around me, inside me, never thinking this would be good, never thinking I'd allow this, not again, not ever, and there it was. Like everything with Creed, I gave him my trust, he gave me beauty.

Slowly and carefully, he slid out. Then I was up and turned, knees back in the back of the couch, facing Creed. I barely got my head tipped back to look up at him before the fingers of both his hands drove into the sides of my hair and back, fisting, and his face dipped close so his nose nearly brushed mine and he was all I could see.

"Now I have all of you. I own every inch of you. Every centimeter. You gave it to me when you were six and it took me twenty-eight years to claim all of it, but now it's mine, Sylvie. Every..." his fingers gave my hair a gentle tug, "single..." another tug and his eyes burned into mine, "*inch*."

Holy shit. How could he be turning me on mere minutes after I had the hugest multiple orgasm in the history of time?

"I take it you *really* like ass play," I noted softly and watched his eyes flare.

Then his head shifted back. His hands slid down to the sides of my neck and he announced, "I'm gonna go deal with this condom. You're gonna go to bed. Take the oil with you. We are far from done."

Excellent.

That gave me a full body shiver.

I grinned before I reached up, grabbed his head, pulled it down to me and laid a hot, wet, long one on him.

I let him go and jumped to my feet on the couch, jumped from the couch to the floor, snatched up the oil and dashed out of the room, my hair flying out behind me, knowing, every second, Creed's eyes watched.

"Oh my God. *Oh my God!*" I cried as my sixth orgasm of the night tore through me, my fingers clenched in Creed's hair as his mouth devoured me.

Seriously, my man was the master of giving head.

Seriously.

As I came down, I felt him nuzzling my belly with his nose and lips. I lifted up on my elbows and saw while I was still in the throes of my climax, he'd swung my legs off his shoulders and now he had his forearms in the bed on either side of me but my hands were still clenched in his hair.

I tugged gently and his head came up.

I drank him in.

Scar and all, he was beautiful.

To tell him this I slid the fingers of one of my hands to his face, running the tips along his cheekbone, down his nose to trail the path of the line of his lower lip. I trailed them over the scar on his upper lip then up again over the scar on his cheekbone, his temple and through the white streak in his hair. Once I'd accomplished this, my other hand slid the hank of hair that had fallen to his forehead to the side, and as expected, it fell right back to its original position.

I didn't get to try again as Creed's big body shifted up over me, settling in, covering me.

He pressed one hand under me so he was braced on one forearm in the bed but still holding me while his other hand curved against the side of my head, thumb sweeping out over my cheekbone and he spoke.

"To respond to your earlier comment, beautiful, yeah, like I mentioned before, I like ass play. But it's not what you think. It's tight, it feels good, absolutely, but that's not it. It's about trust. It's about sharing. It's about giving. For most people it's about losing your inhibitions and opening yourself up to the next level of intimacy. And with you," his face dipped closer as his voice dipped lower, "it's about me giving back what was taken from you and you trusting me to do it. That wasn't huge. That was something so big there isn't a word for it, but the closest I can come to it is that it's beautiful."

He was not wrong, so I agreed, "It *was* beautiful, baby." My arms slid around him and held him tight. "And so are you."

Creed's eyes, already warm, warmed more, warming straight through me before he grinned and stated, "Glad you didn't renege on your part of losin' the challenge."

I grinned back. "Me too."

His thumb moved over my face, my cheekbone, down to my jaw and over my lips as his eyes watched and his grin faded.

Then his gaze came back to me.

"That month I was following you, watchin' you, seein' how you lived, dressed, what you did, I knew somethin' had gone wrong. I didn't know what. I thought you were with Dixon and he cheated on you, didn't treat you right. The only thing I knew, your Daddy lied, you weren't happy."

I contradicted him gently, "Actually, I was happy, Creed."

"Not the way you deserve to be happy," he returned immediately.

I didn't have a reply to that, mostly because it didn't need one. He was right.

He continued to hold my gaze and I knew he read what lay behind it when he whispered, "I'm glad you're happy, my Sylvie."

He gave it to me, kept giving it to me, open, honest, putting it right out there, so I licked my lips and gave it back to him. "I have the only thing I ever wanted lying on top of me, so thanks for making me happy, Tucker Creed."

Creed, being Creed, kept right on giving.

"Right back at 'cha, baby."

Okay, shit, God, *shit!*

I loved this man. I knew it, but way back when, being young, I didn't understand.

Now I did.

I *so* did.

It was time to steer us into waters that didn't include me possibly bursting into tears and blubbering like a big girl.

"So, you're the boss tonight, what's the plan? Are we gonna sleep all oiled up or are we gonna shower before we go to sleep?"

"Sheets are fucked up. We shower, we gotta change them or we'll get oiled right back up again."

This was true, so I gave him the info he needed to make his decision, "I know one thing. I'm not changing sheets tonight."

Creed smiled. "Then we sleep oiled up."

That worked for me.

He rolled to his light, I rolled to mine and I barely had it out before I was hauled back to the middle of the bed, tucked close to Creed.

My body, tired out, relaxed, loose, felt sleepy. My mind didn't.

I was thinking of him following me for a month and wondering, if the roles were reversed and it was me who found him again, how I'd feel. What I'd do. How difficult it would be to stay remote and not approach, especially if I discovered he hadn't left me of his own free will but had been coerced into it.

"How'd you do it?" I asked his throat in the dark.

"Do what?" Creed asked back.

"Follow me, watch me, go through my shit and keep distant? If it was me—"

His voice held a hint of humor and a hint of hardness when he cut me off. "You would have shot me."

I tipped my head back and grinned at his shadowy face. "Yeah. But if I figured it out, if I learned it was as it was, I wouldn't have been able to do it."

His arms around me pulled me deeper into his warm, hard body as he replied quietly, "If it was you, except for the scar, I haven't changed. Got older but not changed. There wouldn't be a reason to delay approach. You..." he trailed off and didn't speak again.

"I changed and that freaked you out?" I guessed.

"You did and you didn't, but the way you did meant my approach needed to be cautious. That tough skin, those sharp edges, both of them you had in a way a man could work a lifetime and not break through, proceed with caution and still get sliced to shreds. I wanted you back and I needed to find the right way to finesse that. When I went through your house, I saw you'd kept my

247

necklaces so I had hope, but I knew I couldn't go gung ho. I had to understand what forced the change in you and I had to get that from you so I could form a plan." His hands slid up my still slick back. "Which is what I did."

And I was glad he did.

I pressed closer and said softly, "It killed."

His hands stopped moving so his arms could wrap around tight. "Yeah, watchin' you. Followin' you. Goin' through your stuff. Knowin' your life didn't go as I was promised it would, but something went down that was not good, yeah. It fuckin' killed."

I closed my eyes and shoved my face in his throat.

"It's also over," he went on.

"It's over," I agreed, holding him close.

"And bottom line, it meant you weren't in Kentucky livin' a good life without me, but open for an approach. It might have sucked for a while, but now we got the future we both didn't think we would ever have, so it was worth every fuckin' minute."

I didn't experience what he did, watching me, following me, but I suspected he was right about that, too.

"Yeah," I replied quietly.

"Yeah," he repeated, gathering me even closer.

I lay in his arms and knew I'd been giving. I knew I'd let him in. I knew he understood this and it was making him happy.

But I didn't know if he understood it all.

So I gave it to him.

"Creed?" I called.

"Right here, baby," he whispered.

Yeah he was. Right there. Now and forever.

Now and forever.

I tipped my head so the bridge of my nose rested along his jaw and whispered back, "No matter what's in our future, no matter if our luck stays good or turns back to shit, from this moment to your last on this earth, know down to your fucking soul I love you. I trust you. You make me happy. There's been no one but you and there never will be. Okay?"

I felt him lift his head then I felt him move so he could bury his face in my neck and his voice was gruff when he murmured into my skin, "Okay, my Sylvie."

I drew in breath then reached with my lips to brush them against the skin of his neck.

He settled back, kept me close and ordered gently, "Sleep, baby."

"Right, Creed."

In Creed's arms, sated by his lovemaking, knowing I'd wake up to him tomorrow, my mind cleared, and as I'd been doing all night, I did as ordered and slept.

Chapter 20

A Few More Months

A cool spring evening in Kentucky, seventeen years earlier. Creed is twenty-three, Sylvie is seventeen...

"I hate him."

Creed's hand slid soothingly up my spine. "I know you do."

It was late at night and we were lying in the dark in Creed's twin bed.

I had not had a good day.

It started with my Mom calling for the first time in ages to tell me she was divorcing her husband and asking me if I wanted to come out to California after I graduated.

To this I told her that I'd lived without her in my life for years, she'd left me to Daddy and the stepmonster, and now that she was again facing being alone and lonely and needed me, because she abandoned me when I needed her, I wasn't available to plug that hole. I used different words, but she got my drift and informed me that she wasn't surprised, seeing as he'd raised me, that I'd turned out just like my father.

Then she hung up.

A totally *awesome* phone reunion with Mom.

Not.

Since I'd called Creed to tell him about the conversation with my Mom before coming over, to make my day better he drove us an hour and a half into the city so we could have an actual going out date and not be seen.

This made my day better, obviously. It got even better when Creed shared his Mom had a new man and she was spending her nights messing up his house and life, which meant our evenings would be clear of her.

He also shared that he talked with a realtor about putting his house on the market. He further told his mother he was doing this and told her she was going to have to pull herself together, find a job and a place to live because he was moving into his own pad.

Kristen Ashley

Since she was drunk and she had a new guy to mooch off of, she didn't react. She would, when she used her guy up and he sent her packing but by then, hopefully, it would be too late.

I knew I shouldn't feel that way about Winona Creed. I knew I shouldn't want, even wish that Creed would scrape her off even before he would do it because we were leaving. I knew it made me not a nice person. But she'd never done anything for Creed, so I figured turnabout was fair play.

After our date, after we made out by my car and after I went home, my day being salvaged by Creed (as usual), it went straight to pot again when Daddy and the stepmonster fighting woke me up.

It was its usual loud and vicious then I heard the thump, and I knew from years of experience this was the stepmonster-hitting-the-wall thump, not the stepmonster-hitting-the-stairs-or-floor thump.

So I did what I always did. Got up. Got dressed. Snuck out.

And went to Creed.

Now I was lying on my side in his bed, my cheek to his chest, my arm around his belly. His arm under me, curled around, fingers stroking and our legs were tangled.

"I hate her, too," I told him.

"Shouldn't hate her, beautiful. Pity her, but no reason to hate her."

I lifted up and looked down at his beautiful face in the shadows. "She went after him. She broke up his marriage to my Mom. She didn't get what she thought she'd get, but she stayed so she could have what he could give her. She's a drunk. She's miserable and there are not enough shoes and purses and jewelry in the whole world to make it worth him treating her like garbage and beating her."

"She's got nowhere to go," Creed pointed out.

"She's got a brain and legs that work, she can find somewhere to go," I returned.

Creed's arm curled tight around me and he pulled me up and partially over his body so we were face to face.

"You see it as easy, but your Daddy's got a long reach," he reminded me, but I shook my head.

"I told you what they were fighting about tonight, Creed. He's got *another* new woman and he isn't even trying to hide her. He won't miss the stepmonster

252

if she went. He'd just replace her. She's willing to do anything to keep her position and that's just crazy."

"Seems that way to you, baby, but it isn't. It's bigger than that, what he's doin' to her, for years, fuckin' with her head." His arm gave me a squeeze. "I get you, how she went about worming her way into his life. That was not cool, but the punishment isn't worth the crime. I remember her, way back then, before she connived her way in and he dragged her down. She was somethin'. Now she's broken. All she knows is the life she has with him. She has no skills, hasn't worked in over a decade. She's got a great house, a great car, great clothes, status in town and your Daddy's a powerful man. We can look from where we are and say without a doubt the devil she doesn't know is better than the devil she knows. She's buried so deep under all that shit, no way she'll see it that way."

I hated to admit it, but Creed was right. So I didn't admit it and just settled, cheek to his chest again.

Creed's hand started stroking my back again.

Then he asked, his voice cautious, "Your father still freaking you out?"

I knew what he was asking.

Daddy's behavior had long since stopped freaking me out, but he was different lately. Weird. Wired. His eyes bright in a way I didn't like.

I'd seen it before. For years it had been happening, although not frequent. The change. Him being more energetic than usual, happy. Now, it was happening a lot more and sometimes, when he wasn't that way, he seemed agitated, strung out.

He would also have lots of phone conversations that were on the hush-hush, hidden. He'd jump if you entered a room he was in and he was talking on the phone, and he did it like he was guilty or something.

He wasn't like that. Ever. He had swagger. He didn't care what people thought about him, the way he acted, what he said. He didn't hide anything.

Now, he was and the fights with the stepmonster were far more frequent. They never went away, but those two had settled into a routine animosity. It was usually only when he came home drunk or she found out he was cheating on her when things got ugly.

It was happening all the time these days.

"Yeah," I told Creed.

"Wide berth, beautiful," Creed advised.

I nodded, cheek sliding against his chest.

I could do that. I'd been doing it for years. I could do it for a few more months.

"You know," I told his chest, "you've had this bed since you were a little kid. You should get a bigger bed."

"I will, in a few months, when we're gone and I'm buyin' one for the both of us."

See?

There it was. Creed making me feel better.

I smiled into his chest.

"Soon," I began, "we'll have to open the windows. We lay like this, we'll hear the crickets. We meet at the lake, we'll hear the frogs."

His hand stopped stroking and his arm curled around me as he murmured, "Yeah."

"Soon after that, no more sneaking. No more driving an hour and a half to have dinner. Just you and me, a big bed, a new puppy then Kara and Brand and a big happy family."

His arm tightened. He pulled me up and over him so we were face to face again and he repeated a quiet, "Yeah."

His face was illuminated only by the moonlight, but I could still see the hair had fallen over his forehead. I lifted a hand to shift it away and for once, since he was lying on his back, it stayed where I put it.

That almost made me smile, but what I had to say made certain I didn't.

"I have to go back."

"I know."

I sighed and felt Creed do the same before both Creed's arms stole around me. He rolled me so he was mostly on top and he kissed me, slow and sweet.

He was good at good-bye kisses. Great. Fantastic. I'd had a lot of them.

Too many.

I'd be glad when the day came that I got them few and far between.

With clear reluctance, Creed rolled us both out of his bed, then he waited until I put my jacket on. We walked, silent, hand in hand out of his house and through the woods to my back gate.

There, as always, he stopped me, turned into me, and, as always lately, he bent low, framing my face with his hands, and he kissed me light and sweet.

A different kind of good-bye kiss, not as good but just as precious.

"See you tomorrow, Creed," I whispered.

"Tomorrow, baby," he whispered back.

I grinned up at him, but I knew it was fake.

So did Creed.

But still, with no choice, he let me go. And with no choice, I went.

A few more months.

Just a few.

Then Creed and I would be free.

Chapter 21
Tomatoes, Toe-mah-toes

Present day, six days later...

Creed lay on his stomach, hand shoved under the pillows. His leg cocked, face turned toward me, eyes closed.

He was still sleeping.

I was on my knees in the bed beside him, watching.

The covers were pulled up to his waist. I knew what lay under them was naked, but as I looked that way, all I saw was our lake, our pier and my name in flowers painted on his back.

Lifting a hand, I started between his shoulder blades and trailed a fingertip lightly down his spine. When I got there, I traced my name backwards, starting with the "e". I knew he came awake at my first touch, but I took my time, studying the tat, my finger's movements. As I finished the "S", my finger slid across the top of his ass and down, taking the covers with me.

I felt my vagina spasm as I exposed his fine, sculpted behind, and my eyes drifted back up his back, to his tat, to his eyes, seeing their startling blue on me. He hadn't moved. Just his eyes had shifted to me, and the look in them made my gut pitch.

God, how could he make lying there on his stomach hot?

I didn't know. He just did.

That was Creed.

"Hey," I whispered.

"Hey," he whispered back then moved, swiftly.

Knifing partly up, his arm snaked out fast, hand hooking me around the back of my neck. He pulled me down to him and kissed me, hard and wet.

I experienced another highly pleasant vagina spasm before he lessened the pressure of his hand on my neck, allowing me back three inches.

When he did, I declared, "I hope I never, ever get used to you sleeping next to me. I hope I never, ever get used to waking up next to you. And I hope I never, ever lose thinking how every kiss you give me is pure beauty."

I watched his eyes, still slightly sleepy, flare before he murmured, "Jesus, Sylvie."

I held his gaze and warned softly, "You should always be ready."

I caught a nanosecond of his brows drawing together before I flew backwards. Breaking from his hold, my quickness and momentum making it so when I hit my back, I could curl my legs and hips over and do a backwards somersault. I landed on my feet by the side of the bed. Reaching down, I grabbed the two Nerf blasters and a bunch of ammo packs I had stored under the bed. I tossed one toy gun on the mattress with some reloads before I lifted my gun and took aim.

I half expected Creed to balk. He said he didn't play at work.

This would be totally unfun.

Luckily, the minute I lifted my fake weapon, he went back on this declaration. I knew it because his arm shot out, he grabbed the gun and rolled, disappearing with a loud thump on the other side of the bed.

It should be noted, he did all this before I even got a fucking shot off!

Shit!

He was good. Even at Nerf!

Wearing my undies and cami, I darted out the door, plastered my front to the wall by the side of the jamb and peered around, me and my gun.

A Nerf dart shot by me, so close I could feel the whiz of air kiss my cheek.

Shit!

He was seriously good.

I pulled back and fired off two blind. I heard heavy footfalls which meant Creed was on the move, so I dashed down the hall to find cover.

I hit the living room and threw myself behind the couch. I shoved one reload into my panties, kept the other in hand, and when I heard Creed coming down the hall, I lifted up, aiming at the doorway.

He hit it wearing faded jeans only partly done up and I immediately unleashed a hail of dart fire. One glanced off Creed's shoulder, another off his arm before he returned fire and disappeared behind an armchair.

I ducked behind the couch, reloaded and got up to a crouch, peeking over the back, not seeing Creed. I straightened further, backing away, gun pointed in his direction as I headed toward the entryway.

I heard a, "Meow," and spared a glance down at Gun who was sitting in the entryway looking up at me.

Her "meow" was not a "what the fuck are you doing?" meow. She was used to my whacky behavior. Although I'd never had a Nerf fight in the house, my whacky behavior had run the gamut so she wasn't alarmed. Her "meow" was a "when the fuck are you gonna feed me?" meow.

I looked back Creed's way, still backing up as I muttered, "In a second, Gunny."

"Meow," she replied, unimpressed by the fake gunplay or the fact that her kickass Momma and a huge badass alpha were engaged in a Nerf fight. All she cared about was she was hungry.

"Promise," I told her and saw Creed shoot from behind the armchair, moving in a crouch, gun up and firing my way.

One hit me in the stomach and I got off three shots of my own before I disappeared in the dining room.

"Gut shot," I heard Creed call, and he was right. If there were rules, which luckily there weren't, he just won.

But I was having too much fun.

"I'm still standing!" I shouted back.

I zoomed to the kitchen, took cover behind the bar and had my gun up, braced on the bar, eyes to the doorway when Creed entered. Another hail of gunfire, from him and me, before he took cover behind the dining room table.

At that point, all hell broke loose. Nerf darts hitting the dining room table making papers fly, Nerf darts striking the bar and flying over my head. They were everywhere.

It got to the point I had no reloads, and I knew Creed didn't either because he'd stopped firing. As I scrambled around the kitchen floor to grab darts to refill, I heard Creed moving through the dining room, his treads fast and thundering.

Shit, he was on the attack.

Nerf done, we were going hand to hand.

Awesome!

I threw the gun aside, braced in a crouch, and as he rounded the bar I sprung up and launched myself at him.

I hit him dead on. Snaking one arm around his neck, one around his back, holding on and, upon taking my weight, he fell back a step. I rounded his legs with a calf and slammed in behind his knees, succeeding in taking one out. His big body pitched to the side. His arms curled around me and we went down

259

to the kitchen floor, Creed's shoulder slamming heavily into it, me slamming heavily into Creed.

Even as I moved to gain an advantageous position, I asked, "You okay?"

His answer was to roll me to my back, his weight on me.

He was okay.

He didn't get the chance to settle before I managed to buck him off and thus commenced the tussle. Creed didn't hold back, I didn't either, and we were grunting and breathing heavily before I, not entirely surprisingly but also annoyingly, wound up pinned to the kitchen floor on my belly.

Shit!

"Give?" Creed asked.

"No," I answered on a heavy breath, arching my back and cocking a knee to try to get it under me in order to lift up and use my weight to throw him off.

"Baby, you're beat," he informed me.

"No, I'm not," I informed him, straining against his weight.

His hips slid off, then my panties were yanked down and I went completely still so my body could enjoy being rocked by a mammothly pleasant vagina spasm.

"Give?" Creed asked again.

"No." This time it came out on a breathy breath.

His hand shot between my legs, finger honing in on my clit.

Fuck, that felt good.

My hips jerked.

"Give?" he asked, now his voice was all rough, no smooth, totally hot.

Oh yeah. I gave.

"Yeah," I gasped.

"Please, God, tell me you're off your period."

I'd had my period the last few days, an unfun circumstance normally, a really unfun one when I wasn't big on having sex during it, which meant I didn't get to have sex with Creed. He got me off with his fingers, I got him off with my hand and mouth, but it wasn't the same.

Now I was back.

"Yep," I gasped again. His finger moved back and plunged deep.

Nice.

I moaned into the floor.

I was ready for him *now*. It had been four days. I needed him inside.

"Now, please, God, tell me you got a stash of condoms in the kitchen," Creed went on.

Alas, I did not, but after he fucked me, I was stashing them everywhere around the house. Under seat cushions. Taped to the bottoms of tables. There would not be an inch of space in my house where a condom would be out of reach.

"No," I answered.

"Fuck," he clipped, and I felt his finger start to move out.

I whipped my head around and looked at him over my shoulder. "Don't. I can't wait, Creed. Fuck me now and pull out. It'll be cool."

His finger did lazy strokes as his face dipped close to mine and he replied, "Baby, pulling out does not work."

"Our luck has changed. It'll work for us."

"Sylvie, you just finished your period, but pulling out does not work. Even a day after your period, let's not take chances."

I saw his mouth moving, but I wasn't sure he was speaking, and this was because I was focused on all I was feeling.

God, *God,* even lazy stroking, not having his cock but having his face that close to me, his finger inside me was doing a number on me.

I needed him. So much, I couldn't focus on this shit.

I needed to move us on, immediately.

In order to do that, I announced, "Okay, so it doesn't work and you get me pregnant. It isn't like we both don't want kids. It happens, I won't be sorry."

His finger stilled.

No!

"Creed," I whispered, and it came out sounding like what it was. A plea.

I started to lift up, but his voice, a rough, low, vibrating growl I'd never heard before stopped me.

"You wanna get pregnant now?"

His words, the tone they were uttered in, performed a miracle. It took me out of what was happening to my body and into the conversation, and I realized what I said.

When I did, I realized I meant every word.

"Absolutely."

Creed stared into my eyes.

I stared back.

Then his finger disappeared and I whimpered. The feeling of loss was cut short when he yanked my panties back up. He shifted, rolled me and then lifted me in his arms. When we were up, he started moving, carrying me like a groom carries his bride over a threshold, his strides long and swift, his destination clearly the bedroom.

I slid my arms around his shoulders and asked, "Creed, where are you going?"

"I'm taking you to your bed. We make a baby, Sylvie, we do it making love. Not fucking on the kitchen floor."

Of its own accord, my hand slid up his neck into his hair, cupping the back of his head spasmodically as goose bumps rose on my skin.

When we made a baby, we did it making love.

Making love.

Making a baby.

What I wanted. What he wanted. What we'd planned.

Sixteen years late.

But, thank God, not too late.

I felt my lip start to tremble and I bit it so the feeling welling up inside me didn't overwhelm me. I didn't want to cry. I wanted Creed to plant our baby in me while he made love to me.

How a Nerf fight ended up like this, I didn't know.

Just that, as with everything, as always, while experiencing something wonderful, only Creed could make it *more* wonderful.

He set me in the bed and immediately covered me with his body.

Creed's hands started moving on me, mine on him, and his head was descending so he could kiss me, when Gun pranced in, stopped and stood by the bed.

"Meow."

Creed's lips were brushing mine when I whispered, "She wants breakfast."

"She can have breakfast after we try to make a baby," he replied, not whispering.

I grinned.

I was down with that.

Creed did not grin.

He slanted his head and kissed me.

Then he made love to me.

"*What?*" Charlene hissed.

We were sitting on her couch in her living room. Creed was outside mowing her lawn.

After Creed made love to me, we took a long shower where Creed paid more attention to me, giving me a slow, sweet orgasm and taking his time doing it. We then got dressed and went over to Charlene's to help her with breakfast, and after, Creed went out to mow her lawn.

So he could concentrate and not run over anything precious with the lawnmower, like, say, children, the kids were inside with us, doing something in their rooms which was likely destructive (except Theo, he was taking a nap). Charlene was ignoring this because I was laying it out, starting with imparting on her the fact that Creed and I had decided not to delay in trying to start a family.

It was Saturday. I'd been home nearly a week after making my decision to move to Phoenix and I hadn't yet told her I was moving to another state. I hated to admit it, but this was because I was chicken.

It seemed clear Drake Nair was out of town and we found no rumblings that he was still scheming against Knight. We also had no indication whatsoever that Nick had anything to do with Nair's plot, or even held any ill-will against his brother.

Therefore, Knight released Creed.

This meant Creed needed to go home, see to his own business. We discussed it and although he could give me a week, he had to get home and work. I had to stay in Denver, put my house on the market, finish the jobs I was still working on and shut down my business.

This was going to suck, being away from him for the first time since I got him back.

Creed thought it sucked, too, and he was somewhat vocal about that.

Regardless that we both thought it sucked, there was no way around it. We'd have to be separated, for weeks, maybe even a couple of months, with quick visits the only thing breaking our separation.

See? Sucked.

I also had to tell Charlene I was abandoning her.

It was arguable, but this might suck more. I'd get back to Creed. I was losing Charlene, Adam, Leslie and Theo, and they were losing me.

I felt shit about this because I promised I'd be there for her. I also felt shit about this because she was doing my admin part-time. She needed the money and that would die away.

Creed, being Creed, solved this problem. He farmed his admin out to an agency. He had no emotional ties to them and it was also part-time. He said it didn't matter who did it or where they did it, which meant he could yank it from the agency and give it to Charlene.

But that didn't solve the problem of her losing her lawn guy, her morning helpers or the moral support coming from next door.

In my heart, I knew she'd survive. She was that kind of person. It might take a while to get used to it, but she would eventually find her way to the bright side of life. I also knew that she'd be happy for me, finding Creed, living my life with him, starting a family.

So it wasn't about Charlene, as such.

It was about me.

I'd miss her.

Back in the day, when Creed disappeared and I found myself owned by Richard Scott, all my girlfriends abandoned me. I didn't really blame them. Suddenly, without an explanation, I was what the town saw as the local pimp and drug dealer's girlfriend. Although Jason Dixon had been telling people for ages he banged me, no one believed him and no one, but no one, not even my girlfriends, knew about Creed.

Needless to say, being with Richard did not do wonders for my reputation.

People talked about me. People speculated. People said shit things behind my back, gave me ugly looks, sometimes even said things straight to my face. I'd learned to live with it and I'd learned to live without friends.

That didn't mean having one again didn't mean everything to me.

Fortunately, two days after Knight released Creed, Hawk Delgado called me. He had a job and not only was he interested in contracting with me, he also asked if Creed was still in town. Since Creed was and since Creed was good with hanging around longer and taking another job, Hawk hired both of us.

The job paid well and Hawk expected it to last a month so I had a reprieve. More time with Creed in Denver. More time to get my shit sorted. A couple more weekends with his kids before I moved in completely.

But I had to tell Charlene. She had to prepare.

And I had to prepare to lose her and the kids.

"Creed and I are trying for a baby," I repeated what I'd said two seconds before.

Charlene blinked at me.

Then she turned her head to the window and stared blankly out of it.

I turned my head that way, too, and saw Creed's tee drenched in sweat, the ends of his hair wet and curling around his neck. He had mirrored shades on and they looked really fucking good on him.

My mouth started watering.

"It's been three weeks, honey."

Charlene's words came at me and I looked at her again.

"I know," I replied.

She shook her head and reached out to curl her hand around my leg. "I get this. I get him. He's a good guy. I get that. I get your history. I get it all, but, Sylvie, listen to me. A baby is a big deal."

"I know that too, Charlene."

"It changes your whole life. It changes the whole *world*."

I put my hand on hers, leaned in and repeated, "I know, Charlene."

Her hand turned and her fingers curled around mine. "I know you know, but I also know you *don't*. A baby changes your body. It changes your relationship. It changed the rhythm of your day. You have a child, you can't drink as much as you do. You absolutely can't smoke. He's got two kids. They've met you once. They—"

I cut her off, "Creed loves them and they love him and they like me. They'll be cool. He'll take care of them. We both will."

Her hand gave mine a squeeze. "You haven't even settled into there being a you two again. Nine months, ten months, a year, most of that pregnant, you won't be able to do that."

She knew. I explained after we had our drama and got back together that Creed and me were, well, back together. Charlene was Charlene. She said little except she was happy for me.

But, right now, she didn't get it so I explained, "There was never a time when we *weren't* settled into the two of us being *the* two."

Her head tipped to the side. "What?"

I leaned closer, lifting her hand and holding it to my chest. "This is Creed."

"I know, but—"

I shook her hand before I pressed it to my chest. "Charlene, babe, *this is Creed.*"

She held my eyes as her lips parted.

She was getting me.

So I helped her get the rest of the way. "There's no one but him. No one. I want our future, the one that was stolen from us. I want it for me and I *need* to give it to him. He was..." I hesitated, having shared a bit but not entirely, and deciding not to, for Creed. "I can't say. What I can say is that I explained, it all came out and we worked it out. What you can guess is we're together, so the reason he disappeared was understandable. So understandable, there's not even anything to forgive."

She sucked in breath.

Yeah, she was getting me.

I went on.

"It's debatable who suffered worse," I told her and she closed her eyes. She opened them when I continued, "And now that's done. I want his baby growing inside me. I want a home. I want a family. I want to let Creed give that to me because Creed *needs* to give it to me. It's what we'd planned. It's what we'd dreamed. It's what we went through hell for and it's what we're gonna *have* and we're not going to wait. Not a month. Not a year. Now."

"Your Dad did something to him," she whispered her guess.

"My Dad did something to him," I replied.

She licked her lips and turned her face back to the window, but she held my hand tight. This time, I watched her face work instead of looking outside to watch my man work.

It took some time, but finally she said quietly, "You should move to Phoenix. He should be close to his kids and your baby should be close to his or her brother and sister."

See?

So totally told you that Charlene would want that for me.

"I am," I said quietly back, and her eyes came to me. They were stunned, but they were also assessing. "It's decided. Creed's going to transfer his admin to you so you won't feel that financial hit and—"

I stopped talking when her eyes filled with tears.

Then I started talking fast. Holding her hand still to my chest, I leaned close and said gently, "I'll come up. So will Creed. I mean, he can't come up every two weeks to mow your yard, but we'll come up. Take the kids so you have time and—"

Charlene interrupted me.

"You're happy."

I blinked and asked, "What?"

"I didn't see it. Or, I should say, I didn't believe it." She swallowed. "Now, I see it."

"Charlene—"

She yanked her hand from mine but then grabbed me by the shoulders, pulled me close, wrapped her arms around me and gave me a hard hug.

I felt her body jerk with her sob as her voice broke with it when she said, "Always, I saw it, that hurt in the back of your eyes. Like you were lost in a way you couldn't get found." She gave me a squeeze. "Now it's gone. You're found and I'm so happy you're happy, Sylvie."

God, friends... freaking... *rocked!*

Suddenly she pulled back, but her hands framed my face and she yanked mine close to hers. "I want you to make lots of babies. Lots and lots of them. You're so cute and pretty. He's so handsome. They'll be beautiful. They'll be brilliant. They'll be loyal. They'll be funny. They'll be *fabulous.*"

Shit, I was *so* over this. Now Charlene was gonna make me cry.

"Charlene—" I started, my voice sounding hoarse, but that was all I got out before she pulled my face even closer to hers. Her wet, shining eyes were all I could see.

"Make him give you lots of babies. Make him, Sylvie." It sounded like she was begging.

I didn't think I would have a tough time convincing Creed to do this, but still, I gave her what she wanted.

"I will, Charlene."

She let my face go so she could throw her arms around me again and give me a deep, sweet, close hug.

I held her back just the same.

She did it sobbing quietly.

I did it breathing deeply.

We kept doing this until we heard shouting from outside, "Who the fuck are you? That's *my* lawn, asshole."

We both shot away from each other, our heads turning, and I stared as I saw Douchebag Dan stalking toward Creed.

I reacted faster and moved quicker than Charlene, who was sitting frozen on the couch, staring outside, her mouth hanging open.

My eyes went back to the window to see Dan advancing on Creed, who'd stepped away from the lawnmower and turned his not unscary attention on Dan. I grabbed Charlene and shook her firmly but gently.

"Kids," I hissed and looked down at her to see her tear her eyes away from the scene in the yard to bring them to me. "Keep them in the back. Don't let them hear their Dad."

"But, Danny's back. I should go out—"

"Kids, Charlene. Now."

She held my eyes a second before seeing the wisdom of my instruction and nodding.

I took off.

I hit the front door just in time to see Dan, for some Douchebag Dan reason, rearing a fist back and aiming a punch on Creed.

A second later, I stifled a laugh, but not my smile, when Dan ended this maneuver on his belly in the turf with his arm yanked up his back and Creed's knee in his spine.

"You can't assault me on my lawn!" Dan yelled.

"I can defend myself when you try to assault me, moron, and if you don't shut the fuck up and calm the fuck down, I'll show you what assault actually is," Creed returned.

This exchange went down as I was making my way to them and it ended when I stopped three feet away.

"What are you doing here, Dan?" I asked, and Dan twisted his neck, yanking it back in a way that looked kind of painful since he hadn't quit struggling so Creed hadn't loosened the pressure.

He looked up at me.

"Who the fuck is this guy?" he snapped.

"Charlene's new boyfriend," I lied and Dan's eyes widened to huge and his mouth dropped open.

"Sylvie," Creed rumbled.

I grinned at him with him shaking his head, his lips twitching.

Then I looked back at Douchebag Dan to inform him, "She traded up."

"Get him off me," Douchbag Dan demanded, still struggling.

"Uh... just a reminder. He did tell you that if you shut the fuck up and calm the fuck down, he'd let you up."

"He told me he'd *assault* me if I *didn't* do that."

I shrugged. "Tomatoes, toe-mah-toes."

Dan scowled at me as best he could, seeing as his face was mostly in grass. Then he said, "Okay. Whatever. I'll calm down. Tell him to let me up."

I looked back at Creed who was still fighting a smile. "Although you aren't deaf, just in case you missed it, he says he'll calm down. You can let him up."

Creed's grin broke through and he waited a full five seconds before he pushed off and straightened away from Douchebag Dan. This, incidentally, made me love him more, and I already loved him a whole fuckuva lot.

Dan struggled to his feet, swiping at grass clippings on his clothes as he took a healthy, and wise, step back from Creed while glowering at him.

"Are you seriously seeing my wife?" he asked.

"Yeah," Creed lied. "She's hot," Creed did not lie.

Dan looked to the house, muttering, "I don't believe this shit."

"I don't know what's not to believe, Dan," I stated. "Life goes on. Bills need to get paid. Women need to get laid. Lawns need to get mowed. Bonus for the kids, Tucker here," I indicated Creed with a swing of my hand, "actually likes them."

I saw Dan blanch even as his eyes narrowed on me.

"That wasn't cool, Sylvie," he said quietly.

Oh shit. I was getting mad.

I knew Creed knew it because he took a step toward me, but I didn't tear my eyes from Douchebag Dan.

"Are you kidding me? *That* wasn't cool? *You* left them," I reminded him.

"Maybe my head was screwed up, but she's fuckin' another guy!" he shot back. "I've only been gone two months, for fuck's sake."

I leaned toward him. "Two months and a week, *Dan*," I clipped. "You won't know this because you didn't do fuck all while you were here, so let me

269

educate you. That extra week is a lot when you got three kids to take care of, one a toddler, one special needs, and you got a lawn to mow, storm windows to take out, faucets that leak, a mortgage that needs to get paid, a car that needs fixed and a second job to get so you can try to make ends meet. You didn't even leave her the new TV so she could hock it and maybe buy groceries for a couple of days."

"I wasn't gone long and she had the savings," Dan returned.

"She had *half* the savings, Dan, and no word from you. She had no idea you'd come back. Hell, you didn't even give her a heads up you were going."

"Then she's blind and deaf, Sylvie, and you're her best friend so you fuckin' know it," Dan shot back.

I hated to admit it but he was right, even though the action he took wasn't.

"So that's okay, your nonverbal, man communication shoots by her because she's got three kids to take care of and a full-time job? She should have known something was wrong and fixed it? That lets *you* off since *Charlene* didn't make the effort to drag it out of you?" I threw an arm out. "Jesus, Dan, if you're serious about that crap you're more of a douchebag than I thought, and I thought you were the King of Douchebags."

"You don't get how it is," he retorted.

Oh yeah. He was pissing me off.

"Clue in, Dan," I ground out. "I've been over here nearly every morning since you took off. I only have forty-five minutes a morning of it but I *still* know how it is. I also know your wife does not complain. She loves those kids, that house, her family, her life, and she used to love *you*. You fucked up, asshole, *huge*."

"Sylvie, go inside. See to the kids. Get Charlene out here."

This was Creed ordering me around, and in doing so, we'd discovered a time when I wasn't real fond of him being bossy.

Therefore I replied, "No way."

"I'm not moving, and if I don't like how it goes down between them, he's gone and she's inside. Yeah?" Creed returned.

I took in a big breath and countered, "How about if you figure *I* won't like what goes down, he's gone and she's inside?"

"Sylvie, just go get Charlene," Creed kept being bossy.

"Creed—"

"Woman, there is no way in fuck I'm gonna let this motherfucker who walked out on his wife and kids pull shit on her," Creed declared before he stressed, "No fuckin' way. You know that. You know me. You got nothin' to worry about. Now, baby, go the fuck inside, get Charlene and see to the kids."

"Baby?" Douchebag Dan asked at this juncture, and I controlled my blood pressure by looking at him, which didn't exactly help.

"I forgot to mention, he's my man, too. We do three-ways. They rock. See? You totally missed out. You hung around and acted like a decent guy, who knows what would have happened?"

After delivering that, verbally marking my score at the look of shock and hunger that cut through his features, I ignored Creed looking to the sky and shaking his head and stomped into the house.

I found Charlene, guided her away from the kids and held a low-voiced conversation with her in the living room.

"Right, you go out but, Creed is not leaving, and, Charlene, I love you, he loves me, he cares about you and those kids, so he's not gonna leave you alone with Dan in order that he can be close to see to you. You listen to what Dan has to say, but warning: if Creed doesn't like his bullshit, it's done."

"But he's back and—" she started and God, God, *God* she needed to clue in!

I grabbed her by either side of her neck and gave her a gentle shake. "Trust me. Trust Creed. Dan says his head was screwed up and maybe he's not lying. If that's the case and he's got his shit sorted, Creed will get that and roll with it. If it's not, Creed will sniff it out and Dan will be on his way."

She held my eyes.

I held hers back.

She said nothing.

I didn't either until this lasted awhile so I whispered, "Babe, trust us."

She licked her lips before she nodded.

I squeezed her neck and let her go.

She was walking away when I called her name and she turned back.

"Uh... FYI, Dan thinks Creed's your new boyfriend, he's mine too, and we do three-ways."

Her mouth dropped open as her eyes went huge.

I grinned at her then went to find the kids.

Adam, Theo and Leslie were strapped into their car seats in Creed's truck and I was making goofy faces at them through the windows. Once I got big smiles, I stopped doing that, rounded the hood and went to Creed's open window.

"You got them?" I asked quietly.

"I got them, you get her," he answered quietly.

I nodded before saying, "Love you, babe."

"Back at 'cha," Creed replied. I smiled at him, slapped the side of his truck with my hand and stepped away.

Creed pulled away.

I moved to Charlene's house.

I found her in her bedroom, the drapes pulled, the room dark. She was face down on the bed and she'd already been through a half a box of Kleenex, the tissues rumpled and strewn all over the bed and the floor.

Suffice it to say, Douchebag Dan had not got his head screwed on straight. Even Charlene cottoned onto the fact that Dan was home because Dan had underestimated what it would cost to set up a new life without the ball and chain of home, spouse and family. He'd run out of money and had nowhere else to go. This being the case, Creed didn't send him packing. Charlene did.

When I arrived in her room I climbed right into bed with her, shifting until my front was flush with her back and I wrapped my arm tight around her waist, holding her close.

"We'll get you through this," I whispered.

"He's a dick," she whispered back, her voice trembling.

"Yep," I agreed. "He's also gone. You feel this for a while then you move on."

Her body bucked against mine with her sobs but I just held on.

We lay together silently for long minutes before she asked softly, "What if he's my Creed?"

Seriously?

I loved her, but she had to *clue in*.

"He isn't your Creed, and I know this because the true Creeds of this world are out doing things like my Creed is doing: taking your kids for lunch and ice cream and to a park so you have time to get yourself sorted. They do not take off, shirk their responsibilities, come home after over two months and not even ask to see their kids. He isn't your Creed, babe. Maybe there's one out there for you. It just isn't Dan."

I heard her stuttering breath before her head moved on the pillow indicating she was nodding.

"I'll stay until your shit's——" I started, but stopped when she turned in my arm and wrapped hers around me.

"You won't. When you're ready to go, you'll go. I'll be okay. You be happy."

"Helping you out makes me happy," I informed her.

"Not as much as being with Creed."

That was the truth.

"Charlene, girl——"

She shook my body with her arm. "You aren't going tomorrow, right?"

I grinned at her through the dark and confirmed, "Right."

"When my eyes don't feel puffy and my stomach doesn't feel funny and my heart doesn't hurt so damned much, we'll talk. We'll plan. We'll figure it out. I'll find my way and I know you'll help me. It doesn't feel fine now, but it will be. It always is."

"Yeah," I agreed softly. "It always is."

"I hope my fine doesn't take sixteen years, though," she told me, and I grinned again.

"I hope so, too."

She nodded and didn't grin back. She dipped her chin and stared at my chest.

I lifted a hand and pulled her hair away from her face and neck. Then I wrapped my arm around her again and held tight.

Once I did that, I said quietly, "Love you to bits, Charlene."

"I know, Sylvie," she replied quietly back without looking at me. "Love you, too."

I held her close and listened to her take another staggering breath.

And I held her close until she fell asleep in my arms.

And I held her close for a while after.

Kristen Ashley

Then I got up and left her sleeping. I closed her door, and as quietly as I could, I cleaned her house.

"Got a firm on retainer. I'll call them. They have a divorce lawyer who's a fuckin' piranha. This asshole left her with three kids, one Down's, that guy'll nail his balls to the wall."

I was sitting on Knight's couch in Knight's office with my cowboy booted feet up on his coffee table.

Knight was standing at his window, looking down at his heaving club.

It was late. Charlene's kids were home, fed, pajama'd and put to bed. Creed was outside in his truck waiting for me to chat with Knight. I was upstairs doing that, having asked him if he could help Charlene out in some way, and also telling him that I would soon be moving to Phoenix to be with Creed.

As suspected, Knight stepped up for Charlene. It wasn't just hookers he looked after. He wasn't big on any woman getting screwed over in any way that could happen.

I smiled at him. "You rock."

Knight didn't smile at me. I guessed this was because he really didn't like it when women got screwed. He was pissed Charlene was going through this, even though he'd met her only a couple of times, so he barely knew her at all.

When Knight didn't say anything, I offered, "If I have free time from Hawk's job, I'll work for you the next month for free if you set that guy on Dan."

"Did you miss the part about them being on retainer?" he asked.

"No," I answered.

"It's covered, Sylvie."

Yeah. Knight totally rocked.

I smiled at him again, but this time it was bigger.

Knight turned his head away and looked out the window.

Weird.

He could be intense…

No, strike that. He was pretty much always intense, but he wasn't broody. He spoke his mind and didn't hesitate to do it when he had something to say. He wasn't a man of few words. He had words and he used them.

So, as I noted, this was weird.

274

"I'll take on Creed."

This came from Knight, directed toward the window, but meant for me. "What?" I asked.

He turned to me. "I'll take on Creed. Make it worth his while. If he's got to take extra time to go down to Phoenix and see his kids, he'll have it. I always need good men, men I can trust. He's a man like that."

I stared at him, my breath failing me.

He didn't want me to leave.

He was trying to make it so I'd stay.

Holy shit!

I didn't know what to do with this.

"I…" I started, swallowed, sucked in breath then told him quietly, "He doesn't agree with what you do."

Knight tipped his head to the side. "He doesn't agree?"

I shook my head. "He believes you do what you do with integrity, but he doesn't agree with what it is you do. He won't work for you, and even if he would, it wouldn't be fair to ask him to leave his kids. He loves them. For me, I believe he'd do that, but it would tear him apart, so I won't make him."

Knight held my eyes a second then looked back out the window.

I took in another breath as I pulled my boots from his table, put them to the floor then leaned my elbows into my knees.

"I'll come back, visit you and Anya and Kat," I told him.

"Got a lot to be thankful for," he told his window, his words confusing me. "A good woman, beautiful daughter, work I believe in, money, men around me I trust." He turned back to me. "Still, you left, that hole will not be filled. Not ever."

Holy fucking shit!

I felt my throat start to close and forced through it, "Knight," but that was all I could think to say.

Knight held my eyes, and I was so undone I let him, and I did it silently.

Finally, he spoke.

"We'll visit you, too. But, warning Sylvie, we're not comin' down there in the summer. I've been down there in the summer. It's torture. Maybe Thanksgiving. Anya gets off on holidays. She'll like that."

"Creed has a big table," I said quietly.

"You cook?" he asked.

"When forced," I answered, and finally got a lip twitch from Knight.

"Creed cook?" he went on.

"Absolutely."

"Then it's a plan."

I stood, and was going to move to him, but I found my feet failing me. All I could do was stand there, staring at one of only two men in my entire life who really, truly loved me.

So I decided it was time to give that back.

"You know, I love you, Knight."

"You could have been one of my girls."

Again, that wasn't the response I was expecting.

"Say again?" I asked.

"You came to Denver, after that shit went down with you, if that had broken you, you could have found me for another reason. You didn't. You didn't let that shit break you. You didn't bow to it. You fought it. You didn't become one of my girls. You became the woman who protected them. That says a lot about you, Sylvie. I respect that. I respect you. I respect that you're professional, I can trust you, but you still got a personality, a sense of humor. After that shit happened to you, you kept that, you kept you. I respect that, too. I respect that we had an attraction, and, not like a lot of women, when we found we didn't suit, you didn't let that shit turn catty or destructive. You let it go, you kept us solid and it means somethin' to me you shared your shit with me. You trusted me with it. You trusted that me knowin' it wouldn't alter our relationship. That was an honor, Sylvie. I know you haven't given that to anyone but me and Charlene, and, babe, it was an honor you chose me."

Told you Knight could talk.

And that was nice and all, *really* nice, but I was a little put out he didn't say it straight. He always said it straight.

Then he said it straight.

"We been through a lot and you earned a piece of my heart, babe. It's all yours and always will be."

I pressed my lips together.

"You cry, I'm tellin' the boys," he warned.

I unpressed my lips and glared at him.

He smiled at me.

"Come here," he ordered.

I went there, and when I got close Knight Sebring's arms folded around me.

Mine folded right back.

We'd hugged only once in the time we'd known each other, and that had been when we were drunk and I told him all about Creed.

It felt better not being drunk and after I got Creed back, even if that meant I was semi-losing Knight.

"I'll miss you, Sylvie," he whispered into the top of my hair.

"I'm not leaving tomorrow," I told him.

"Then I'll enjoy you bein' a pain in the ass for as long as it lasts."

I sighed, but it was fake and both of us knew it.

Knight gave me a squeeze then he let go and I stepped back.

"Gotta get to my man," I said.

"Go," Knight replied.

I nodded, lifted a hand, squeezed his bicep then moved to the door.

I stopped at it and turned back. "You know, I agree." I shook my head. "That's not true. I don't agree, exactly. I believe. I believe in what you do, Knight."

"I know," he told me.

"The Serenas though, before they begin—"

Knight cut me off. "Know that, too, Sylvie."

I studied him and I knew. He felt what happened to Serena. He felt it deep. He knew she had no business in the business.

"We're instituting better screens," Knight explained, and I knew what that meant. A girl came to him, she wouldn't work unless she understood the life and could take it.

"Right," I muttered before, "You got work to throw my way, I can take it on and do Hawk's job, I'll take it and be a pain in the ass while doing it."

"Would expect nothing less," Knight returned.

"You'd be right," I replied.

He shook his head and jerked his chin to the door.

I shot him a grin and walked out of it.

I was down the steps, through the club and out the backdoor before I let it hit me. And when it did, it nearly brought me to my knees.

Kristen Ashley

I loved the life I had in Denver and the people I shared it with. I was only moving a state away, but that didn't mean it didn't hurt like a mother knowing I had to let it go.

I saw Creed standing outside his truck, leaning back against it, having a smoke, probably doing this because he was worried about me.

He studied me as I walked through the streetlamps toward him and he flicked his cigarette into the alley when I was three feet away. He saw it on my face, I knew, and that was why he pulled me straight into his arms and held me tight.

"He's gonna help Charlene," I shared, snaking my arms around him.

"Not surprised."

My arms tightened around him.

"That sucked," I said into his chest.

"I bet."

"I'm not gonna cry," I stated.

"All right."

I sucked in breath.

Creed whispered, "I love you, Sylvie. Thank you for doin' this for me, baby. I know you know, but I'll say it clear, it means the world to me. Just like you. All I can promise is, a day won't go by where you won't know you got that from me."

At that, I started crying silently.

I did this while Creed held me, and I kept doing it for a good long while.

Through it, Creed never let me go.

Chapter 22

My Creed

A hot summer night in Kentucky, sixteen years earlier. Creed is twenty-three. It's Sylvie's birthday, she's just turned eighteen...

I was in the warm, midnight blue waters of the lake when I saw his truck drive up, the headlights bright, cutting through the cloudless night.

I treaded water and watched the lights go out on his truck. I kept doing it as I watched his tall, shadowed form stalk through the dark toward the pier.

I adjusted my position and kept my eyes on him as I heard his boots fall on the wood slats while he made his way to me.

At the end, he stopped and I felt his eyes on me through the dark.

"Baby, what the fuck?" he asked, sounding irritated. "We got all of six hours before we're home free. Why did you call me and what the fuck are you doin' in the lake?"

"What time is it?" I asked back.

"What?" he returned.

"Creed, honey, what time is it?"

He looked to his watch then back at me. "Can't see shit, so I don't know but I left the house at two fifteen."

I did a lazy breast stroke and when I made it to the end of the pier, I lifted a wet hand and curled my fingers around the edge, tipping my head way back to keep my eyes on Creed.

"I was born at two oh four."

His patience waned. I knew this when he asked, "Sylvie, again, what the fuck?"

"I was born at two oh four."

Creed said nothing, but I saw the line of his body go completely still.

He understood me.

"I'm legal, baby," I told him softly.

I barely got out the word "baby" when he crouched low and leaned forward. His hands went under my pits and he hauled me clean out of the water.

Just as suddenly, he was down and my wet, bikini-clad body was on him and his hands were on me.

All over me.

Finally.

I'd wanted this for as long as I knew it was mine to have. I'd wanted to give this to Creed for as long as I knew it was mine to give. For a year, we'd held back.

The floodgates opened and it all rushed out, beautifully.

But not perfectly.

He started by kissing me then he reached out and grabbed the blanket I brought, pulled us up to our feet and covered the pier with it.

After he did that, back down we went, this time, Creed on top of me.

A place I loved him to be.

Creed, being Creed, gave and gave, with his hands, his mouth, his fingers, his tongue, even his teeth. Gentle, slow, sweet.

Restrained.

I knew it cost him because I felt his tenseness, heard him stifle the noises he would normally make, probably so he didn't scare me.

My hands up his shirt tensed against his sleek skin.

"Let this be everything it's meant to be, Creed," I whispered into his neck.

"Want it to be the best it can be for you, Sylvie," he whispered in mine.

"It's you. There's no other way it can be."

His head came up and I felt his eyes looking down at me.

"What do I do?" I asked.

"Whatever you want," he answered. "Do what comes naturally."

I shoved my hands in his tee and pulled up.

Creed arched his back and lifted his arms.

I pulled his shirt off.

Amazing.

All that smooth, muscled skin in the moonlight.

Amazing.

I put my hands to it.

Not amazing.

Sublime.

Creed kissed me.

Even better.

He rolled so I was on top and I used my hands on him, my mouth, my fingers, my tongue, even my teeth. Just like he did on me.

He rolled us again so he was on top, he did the same to me and I felt it building. Building so much, I couldn't stop the noises from escaping my throat. Little whimpers, low moans, breathless gasps.

Creed's lips on mine, he told me gently, "Gonna put my hand between your legs, beautiful. Are you ready?"

"I'm ready," I breathed.

His hand slid down my belly and I shivered, waiting, braced, anticipating, *needing,* but he stopped with his fingertips at the top edge of my bikini bottoms.

"You sure?" he checked.

"Baby," I gasped. "I'm ready."

His hand slid in.

My neck arched.

Oh wow.

Wow.

His finger hit me right at the perfect spot and my hips bucked violently.

I liked that.

A lot.

His finger retreated.

No!

"Jesus, I hurt you, Sylvie?"

"No," I panted, my hands moving on him, feverish, communicating. Then I gave it to him verbally. "Please," I whispered.

Apparently he needed no further encouragement. I knew this because his hand slid back in and his finger went right where I needed it.

My mouth opened on a silent moan.

Yes, this was good.

Now, it was perfect.

His finger moved on that sweet spot between my legs as his mouth moved on my neck, his tongue traced my jaw. Then, just as it built so high it crashed over, obliterating me with its sheer beauty, his mouth took mine and his tongue slid inside.

Yes.

Utterly.

Perfect.

As it slowly receded, I felt Creed's finger move tenderly away then his hands went to the string ties on the sides of my bikini. He pulled them and I felt the material loosen around my hips.

"Gotta have you, baby," he murmured against my mouth, his hand doing something at the back of his jeans.

"Okay," I whispered.

"I'll go slow. Be gentle," he promised.

"Okay," I repeated.

"It may hurt, beautiful," he warned. "I'll try to—"

My hands slid up his back into his hair and I curled them around the back of his head as I lifted mine, my lips to his and I urged, "Creed, baby, it's okay. I want it. I've been waiting forever for you to make me *really* your Sylvie. So, please, *please* make me your Sylvie."

I heard, just as I felt, his deep groan.

Yes.

Yes.

Utterly *perfect.*

Then, at the end of our pier, surrounded by our lake, my Creed set about making me *really* his Sylvie.

And he really became my Creed.

"We should just leave."

That was Creed.

We were at the end of the pier. I had my legs curled under me, my bikini bottoms back on, Creed's tee covering the rest of me. He was wearing his jeans, rolled up, his legs over the side, feet in the water. I was resting against him, my arms around his middle, my cheek to his chest. He had his arm curled tight around me and we were studying the lake.

"Just leave?" I asked the water.

"Get in my truck," he answered. "Go."

I closed my eyes and drew in a breath.

Then I reminded him, "I've got a bikini, Creed. Shorts, a tank, flip-flops. That's it."

"That's all you need. That and me."

He was right.

But what he wanted to do was wrong.

I pulled my head away from his chest and tipped it back. As I did, his arm tightened around me, pulling me closer, and his chin dipped down so he could study my face in the moonlight.

"The plan is we meet here, eight thirty tomorrow after I tell Daddy I'm leaving," I reminded him.

"We should change the plan."

"Creed—"

His arm got super tight as he pulled me and twisted me so my bottom was in his lap.

Then he stated, "You don't owe him that, beautiful. You don't owe him shit."

"He's my father."

"He's no father."

This was true.

Darn.

To buy time, I watched as I slid a hand up his chest, the skin warm and smooth, the muscle underneath hard and defined. I loved every inch. So I memorized the feel, knowing I'd be able to call that up anytime, always, for the rest of my life and remember it. Remember tonight. Remember every second. Every single second of my first time on the pier, by our lake, making love with Creed.

I pulled in a deep breath before I replied, "It wouldn't feel right."

"Too good of a girl," Creed muttered, and I looked up at him to see his eyes on the lake.

"He doesn't deserve it, but I'm not what my mother said. I'm not like him. I couldn't live with myself if I just up and left. Didn't tell him I was going. Didn't tell him I wasn't coming back. He's not much of a father, Creed, but maybe somewhere in there, somewhere deep, he'd worry, and I'd worry about that. At least, if he knows, I won't have that worry."

I heard and felt Creed heave a deep sigh, but he didn't speak.

I snuggled closer. "I'm all packed. First thing, I'll tell him and then I'll meet you here."

His hand slid up my back and into my damp hair before he murmured, "You're mine now, beautiful, in all the ways you can be. What we just shared, I

283

loved it, it was right. Being here, our place, it was perfect. I want more. I want it all. I'm tired of waiting."

I was too.

Still.

"Just a few more hours," I whispered.

Creed's hand cupped the back of my head so he could shove my face in his chest as he replied, "This proves it, baby. Nothin' I won't do for my Sylvie."

I grinned against his chest and my arms around him gave him a squeeze.

I turned my head and pressed my cheek against his skin before I called it down.

"So, your friend has power of attorney to sign the papers to sell your house next week. I'm packed. I'll tell Daddy, come here," I gave him another squeeze, "you'll give me my necklace, we'll eat frozen Snickers bars for breakfast and then we're gone."

"Gotta find somethin' different for you," he muttered. "I'm thinkin' I don't like you knowin' what you're gonna get for your birthday for forever."

My head jerked back and my eyes honed in on his face. "If you ever, *ever* get me anything but my peridot pendant, Creed, I… I… well, I don't know what I'll do, but I'll be super, extra pissy."

I saw the white flash of his teeth. "Wouldn't wanna make you super, extra pissy."

"Don't joke. I'm serious. Those necklaces are the only things I own that mean a thing to me."

I saw the white flash of his teeth disappear right before I heard the guttural tone of his, "Jesus, Sylvie."

"And they always will be," I finished.

Both his arms closed around me tight. My head tipped back, his dipped down and he kissed me, hard, wet and long. A new kind of kiss. An unrestrained kiss.

Pure beauty.

Unfortunately, it didn't last forever like I'd like it too. Creed broke it.

Then he murmured, "Let's get you dressed and home. Our life starts in about four hours. Don't want you nodding off when it does."

"Probably a good plan," I agreed, smiling at him.

I caught his smile back at me then he shifted, we were up and he placed me on my feet.

He held my hand as he walked me to my clothes. I gave him his shirt. He gave me my bikini top. He tied the back for me and I pulled on my tank and shorts and slipped on my flip-flops. Creed grabbed the blanket and again he held my hand as he walked me to my car.

At the door, again, he kissed me. This one I'd had before.

A good-bye kiss.

I savored it because it was the last one.

The last good-bye kiss ever.

Tomorrow, there would be nothing but the-rest-of-our-lives kisses, free and easy.

"Sleep good, beautiful," he muttered against my mouth.

Like I was going to sleep.

Not.

"You too, Creed."

"Soon, baby."

"Soon, Creed."

His arms gave me a squeeze. "Love you, Sylvie. Didn't think I could do it more, but after what you gave me tonight, know it can be more until infinity."

Oh.

Wow.

People in town thought Winona Creed was a redneck hick, a floozy, stupid and a loser.

Creed fell very, very far from that tree. What he said might not rhyme but still, it was poetry.

"I love you too, Creed. Seems like I've loved you forever, but I know that I will love you that way. Forever."

I wasn't as good at it, but Creed didn't seem to mind. I knew this when he bent his neck and gave me another good-bye kiss, soft, sweet and short.

Okay, so *that* kiss was the last one.

In my car, I waved, staring at his shadowed form in my rearview mirror, feeling light, feeling free, feeling happy, not having any clue I wouldn't see that tall, muscled frame for sixteen years.

Not having any idea.

And feeling so happy when I stole into the dark house I grew up in, through the foyer and up the stairs, thinking it was for the last time, I didn't feel Daddy's eyes watching me.

Chapter 23
You Can't See It

Present day, six days later...

They had him chained to the floor, cheek to the cement, tape on his upper and lower eyelids, stuck to his lashes, holding his eyes open.

So Creed saw her when they pushed her down and chained her to the floor six feet away.

At first glance, he thought she was me. Same hair. Same build. Same face shape. Even the same colored eyes.

She wasn't me.

Daddy held his head down so Creed couldn't even turn it. The tape held his eyes open so he couldn't shut the visions away. There was no way he could close out the screams.

No.

He had to watch.

Watch as they ripped her clothes away.

Watch as, for hours, repeatedly, brutally, they raped her.

Watch as she fought the chains, strained, shrieked, begged.

Watch as the blood flowed from between her legs, where the chains gouged into her wrists, her neck, her ankles.

Watch as the fight left her, the light died in her eyes and she lay, her head turned, her gaze locked to Creed's as they kept at her for hours, one after the other and then back again.

Five of them.

Then they were done.

"You know," Daddy whispered into Creed's ear, "you take her, you think to escape me, you know I'll find you."

He knew. Daddy had a lot of money. Daddy had a long reach.

Daddy kept talking.

"I've tried to talk sense into you, but it's come to this. You've already sullied her, taking her virginity. You take her, Tucker, I'll find you. I'll bring you both back. You take her, she'll mean nothing to me. If you take her, I'll bring you back and I'll make you watch like you did just now as they do the same to Sylvie. But she'll be safe if you leave her be."

This time, Creed didn't say, "never".

His eyes forced open, his head still held down, he had no choice but to stare into the girl's eyes. The girl, so young, maybe seventeen, maybe even sixteen, my hair, my body, bloodied, bruised, violated, the light in her eyes extinguished.

So like me.

So very like me.

He knew, if Daddy would do that to her, he'd do it to me.

Creed's voice came, weak, raspy, "Promise me."

Daddy's hand left his head, but she didn't look away so Creed, now free to move his head, didn't either. He gave her his gaze, the only thing he had to give, the only thing he had to offer her as even a scrap of comfort as she endured a nightmare.

"Promise?" Daddy asked.

Creed stared at the girl who was almost me.

"She'll be happy."

Quickly, Daddy declared, "I promise, Tucker, she'll be happy."

"Swear it."

"You leave, never come back, never phone, never try to see her, I swear. She'll be happy. I'll do everything in my power to make sure she's happy. You come back, phone, ever, *ever* try to contact her again, she'll be lying there as that girl is and you'll be lying right where you are, watching."

"Just make her happy."

"I'll make her happy."

Creed stared into the girl's eyes and watched the fresh tear roll over the bridge of her nose, drop and mingle with the blood on the cement by her face.

So me.

So very me.

"Then I'll leave."

I shot up in the bed, and not thinking, my skin prickling, cold sweat trickling between my breasts, I jumped to my feet, and for some reason hurdled over Creed's body. My feet landed on the other side of the bed and I bounded to the floor. My foot lifting to run, flee, escape like that girl sixteen years ago was me and I had the chance, one shot, to get away before they destroyed me.

Creed's arm hooked my waist and I flew backwards. Landing in the bed, Creed rolled over me.

"It's a dream, Sylvie. Just a dream," he said what he'd said over and over again when I woke up after a dream assaulted me.

"I know those men. I know those men," I panted, my breath coming fast, sharp, heavy, hurting as it tore up my throat and out of me. "I know them… knew them. Served them beer. Nachos. I knew those men, Creed."

"Beautiful, what are you—?"

"The men, Richard's men, those men who Daddy forced you to watch raping that girl who looked like me."

"Fuck," he clipped then bit out, "You're dreaming that shit."

My hands drove into either side of his hair and held tight. "I knew them. I brought them beers while they watched games on Richard's huge ass TV."

"They're out of your life, Sylvie."

"I knew them."

"Baby, they're gone."

"*I knew them!*" I shrieked.

Creed stilled then he rolled, sitting up, forcing me to straddle him, but his arms clamped tight around me.

"Calm down, Sylvie," he ordered firmly.

"I can't, Creed."

"You gotta try, baby."

"I *can't*, Creed. It's hideous."

I stopped speaking, shook my head and struggled in his lap. I had too much energy. I had to move. Pace. Run. Sprint. Stand up and scream.

Creed held firm and wouldn't let me, so I gave up and kept talking.

"I can't believe they did that. I can't believe they *taped your eyes open* and *made you watch*. I can't believe they found someone who looked like me and hurt her like that. Just because she was unlucky enough to look like me and they needed to make a point, hurt her in a way she'd never get over. Alter her life forever and you didn't even know who she was. They probably didn't know who she was!"

"I know who she was."

That made me go still.

"You knew her?" I asked quietly.

"Not then," he answered. "After. When I got into the business. When I had the resources. A few years later, I tracked her. She was from a county over. She was the girl in the picture with Dixon who I was too fucked up to note really wasn't you."

"Is she okay?"

Creed didn't answer.

"Is she okay, Creed?"

Swiftly, like pulling off a Band-Aid, he gave it to me.

"She committed suicide two days after they released her and me."

I closed my eyes, and not able to hold it up, my head fell forward and slammed into his collarbone.

"Maybe the best thing for her, baby," he whispered. "She went home."

"You don't believe that," I replied.

Creed said nothing.

I was right. He didn't believe that. He was just spouting that shit to make me feel better.

"God, if they weren't dead, I'd kill them," I told his collarbone then lifted my head. "Or, in Richard's case, I'd kill him *again*. Though this time, I'd find a better way to do it."

"When you told me what went down, Sylvie, and while you were deciding whether or not to listen to me, got a buddy who has a buddy back home. I made a call and he made a call, and his buddy looked into that shit. You hit Scott's jugular. Report says he bled out in minutes. Seems you found the best way to do it."

"Right, then, I'll amend. If I knew he was even *more* of a heartless sociopath than I already knew he was, I would have made it last a whole lot longer."

"Baby, I've said it before, I'll say it again. It's over and you keep dreamin' this shit so you need to see somebody."

"I'll call someone."

"Yeah? When?" he shot back. "We been back here two weeks and you haven't called anyone."

"It's been a little busy and the kids come up today. Not to mention, soon, I'm moving so why start now when I'll have to find someone in Phoenix?"

"So you won't wake up in a cold sweat and leap over me, runnin' to God knows where to do whacked shit that freaks me way the fuck out."

He had a point.

"I haven't had a dream in days. Maybe they're waning," I suggested.

"He tied you down. He took you repeatedly," Creed returned. "He violated you in ways you didn't want. He controlled you. Sylvie, I am no psychologist and you got a heart of gold. You don't know that girl, you weren't there. It was nearly two decades ago and she is very dead, and I still know you feel for her, but this isn't about her. This is about you. This is about you learning I watched that happen to her and then I learned that pretty much the same thing happened to you for *six fuckin' years.* You givin' me that shit and remembering it happened to you, both are fuckin' with your head. I do not have the tools to sort that. You have got to find the tools to sort that. People in counseling move all the time. Psychologists know the drill. They start therapy and they transfer you to a new doctor, but you gotta start therapy, Sylvie. You gotta work this shit out. For you. For me. For the family we're making. For Charlene. For Adam. For everybody."

Fuck it all, I hated it when he was right, and it happened a lot.

So I did the only thing I could do.

I snapped my, "Okay."

"That okay is an okay as in, you call to-fuckin'-day. I'm standin' over you, Sylvie. Clock strikes nine in the morning, you're on the goddamned phone finding a therapist you think you can work with."

"Fine," I bit out.

"Don't think I'm joking."

I didn't think that. His tone told me he absolutely was not.

"I said fine," I clipped.

"Jesus, this shit makes me wonder if I should have just let you think I left you."

My blood turned cold.

"Don't say that."

"It's haunting you."

"Don't say that."

"It's bringing it all back. You had it under control. Now it's in your face."

"*Don't say that!*" I shouted, jerked away, breaking free from his arms. I jumped to the side of the bed only to lean forward and point at him. "If you didn't tell me, I'd never have let you back in."

"Come back to bed, Sylvie."

I swung my arm out. "You didn't tell me, we wouldn't have this."

He leaned toward me, his tone cautious, and he ordered gently, "Baby, come back to bed."

I ignored him and carried on, this time my voice hoarse, beginning to grate, sounding like it would break, "You didn't tell me, I wouldn't have you."

"Sylvie, come back to me."

My voice was abrasive when I declared, "I'll take nightmares every night for the rest of my fucking life if it comes with waking up to you."

He reached out a hand and caught mine, but I leaned back, putting my weight into tearing free.

I couldn't because Creed held tight.

"I shouldn't have said that," he whispered. "I'm sorry I said that, beautiful. I should never have said that."

"I watched you in my rearview mirror," I told him.

He pulled on my hand and his voice was gruff when he pleaded, "Baby, fuckin' please, come back to bed."

"I was so happy."

"Jesus, Sylvie."

"I sat on that pier for hours the next day. It was so hot, the Snickers bars melted in their wrappers. I got sunburn."

His hand tugged at mine and his voice was harsh when he said, "Fuck me, Sylvie, please, come back to bed."

"I looked everywhere. I couldn't find you."

"Fuck."

"Days, I looked and I couldn't find you."

"Baby, please."

My voice broke on my repeated, "I couldn't find you," and Creed was done.

I knew this because he yanked on my arm and I went flying to him. Then I was in his arms in bed, tucked mostly under him, one of his hands cupping the back of my head, pressing it into his throat, both arms holding me tight.

"I couldn't find you," I whispered into his skin.

"I'm here."

"You always protected me."

"Fuck me, fuck me, fuck me," he murmured into the top of my hair.

"When Daddy gave me to him, I knew you'd come back and take me away. Take care of me."

"Fuck, Sylvie."

"You didn't come back."

Creed said nothing.

I lay in his arms and it hit me what I was saying and what it must sound like.

"I don't blame you," I told him quickly.

Creed said nothing.

"After that, what they did to that girl, I would have done the same thing," I declared.

Creed said nothing.

"You did what you thought was right. You couldn't know. We didn't know Daddy was hooked on blow. Hooked so bad, in so deep, he had to pay Richard off with me."

Creed said nothing.

"Creed."

Creed rolled over me, and by the time I turned in bed I heard what I suspected was the lamp from my nightstand crash against the wall.

Then I heard his roar, "*Fuck me!*"

I shot out of bed, pressed myself to his back and circled his middle with my arms.

I pressed my face into his skin, into my tat. "Sorry, baby, sorry, so, so, sorry. I should have shut up. I shouldn't have kept talking."

He twisted in my arms and his big hands cupped either side of my head, jerking it back with only a modicum of gentleness, and his shadowed face was all I could see.

"You work that shit out, Sylvie, you work it out and you do it *with me,*" he growled.

"Okay." I thought it best to agree immediately.

"You give me everything you got, I'll deal."

"Okay," I agreed again, immediately.

"They took a month from me. They took *six years* from you. I'll deal."

"Okay."

He used his hands on my head to yank me forward and I did a forced face plant in his chest before his arms wrapped around my head.

293

When I felt his chest expand with a huge breath then release I felt it safe to note, "They took a month from you, six years from me but they took *sixteen* years from *us*."

"Yeah. And we'll both deal with that shit by me makin' love to you, planting my baby inside you, and both of us, when we make more, *all* of us livin' free, easy and happy for the rest of our lives, exactly how they did not want us to be."

It was easy to agree to that one.

"Okay."

Creed didn't let me go and I let him hold me.

This went on awhile. So long I decided to move things on.

"Uh... Creed?"

"Right here, Sylvie."

"This might not be the time, but I'm thinking at least three kids, maybe four."

His body turned to stone.

"Okay, three," I said hurriedly.

Creed said nothing.

"Right, then, two. But, warning, I'm sticking on two."

Creed still said nothing.

"Though, if it's two boys, we have to go for a girl..." I paused, "and, uh, vice versa."

Creed stayed silent but started walking me backwards to the bed. We weren't too far so we went down in two steps, me on my back, Creed on top of me.

After we bounced twice and settled, Creed spoke.

"You want four kids, we best get to work, baby."

I grinned.

There it was. Creed made it all better.

Unfortunately, he went on, "We stop at three, you get to an age where four isn't healthy."

Seriously?

"I'm not old, Creed."

"Gotta have two years in between."

"Is that a rule?"

"Yes."

Seriously. Sometimes a bossy badass was annoying.

"Creed—"

His head was descending and I stopped talking when it froze in its descent for a moment before he dipped his chin and looked at me through the dark.

"It's two oh five," he announced weirdly.

"What?" I asked.

"It's two oh five, baby."

"Okay," I said slowly, not understanding the information he seemed intent on imparting on me. Or, more to the point, not understanding why he seemed intent on imparting this information on me.

His lips came to mine. "You're a minute into your thirty-fifth birthday."

Oh. Yeah.

Right on!

"Yippee," I whispered against his lips. I was pretty sure he was going to kiss me, but he rolled, got on his ass, did something in the dark by the night-stand then he came back to me.

His hand trailed down my arm and found my wrist, lifted it and turned it so my hand was palm up.

I felt a box set in it.

"My girl's green," Creed murmured.

Oh shit.

Oh crap.

Oh fuck.

I had this back, too.

Not that I forgot it, just that I had it back.

I had it back.

Finally.

Tears clogged my throat and through them, I pushed out a weak, "Creed."

"Open it, Sylvie."

I sucked in breath and started to shift up. Creed moved to my side. I got up on my ass, and in the dark, I opened it. I didn't even look at it, not that I could see it if I tried. I just pulled it out, tossed the box aside and my fingers slid along the chain until I found the clasp.

"Will you lift my hair, baby?" I muttered, and Creed moved to do as I asked.

When he shoved a hand under and lifted the mass up, I clasped the neck-lace on and felt its cold settle next to the one I was already wearing.

My eyes went to him. "Love it."

My hair tumbled down. I felt his hand cup my jaw and there was a smile in his voice when he remarked, "You can't see it."

"Don't care. Still love it."

For a moment, yet again, Creed said nothing.

Then he said something, he just didn't use words.

He moved into me, covered me and used body language.

Magnificently.

Thus my thirty-fifth birthday, unlike any of the thirty-four before, except one, started perfectly.

This was it.

The life.

It was evening. I lay on my back in my backyard, elbows in the turf, bare feet crossed, gut filled with Creed's homemade, shredded chicken barbeque sandwiches, store bought macaroni salad and Charlene's birthday cake. I was watching Brand and Kara play with Adam and Leslie. Creed was lying in the grass twenty feet away letting Theo use him as a jungle gym while Charlene was in my kitchen. She had put her foot down declaring I was not allowed to do the dishes on my birthday (not that I would; they could wait a day or three) so she was doing them.

I lounged thinking that I loved this. I only ever had a hint of this feeling, spending time with Creed and his kids in Phoenix, but I got it.

This was what family felt like.

This was what friends *and* family felt like.

This was what it felt like to be surrounded by people you loved who loved you (mostly; Kara and Brand probably weren't there yet, but I hoped they some-day would be).

Outside of having Creed, this was the best feeling in the world.

And when he and I made our babies and Kara and Brand got to know me, it would only get better.

I'd had eleven great birthdays. The ones I spent with Creed growing up.

Those were great, but this one was better.

Further, it was official. Creed's kids were good kids. Maybe Creed gave them a heads up and some instruction, but they didn't even blink when they met Adam. They also didn't treat him any differently.

Kara, especially.

I was surprised, considering her age, but she seemed to have a natural ability both to look out for Adam without making it seem like she was while at the same time she included him.

It was pretty awesome.

It had been Creed's idea to bring the kids up to Denver. He said it would be a before-going-back-to-school mini-vacation for them because they'd never been here before. We were going to Elitch Gardens amusement park the next day and the Butterfly Pavilions on Sunday before he had to put them back on a plane.

He said that he also wanted to them to come up because even kids absorb things, witnessing people in their element and meeting the people who meant something to them. So it would be an opportunity for them to get to know me better.

It was my decree that they were staying in a hotel. Firstly, my second bedroom was still a pit and I hadn't had the chance to clean it out. I also thought it was way too soon to introduce them to the kind of intimacy Creed and I sleeping together would communicate.

Creed agreed, but only with the stipulation that I join him in his room (he and the kids had adjoining rooms) when he called to tell me they were asleep.

But the whole weekend, outside of the nights, would be spent together.

I was looking forward to it. Not only because I fucking loved roller coasters, and they had tarantulas you could hold at the Butterfly Pavilion and tarantulas weighed about an ounce, they were furry, cool and I thought they were the shit. But also because I got a birthday weekend like I'd never had before.

Filled with family.

I heard dishes clanking in the kitchen while I watched Creed roll to his back, grab Theo and toss him in air repeatedly, making Theo giggle. I hoped like all hell all the unprotected sex we were having meant I'd soon see him again doing just that.

But with our baby.

I was so focused on this, when Brand threw himself into the grass beside me, my body jerked and my head whipped around.

Kristen Ashley

"Hide and seek is for babies," he declared, and my gaze moved into the yard to see, with difficulty but also patience, Kara organizing the game with Adam and Leslie.

"I don't know," I replied to Brand. "Seems like it'd be fun to me."

He grinned at me. "A squirt gun fight would be fun."

I grinned back. "Yeah," I agreed. "Little too late for that, though. Charlene and the kids'll be heading home soon."

He looked into the yard. "Bummer." Then his eyes came back to me and he suggested, "We could do it when they leave."

"I don't have any squirt guns," I informed him, making a mental note to put that on my shopping list and stock up.

"Does Denver have stores?" he asked cheekily.

"Uh... yeah," I answered.

"Then I get to ride with you in your 'Vette when we go get 'em."

My grin became a smile. "It's a plan."

He looked back at the yard and stated, "It'll be so cool when you move in with Dad and we move in with you guys. Squirt gun fights all the time."

I stared at his profile, forgetting how to breathe.

I forced myself to remember and asked a wheezy, "What?"

He looked back at me with another grin. "Kara says you're gonna move in, and when you do, we're gonna move to Dad's. He has a better pool and *he* likes football, so we can watch it on the big screen. Not like at home where Mom makes me and Van watch it outside on the smaller TV." He paused then finished, "Oh, and you have a 'Vette, which is *way* cooler than any of Dad's *or* Mom's *or* Van's cars."

I blinked at him before I cautiously asked, "You're, uh... moving in with your Dad?"

He nodded and looked back at the yard. "Yup. Kara says you're Sylvie and we know what that means."

Holy shit!

"What does that, um... mean?" I asked, and his eyes came to me.

"You're on Dad's back."

God, Creed was right. His kids were far from dumb.

"Brand—" I started, but he interrupted me, not that I knew what I was going to say.

298

"Kara says you're, like, *the one*. She says Dad's been waitin' for you to come back for, like, *ever*. She says that now you're back, Dad will be happy and he'll want us all together. She says Mom couldn't hold on to him because she wasn't you. Now he has you and we can be a family again. Least that's what Kara says."

He looked back to the yard as I mentally scrambled to figure out what to say, what to do, at the same time sending vibes to Creed in an effort to get him to come over and rescue me from this crazy, landmine filled conversation.

Even as I scrambled, Brand, being Brand, kept talking, and when he did, he gave me the remaining puzzle pieces as to why Kara and her Mom didn't get on and why Kara attached herself to his hip when she was around Creed.

"Kara says Dad's the best guy on earth and I agree. Totally. Only the best girl for the best guy, she says. She says she wasn't surprised when she met you because you're like Dad. Cool and pretty but fun." He shot another grin at me. "Dad can be kinda strict."

"Uh..." I mumbled.

Brand kept talking.

"Mom's cool, too, I think. Kara and her, though..." he shrugged and looked away. "I like Van, but Kara says he's no Dad. He isn't, but he's okay. I like him, but I think he tries too hard with Kara and that's kinda lame. I mean, he should be with her like he is with me, you know, natural-like." He shook his head. "But he isn't."

Van, obviously Chelle's husband, wasn't with Kara like he was with Brand, I suspected, because Brand liked him and he didn't have to try.

Brand continued blabbing.

"Kara says a woman like Mom gets a man like Van and a woman like you catches the eye of a man like Dad. She says it's going to be *totally* awesome when we move in with you guys because we'll be cool just like you. I love her, but Mom and Van aren't cool. Mom and Van are, like, totally *normal*."

Shit.

Shit, shit, *shit*.

Brand wasn't done.

"Kara blames Mom for Dad leaving. She always did, you know. I didn't get it, but after we met you and she explained it, I did. Mom couldn't hold him because Mom wasn't you. I miss him, but Kara, she like, *really* misses him. She's a pain, but she's my sister and it kinda hurts to watch."

And there it was.

Kara blamed Chelle for Creed leaving.

Shit.

Shit, shit, shit!

"She's a whole lot better now," Brand finished.

Shit.

Well, I guessed I couldn't ease my way into being a part of the family. Not with these people. They were sucking me into the big stuff right away. All of them.

Crap.

"Brand," I called.

"Yeah," he answered.

"Look at me, would you?"

He looked at me.

I took in a breath.

Then I laid it out.

"I gotta tell you, straight out, that I gotta talk to your Dad about what you just told me."

His head tipped to the side. "Why?"

"'Cause I'm not real sure how you and Kara think it's gonna go is how it's gonna go."

He looked a little confused and a little scared as he studied me. "Are you and Dad not, like, hooked up? I mean, are you not the Sylvie from his back? Before we met you, he told us your name and he told us that he'd known you from a long time ago, so we just figured you were that Sylvie."

Shit!

"We are hooked up," I said quietly. "Very. And I am that Sylvie. It's just that I need to tell him what you and Kara expect for your future. Or, maybe, if you feel up to it, you both should talk to him about it. That would actually be better."

The confusion left, the fear escalated, and I knew I was not handling this well at all.

God, should I call Creed over?

"Does Dad not want us to live with him?" Brand asked.

I so totally should call Creed over, but I couldn't since I figured the priority was dealing with Brand's escalating fear immediately.

"He does," I answered. "Definitely. He misses you kids. He talks about you lots. He loves you to bits. But, it's just—"

"Do *you* not want us to live with him?"

God!

What the fuck should I do?

Crap. I had to do what I always did.

Give it to him honestly.

"Yes," I stated. "In a perfect world, yes. I think you kids are the business. You're funny and smart, and if I get some practice in, I am *so* getting my fair share of the pizzookie."

That got me a small grin. I took heart in that so I kept going.

"So if you were around, I'd have lots of practice. But I've also met your Mom and I liked her a lot. She's awesome. She still cares about your Dad and she totally loves both of you. For your Dad to have you, that would mean her losing you. It sucks, babe. You're young and this is heavy stuff. My Mom and Dad were divorced and it's not fun, sharing time, wanting both, only getting one at a time."

Okay, part of that was a lie, but I had to roll with it, so I kept doing that.

"And, for a while, until you're old enough to do it for yourselves, your Dad and Mom have got to decide what's best for you. I'm here to listen and happy to do it, but they make the decisions. You just gotta tell them where your head is at, and I don't just mean you. Kara too. Your Dad has told me she and your Mom kinda don't get along, and it worries your Dad, and probably really worries your Mom. She should know what's up with Kara so she and your sister can work that out. You with me?"

"I think so," Brand replied.

I nodded. "So, you do what you want, but I suggest you talk to your Dad about all this. I don't want to burst your bubble, but it's the right thing to do. That said, sorry if it freaks you out, babe, but I'll be telling your Dad about this. Sometimes we're gonna have just you and me talks. Hopefully, I'll get the same with Kara. But sometimes, if it's really important, like this, I'll have to make the decision to tell your Dad, and I hope you trust me to do right by you when I do."

His mouth moved around and he looked at the yard. I looked too, and saw that Creed totally missed my vibe and was now, with Theo on his shoulders, playing hide and seek with Adam, Kara and Leslie.

Kristen Ashley

Shit.

When I got nothing back from Brand, I looked at him and asked, "Brand, you okay?"

"I think I'll talk to him."

Like his Dad, something weighed heavy on his mind, he went silent in order to think about it.

And he just proved he was a smart kid and brave.

Thank God.

"You think I should talk to him, just me and him, or do you think Kara should be with us?" he asked quietly.

"I don't know you guys enough to know how to answer that," I replied honestly. "What do you think?"

"She might clam up if she's there. She might get mad if I talk to Dad behind her back."

"Then there's your answer."

He looked at me. "What?"

"If she makes the decision not to participate in the discussion, it's her decision to make. But you should try not to make anyone mad, and if you know it might happen, you should avoid doing what you're gonna do to make them mad. There are times, but it's rare, when it's okay to talk behind someone's back or break a confidence. This, just my opinion," I shrugged, "is not one of those times."

"I'll talk to him when she's there," Brand decided.

"Good call," I muttered.

We fell silent.

Theo's giggle pierced the air.

"You're really, pretty, totally cool, Sylvie," Brand whispered into the silence.

Okay, good.

No, fucking *great*.

I survived that minefield.

Fucking awesome.

"You're really, pretty, totally cool, too, Brand," I replied.

"Awesome," he kept whispering.

I grinned.

Adam found Creed and Theo, not hard since Theo was making so much noise, and it was Adam's turn to giggle.

Yes, this was it.

The life.

My grin turned into a smile.

Creed stifled the groan of his orgasm in my neck.

I held on with all four limbs as he did, and I kept holding on as he stayed seated inside me and came down.

When his breathing started to even out, I whispered, "Right, I seriously liked it, in a big way, but what was *that?*"

It was late. A lot later than I expected to be in Creed's bed, in his hotel room with Creed. It was also hours later than I expected to get his call and I didn't expect his call to include him saying, "Get over here. Now. Bring the oil," before he hung up.

I got over there as soon as I could, which, admittedly, included me driving a little bit more than my normal crazy, and I brought the oil.

The minute I arrived, I barely knocked twice before the door was opened, I was in and Creed was on me.

He didn't speak. What he did do was do me up the ass, fuck me normally and make me come three times before he found it.

I let this happen because he was being silent and broody, except a lot hotter since he was fucking me while doing it.

Now, I wanted to know what was going on.

He lifted his head and declared, "You're staying with me in two weeks when we go down to Phoenix. No more of this hotel bullshit."

"Uh," I proceeded cautiously, "not sure I'm down with that, baby. It's too soon."

"If Brand lays shit on you like he laid on you tonight, then it's not too soon."

There it was.

They had the talk.

"Tell me what's happening," I encouraged on an arm squeeze.

He pulled out gently and rolled off to settle on his back in the bed. Once there, he lifted both hands and swiped his face.

I rolled to my side, plastering my front to his, and got up on a forearm.

"Creed, baby," I called.

He dropped his hands, rolled toward me and got up on his elbow, head in his hand.

"You told me that shit went down, and since you suggested the kids have a chat with me, they did."

I dropped down to lie like him and prompted, "Okay."

"So they shared their shit and I was right. Kara likes you. Rabidly. She thinks you're the key to gettin' me back. And, as you know, she thinks her Mom's the reason why she lost me."

"Right," I said softly when he stopped speaking, so Creed started speaking again.

"I had no choice but to share that shit with Chelle. This meant I had no choice but to listen to Chelle bawlin' her eyes out and workin' out with her what we're gonna do about Kara. This, for some fuckin' reason, led to her goin' back over, *a-fuckin'-gain,* how she trapped me into marriage and how I needed to be free of the burden of guilt for our marriage not workin'. Except, unlike the seven hundred fuckin' times we went over that shit before, she wouldn't let it go. She kept at me. For-fuckin'-ever. It was only when I said I'd let that go did she calm down. Then she started up again bawlin', but this time it was about how happy she was for me and how you were the shit 'cause you bein' around meant we were workin' all this out."

When he stopped talking, I remarked, "None of this sounds bad, Creed. Why are you in a mood?"

"'Cause I gotta work all this shit out, and I have no fuckin' clue how to explain to my daughter that she's got a great mother who's a good woman she should learn from and emulate, and bein' a girl, she needs her Mom growin' up. Therefore, she is not movin' in with you and me."

"Can I suggest that giving a little might get you all a lot?"

His brows drew together. "What?"

"Creed, you see your kids four days a month. I get that your work makes that the way you have to go, but you'll have me partnering with you *and* living with you, so maybe you'll have more time to be with your kids. If Chelle's down with restructuring custody, maybe you two can do joint or you can have a day or two a week. If they've got a ways to go for school and you're busy, I'll be all over getting them to and from school, but more time with you may help Kara out. If Chelle gives that to her daughter, it may help her to see her Mom in a different light. And," I grinned, "I'm awesome and you love me, but I'm not her Mom. She's young, she may not get it for years, but I figure she'll get it eventually that Chelle is really the shit and all that will work itself out. You all just need to power through it. Girls are complicated, but if we have a brain in our heads, which Kara does, we straighten ourselves out in the end."

His eyes drifted over my head and he stared unfocused into the room a moment before he muttered, "Chelle'd work that out with me."

I figured Chelle would do just about anything for Creed *and* her kids, but I kept my mouth shut.

He kept musing over my head. "And I'd get to see my kids more."

"And they'll get to see you. An all-'round winner."

He looked back at me and said softly, "You're gonna be a good Mom."

Jesus, I hoped so.

"If we're lucky, we'll find out that's true sooner rather than later."

His arm snaked out and wrapped around me, pulling me toward him, off my elbow and tucking me under him as he rolled into me. "Doesn't have to do with luck. We gotta put the effort in," he told me.

We certainly were doing that.

"As you know, I'm all in on that plan," I shared.

He smiled down at me.

I lifted a hand and ran a finger down his jaw as I said quietly, "Don't know where you're at with it. I told you Chelle told me all about it. I'm just going to say for the record, she's right. She deliberately trapped you into marriage and knew through your time together she didn't have your love."

"Can't trap a man who agrees."

I shook my head. "Oh yeah, you can."

"Sylvie—"

I cut him off to ask, "Did you tell her you love her?"

I watched his jaw get hard before he forced out his, "No."

"Not ever?"

He drew in breath then admitted, "Found other words that implied it but didn't say it."

"Then you didn't lie."

"She didn't hold me at gunpoint at the altar," Creed pointed out.

"Babe," my hand slid down to the side of his neck and curled around, "you're Creed. You've always been Creed. She fell in love with you and did it hard, so even drifting after losing me, my guess is you were Creed with her, too. And the Tucker Creed I know would never knock up a woman and not do right by her. My guess again, she knew that and played on it. People do shit when they love someone. It wasn't cool, but it was understandable. That said, you gotta let that go. You both played your part in that doomed marriage. If you let it go, maybe she can let it go too. You'd be doing her a favor, and I think if you two worked that shit out, your kids would feel that ease between you and it would work out for them, too."

Creed stared down at me and asked, "Jesus, baby, when'd you get so fuckin' smart?"

I grinned up at him. "See, when I was six, I met this worldly eleven year old who was wise and took care of me and taught me everything he knew."

As I spoke, I watched Creed's eyes flash, his face harden with intensity and I felt his body tense against mine.

When I was done talking, he said softly, "Fuckin' love you, Sylvie."

I kept grinning. "Fuckin' love you too, Tucker Creed."

Then I lifted my head, touched my mouth to his and only moved back an inch before I said quietly, "Thank you for giving me a great birthday."

I watched his face get soft and I fell back to the pillows just in time for his hand to come up. His finger touched my new (totally beautiful), pendant then it slid under it and twisted the chain gently before he replied, "You're welcome, beautiful."

My grin got bigger, but it didn't last long.

This was because Creed dropped his head and kissed me.

Therefore, my birthday started great (notwithstanding the shitty dream) because of Creed.

And it ended great, too.

Because of Creed.

Chapter 24
Come Back to Me

A hot summer night in Kentucky, sixteen years earlier. Sylvie is eighteen...

I sat on the pier in the moonlight, staring at the water.

I couldn't find Creed.

I'd spent hours at the pier the day before, waiting, waiting forever. The Snickers were ruined. My skin was burned.

Creed didn't show.

I went to his house. He wasn't there. His truck wasn't there.

I went back to the lake, waited and waited, and nothing.

I was worried.

Creed would never leave me.

Never, never, *ever.*

Something was wrong.

I called him but he didn't answer. I called him again and he didn't answer. And again. And again.

When it got late and he didn't show, I went back to his house. I broke in the window and lay in his bed, waiting. I hoped he'd come home, but I also couldn't go to my house.

I told Daddy I was leaving. I told him I wasn't coming back. He was really angry then he got all calm and tried to talk to me. I told him I wasn't going to change my mind and he let me go. He even said I could keep my car.

It was kind of strange how easily he let me go. I mean, it wasn't pleasant, but it wasn't as hard as I imagined it would be.

So when he let me go I went, but I told him I wasn't coming back and I couldn't. I couldn't go back. I had a life to begin with Creed and I had a life I hated that had to end.

But Creed didn't show.

The next day I went back to the pier and waited again.

I didn't know what to do.

No one knew about us and Creed wanted to keep it that way just in case Daddy sent someone out looking for us, so I couldn't ask his friends. I told

Daddy I was leaving, but as Creed told me to do, I didn't tell him I was leaving with Creed.

Creed had worked out his notice the week before to get ready to leave, but he would also be angry if I went by to the factory, so I couldn't go there, either.

So I got in my car and drove around, drove everywhere. Went into the stores and diners and swung by gas stations to check and see if he was around, even if his truck wasn't outside.

He wasn't in the stores or diners.

He wasn't anywhere.

Worried, scared, feeling truly alone for the first time since I was six, I did the only thing I could do.

When it got late, I went to the bar. I stood outside until someone showed and asked if they'd go in, find Winona Creed and send her out to talk to me. I found someone, they went in and she teetered out and proved what I knew. She paid absolutely no attention at all to her son and she cared about him even less.

When I asked her if she knew where he was, she threw out an unsteady hand, which made her list to the side before she righted herself, and she stated, "He lef'. Goin' somewheres. Doan know wheres. Just know he sold the house an' he gone." Then she squinted her eyes to focus on me and she asked, "Whas' a Bissenette doin' askin' after a Creed?"

I didn't answer that. I asked, "He left?"

She nodded unsteadily. "He gone."

"Are you sure?" I asked.

"Sure I'm sure, gurl. He's my boy, ain't he?"

No, he was *my* boy.

And he wouldn't leave without me.

Would he?

Would he take my virginity then take off without me?

No.

No way.

Creed wasn't like that. Creed wasn't like other guys.

Not Creed.

Not my Creed.

"Thanks, Mrs. Creed," I mumbled, moving away.

"Whatever," she mumbled back and lurched into the bar.

I went to his house. I drove around town and then I went to the pier.

No Creed.

I sat on the end, my feet in the water and my head spinning. I didn't know what to do. How could he disappear? No one just disappeared. Should I talk to the police? Should I risk Creed getting mad at me and talk to his friends?

Oh God, I didn't know what to do. Not only didn't I know what to do to find Creed, I didn't know what to do without him.

There didn't seem a time when he wasn't there.

I didn't *want* there to be a time when he wasn't there.

And I was terrified. Two days, no Creed. Something was wrong. Very, very wrong. I felt it in my bones. He'd never leave me. Never disappear. Never make me wait to start our new lives.

Never.

Something was very, very wrong, and that something had to do with taking Creed away from me.

I stared at the lake, our lake, the place we met, laughed, swam, ate, necked and made love.

"Come back to me," I whispered.

I closed my eyes tight, using everything I had, praying hard, hoping, when I opened my eyes I'd feel Creed moving toward me.

I opened my eyes and saw lake.

I twisted around and saw the dark grass, wood and pasture, all empty.

I twisted to the other side.

More empty.

No Creed.

I twisted back to the lake, my lips trembling, my nostrils quivering.

"Come back to me," I begged, the tear slipping over my eye and gliding down my cheek.

I fell asleep on that pier.

Creed never came back to me.

Three days later...

I paced the room.

How did this happen?

How was this happening?

And where was Creed?

He had to be out there. Maybe he'd heard something was wrong. Maybe he knew Daddy knew about us. Maybe he was working to save me.

He had to save me.

There was noise outside. My heart jumped and my gaze swung to the locked door of the room I'd been held in since Daddy found me.

The door opened and my father and a man walked in.

Daddy led the man to me. He couldn't meet my eyes.

The man was looking at me.

I stared into his eyes and I did not like what I saw. Not at all.

Not at all.

My stomach clenched so hard, I thought I would throw up and I backed up, up, up, up, until my body was in the corner.

"Sylvie, I'd like you to meet Richard Scott," Daddy said to my shoulder.

Richard Scott smiled at me, and I did not like that smile. Not at all.

Not at all.

He came toward me. Daddy looked to the floor and I pressed myself into the corner.

Oh God.

Oh God!

Where was Creed?

Chapter 25

Consider It Done

Present day, eighteen days later...

I sat on a tall stool at the bar in a swank restaurant staring at myself in the mirror behind the bar, and not much liking what I saw.

My hair was three times its normal volume and I had five times as much makeup on. I was wearing a skintight black dress that left absolutely nothing to the imagination. It had a straight bodice that sat low and tight, making my not-altogether-spectacular cleavage nearly spill out, and thus, exposed cleavage, as everyone knew, miraculously became spectacular. It also had spaghetti straps, and the little ruffle (yes! a ruffle!) at the hem was the only thing that, when I was standing, saved me from having my ass cheeks hanging out. Sitting, it was a disaster. In other words, near-to crotch shot. Last, on my feet were spike-heeled, bronze sandals that I had to admit were hot, but they fucking killed, even when I was sitting.

Serious yuck.

So not me.

Suffice it to say there was nowhere, as in no-freaking-where, to stash a weapon.

This meant I felt exposed in more ways than one, and it sucked.

The only good thing was, I'd had my mani/pedi done the day before, and in that getup they looked *awesome*.

My eyes slid to the art deco clock behind the cash register, and I dipped my chin and muttered into the microphone taped between my shoved together and pushed up tits, "He's half an hour late."

In the transparent ear bud receiver tucked in my ear, I heard Hawk Delgado's deep voice reply, "He'll show."

It was go time on Hawk's job and I was meeting the contact to set up the principals in order to bring them down.

I was antsy for action.

This was partly because I hadn't had a drink or cigarette in two weeks. I didn't know if I was pregnant, but the amount of effort Creed and I were putting into making me that way meant that undoubtedly would happen (I hoped), and I wasn't taking any chances. As the days went by, it was getting better, but I wasn't there yet.

This meant I was in a bad mood.

Further, shit was falling into place and I wanted this job done.

I put my house on the market, and miracle of miracles, I got an offer that was acceptable within a week. This, I figured, was because I didn't really give a shit what it sold for, so the buyers got a screaming deal, but whatever.

Money didn't mean anything to me.

Starting my life with Creed did.

I'd set up an estate auction to sell everything even though most my shit was junk. Still, there were people who liked junk and I needed to unload it, so they were going to get their chance to have mine. Lucky me, this gave me my chance to kiss that crap good-bye.

As for Charlene, she'd made the decision to move back to her hometown. She had a brother and parents there that were concerned about her and too far away to help out. Her Mom was semi-retired so she could help take care of the kids, and her brother owned some asphalt company and he needed an office manager. All she had to do was sell her house, pack up and go. When she unloaded the house, Creed, me and the kids were going to come up and help. Then his kids would go back to Phoenix and Creed and I were going to help drive her down to New Mexico.

I was ecstatic about this decision. First, she'd be close to a number of people who would have her back. Second, her family lived in a burg that was a good haul from Phoenix, but it was a fuckuva lot closer than Denver.

Douchebag Dan was *not* ecstatic (which made me more ecstatic). He'd quit his job to start his new life and now was struggling. He wanted his piece of the house and he was balking at child support. On the flipside of that, Knight's piranha attorney wanted to assist him in finding a way where he could fuck himself and the man was a master at this task.

Douchebag Dan was screwed. Knight's attorney was already eating him alive, taking his time, making it tortuous and enjoying every second.

So was I.

Charlene hated it being ugly and the kids were subdued in response to their Mom trying, but not exactly succeeding, in hiding her heartbreak. So I hid the fact I thought it was the fucking bomb that Dan was squirming. It would be over soon. She and the kids would be with people who cared about them, she had a job, the extra income from Creed's work and Dan would be forced to bend over and grab his ankles.

All was right with that world.

It was also right in mine. Chelle had immediately agreed to Creed getting the kids more when he returned to Phoenix. He'd have them every other weekend and Tuesday night through Thursday after school each week. When we went down there last weekend, it was clear the kids were thrilled with this.

I had been right. Chelle reported to Creed that when she told Kara and Brand that she and Creed had decided they'd spend more time with their Dad, Kara thawed toward her mother. She just wanted more Creed time. Chelle giving it to her, and Creed sitting them down and making it clear that was a decision he and Chelle made because he wanted to spend more time with them (and Chelle wanted them to have more of their Dad) made her the good guy for once.

Further, Creed finally accepting that Chelle held some guilt for the collapse of their marriage and letting go of the burden he held meant that their relationship had also changed. They didn't phone each other every day to have a gab, but the baggage weighing on them was gone. It wasn't hard to feel the ease that generated not only between those two, but the kids sensed it too.

What made really fucking good infinitely better was that Creed was, in his badass way, over the fucking *moon* about all of this. He'd see his kids more, shit was sorted with his ex and he was going to have me.

Never, not in my life, not once, had I seen him this relaxed and happy. I knew why, but that didn't mean he didn't tell me that he not only had it all, but he seriously got off on the fact that, for the first time in sixteen years, our future was bright.

I loved that, fucking *adored* that he finally had that. He was a good man. He deserved it.

So, outside the occasional nic-fit, life was good.

As for me, Creed being pushy as well as bossy meant that, twice a week, I was seeing a therapist. I'd had five appointments and the first three didn't go so well because I thought it was hogwash. I felt that all I really needed was Creed and eventually I'd work through my shit and get on with life.

At the end of my third appointment, my therapist told me he sensed I thought it was hogwash and suggested I didn't trust him, thus he couldn't help me, and asked me if I'd like him to refer me to someone else.

Kristen Ashley

I dug his honesty and the fact that he wasn't willing to take my money even if I was shutting him out so he'd never help me but still get paid for it.

In other words, he broke through.

The next two appointments weren't great either, but only because reliving that shit sucked.

That said, there was something about unloading it on someone objective, watching the expressions on his face mirror some of the shit I felt bottled inside, not having to worry about what I said or how I reacted hurting him or affecting him like I would if I shared it with Creed, or even Knight or Charlene, that was such a massive relief, it was hard to express.

What it was, was instantaneous.

After the first appointment where I shared, I left feeling almost fucking giddy. The next, the same. My doctor warned me that when I began to dig further into what happened in order to move past it, I would have times when I would not feel giddy. Where it would be difficult, draining and even painful. I got that. It was just good to know that therapy actually worked. I was in the hands of someone who knew what he was doing and it was about me and only me, unloading a huge wad of crap and I didn't have to drag anyone I loved into it.

Not to mention I had not had a single dream since I decided to trust my psychologist, which in and of itself was worth the money.

So all was good in Creed and Sylvie Land. My house was sold. My shit was going to be sold. Charlene and the kids were going to be in a good place. Most of my jobs were sorted and Charlene had billed so those files could be closed. Creed's shit was sorted. And after tonight, when hopefully we'd tie the bow on Hawk's job, I figured I had about a week of crap to deal with, then I was in my girl and driving down to Phoenix to finally, fucking, fucking *finally* begin my life with Creed.

I couldn't wait.

So I wanted this done.

Now.

I lifted the martini glass I'd asked the bartender to fill with cranberry juice, took a sip, put it down and murmured into my microphone, "This dress sucks."

"Shut it, Sylvie," Hawk ordered in my ear.

I didn't shut it.

I muttered, "And I'm sitting down and these shoes *still* hurt."

"Quit bitchin'," Hawk replied.

"I didn't sign up for this crap," I told him, which was a lie. It was anything-goes with my jobs and this wasn't the first time I tricked myself out. Usually it was to be a honey trap, though I didn't take that role all the way, ever.

This time, it was different.

"You're gettin' paid, babe, *and* I bought the fuckin' dress and shoes you get to keep. Stop moaning," Hawk returned.

Like I would ever wear this dress again.

The shoes… that was a different story.

I didn't tell Hawk that.

"I hope you read the fine print in my contract that says if I have to show cleavage and wear shoes with a heel over three inches, my rate doubles," I shot back.

"Baby," another voice came into my ear and this was my man's, "shut the fuck up. Concentrate and don't sit there muttering into your tits, makin' it look like you're waitin' to fuck over some asshole. He sees you doin' that shit, these guys we're hunting will take you out, and tonight is not my night to lose you."

That made me shut up, and my eyes slid down the bar to take in the reflection of Creed sitting alone across the restaurant in a semi-circular booth with a martini glass in front of him, too. He had his hand resting on the table next to the glass and the liquid was so high, I knew he hadn't brought that glass to his lips.

I was not surprised. Even undercover, he wasn't a vodka man. He was all about beer and tequila.

Like me.

His eyes were aimed at the room, not me, and since I didn't have anything better to do, I felt it safe to study him in the mirror.

An excellent way to pass the time.

He was in a suit, and I'd never seen him in a suit, not even back in the day.

Needless to say, he rocked it.

Hawk didn't buy that suit for him. It was Creed's. It was also made for him, as in literally. And earlier that night, when I touched the lightweight wool fabric, it was so plush and fabulous, I wanted to rip off my clothes, rip off his jacket, wrap it around me and roll around in it naked.

Alas, this option wasn't open to me. Still, I told Creed and I did this with intent. As suspected, when I imparted this information on him, Creed's eyes flashed and then they promised I'd get that opportunity, just later.

Another reason I wanted this job done.

He also had on a tailored shirt, opened at the collar, in a color that matched his eyes. This brought into stark relief not only his tanned face and the strong, muscled line of his throat, but also his rugged, scarred features. It too was made for him, and fit so well it hugged his abs, ribs, chest and shoulders in a way that, if it breathed, I'd be jealous.

He had his gun in one side of his shoulder holster, my gun in the other, a .22 in an ankle holster and a knife in his other boot.

In other words, he was seriously strapped, and that was good since he was the man who had my back.

After telling me off, I heard him say to Hawk, even as I watched him through the mirror and saw his lips did not move, "Do you have any visual at all?"

"Negative," Hawk answered.

Creed and I were inside. I was the contact. Creed my backup, who would eventually follow me, hopefully undetected, to where the "deal" would go down.

Hawk and his boys were outside. Hawk on the prowl with his main man, Jorge, and another of his crew, Mo. He also had men in a surveillance van and eyes on the street, the back alley, the entrance of a nearby parking garage and the men's bathroom.

I suspected (accurately) that Hawk was even more ready than me for this to go down. I suspected this because Creed and I had come in on the tail end of a job Hawk had been working for five months.

Apparently, some socialite in LA thought of her Mexican nanny as part of the family. She learned that her nanny's sister, who had made a connection in Mexico to try to gain entry into the USA, had disappeared in the middle of attempting to seal this deal. Understandably, the nanny was beside herself and the socialite pulled Hawk in.

He investigated and found this happened often over the border to Mexican nationals so desperate to leave or to join loved ones that they didn't check out the folks they handed their cash over to and thus they lost their money and their freedom.

Hawk wasted no time and got a lock on the slavery ring *and* the sister, and it was sheer luck she was in Denver, Hawk's home turf.

Extracting her safely was another matter which took frustrating amounts of time, because it also took extreme amounts of preparation and finesse.

The part, or one of them, that made this job delicate was that, considering these folks were trafficking humans in the US of A, local cops had aligned with a federal task force to take down the entire ring which was operating multi-state. On the other hand, Hawk only had one mission, to recover the sister. So the task force wanted Hawk to back off. Hawk wanted to get the sister back to her family. There had been some butting of heads, but Hawk Delgado was the kind of man who didn't back down.

So he didn't.

Enter me, posing as a madam of sorts on the buy for new talent. It had taken weeks and lots of work to build my false reputation as a viable buyer. Now that was done, I was to meet the contact tonight and he would take me to where they held their stock of available humans. I would confirm the girl was there, make the deal and skedaddle. Then Hawk and the boys would swoop in and recover the girl.

Easy.

I hoped.

"Visual. Front. Street. Mercedes parking three cars down from door," Mo grunted into his microphone.

"Go time," Hawk growled.

I sucked in a breath then lifted my glass to take a sip. My eyes slid back down the bar to the mirror where I could see Creed. His eyes were on me, intent, burning into my back.

He jerked up his chin.

I tipped my lips up slightly.

His eyes went to the door.

I put my glass to the bar and discreetly plucked the bud out of my ear, reached in my cleavage and grabbed my microphone, ripping it and the tape off and away.

I set them beside me on the bar, and instantly a waitress Hawk primed slid by, hand out. She covered the apparatus, walked behind me and it was gone.

I put my fingers to the slim, gold watch at my wrist, flipped a tiny switch on the side and the microphone engaged. Hawk had given me that watch. It had a microphone and GPS.

They'd pat me down, definitely. I had to go in unwired, no communications, but I had Creed as a tail and the watch Hawk gave me. They could hear what was happening with me and they would know where I was at all times. I could not hear what they were up to nor know where they were.

I impatiently started to tap the toe of the foot hanging from my crossed leg and studied the watch.

Two minutes later, I heard, "Collette?"

My head turned and my eyes hit the man who acted as a middle man to sell humans.

Motherfucker.

I buried my sneer, smiled a small smile and extended my hand.

It was go time.

⚜

The minute I hit the warehouse, I knew I was fucked.

This was because I was meeting the principals, and amongst them was Nick Fucking Sebring.

Shit, shit, *fuck*.

His eyes came to me and they widened momentarily as I braced, mentally preparing to run and about to scan the environs for a makeshift weapon or cover I could use until I could get my lips to my watch and alert Creed and Hawk to the situation.

But as I thought this, I saw his face go blank. He didn't call attention to me and stared at me like he'd never met me before when he had, numerous times. I'd been working for Knight for years and Nick used to work for him too, so our paths had crossed.

Fuck, how had Creed and I not clocked this?

Fuck, *fuck*.

Creed said Nick didn't keep good company, but seriously, these were nasty motherfuckers and we'd been all over his ass, Creed for over a month.

Seriously. How had we not clocked this?

"I take it you're Collette?" one of the other dudes said to me on his approach.

I took a step back, surveying him, cold shoulder. There was no rule saying I had to be a friendly flesh peddler. I also did a quick head count. With the middle man, the leader of the gang who was approaching and Nick, there were three other men.

Too many.

Fuck.

When I didn't offer mine, he dropped his hand. My mind scrambled for some code to tell Creed and Hawk there was a possibility I'd be made and my eyes went to Nick.

"How many people need to be here for us to make this deal?" I asked, giving Creed and Hawk the information that the bad guys were fully staffed.

"That gentleman is a new recruit. He's in training," the dude answered, and my eyes cut to him.

"If you were using this transaction for training purposes, I should have been informed."

"From the background check we did on you, you're aware we're exceedingly cautious. We've done an equally exhaustive check on him. You have nothing to be concerned about," he replied.

"I'm exceedingly cautious as well and I don't like surprises," I fired back.

He inclined his head. "That's understandable. Would you like to terminate now?"

Shit, shit, *fuck.*

If I didn't see those girls, Hawk's entire operation was a bust. Or he had to follow through, maybe not get his girl, but definitely get a lot of shit from the Feds and possibly fuck *their* operation.

I decided to call his bluff. I held his eyes, lifted my chin slightly in an affirmative and replied, "Thank you for your time."

I turned, again lifted my chin to the middle man and began to make my departure, hoping like all fuck they needed a buyer and bad. I didn't know the market for human trafficking. It could be a buyer's market. If my luck was bad, it could be a seller's.

"Collette," he called.

Thank God.

I turned and leveled my eyes on him.

"Would you be more comfortable if Mr. Cardinal wasn't here?" he asked, indicating Nick.

Mr. Cardinal?

What the fuck?

"Or," the man went on, "would you be more comfortable, considering we're aware that Mr. Cardinal is a confidential informant for the FBI, that we dispatch him in your presence rather than after our deal is done as we'd planned to do?"

Terrific.

My eyes moved to Nick, who had gone pale, which probably partially had to do with his obviously having been made, but mostly it had to do with the man standing behind him with a gun held to the back of his head.

Shit.

Shit.

Fuck!

God, please, please, God, let Creed and Hawk have heard that in the microphone.

"I'm not fond of mess," I told the man.

He inclined his head again. "Then we'll take him away while we see to business."

To that, hurriedly but trying not to sound hurried, I stated, "I'm also not fond of something happening I can't see nor being involved even remotely in felonies that have nothing to do with me. I have a business. I'm seeing to business. We conduct our business, we're done. I don't want to be dragged into your mess. When I'm not here, do what you wish. That's *your* business, but I'll ask you to put a hold on it while we complete our transaction."

He inclined his head yet again, and that was beginning to grate on my nerves but I couldn't concentrate on that.

I had to buy Nick time, and I had to hope that first, Hawk, Creed and the boys were adjusting the operation not only to recover the girl, but to extract Nick. And second, that Nick was somehow wired so whoever he was working with knew he was in jeopardy, because he sure as fuck needed the cavalry.

"So you'd like him to witness the transaction?" the man asked, and I arched my brows.

"I'd like to stop talking about your problems, complete the transaction and be on my way," I answered.

320

"As you wish," he muttered, and his whole gentlemanly act when selling humans made my gut clench, which was no good since it was already in knots because this shit was fucked. There were more of them than I expected, I had no weapon and I had no way to communicate to Nick that I would have his back.

Instead, I gave him a blank look as I followed the head honcho speaker of the group deeper into the warehouse.

"It's surprising you'd come here alone, Collette," the man remarked as we walked, and I felt the others following us.

"Perhaps you can also refrain from commenting on how I conduct my business," I suggested, not liking the darkness we were moving into.

"A small woman like you, all heels and hair, it seems foolhardy to me," he noted.

This was not good.

"What I've learned is foolhardy is men who see all heels, hair and stature, make assumptions and thus underestimate the situation," I retorted.

He was silent a moment as he led me into the shadows before he muttered, "Indeed." Then, "You weren't followed, no one at your back, patted down and no weapon. I think you can understand how assumptions could be made."

There it was. Creed, again, genius. He wasn't made, but I knew he was out there.

"What I understand," I returned, "is that it would be bad business to whack a potential good customer."

There was a smile in his voice when he repeated his, "Indeed."

Asshole.

He stopped, so I stopped, as did everyone else.

"Flashlight," he ordered, and I saw movement. Then I saw the beam hitting a massive, wooden, freight crate.

God, they had them in a crate.

A fucking *crate*.

How did people like this sleep at night? How did they stop themselves from jumping off bridges? How did they not spontaneously combust with guilt and shame?

The middle man I met at the bar scurried forward, lifted the latch and swung the big door open. The seller moved in and trained his flashlight inside.

I got as close to him as I could stomach and looked. I clocked her immediately. I also clocked there were at least two dozen of them. They were barely clothed, clearly not allowed to bathe, had nothing but a few ragged blankets to make that crate even slightly comfortable, and all appeared underfed.

They looked beyond miserable. They looked lost, terrified out of their minds and totally beaten.

Blood roared in my ears and it took everything I had to check it and carry out the game.

Therefore, I uttered the code words that would mean the team should proceed with the extraction. "I'll take two. That one, right side, third in and the one at the back in the middle. The others are too skinny."

I barely got out the word "skinny" when an alarm sounded and I saw flashing red lights throughout the warehouse. A nanosecond later, I was suddenly blinded when all the lights in the warehouse were switched on, bright and overpowering.

Fuck, shit, fuck.

Too soon. They wouldn't breach now. Not until I was clear. No way. No fucking way.

Something was wrong.

I braced on an aching foot in order to whirl and run, but was hooked by the seller with an arm around my waist. I heard the door to the crate swing shut, pinning in the girls, even as I saw Nick turn on the man who had a gun on him and grab the gun.

They started grappling as the seller tugged me back and another henchman turned on Nick and the man he was struggling with and opened fire.

Shit, fuck, shit, fucking fuck, fuck, *fuck!*

I whirled in my captor's arm, hand up, and clawed his neck. He let out a howl of pain. His arm loosened, I lifted a knee high, suddenly thankful for my short skirt that gave me range of motion, and caught him sharp in the gonads. He yowled, I tore free and fucking *ran.*

In these bare seconds, all hell had broken loose in the warehouse. Clearly, there were more bad guys lurking, and it was equally clear an operation had been launched to seize the warehouse. There was gunfire coming from everywhere; shouts, boots hitting the concrete floors, pandemonium.

The man Nick had been grappling with was down and bleeding from a wound in his chest.

Nick had disappeared.

Not surprising he didn't take my back. He might for some reason be acting as a CI to the Feds, but he'd always been all about himself.

But I was fucked. I had no weapon. There were operatives in play who
may or may not know I was a plant. And I had to find my way out of this warehouse so I could have the future I'd waited sixteen years for.

So I ran, using crates for cover and checking that the coast was clear
before making my way to the next one, doing this and making a mental note
actually to add the line in my contract doubling my hourly rate if I had to wear
heels.

This and escape were my thoughts when I was caught around the chest
and hauled back into a man's body.

Fuck.

Before I could begin to execute maneuvers to get free, my heart stopped
beating. My stomach plummeted and my world rocked when Creed appeared
in front of me, gun raised, just as I felt the muzzle of a gun against my temple.

Fuck!

One second after that, Creed's gun discharged. The arm around my chest
loosened and the gun at my head went away as the man behind me shouted in
pain when the bullet ripped through his thigh.

One second after that, I cleared him and started running to Creed.

And one second after that, my world exploded.

This was because two shots were fired. Not from the man Creed brought
down, but from another one who hit our scene from behind. They whizzed by
me and hit Creed. Blood sprayed in a hideous cloud from his neck and his chest
jerked back before he fell back, landing heavy without even attempting to break
his fall.

"*No!*" I shrieked, still running toward him.

More bullets flew and I dropped to the side of my hip, sliding toward
Creed like I was stealing a base. I yanked the gun out of his motionless hand,
twisted, lifted, aimed and fired two kill shots. One directly in the face of the
man who shot Creed, one through the throat of the man who grabbed me and
was on the ground, recovering and aiming his weapon at me.

Two lives extinguished, two more lives taken by me.

I didn't give it a thought.

I turned, pulled myself up on my knees, dropped the gun with a clatter
and bent over Creed.

My Creed. My beautiful, beautiful Creed, on his back, eyes closed, not breathing, blood pooling from the wound in his neck.

I covered the wound, put pressure on and shouted, my voice a piercing screech, *"Man down! Man down! Man down!"*

I stopped screaming and bent over Creed, my face in his face, my hand not engaged in putting pressure on his neck running over his chest, searching for another wound as my heart pounded in my chest, my pulse beating so hard in my neck, it felt like it would tear through, my throat burning, my world ending.

"Tonight's not my night to lose you, partner," I told him. "Tomorrow's not my day to lose you, either." I lifted my hand from his chest and brought it down in a fist over his heart, my voice now shouting, "Never, never, never again will there be a time when it's my time to lose you!"

Creed said nothing and his blood flowed warm against my hand.

Fuck me, fuck me, fuck me.

I knew that feeling. I'd seen it before. That blood, all that blood.

Richard bled out in minutes. I watched. It seemed his life flashed, then gone.

Not Creed.

That was *not* going to happen to my Creed.

Fuck, God, please don't take Creed away from me. Not again. Not again. Not ever again.

I bent over him, my hand leaving his chest. I held the pressure to his neck with my other as I vaguely heard the gunfire die out, running feet around us and I put my lips to his ear.

"Come back to me," I whispered. "Come back to me." Tears hit my eyes, spilling over instantly as Creed didn't move. "Goddamn it, Creed, *come back to me!*"

"Jesus, baby, calm down," he wheezed and I blinked.

Then I jerked up and looked down into his opened, beautiful, stunning, amazing, beloved blue eyes.

He sucked in another breath and knifed up to sitting. Automatically I sat back on my calves to give him room and my hand dropped from his neck as his hands went to his chest. He tore open his awesome shirt, buttons flying everywhere, then reached in and yanked. I heard Velcro tear as he unstrapped his stealth-fit bulletproof vest.

When had he put on a vest?

And how had I not felt it?

"Fuckin' hell, that hurts like a goddamned mother," he bitched breathlessly.

I stared.

He sucked in another breath, then another one, before he lifted up his hand, put it to his neck, took it away and stared at the blood.

His eyes came to me. "Flesh wound."

Before I told my hand to do it, and mark me, if I had my head together, I *still* would have told my hand to do it, I lifted it and slammed it, hand flat, into his chest. I ignored Creed's pained grunt and jumped to my feet.

Pointing down at him, I screeched, "*You're getting a job as an accountant!*"

Creed blinked then grinned.

Blood roared in my ears.

"Fuck, thank God Gwen isn't a badass," I heard Hawk mutter, referring to his wife. "I would not tolerate shit like that on a job."

"I hear you, brother," Jorge muttered.

I looked to cargo pants, boots, skintight Under Armour-wearing, dark haired, intense black eyed, hot guy commando Hawk Delgado, got a load of his two phenomenal dimples telling me eloquently he found me amusing and I spat, "Shut your fucking trap, Hawk."

He lifted his hands in surrender, but, I noted, his dimples didn't go away.

Fuck me.

It was time to save face.

As Creed pushed to his feet, I looked around and asked sarcastically, "Is everyone enjoying the show? Or is anyone thinking maybe now's a good time to rescue the two dozen women locked in a wooden freight crate? Or is that just me?"

"The DPD and Feds are seein' to the girls," Hawk informed me.

"Well, that's good," I returned.

"And seriously, Sylvie, you got great aim, babe, but you make a mess," he continued, indicating the dead men scattered around.

I didn't look at them. Refused to look at them. They had ceased to exist until I got back to my therapist.

But I did shrug.

Hawk grinned.

Then he finished, "And, just FYI, personally, I'm enjoying the show."

I glared at him.

"Me too," Mo, who was also standing around and watching, added.

Someone kill me.

Creed threw an arm around my shoulders.

I stepped sharply away from it and jerked my head back to look up at him. "I'm not talking to you, and you're not touching me until I'm not pissed at you anymore."

His brows shot together. "Beautiful, why the fuck are you pissed at me? *I* didn't shoot me."

"Grab the wrist, yank it out, head butt to the chin, spike heel into his foot, Creed," I snapped. "I know how to get away from being held at gunpoint. You didn't need to open fire."

"I had on a vest and I got fuckin' good aim," Creed shot back.

"You also had another shooter on the approach," I returned.

"You think I didn't see him?" Creed asked, sounding insulted.

"I think *I* didn't see him since my back was to him, and I had other things occupying my attention, like, say, the gun being held to my head," I retorted.

"And *I* think I got a partner who knows what the fuck she's doin', so even though he nailed me, Sylvie, clue in, two dead guys are lyin' on the floor ten feet away, one with his face blown off. I knew, I covered you, you'd cover me and I was right. I covered you, you covered me."

Wow, that was nice.

I didn't say that.

I said, "You might want to use your words like, say, calling, '*Shooter!*' You think? Maybe?"

"I reckoned, when he shot me, you'd get there was a shooter."

Oh my God!

Really?

"When did Grandpa turn into 'Take His *and* My Life in His Hands Maverick Hot Guy'?" I asked.

"When I took my first job. And Sylvie, warning, another Grandpa crack and your bare ass feels my hand."

Shit, that got a tingle.

I ignored the tingle and snapped, "Get shot again and you won't see me naked for a week."

"Baby, it was under control," he replied.

I pointed at the blood dripping into his suit coat and shirt. "Yeah? Really?" I asked mockingly, then went on to inform him, "This I know, I'm not taking that to the dry cleaners, and I do *not* sew buttons back onto shirts."

"Seriously?" he asked back. "Are we having this conversation?"

"Yes, we seriously are," I clipped my answer.

"Yo, Bogey and Bacall, it may be a flesh wound but it's still bleeding, so will you two wind up this bullshit bickering and maybe we can get our man some medical attention?" Hawk asked fake politely, and I turned my scowl to him.

Hawk withstood my scowl with no apparent effort so I gave up. I crouched down, unbuckled one shoe, stood up, slipped it off and threw it overhand into the warehouse. I repeated this maneuver with the other shoe but grabbed Creed's gun on the way up.

Then I cut a frown through all the men and started to stomp away.

As I stomped away, I heard Creed say, "Favor, Delgado. Send a man after those shoes. I'm gonna need them later."

To which I heard Hawk reply, "I hear you, man. Consider it done."

Which meant, as I stomped away, I did it rolling my eyes.

But I also did it thinking Creed would probably get creative, me in those shoes. And on my back or knees, they probably wouldn't hurt too much. Or, alternately, me lying over his thighs getting my first spanking.

Then again, if any of those scenarios occurred, I'd be feeling other things so my mind wouldn't be on those fucking shoes.

This meant, my thoughts having turned pleasantly, when I exited the warehouse at the same time I felt Creed's big, warm hand catch mine and hold tight, I wasn't pissed anymore.

I was smiling.

Epilogue

Dreamweaver

I felt the crack of Creed's hand on my ass. My body jumped and fire shot between my legs.

"Spread," he growled, and instantly, I did as he said.

I was draped belly down over his thighs, naked except my bronze sandals, and Creed was spanking me. This was after he spent some time doing other delicious stuff to me.

No sooner had I opened my legs than Creed's hand dove in. His fingers scored through the wet, rasping across my clit, and since I was beyond ready, my head flew back and I came.

Hard.

Still coming, suddenly I was flying through the air. Creed lay back on the bed, his legs still over the side, feet on the floor, and suddenly I was on top of him, my pussy to his face, his hard, thick cock right in front of me.

"Suck me off," he ordered, voice thick. I moved, lips latching around the tip. Immediately I sucked deep.

He lifted his head, buried his face in my pussy and groaned against me.

Then, his hands at my hips yanking me down, he commenced eating me. My head bobbed, sucking, stroking. I engaged my hand and gave him everything I had as he devoured me.

I came in his mouth.

Creed returned the favor.

After, coming down, he lapped. I licked.

He let this go on awhile before I was up again. Creed repositioned so we were righted in the bed, my head no longer at his crotch but at his throat, and he settled us down, him on his back, me partly on him, partly pressed to his side with his arm around me.

"You take it up the ass. You like to be spanked. And you swallow. Seriously, Sylvie, you were born for me," he muttered.

I lifted my head and looked at him. "That was hardly hearts and flowers."

Creed grinned at me. "A man finds a woman who swallows, that alone, for a guy, is totally fuckin' hearts and flowers."

I rolled my eyes.

Creed kept talking.

"Add gettin' off on bein' spanked, we're talking rainbows and pots of gold."

Again, I rolled my eyes.

"Takin' it up the ass and beggin' for it every time, baby, seriously, you and your body, slice of heaven."

"Not sure any of that will make it into poetry books, hot stuff," I informed him.

"If badasses read poetry, it'd be a bestseller."

I couldn't argue that.

"I just came hard twice, stop annoying me," I ordered.

He transferred his gaze and grin to the ceiling, muttering, "Anything for my Sylvie."

That got me a tingle. Not the usual one, but a great one all the same.

I settled in, cheek to his chest, and saw the still-ugly, livid, blue and purple bruise edged with yellow that marred him where the bullet hit his chest.

I tipped my head back, my cheek sliding against his skin and saw the bandage that covered the stitches at his neck.

That would make another scar.

My arm stole around his gut as I righted my head and sighed.

If I asked, he'd become an accountant (or something) for me. I knew it. All I had to do was ask.

But then he wouldn't be Creed.

"I'm okay," he said quietly, reading my thoughts.

"I know."

"You're okay," he went on.

"I know."

"We're together, we'll always be okay, Sylvie. Always. It's when we're not together that we're not. You with me?"

"Yeah," I said softly, giving his gut a squeeze.

I was with him. I was *so* with him.

Gun jumped up on the bed, looked at me, looked at Creed, understood who her chances were better with and said to Creed, "Meow."

She was right.

Creed moved, sliding out from under me, muttering, "Be back. Getting Gun some treats."

I looked at Gun and shook my head.

She didn't spare me a glance.

She pranced out of the room behind a naked Creed.

I rolled to my back on the bed and stared at the ceiling, realizing my ass burned a little.

It was then I smiled.

Seven days later...

"Your round, Pip," Live declared, grinning drunkenly at me.

"It was my round last time," I replied, staring soberly at him, thinking it was seriously unfun being out with the guys and not drinking.

"I know. You're leavin', you're not gonna be around. That means you gotta get 'em in before you go," Live returned.

"That makes no sense, Live," I informed him.

"Makes perfect sense to me," Tiny put in.

I glared at Tiny then declared, "I'm not even drinking so I'm definitely not buying another round."

"You're supposed to stop drinking *after* you *know* you're knocked up," Live educated me. "Not when you *think* you are."

"Man, were you not there when I explained my history with Creed? I'm not pushing my luck," I shot back.

He swung his beer around, slurring, "Mishin' out."

He was wrong. I'd so take a healthy baby over a drunken night out with the guys. Absolutely.

"Go home."

This came from behind me and I turned, looked up and saw Rhash standing there.

"What?"

"You got a long drive tomorrow. It's after midnight, you aren't drinkin' and these guys are three sheets, so in about ten minutes, they won't even know where they are, much less why they're here. So go home," Rhash answered.

"Do I have to give out hugs?" I asked.

"Fuck, no. You hugged me, I might puke," Live answered the question I asked Rhash, and I turned back to him.

Tiny grinned stupidly at me. "You can hug me."

"I'm not hugging anyone," I declared.

"Aw, come on, Pip. Give me a hug," Tiny encouraged, lumbering toward me.

"Tiny, stand down," I ordered, retreating.

"A little one?" Tiny asked.

"Fuck off," I snapped.

He lifted his hand with his thumb and forefinger an inch apart. "A teeny, eeny, one?"

Jesus.

I put my hands to the massive wall of his chest and pushed. "Fuck off, Tiny, or I'll shoot you."

His hand shot out, curled around my neck and his face was suddenly all I could see. "I'll miss you, girl."

As fast as it happened, he turned and lumbered away.

Live caught my eyes and tipped up his chin before he looked away, swallowed, and jerked his chin up again at the bartender to order another beer.

My eyes slid through the guys and I got more looks, chin lifts and then they turned away.

They were all going to miss me.

I felt a lump form in my throat.

"Go home," Rhash said quietly from beside me, and I looked up with him. "Right."

He held my eyes.

I lifted a hand and placed it on his chest.

"Quality, Pip," Rhash was still talking quietly, "you are pure quality."

I pressed my lips together, pressed my hand in his chest and jerked up my chin.

Then, before I lost it, I said not a word, turned on my boot and left.

As I was walking to my girl in the parking lot, I saw it.

A shiny, black Aston Martin.

My lungs started burning.

For over a week Knight hadn't returned my calls. At first, this was unsurprising. It happened often, he was a busy guy. Then it got kind of annoying.

Then it hurt.

He knew Creed took off a few days ago to get back to life in Phoenix and prepare for me to join him there.

He knew I didn't like to be separated from Creed.

He knew that tomorrow, I was climbing in my 'Vette and driving away from Denver and everything that meant whole worlds to me.

Including him.

Now he was standing in the dark, hips against his superior, high performance vehicle, and I knew his eyes were on me.

I started to move toward him, but saw his head in the streetlamp shake once and I stopped dead.

We stood there staring at each other through the lights illuminating the parking lot, and we did this for some time.

Finally, Knight pushed away from his car, turned and opened the door.

He was beginning to fold his long body inside when I shouted, "Bottom of my soul!"

I heard his door slam. The car purred to life and he shot around in a tight circle. He stopped with the driver's door beside me, his window down.

He looked out and said softly, "Bottom of mine, Sylvie."

Then the window whirled up and he purred away.

Total badass.

Total cool.

Totally fucking sweet.

I went to my girl, opened her up, slid in and rested my forehead on the steering wheel.

Creed had wanted to come up, be with me while I said my good-byes, ride with me on the way down. I told him he needed to get back to his life. His kids and I wouldn't be far behind, but I *would* be okay without him.

I was wrong.

I sucked in breath, lifted my head, started her up and headed to Charlene's, where I was sleeping on the couch because my house was empty.

The next day, early. . .

I stood in the back room of my house, Adam leaned heavily into my side.

I hated my house.

I loved this room.

I had Creed for the second time in this room (and a few other times, too).

I saw his tat for the first time in this room.

And right then, I was standing with a little boy I loved so much it hurt leaning into my side in this room.

I put my hand on his head and slid it down his hair to curl around the back of his neck.

"Is Gunny okay?" he asked the room.

"Yeah, baby. Tucker said she made the trip just fine in his truck," I replied.

He looked up at me. "Mom says you're gonna come to visit us at Grandma's."

I nodded. "I absolutely am."

"Will you make me Cocoa Puffs?" he asked.

"Yep," I answered.

"Will Tucker bring donuts?" he asked.

"Absolutely," I answered.

He grinned. "Good."

"Good," I whispered, sliding my hand to his cheek.

He tipped his head to the side and asked, weirdly, "Sylvie, do you know what love is?"

I stared into his face and answered softly, "I do, Adam. I absolutely do."

He stared into mine and replied just as softly. "I do, too."

That was when I knew.

I knew.

I had to lose Creed and endure Richard so I could have Adam.

And Knight.

And Charlene, Leslie, Theo, Ron, Rhash, Live and everybody.

So that was also when I knew. . .

It *so totally* sucked.

But it was worth it.

Sixteen hours later...

I barely got one wheel over the curb in my turn into Creed's drive before I saw his garage door go up.

The Expedition was to one side in the garage. The sedan was parked out in the drive. Creed was walking out the door that led to the kitchen.

My heart skipped.

I rolled my baby in, turned her off and exited, a stray candy bar wrapper falling to the cement of Creed's garage floor.

I'd pick it up later (maybe).

That was my last thought before my feet left the ground. An arm around my waist holding me close, a hand shoved into the back of my hair pulling my face down and Creed kissed me.

I slid my arms around his shoulders and kissed him back.

We did this a while.

When we stopped, I opened my eyes and looked into his blue ones just as he said gently, "Welcome home, beautiful."

Home.

I smiled.

Two minutes later...

Hand in hand, Creed walked me through the dark house into his bedroom.

One light was on at Creed's nightstand, and at what it illuminated, I stopped dead.

Holy shit.

Holy shit!

"How's that for hearts and flowers?" Creed murmured, and I tore my eyes away from his huge bed that looked entirely covered in deep red, velvety soft rose petals to tip my head back and look at Creed.

I opened my mouth.

I closed it.

I opened it again.

I closed it.

"Fuck me, she's speechless," he kept murmuring as he grinned down at me.

"I… holy shit," I muttered, and his grin turned into a smile.

I pulled my hand from his and walked to the bed. "Jesus, babe, how many flowers did you have to pluck to do this or can you buy just the——?"

I stopped talking abruptly when I saw it.

In the middle of the bed, a black velvet box, opened. And in black satin sat a humongous, princess cut diamond ring, set in what looked like platinum, inlaid with more diamond baguettes around the band.

It was stunning.

It was exquisite.

It was *huge*.

"Holy shit," I breathed.

Creed's arms wrapped around my chest from behind and I felt him arch so his lips could be at my ear.

"Gonna do it, go big," he whispered.

I agreed. I *so totally* agreed.

That rock was completely ostentatious. It had to cost a mini-fortune.

I fucking *loved* it.

"How you feel about marrying me?" he asked in my ear.

"How I feel is Vegas is a six hour drive away so that's not outside checking off our to-do list for tomorrow. That and stopping by the grocery store so I have Cocoa Puffs."

Creed's arms squeezed me reflexively.

Then he burst out laughing.

Then he picked me up and threw me on the bed, and as I bounced, he put a knee in and joined me. He tagged the ring case and pulled out the ring. He threw the case aside, shoved the ring on my finger and, eyes on mine, he kissed it.

My heart swelled.

Then he used his hand around mine to yank me to him.

Other things swelled.

Then he made love to me on a bed of rose petals.

Seriously.

My man.

Was.

Genius.

⚭

Three weeks later...

I was pacing the bathroom, phone to my ear, white stick in my hand.

"Nothing's happening," I told Charlene.

"Honey, you just peed on it. I heard you. And, by the way, I love you, but I never want to hear you peeing again."

"Charlene, you've heard me peeing in bathroom stalls in bars. This is no different," I replied.

"Oh, right," she mumbled then, "Adam's here. You want to talk to him?"

"No!" I hissed. "I'm waiting for a plus sign, Charlene. I love him, but I can't talk to Adam while waiting for a plus sign on a pregnancy test. Jeez."

"Oh, right," she mumbled then I heard her cover the phone, but not well because I also heard her say, "You can talk to Sylvie next time she calls, okay, honey?"

"Okay, Mom," I heard Adam say then a shouted, "Hi Sylvie!"

God I loved that kid.

I couldn't think of that now. I was busy staring at a plastic stick.

Charlene came back to me. "Anything?"

"No," I answered.

"Give it time."

Fuck. The suspense was killing me.

"Should I shake it?" I asked.

"I don't know. What does the box say?"

I snatched up the box and it didn't say anything, so I dropped the box and snatched up the instructions and read them.

"It doesn't say anything about shaking. It just says one to three minutes. How long has it been?" I asked.

"Well, definitely over one minute but not over three."

Shit.

I dropped the leaflet and stared at the stick.

A plus sign showed.

Holy shit.

I was pregnant.

Holy shit!

I was pregnant!

"I'm pregnant," I whispered.

Silence, then more silence, then a soft sob.

"Charlene," I said gently, "I need to go tell Creed."

"Go. Go make a good man happy," she replied quietly.

Right on.

A fabulous way to start the day. Making a good man happy.

Better, he was *my* man.

"Love you, babe," I told Charlene.

"Love you too, Sylvie," she told me.

I beeped off my phone, put it on the bathroom counter and wandered into the bedroom, down the hall and to the kitchen.

Creed's back was to me, bare. His tat on display, his hips and legs encased in faded jeans.

God, he was hot.

He obviously heard me coming because he asked the inside of the fridge, "Cocoa Puffs or are you gonna join me in eggs and bacon?"

"You should always be ready," I told him.

He closed the door instantly and turned.

I tossed the stick across the kitchen and he caught it.

I watched him look at it.

I watched his body still.

And finally, I watched his head come up and his eyes lock on me.

"Dreamweaver," he whispered.

"You bet your ass," I replied, smiling huge and not even close to whispering.

He dropped the stick on the counter and started stalking toward me.

I started backing up, sharing, "Creed, I peed on that."

"Later, I'll get the Windex out."

Good call.

He kept stalking.

I kept backing up.

Finally, he lunged, and I turned and ran.

He caught me two feet from the bed, tackling me, and we both went down on the mattress.

This time, there were no rose petals.

Still, it was *awesome*.

Then again, it always was.

◦❦◦

One month later...

"Partner, this sitting in the getaway car is for the birds," I said, my voice going straight to Creed's earpiece.

"Shut up, Sylvie, I'm breaking and entering," Creed said back, his deep, smooth yet rough voice filling the cab of the Expedition.

"I'm just saying, next B&E job, I get to do the B&E," I declared.

"You can do the next B&E that happens when you aren't pregnant or nursing," he replied and I blinked.

Then I snapped, "I'm not nursing! Nothing latches onto one of my breasts except your lips."

"Now she's making me hard while I'm breaking and entering," Creed griped.

"We're talking about breast feeding, Creed," I returned.

"We're talking about my lips and your tits, Sylvie," he shot back.

He had a point.

I shut up.

Then I waited, staring at the building Creed was breaking into, waiting for an alarm or a siren or anything while scanning to make sure he continued to have privacy, no cars or passersby.

There was nothing.

Ten minutes later, I saw his shadow jogging toward the Expedition.

Not surprisingly, it jogged to the driver's side.

He pulled open my door and ordered, "Scoot. I drive."

"Other side, Creed. You got to break in. I get to drive."

"Baby, scoot," he clipped.

"I'm not moving."

"It's one o'clock in the morning and I just nabbed a hard drive with stolen formulas that are patent pending and worth seven hundred million dollars, and now I'm standing by a truck arguing with my woman. Seriously?" he asked.

"Other side, Creed," I answered.

He moved, swiftly, and I found my seatbelt was unfastened and my cowboy booted feet on the ground.

I glared up at him.

He angled into the truck and looked down at me.

"Other side, Sylvie."

"You're a pain in my ass," I hissed.

"Right back at 'cha, baby."

I narrowed my eyes.

Then I stomped to the other side and dragged myself in.

"Let's roll," I snapped.

Creed rolled.

I scowled as the landscape passed by.

Then I announced, "I'm putting out my own shingle. You're too bossy."

"You're welcome to do that, Sylvie, when you're not pregnant or nursing."

"I'm not nursing!" I bit out.

"We'll see," he muttered.

I rolled my eyes.

Creed turned on the radio then switched it to news.

I immediately leaned forward and switched it to country.

"Pain in my ass," he murmured.

"Bite me," I replied.

Silence.

Then Creed burst out laughing.

I was in a bad mood, but still, I liked that sound so much, I couldn't stop myself from smiling.

But I did it with my head turned to the side window so Creed couldn't see.

Five months later...

The lady behind Bashas' bakery counter handed Creed the bag of donuts.

I snatched it out of his hand and opened it. I pulled out the chocolate-covered chocolate buttercream-filled donut and opened my mouth huge, shoved in as much donut as I could get, bit down and chewed.

Creed stared down at me.

I stared up at him and chewed.

Creed looked to the bakery lady.

"She's eating for two," he shared.

Her eyes went down to my enormous belly then they went back to Creed.

"This was not lost on me," she replied.

I swallowed and shoved more donut in.

"Give us another of those, would you?" Creed asked.

"On it," she muttered.

My Creed.

Totally genius.

I shoved more donut in and Creed looked back at me.

Through donut, I announced, "While we're here, we need to pick up some Snickers."

Creed blinked.

Then he tagged me behind the head, forced me to do a face plant in his chest and burst out laughing.

Four months later. . .

"I feel the hot coming through my shoes," Kara and Brand's cousin whined.

My eyes swept to Kara and Brand.

Kara was looking at me, lips twitching.

Brand was pressing his together, probably so he wouldn't say anything.

He lost this fight and opened his mouth, but not a word came out before. . .

"Brand," Creed warned low and I looked at him to see him tuck our son, Jesse, tighter to his chest.

I loved that.

Loved it.

I looked back at Brand and his face was red. Not from embarrassment, but from trying to keep his mouth shut.

I burst out laughing.

Creed

Thirteen months later. . .

Creed shut the door on the rental, his other hand curled around the handle of the cooler.

He moved through the trees into the grass, feeling the warmth of the sun shining on his head and beating through his tee.

He walked through the grass, his mind registering the cool of the turf on his bare feet.

Something you didn't get in Arizona.

Something you got in Kentucky.

He lifted his head from his study of the grass, his eyes took in the scene and his body rocked to a halt.

Brand was in the lake, screwing around, able to entertain himself just as he was skilled at entertaining others. He was happy to be swimming on his own.

Kara was in her bikini at the side of the lake, feet probably sunk to the ankles in mud. Still, she was smiling and bouncing in the water, a giggling, squealing Jesse in her arms.

Sylvie was sitting at the end of the pier in shorts and a cami, her tanned legs over the side, her arms behind her, weight in her hands, head tipped back to the sun. The huge rock that he'd placed a diamond encrusted band under in Vegas two months after she moved to Phoenix blinking in the rays.

As he suspected, neither of his kids had a problem with him making Sylvie his wife. They also didn't blink when told they were getting another sibling. Brand had two new people to jabber to and Kara had two new people to love.

They were happy.

Sylvie was happy.

So was Creed.

He forced himself to come unstuck and started moving again, thinking what he thought when Kara was put in his arms. When Brand was set there. When he tucked his and Sylvie's bundled Jesse close. When he studied his Sylvie, sleeping in sheets filled with rose petals.

He was thinking his Dad would like one fuckuva lot all the love that Creed had created, but better, earned.

"You got him?" he called to Kara as he put his foot up on the pier.

"Yeah, Dad," Kara called back, and shit, she was growing into her beauty. A year, two, he was going to be fucked.

God, he hoped the kid in Sylvie's belly was another boy.

Please, God, he prayed, let it be another boy.

He moved down the pier and saw Sylvie had twisted her torso just slightly, but her neck all the way around. Her arms were still behind her. The diamonds he gave her twinkling. The green at her neck sparkling.

Every day, every single day, she wore his green.

Every day.

She smiled at him.

Warmth that had nothing to do with sun radiated down the pier and saturated him all the way through.

Creed smiled back.

There she was, his woman wearing his ring, his green, with his baby in her belly, sitting at the end of their pier.

His Sylvie.

His dreamweaver, able to weave dreams doing nothing but sitting on a pier and smiling.

The way it always was.

The way it always would be.

He stopped at the end by his wife and put the cooler down. She instantly flipped the top open. Creed bent and rolled up his jeans.

When he got them up, he settled at the end of the pier with Sylvie, his feet in the water, and he saw hers were covered to her ankles. Her watery toes painted a bright pink, the same color that was on her nails. His feet were covered up to the tops of his calves.

She handed him a frozen Snickers bar. He took it and she tore into hers.

Pregnant, his woman could eat. He'd never seen anything like it. She consumed everything in sight.

She also didn't slow down, and she was nourishing two so she needed a lot of energy.

Then again, not pregnant, his woman could eat.

She just ate like she lived, consuming life and enjoying the fuck out of it.

It was one of the myriad reasons he loved her.

Creed ripped open his candy bar and slid his arm along Sylvie's shoulders.

She leaned into him, head to his shoulder, and bit hard into her Snickers.

Creed followed suit and his eyes moved to the lake.

They were back in Kentucky because they told the kids a little of their history and Kara and Brand were curious about where their Dad came from. Something, for obvious reasons, he had never shared much about. Something, because of this, they'd always been curious about.

Now they were in the lake that, since they could cogitate, they'd seen on their father's back.

Creed didn't want to come and Sylvie kept her mouth shut, even though he knew she didn't want to come either. She did this so he wouldn't put his foot down and not come, and therefore not give this to his kids.

Sitting there, eating a frozen Snickers bar, holding his pregnant Sylvie on the spot where he gave her her first green, practically on the spot where she gave him her virginity, his three kids splashing around him, he wondered why the fuck they hadn't come sooner.

"We need a dog," Sylvie said through frozen chocolate, caramel, nuts and nougat.

She had said this repeatedly since approximately seventeen hours after moving into his house in Phoenix.

"Gun would hate a dog," he replied, having said this repeatedly since approximately seventeen hours after she moved into his house in Phoenix.

"You spoil that cat like she was your child," Sylvie bitched and bit off another hunk of candy bar.

"Does she depend on me to eat?" he asked.

"Creed."

That was all she said.

That meant yes.

"Does she depend on me to keep a roof over her head?"

"Jesus," she muttered.

"Does she depend on me for affection?"

"Partially. She also depends on me, Kara, Brand, and now Jesse," Sylvie returned.

Creed ignored that.

"Does she depend on me to enforce rules so she gets along in our household?" Creed kept going.

"Like Gun follows rules," she mumbled.

Creed ignored that, too.

"So she's like another child, and if a dog's gonna make her unhappy, we're not gettin' a fuckin' dog."

"Jesse loves dogs."

"Jesse's gonna have to wait until he has the body coordination to feed it to get one."

"You're so strict," she muttered.

"I'm a Dad. That's what Dads are."

She pulled slightly back so she could tip her head to look at him.

When her green eyes locked with his, quietly, she said, "Creed, I want a dog."

To which Creed immediately replied, "When we get home, I'll get you one."

She grinned.

Creed bent his head and kissed her.

Her lips tasted partly of Snickers, but mostly of sun...

And Sylvie.

Thirteen hours later...

Creed stood beside the bed in the dark.

Sylvie was in it, on her side, her legs curled up.

Jesse was in his Diamondback pajamas on his back, tucked to her front with her arm around him. He had his arms over his head, his legs splayed out, his little fist tucked against Sylvie's lips.

Carefully, Creed pulled the sheet up to his wife's waist before he turned to his bag, dug into the bottom and pulled out the envelope and the flashlight.

Silently, he left the room, the hotel and got in their rental.

Then he drove.

He entered from the south side and parked where his research told him it would be.

He shut down the ignition and sat in the car.

"Understand why I gotta do this," he said into the car.

As ever, over the years when Creed spoke to his father, Brand Creed didn't reply. And as ever, over the years when Creed spoke to his father, he hoped like Christ his father heard.

And this time understood.

Creed got out, turned on the flashlight and illuminated the headstones as he walked until he found it.

Bissenette.

He turned off the light and shoved it in the back pocket of his jeans. He ripped open the envelope and sprinkled the grass with its contents.

Jesse's hair. Not the first that had been clipped. That was pressed in a frame that sat on Sylvie's nightstand.

But it was his.

Jesse's.

A Jesse made by Sylvie and Creed.

Once the hair was out, Creed rumpled the envelope, and for the first time in his life, he littered by throwing it at the base of the headstone.

He stared at the grave.

Sylvie's father had died of a heart attack at an age too young for a good man to leave this world, but way too late for the man he was.

"I win, asshole," Creed whispered.

Not surprisingly, there was no reply.

Creed didn't need one nor did he wait for one.

He turned on his boot and went back to his family.

Two years and four months later...

"It's good you have a big table," Knight muttered, and Creed looked from the stove to the man standing, hips to the counter, bottle of beer in hand, surveying the scene.

He looked over his shoulder.

Outside he could see Brand and Adam with Charlene's new man. God only knew what they were doing, but not surprisingly, whatever it was, Adam was smiling and Brand's mouth was moving.

Inside, Anya was chasing after Theo, Leslie, Kat, Jesse and Rayleigh, Creed and Sylvie's petite, wild, curly blonde-haired daughter, and Kasha, Knight and Anya's second girl.

Anya had company. Sylvie's white West Highland Terrier was jumping around, panting and barking at Anya and the kids.

Kara was sitting in an armchair, phone glued to her ear, talking either to a girlfriend or one of her—God help him—boyfriends.

Yes, he said *one of.*

Jesus.

Charlene and Sylvie were on the couch, gabbing.

He looked at Knight, who was still looking through the full house, his expression not giving anything away.

"Sylvie says you're not big on holidays," Creed muttered as his eyes went back to the stove.

"Wasn't."

Creed looked back to Knight at his answer.

"Wasn't?" he prompted.

"Got three women in my house who go wild for every holiday. Swear to Christ, Creed, even when the red, white and blue M&Ms make their appearance for the Fourth of July, they act like Uncle Sam swooped in and personally asked them to watch the fireworks at the White House with the President. It's impossible not to be big on holidays with those three dragging me in their wake."

Creed grinned back down at the stove.

Knight was totally fucking full of shit.

Not about the part where he didn't give a shit about holidays. He probably didn't.

He gave a shit about his girls and he'd do anything that would make them happy. Even eat red, white and blue M&Ms and take them to see fireworks.

"Kara!" he called. "You wanna give your Dad a hand?"

"Be right there, Dad!" she called back.

Translation: She'd get off the phone when the turkey was on the table.

He turned his head and pinned his eyes on Sylvie.

"Baby? Preparations are coming to a head. You gonna help out?"

She had her hand on her enormous, again-pregnant belly, and her eyes on him.

When he stopped speaking, her mouth moved to say, "Who did you marry?"

No help there.

"I'll help, Tucker," Anya offered.

"Me, too," Charlene pushed up from the couch.

Creed looked back at Sylvie and lifted his brows.

She grinned and leaned down to snatch Kasha up in her arms and give her a snuggle.

Right.

Again.

No help there.

Knight moved out of the room, and as he did he tagged Rayleigh, swung her up in the air and made her laugh.

No help there, either.

A miracle occurred when, fifteen minutes before the food would be set on the table, Kara got off the phone and joined them in the kitchen.

Seventeen minutes after that, the table was covered in food and surrounded by people. Some of the kids were sitting on stools at the bar, others were in highchairs.

It was not surprising when Brand piped up and asked for a chance to run his mouth.

"Dad, can I say the blessing?"

Creed jerked up his chin. "Have at it, son."

Brand, Anya and Charlene all looked to their laps.

Sylvie's eyes went to Creed.

"Dear God," Brand started. "Thanks for health and food and family and friends. Oh, and love, I guess. Amen."

Creed's firstborn son lifted his head and reached immediately for the potatoes.

Creed watched Sylvie's shoulders start shaking.

He grinned at his wife.

"Mommy! I wanna sit by Adam!" Jesse shrieked.

Sylvie shot out of her seat.

His wife spoiled the dog and her son.

Creed spoiled the cat and his sweet little Ray.

Both of them, in different ways, spoiled Kara and Brand.

Kara and Brand spoiled all of them.

The perfect family.

Finally.

Creed drew in a breath and grabbed the platter of meat.

One year and nine months later. . .

Creed sat at the end of their pier, jeans rolled up, feet in the water, and he stared at the moonlight glinting on the lake as Sylvie burrowed her shoulder into his side.

He wrapped his arm around her.

When he did, Creed remembered the first time she did that, in the woods when he told her he intended to be Creed.

He felt his lips tip up slightly and curled his wife closer.

She didn't put her feet in the water. She curved them under her. Since he'd just finished making love to her, she was wearing nothing but her panties and his tee, and he remembered the last time he had that, too.

Vividly.

Years, the memory of his Sylvie finally becoming all his at the age of eighteen had been bittersweet.

Now it was just sweet.

She snaked an arm around his gut and shoved closer even as she asked, "Do you think we should get back to the hotel?"

"Kara's got 'em, baby," Creed muttered, and he was right. His girl would look after the kids. All of them, even Brand, were with her in their adjoining suite.

"You wanna stay," she murmured.

Yeah, he did. He always did. Every year, when they came back and he brought his Sylvie out here in the moonlight, he wanted to stay as long as they could.

So they did.

"Yeah," he answered softly, and she snuggled closer.

His Sylvie.

Their spot.

Their lake.

Their pier.

No more bitter, just sweet.

Yeah, his Sylvie, weaving dreams.

He drew in a deep breath and felt every millisecond of its release as he stared at the water, holding his woman pressed close.

He did this a while.

Then he was done doing it and he turned into her. She knew his intent and she tipped her head back to prepare.

Creed took her mouth.

Then he moved her to the blanket he spread on the pier.

There, again, he made love to her.

And when he did, Tucker Creed finally gave Sylvie Creed everything she wanted.

Because when they made love in the moonlight on their pier, he planted inside his wife, his Sylvie, baby number four.

Thus proving, yet again, Tucker Creed could also weave dreams.

*The Unfinished Hero Series will continue with the story of **Raid.***

Made in the USA
Lexington, KY
26 May 2015